STAR
CURSED

DON'T MISS THE FIRST BOOK IN
THE CAHILL WITCH CHRONICLES

BORN WICKED

THE CAHILL WITCH CHRONICLES

STAR
CURSED

JESSICA SPOTSWOOD

G. P. Putnam's Sons

An Imprint of Penguin Group (USA) Inc.

G. P. Putnam's Sons • An imprint of Penguin Young Readers Group.
Published by The Penguin Group.
Penguin Group (USA) Inc., 375 Hudson Street, New York, NY 10014, USA.
Penguin Group (Canada), 90 Eglinton Avenue East, Suite 700, Toronto,
Ontario M4P 2Y3, Canada (a division of Pearson Penguin Canada Inc.).
Penguin Books Ltd, 80 Strand, London WC2R 0RL, England.
Penguin Ireland, 25 St. Stephen's Green, Dublin 2, Ireland
(a division of Penguin Books Ltd).
Penguin Group (Australia), 707 Collins Street, Melbourne, Victoria 3008, Australia
(a division of Pearson Australia Group Pty Ltd).
Penguin Books India Pvt Ltd, 11 Community Centre, Panchsheel Park,
New Delhi–110 017, India.
Penguin Group (NZ), 67 Apollo Drive, Rosedale, Auckland 0632, New Zealand
(a division of Pearson New Zealand Ltd).
Penguin Books South Africa, Rosebank Office Park, 181 Jan Smuts Avenue,
Parktown North 2193, South Africa.
Penguin China, B7 Jiaming Center, 27 East Third Ring Road North,
Chaoyang District, Beijing 100020, China.
Penguin Books Ltd, Registered Offices: 80 Strand, London WC2R 0RL, England.

Design by Marikka Tamura.
Text set in Carre Noir Std Light.

Library of Congress Cataloging-in-Publication Data is available upon request.
ISBN 978-0-399-25746-9
1 3 5 7 9 10 8 6 4 2

To my brilliant husband, Steve,
who challenges me to be better
but loves me as I am.

CHAPTER
1

I FEEL SUCH A FRAUD.

I stand with Alice Auclair and Mei Zhang in a narrow tenement hallway that stinks of boiled beef and cabbage. We are all dressed alike: black woolen cloaks covering stiff black bombazine dresses, heeled black boots peeping out beneath floor-length skirts, hair pulled back simply and neatly. This is the uniform of the Sisterhood, and while none of us are full members yet, we are on a Sisterly mission of charity. We carry baskets of bread baked in the convent kitchen and vegetables from the convent cellar. We keep our eyes low, our voices quiet.

No one must ever suspect us for what we really are.

Alice knocks. Fine onyx earbobs swing from her seashell ears. Even on a mission to feed the poor, she finds a way to flaunt her family's status. Someday her pride will be her undoing.

I half relish the thought.

Mrs. Anderson opens the door. She's a widow of twenty-three with blond hair a shade lighter than my own and a perpetually harried expression. She ushers us inside, her hands fluttering like pale moths in the November gloom. "Sisters, thank you so much for coming."

"There's no need to thank us. Helping the less fortunate is part of our mission," Alice says, grimacing at the cramped two-room flat.

"I'm grateful." Mrs. Anderson presses my hand between her icy palms. She still wears her gold wedding band, though her husband has been dead three months now. "My Frank was a good provider. We always made ends meet. I don't like to depend on charity."

"Of course not." I give her an uneven smile as I pull away. In the face of our deception, her gratitude makes me squirm.

"You've had hard luck. You'll be back on your feet soon," Mei assures her. The fever that tore through the city in August claimed Mr. Anderson and their eldest boy, leaving Mrs. Anderson to fend for the two surviving children.

"It's not an easy thing, to be a woman alone in the world. I'd take on more hours at the shop if I could." Mrs. Anderson slides the jug of milk into the icebox. "But it gets dark so early now, I don't like to walk home alone."

"It isn't safe for a woman to be out at night." Mei is stocky and short; she has to stand on tiptoe to put a jar of apple butter on the shelf next to the canned vegetables.

"So many foreigners in this part of the city. Most of them can't even speak proper English." Alice's hood falls back, revealing golden hair that waves prettily away from her pale forehead. Looking at her, you'd never guess what a harpy she is. "Who knows what kind of people they are?"

Mei flushes. Her parents immigrated from Indo-China before she was born, but they still speak Chinese at home. She's the only Chinese girl at the convent and conscious of it. I daresay Alice knows that; she has a talent for poking at people's bruises.

The old Cate Cahill would have taken Alice to task, but Sister Catherine only helps Mei unpack sweet potatoes and butternut squash onto the scratched wooden table. Sisters do not have the luxury of losing their tempers—at least not outside the convent walls. In public, we must be models of ladylike decorum.

I loathe these visits.

It's not that I lack compassion for the poor. I have plenty of compassion. I just can't help wondering how they would feel about us if they knew the truth.

The Sisters pose as an order of women devoting their lives to charitable service for the Lord. We deliver food to the poor and nurse the sick. That *is* the truth—but it's also true that we are witches, all of us, hiding in plain sight. If people learned what we really are, their gratitude would turn to fear. They would think us sinful, wanton, and dangerous, and they would have us locked up in the madhouse—or worse.

It's not their fault. That's what the Brothers preach at church every Sunday. Few would risk going against them, and these poor people already have less than most.

No matter how kind Mrs. Anderson may seem, she'd give us up. She'd have to, in order to protect her children. They all would.

"Sister Cath'rine! You're back!" A small boy runs out of the bedroom, his hands full of jacks, his mouth smeared with the blackberry jam we brought last week from Sister Sophia's cellar. Alice shies away from his sticky fingers.

"Good day, Henry." This is my third visit to the Andersons' flat, and Henry and I have become fast friends. He's lonely, I think. Now that his mother goes out to work, he and his baby sister are left with an elderly neighbor all day. It can't be much fun for him.

"Henry, leave Sister Catherine alone," his mother scolds.

"It's all right. He's not bothering me." I take the final item—a jar of juicy red tomatoes, seeds floating in the pulp—from my basket. As I kneel, my eyes fall past Henry to the pallets stuffed with straw ticking. The first time we came, they had a nice mahogany sleigh bed, a matching trundle for Henry, and an armoire, but Lavinia's had to sell them. Now her pretty blue wedding quilt is tucked neatly over her pallet and their clothes are stacked in cardboard boxes.

Henry sits, scattering jacks across the floor and giving me a gap-toothed grin. I'm out of practice, but I was a champion at jacks in my day. A memory flashes through me: Paul McLeod squatting across from me on the cobblestone walk

4

in my garden, the hot summer sun beating down, the smell of freshly cut grass all around us.

Once upon a time, memories of my childhood friend would have made me smile—but not anymore. I treated Paul poorly, and I'll never be able to apologize.

He's not even the one I hurt most. The thoughts hammer at me, relentless.

"I been practicing," Henry announces, tugging at the grimy white shirtsleeves that end halfway up his skinny fore-arms. "Got up to ninesies yesterday. Bet I can beat you now."

"We'll see about that." I settle across from him while Alice and Mei and Mrs. Anderson cram together on the stained, lumpy brown sofa, clasping hands and bowing their heads in prayer. I ought to join them, but my relationship with the Lord is fragile these days. I'm in good health and safe from the Brothers' meddling eyes, but it's hard to feel thankful when everyone I love is at home in Chatham and I'm here in New London alone.

I miss my sisters. I miss Finn. Loneliness carves a hollow in my stomach.

Henry and I are up to sevensies when there's a furious pounding on the door. I freeze at the sound, the red rubber ball bouncing right past my outstretched hands.

The baby stirs in her wooden cradle. Mrs. Anderson leans over her for a moment on the way to the door. "Shhh, Eleni," she says, and the tenderness in her voice makes me miss my own mother.

Mrs. Anderson opens the door to a nightmare of black

cloaks and stern faces. Two Brothers push past her into the flat.

My heart stops. What did we do? How did we give ourselves away?

Alice and Mei are already on their feet. I scramble across the room to join them, and Henry rushes to his mother's side.

A short, bald Brother with a long face and piercing blue eyes steps forward. "Lavinia Anderson? I am Brother O'Shea of the New London council. This is Brother Helmsley," he says, indicating an enormous red-bearded man. "We have received a report of impropriety."

It's not us, then.

Relief courses through me, followed closely by guilt. Lavinia Anderson is a good woman, a good mother, kind and hardworking. She doesn't deserve trouble from the Brothers.

Lavinia presses a fist to her mouth, her wedding ring glinting in the fading afternoon light. "I've done nothing improper, sir."

"That will be for us to decide, won't it?" O'Shea turns to us with a smug, self-important smile. He stands like a bantam rooster with his chest thrown forward, shoulders back, legs spread wide, in the way of a small man trying to seem bigger. I take an immediate dislike to him. "Good day, Sisters. Here to deliver weekly rations?"

"Yes, sir." Alice bows her head, but not before I see the flash of mutiny in her blue eyes.

"It's a pity your charity's been wasted on the undeserving. Poverty is no excuse for wantonness," Helmsley snarls. "Just lost one husband and already setting her cap for another! It's scandalous is what it is."

Mrs. Anderson clutches Henry's thin shoulder, her face suddenly white.

"Do you deny that you allowed a man to escort you home last night? A man who was no relation to you?" Brother O'Shea asks.

"I do not deny it," Lavinia says carefully, her voice quavering. "Mr. Alvarez is a customer at the bakery. He was leaving the same time I was and offered to see me home."

"As a widow, Mrs. Anderson, your behavior must be beyond reproach. You cannot consort with strange men on city streets. Surely you know that."

I bite my lip, face cast down. What other choice did she have—to walk home alone and risk being robbed or accosted? To hire a carriage with money she cannot spare? To beg her employers for an escort? This problem would never present itself to girls like Alice or me. Before we joined the Sisters, our movements were shadowed by ladies' maids and governesses. A proper lady rides hidden away in a closed carriage, not down in the dust and dirt for anyone to stare at and take liberties with.

But Mrs. Anderson cannot afford a carriage or a maid. She has neither parents nor a husband to look after her. What, precisely, would the Brothers have her do? Stay home and starve?

"I wasn't consorting. I mourn my husband every day!" Lavinia insists. Her shoulders are thrown back, her chin is up, and she meets O'Shea's eyes straight on.

"You're a liar." O'Shea nods at Helmsley, who slaps her across the face.

I flinch, remembering the way Brother Ishida once struck me. My hand flies to my cheek. The cut from his ring of office is healed now, but I will never forget the indignity of it—and the vicious pleasure on his face.

Lavinia stumbles back against the cradle. The baby lets out a wail.

Henry launches himself at Helmsley's legs. "Don't hit my mama!"

He shouldn't have to watch this. No child should. "Should we take the children into the other room, sir?" I ask O'Shea, who is clearly the brains behind this visit.

"No. Let him see his mother for the slut she is." O'Shea leans down and grabs Henry's small shoulders, shaking him. "Stop that. Stop it this instant, do you hear? Your mother is a liar. She betrayed your papa's memory."

Henry stops fighting, his brown eyes wide and frightened. "Papa?"

"I haven't!" Lavinia protests, tears coursing down her face. "I would never!"

"Your neighbor reported seeing you arm in arm with Mr. Alvarez," Helmsley continues, looming over her. He must be six feet tall.

Lavinia cowers away from him, pressing back against the peeling blue-flowered wallpaper. "I stumbled over a loose brick, and he caught me before I fell. That's all there was to it, I swear! It won't happen again. I'll be home before dark from now on." But that means giving up several hours of work—and pay—that her little family can scarcely afford.

"A woman's proper place is in the home, Mrs. Anderson," O'Shea says. He releases Henry and turns to Helmsley, sneering. "You see, this is what comes from permitting women to take on outside work. Gives them false notions of propriety. Turns their heads from the Lord."

"Makes them think they can do for themselves just as well as men," Helmsley agrees.

"Do you think I *like* going out to work?" Lavinia shrills, and I want to clap a hand over her mouth. Arguing will only make this go worse for her. "I only took this job after my husband died. We can't depend entirely on the Sisters' charity. We'd all starve!"

"Hush!" Brother O'Shea roars, strutting up to her. "Your insubordination does you no favors, madam. You should be thankful for what you get."

Mrs. Anderson takes a deep breath and offers up a watery smile. "I'm sorry," she says softly, looking at Mei and me pleadingly. "I am very grateful. I'll do whatever you want. I'd swear on the Scriptures, I've done nothing wrong!"

O'Shea shakes his head as though she has committed another grave sin. "Then you would forswear yourself."

A grin settles on Helmsley's ugly bearded face, and I sense a trap closing around her. "Your neighbor said Alvarez kissed your hand when you parted. Do you deny that?"

"I—no, but—" Lavinia sags against the wall. "Please, let me explain!"

"You've told us enough falsehoods for one day, Mrs. Anderson. I think it's clear what's been going on here. We are arresting you for crimes of immorality."

The baby begins shrieking. Henry is crying, too, clinging to Lavinia's skirts.

"We could stop this." Alice's lips barely move. Her voice is so low I can hardly hear her over the commotion, but I catch her meaning immediately.

What she's suggesting is dangerous. Doing magic outside the convent puts every one of us at risk. And mind-magic is the rarest, wickedest kind of magic there is. Erasing one memory can take other, associated memories with it; performing mind-magic repeatedly on the same subject can leave devastating mental scars. Long ago, when the witches ruled New England, they used mind-magic to control and destroy their opponents. The Brothers tell those old stories to keep people frightened of us, though Alice and I are the only two students at the convent even capable of it.

"No," Mei begs, her dark eyes frantic. "Stay out of it. It's not our business."

"Four of them. We could do it, together." Alice's soft hand clasps mine. "Count of three."

What the Brothers are doing is hateful and wrong; it wouldn't trouble me overmuch to use magic on them. But Alice is more confident in her skill than I am. I've never performed mind-magic on more than one subject before, and certainly never on a child. What if we fail or it goes wrong and we damage Henry's mind permanently?

I snatch my hand away. "No. It's too risky."

Then the moment is gone. Helmsley is binding Lavinia's wrists with coarse rope.

"Our work is never done, Sisters. I'm sorry to subject you

to such a scene," O'Shea says, though it's obvious he's rather enjoyed having an audience. He gestures to the fresh bread and vegetables piled on the kitchen table. "You'll want to take that to someone else in need. No point in letting it go to waste."

"Yes, sir." Alice snatches up her basket from the floor and begins to gather up the food.

Mei steps toward O'Shea. "Sir? What about the children?"

O'Shea shrugs, and I cringe at his indifference. "We'll take them to the orphanage if there's no one else to look after them."

"There's a neighbor," I suggest. It's the least I can do.

I hope the neighbor will agree to take them. Two more mouths to feed isn't an easy burden. If Lavinia is sentenced to hard labor on a prison ship, she might be home again in a few years—if she survives the backbreaking work and rampant disease. If she's sent to Harwood Asylum, though, that's a lifetime. She'll never see her children again.

"Mrs. Papadopoulos, two doors down," Lavinia says quickly. "Henry, go with Sister Catherine. Don't worry. I'll be back soon." She gives Henry a smile, smoothing his floppy brown hair, but her voice cracks on the lie. "I love you."

"Stop delaying." Helmsley yanks Lavinia away from her son and out the door. I hear her stumble on the steps, and my breath catches. *Could* I have stopped this? Have I become as cruel and cowardly as the Brothers?

"Come here, Henry," Mei says, reaching for him, but he darts past her.

"Mama! Come back!" He surges after Lavinia like a small,

sobbing lion. Mei scampers after him, and I follow, cursing the steep stairs and my heeled boots.

Outside, Henry runs to his mother and buries his face in her skirt. There's a ragtag crowd gathered: the Spanish and Chinese boys who'd been playing stickball in the empty lot across the street. Above us, curtains twitch, and I wonder which of those nosy neighbors informed on Lavinia.

"Don't take my mama!" Henry begs.

"Don't you see he's scared? Let me say a proper good-bye," Lavinia pleads, reaching for him ineffectually with her bound hands.

O'Shea's thin face is hard. "He's better off without a mother like you."

Helmsley shoves her toward the carriage, and Lavinia trips, falling to the sidewalk in a heap of black skirts and blond hair.

"Take the boy inside," O'Shea orders us, his pale eyes cold.

"Mama!" Henry screams, fighting, kicking Mei as she tries to grab him.

I see the crowd of boys stirring restlessly, grumbling among themselves. I cringe, remembering the last arrest I saw—Brenna Elliott's—and the way onlookers called her a witch and threw stones at her.

One tall boy draws his arm back, and I almost shout a warning as he lets it fly.

The rock smacks O'Shea between the shoulders. O'Shea turns and glares at the group of boys, and I glance at Mei, suppressing a smile.

I've never seen anyone fight back against the Brothers. It's marvelous. Foolish, too—but then they are boys, not girls, and they've got less to lose.

More rocks fly through the air, pelting O'Shea and Helmsley in the back and shoulders, accompanied by angry shouts in foreign languages. O'Shea spins around, bellowing something about respect, then gives up and sprints for the carriage like the coward he is. Helmsley yanks Lavinia to her feet, dragging her down the sidewalk.

As Mei bends to grab Henry, a rock slams into the side of her head. She screams something at the boys in Chinese. I dart forward and nab Henry by the collar. The boy buries his tearstained face against my hip as the Brothers' carriage rattles away with his mother sealed inside. The hailstorm of rocks stops as suddenly as it started. The crowd drifts away; the curtains flutter shut. It's over—for everyone but Lavinia Anderson, whose nightmare has just begun.

"Are you all right?" I ask Mei. Blood is gathering at her temple and trickling down her cheek.

"Sure. One of them's got terrible aim," Mei jokes, but she looks a little unsteady.

"Help Mei into the carriage. I'll take Henry back upstairs and get our baskets," Alice says, appearing behind me. "Mrs. Papadopoulos heard the fuss. She's with the baby now."

Our coachman, Robert van Buren, is running down the street toward us, a newspaper tucked under his arm. He's one of the few people who know the truth of the Sisterhood; his daughter Violet is a student there.

"I saw the ruckus just as I was leaving that store on the corner. I'm sorry, Miss Zhang. I'll get you home right away," he says, handing Mei up into the carriage.

"Does it look real bad?" Mei tilts her head at me, swaying dizzily, before sinking onto the leather bench.

I swallow at the sight of a three-inch gash. "No. Sister Sophia will fix you up good as new." I use my black satin glove to wipe away the trail of blood weaving across her round cheek.

It's a pity Mei can't heal herself. Healing is her specialty; she's one of three girls in Sister Sophia's advanced class who go on nursing missions to Harwood and Richmond Hospital. In my six weeks at the convent, I've discovered that many witches have an affinity for a specific kind of magic: illusions, animations, healing, or memory modification. It's another piece of our history that Mother never bothered to share before she died.

Mei closes her eyes. "Maybe *you* could heal me," she suggests, voice faint.

"Me? I can barely cure a headache," I protest.

She opens her dark eyes and smiles. "I've got faith in you, Cate."

I don't know why; I don't have much faith in myself. But something snaps inside me. When did I become someone who *hesitates* instead of helping? Mei has been a good friend to me. Trying to stop her from swooning in a pool of her own blood seems the very least I can do in return.

"All right, I'll try."

I lean across the aisle, cupping my hand gently over hers. Healing is different from other sorts of magic; there has to be a physical connection. I pull on the threads of magic that coil in my chest, weaving through my body alongside nerves and muscles. I wish it weren't there; I wish I weren't a witch. But it is and I am, and if I can't ever be rid of it, I might as well try and use it for something good.

I think of how sweet Mei is, always the first to offer help. How I would take this pain from her now if I could.

The magic rolls through me, powerful as an ocean wave, warm as a hot bath. It pours out my fingertips, and the unexpected strength of it leaves me limp and breathless. That felt—strong. Formidable.

"Oh," Mei gasps. She turns her head so I can see. Her black hair is still matted and bloody, but the cut is gone. Completely.

"All fixed?" I try not to sound flabbergasted by my success.

Mei searches with her fingertips. After a moment, she beams. "It's not even sore. Thank you, Cate."

"You're welcome. I'm glad to be of—" I've got to brace myself against the seat before I fall. My legs have gone weak and rubbery.

Sister Sophia warned us about this. My stomach heaves, and I lurch for the door just in time. I'm sick right onto the cobblestones below.

I wipe my mouth with my clean glove, then look over at Mei, embarrassed.

"That's a normal reaction to a healing spell," she assures

me, helping me back into the carriage and onto the leather seat across from her.

I curl up on the bench, squeezing my eyes shut and resting my aching head on my arms. Heels hammer on the cobblestones outside, and Alice steps through the open carriage door, dropping the empty baskets at our feet. "What's the matter with you? I didn't take you for the type to be sick at a little blood, Cate."

I clench my jaw and breathe deeply through my nose.

"She healed me," Mei explains. "See?"

Lord, but I wish I were at home in my own bed. Mrs. O'Hare, our housekeeper, would bring me a cold compress for my head and a cup of peppermint tea. I can picture it so clearly I can almost smell the tea; I can almost feel the worn, familiar cotton pillowcase against my face. Tears prick the corners of my eyes. I'm glad no one can see; Alice would laugh at me for acting like a homesick child.

"Perhaps she's not utterly useless, then."

I peer over at Alice as she slides onto the seat next to Mei, crossing her ankles primly as the carriage rocks forward. Her skirts are spotless, untouched by the dust and dirt of the street. I don't know how she manages it.

"Better than you." Mei smooths her black fringe. Bangs are the new fashion; she had Violet cut them for her last week. I was afraid it would look a fright, but it actually suits her. "You can't heal a paper cut."

Alice rolls her eyes. "Everyone knows healing is the least useful kind of magic there is. It figures that would be Cate's affinity."

I sit up gingerly, ignoring her insults and peering out between the curtains, watching the crowds of people swarming down the sidewalk. The noise is deafening: horses and wagons clomping their way downtown, hammers pounding away on new buildings, men's voices shouting in a dozen different languages, street vendors hawking food and clothing.

I'm not a city girl. It overwhelms me. Maura would love the busy rush of it, the thrill of something always new. I miss the quiet of home, the birdsong and the buzz of cicadas. I am lonely here, surrounded by strangers. Without my sisters, without Finn and my flowers—who am I?

I am not who the Sisterhood wants me to be.

"Cate was too much of a coward to do mind-magic back there," Alice scoffs, toying with one of her onyx earrings. "Too afraid to stick her neck out to help people."

"Don't pretend to care about helping Mrs. Anderson," Mei snaps. "You just wanted an excuse to do mind-magic. Sisters are s'posed to be compassionate, you know. Don't you think these people notice the snooty way you look at them?"

"I don't care what they notice," Alice says, wrinkling her patrician nose. "I'm hardly going to pretend they're my equals. They're fools to come here in the first place, the way things are, and greater fools yet to keep having children when they can't afford to feed them."

Mei is shocked into silence. Her father is a tailor; her mother takes in embroidery and raises Mei's younger brother and four younger sisters. Mei said once that she feels guilty for coming to the Sisters instead of going out to work. Her family is proud of her supposed scholarship to the convent school, but they don't know she's a witch.

"Everyone's got troubles, Alice. It wouldn't kill you to show a little sympathy," I suggest.

"Oh, yes, it must be so difficult being Cate Cahill. Lifted from obscurity in your backwater nowhere town. Told that you're going to be our savior!" Alice rolls her eyes again. I hope they'll get stuck in the back of her head someday. "I don't see it, myself. A timid, mousy thing like you?"

It's true that I'm no great beauty—but timid? I almost laugh. I know how to keep my head down and stay out of trouble, and I don't boast of my mind-magic and terrorize the other girls, if that's what she means. In the six weeks I've been at school, I've kept mostly to myself. The Sisters have fallen over themselves to offer me tutoring, so I'm busy morning, noon, and night.

Still, I can't imagine anyone who knows me dubbing me *timid*.

"That's how you see me?" I arch an eyebrow at her.

Alice fusses with the black rabbit fur at her cuffs. Even her Sisterly uniform has fancy touches, though the entire point of a uniform is uniformity. "Yes. Aside from your *supposed* mind-magic, you're still a beginner. If war broke out tomorrow, what on earth could you do? I'm starting to think the whole prophecy is nonsense."

"I wish it were," I admit, glancing out the window as the carriage turns away from the busy riverside streets toward the quiet residential neighborhood of the convent.

One hundred and twenty years ago, the witches who

ruled New England—the Daughters of Persephone—were overthrown by the priests of the Brotherhood. For fifty years, any woman suspected of witchery was drowned, hanged, or burnt alive. Anyone who escaped the Terror went into hiding. There are, at best guess, only a few hundred witches left in New England now. But just before the Terror, an oracle prophesied hope—three sisters, all witches, who would come of age before the dawn of the twentieth century. One, gifted with mind-magic, would be the most powerful witch in centuries. She would bring about the resurgence of magic—or, if captured by the Brothers, cause a second Terror.

The Sisters think that it's me. That I'm the prophesied witch.

I'm not entirely convinced, myself. But they were willing to bargain my sisters' freedom for mine, and I consider that a sacrifice well made.

My mother didn't fully trust the Sisterhood, so neither do I.

Outside, the gas streetlamps flicker to life. We rattle past half a dozen large houses, each surrounded by a manicured lawn, before stopping in front of the convent. It's a gargantuan three-story building of weathered gray stone and arched Gothic windows. White marble steps lead from the sidewalk up to the front door, but in the back, there's a garden, hidden from prying eyes by a high stone wall, filled with flowers and red maples and Sister Sophia's vegetable patch.

"You don't even *want* to be the prophesied witch, do you?" Alice demands, pulling her hood up over her golden pompadour.

"I don't want one of my sisters to die."

Even Alice doesn't know what to say to that.

That's why Maura and Tess and I were separated: the oracle also predicted that one of the three witches wouldn't live to see the twentieth century, because one of her sisters will murder her. The Sisterhood wasn't confident that Maura was in control of her magic. Given the dreadful nature of the prophecy—and, frankly, the nature of Maura's temper—they were afraid she might hurt me. And they aren't willing to risk the safety of their prophesied witch.

I tried to tell them the notion of Maura hurting me is impossible. Ludicrous.

Since our mother died and Father became a shadow of his former self, Maura and Tess and I have only had each other. The Sisterhood doesn't understand how strong our bond is. I would do anything for my sisters.

But I still wake crying from nightmares where I stand helplessly over their bloody bodies.

CHAPTER
2

"THERE YOU ARE!" RILLA STEPHENSON says, bouncing into the modest room we share.

I look up in surprise, lying on my stomach on the narrow feather bed. I've been rereading letters from home. *Letter*, I should say; there's been only the one, and I already know its contents by heart:

> *Dear Cate,*
>
> *Father came home last week. He was terribly surprised to find you gone to New London, but he accepted your decision with good grace. He asked me to give you his blessing and convey his love. He seems thin, and his cough is worse than ever, but he has promised to stay at home with us until after the New Year—though he insists our lessons are best left to Sister Elena.*

After keeping to her room for a week, Maura is now quite recovered. She has funneled her energy into her studies, showing marked improvement. I worry that she is overexerting herself. I have urged her to write you, but she insists you must be having such grand adventures that you care nothing for what happens at home. I know she is wrong in that. I hope she will soon reconcile herself to her place here.

We had an at-home afternoon last week, which was very well attended. I baked a splendid gingerbread, and everyone inquired after you. Mrs. Ishida says she cannot remember the last time a girl from Chatham joined the Sisterhood, and Miss Ishida asked me to convey her particular good wishes.

I miss you dreadfully, Cate. Even with Father back, the house is dull and lonely without you. Penny had kittens in the hayloft, three white and one black, and Mrs. O'Hare keeps chiding me for climbing up to see them; that's the sum of this week's excitement.

I hope that you are well and not too homesick for us. Write me as soon as you can.

With love,
Tess

I picture my brilliant little sister—her blond curls, the gray eyes that don't miss a thing—and a wave of homesickness washes over me. Until six weeks ago, I'd seen Tess every day since she was born. I remember hearing her first shriek—a relief, after a stillborn brother—and the moment I first saw her squalling red face. And Maura—we're too close in age for me to remember a time without her; she's simply always been there to battle me and make me laugh.

I hate the Sisterhood for separating us. I hate the magic for giving them leverage to do it. If we were normal, ordinary girls—

But we aren't. It doesn't do any good to think on that.

"Why don't you come down to the sitting room with me?" Rilla suggests.

I always had my own room at home. It's strange, sharing a bedroom with a stranger. There are two high, narrow beds, two armoires, one dressing table—and absolutely no privacy. Rilla knows I'm homesick, and she's determined to cheer me up. She reads me passages from her frightful Gothic novels; she brings me cups of hot cocoa before bed; she shares the sticky maple candies her mother sends from their farm in Vermont.

She means well, but none of those things can cure a broken heart.

"No, thank you. I've got reading to do; I can't concentrate with all the chattering down there." I sit up, grabbing a history textbook from the foot of my bed.

"Caaate," Rilla groans, picking her way across the cluttered floor. Her bed is beneath the single, arched window; mine is along the wall perpendicular to it. "You can't keep shutting yourself away like this. Don't you want to get to know the other girls?"

Not particularly, no. They're always staring at me as though I'll manifest some magnificent power at any second, and I always feel as though I'm disappointing them.

"Maybe tomorrow?" I suggest.

"You always say that." Rilla jumps up onto her bed. "I know you don't want to be here. *Everyone* knows you don't want to be here. You hardly hide it. But it's almost December—you've been in New London over a month now. Can't you make the best of things?"

"I am! I'm *trying*," I insist, stung.

Since healing Mei two days ago, I've been shifted out of botany—the one class I loved—and into advanced healing. Mei's been partnering with me for lessons and keeps asking me to play chess with her during afternoon tea. Rilla's made a point of sitting with me during meals and in the classes we share, though it would certainly be easier—and more fun for her—to sit with other chattering, laughing girls instead of the one who barely speaks.

Have I ever thanked them for their pains?

"Are you really?" Rilla echoes my thoughts, her tone uncharacteristically tart. She rubs a hand over her cheek, dusted with freckles that remind me of Finn every time I look at her. "I don't mean studying magic and delivering food to the poor; I mean making this your home. Just look at your side of the room!"

Oh. I notice, suddenly, the difference between hers—the yellow quilt with uneven stitches covering her bed, the novels and mugs and dresses scattered everywhere—and mine, which is barren. I never sent for my rose-patterned rug or

Mother's watercolor painting of the garden. I never even un-packed my spring dresses. I tell myself it's because I don't want to take up too much space—but is it, or do I just want to be prepared to pack up and leave at a moment's notice?

"I'm trying to be your friend, Cate. But half the time you act as though I'm some pesky fly you'd like to swat. You never ask how my day was. You've never even asked me how I came to be here!"

The complaints pour out, a litany against me, and I'm staggered. Rilla is so relentlessly good-natured; I had no idea she'd noticed my rebuffs, much less was hurt by them.

"I defend you, you know, when the other girls say you're proud and standoffish. So does Mei. But you've got to start making more of an effort." Rilla swings her legs off the edge of her bed. She's wearing a new dress today—a yellow bro-cade with enormous orange gigot sleeves, an orange taffeta bow at the breast, and orange chiffon ruffles at the hem. It looks well on her. Did I think to tell her that? I get so caught up in my lessons, in missing Maura and Tess and—

"Perhaps sometimes I just want to be alone for five min-utes! Perhaps I have more important things on my mind than who got a new dress, or what mean thing Alice said today," I snap, hunching my shoulders and hugging the book to my chest.

Rilla's face flushes. "That's not all I care about, and you know it—or you *would,* if you ever bothered to talk to me. We all know how bad things are getting, but we don't have to dwell on it every single second. It wouldn't kill you to have a little fun, sometimes."

"Perhaps," I whisper, undone by the disappointment in her voice.

I *could* try harder. Join in the games of chess and draughts and charades after dinner, look through the fashion magazines from Dubai, talk about the Brothers' latest arrests and what the Sisterhood should do next. I know it's what the other girls want from me. I could have friends here, if I wanted them.

But that would mean accepting that this is my home now—that my place is here among these strangers, that my future lies with the Sisterhood, not with Finn. It would require accepting that there's no going back—and despite the ugly machinations they used, despite all my objections, the Sisters were right to bring me here, because this is where I belong.

I take a deep breath, leaning back against the brass headboard and stretching my legs out in front of me. "How *did* you end up here, Rilla?"

She scowls. "Are you asking because you want to know or because you feel obliged?"

"I want to know," I say, truthfully. "And I'm sorry for not asking you before."

"Well. I did something very foolish." Even in the candlelight, I can see Rilla's ears flush red. "There was a boy I fancied. Charlie Mott. He had black hair and he rode a black horse, and he was so handsome! I was desperate for him to notice me. A group of us went on a sleigh ride one Saturday night, and I made sure I was sitting next to him. But Emma Carrick was sitting on his other side, and he put his arm around *her* instead. I was so jealous. It all got a bit out of hand. I wished she weren't so pretty, and then suddenly she *wasn't*; she was hideous! Her face erupted in these awful hives, and her nose grew out to here—" Rilla gestures six inches away from her own pert nose. "When Charlie saw, he scooted away from her right quick. I—well, I couldn't help it. I laughed."

Good Lord, what a goose. But I imagine Finn holding another girl's hand, and my heart twists in sympathy.

"Emma was crying about her nose, and I felt sort of bad about the whole thing, honestly, so I put it back. But then she started screaming her head off about how I'd cast a spell on her because I was so jealous. The boys drove the sleigh down to the church and turned me in. Charlie Mott wouldn't even look at me after that," Rilla sighs.

"But Sister Cora interceded in your trial."

"Yes." Rilla brings her knees to her chest, propping her chin on the yellow brocade skirt. "And she brought me here. Otherwise, I would have been sent to Harwood for sure."

Sister Cora has an extensive network of spies made up of governesses and former convent girls. They send word when they suspect one of the Brothers' accusations of witchery is actually true. If Sister Cora can get there in time, she intervenes on the girl's behalf, using mind-magic to compel the Brothers and the witnesses. Then she brings the girl back to the Sisterhood.

"Do girls ever refuse to come with her?"

Rilla looks at me as though I'm mad. "Why would they? Once you've seen the Brothers turn on you—" She shakes her head, flipping a brown curl away from her face. "We're safer here. We learn to control our magic, and the Sisters protect us."

The Sisterhood was founded in 1815 by Brother Thomas Dolan, as a refuge for his sister Leah. At first, there were only a handful of witches operating in secret behind a smoke screen of piety. Then, in 1842, they decided to take in young witches and teach them magic. Sister Cora was among the convent school's first students. She's been intervening in trials and working to increase our numbers ever since. At present, there are fifty students and a dozen teachers, with twodozen governesses spread out across New England and at least a hundred graduates—like Mrs. Corbett, our neighbor in Chatham—operating as spies. Most girls who study here don't become full members; once they turn seventeen, they go off and live normal lives as mothers and wives.

That won't be an option for me, of course. Not if I'm the prophesied witch.

"Aren't you ever homesick?" I press. "Don't you miss your brothers?"

"I do," Rilla says, glancing at a tintype that she's hung by her bed: herself and her ten-year-old twin brothers, Teddy and Robby; Jeremiah, twelve; and Jamie, fourteen. Five mischievous, curly-headed, freckled little imps. "But it was hard being the only girl, you know, and the only witch. Hard keeping it a secret."

I can scarcely imagine Rilla keeping anything secret. She's such a chatterbox.

"I think Jamie—oh, I'm meant to call him James now, I keep forgetting—might suspect. And Mama knows, of course.

She's a witch, too, but not very good; she can only do a few basic illusions. Not that I'm so much better. I'm sure you've noticed how hopeless I am at animation, and I can't do healing magic at all," Rilla says, blushing. "I'm lucky the Sisters wanted me, really."

"I wish I felt that way. Lucky," I blurt out. Our room has high ceilings, but it feels small and cozy now, with the curtains drawn, the candlelight flickering, and just me and Rilla whispering. "Don't you ever wonder what life would have been like if you hadn't gotten caught?"

"I imagine I would have gone along making maple candies and gotten married and raised a passel of troublesome boys, just like Mama." Rilla tosses me a piece of candy, and I pop it into my mouth. "But I did get caught, so there's no use thinking about that. I've always wanted sisters, and now I've got dozens. I'm happy here."

I lean forward, smoothing the rumpled blue quilt. "You don't mind that you didn't have a choice in it?"

"It's a sight better than being in Harwood." Rilla sighs. "We're warm and fed, and we have a roof over our heads. It's hardly a prison, Cate."

But it feels like a prison to me. Even though coming here was my choice, it really wasn't much of one.

I can't stop mourning the life that wasn't.

I'm not supposed to think about him, but the memories are devious. They sneak up on me without warning; everything seems to prompt them. They play over and over in my head, wonderful and torturous at the same time: Finn, teasing me about reading pirate stories; Finn, kissing me senseless in the gazebo; Finn, asking me to marry him and giving me his mother's ruby ring.

And the last: Finn, as I left the church where I was supposed to announce our betrothal, asking me *why*.

I honestly thought I could marry him and stay in Chatham and be happy.

Stupid. The Sisterhood never would have allowed it. Not when one of the Cahill witches could restore them to power.

What must Finn think of me now?

That line of questioning will only make me miserable.

Rilla's right. I've got to stop sulking.

I stand. "Shall we go downstairs, then?"

"Really?" Rilla pops up like a jack-in-the-box.

"Yes. I'm going to be a better friend, Rilla. Don't give up on me just yet?"

She grins and hops off her bed. "Oh, don't worry. I'm loads more persistent than that."

I'm picking up my books and Rilla's gathering candy to take down to the sitting room when there's a knock on our door. Rilla flings it open to reveal Sister Cora herself.

"Good evening, Marilla. How are you?" Sister Cora's eyes are a vivid blue, like sapphires; they remind me of Maura's.

"F-fine," Rilla stutters, astonished. "How are you, ma'am?"

"I've had better days," the headmistress admits, her lips pursed. "Catherine, could I trouble you to join me for a cup of tea?"

Sister Cora looks like a regal old queen with her shining white hair braided into a pretty crown around her head. She sits in her flowered chair, in a dove-gray dress lined with soft white fur, and she makes small talk. She pours me tea.

She makes me wait.

Worries race through my head. Has something happened to Maura or Tess? Has she learned more about the prophecy? The headmistress does not summon girls to her office to take tea without cause.

"Can I help you with something, Sister?" I ask finally.

She considers me over her gold-rimmed teacup. "I would like to trust you, Catherine."

She says it as though she has her doubts.

"I feel the same about you," I say evenly, smoothing my navy skirts.

She gives a rich, throaty cackle that seems more befitting a barmaid than a queen. "Fair enough. I know you aren't here on your own terms. I would apologize, but that would make me a bit of a hypocrite, wouldn't it? I would like you to trust me, but I understand that such trust is not built quickly. Unfortunately, I'm afraid we haven't much time. Here."

As she hands me the cup of tea, her little finger brushes mine.

The second my skin touches hers, I gasp.

Sister Cora is ill. Sickness lurks in her body, malignant. I reach out with my magic, feel it like a black cloud in her stomach, and wrench away with a sense of self-preservation. My cup smashes on the floor. Tea splashes across my taffeta gown and mingles with shards of white china on the bright green rug.

"I'm so sorry," I say, mortified, but I can't shake my eyes loose from hers.

She waves a hand, and pieces of the shattered cup fly into the garbage bin beside her desk. "You can feel it, then," she says.

"You're ill," I whisper. Even the flickering, flattering candlelight reveals the wrinkles of her face and throat and the blue veins lining the parchment-thin skin of her hands. She must be near seventy.

"I'm dying," she corrects. "Sophia's tried her best, but she can only buy me a few hours' peace. What troubles me most is the question of who will succeed me. It has been agreed that Inez will lead until the prophesied witch comes of age. I will be blunt with you, Catherine. You will be seventeen in March, and I would prefer Inez not guide the Sisterhood any longer than necessary. I need you to understand what is at stake here."

Fear skitters up my spine. I'm not ready for this. I'm used to protecting my sisters, but being responsible for over a hundred witches? I don't know what to do, how to keep them safe. I thought it would be years yet before I was required to step up and lead!

"I'm aware of what's at stake." I stand up, planting my hands on my hips. My fear makes me snappish. "I'm a witch; my sisters are witches; my friends are witches. Do you think I *want* to see girls like us drowned or hanged or burnt? I wish to heaven I knew how to prevent it, but I don't! I don't know what you want from me."

Sister Cora takes another sip of her tea. "If you'll sit down, I'll explain."

I situate myself in the tall flowered chair next to hers,

wrapping both hands around the new teacup she gives me. The convent is a thoroughly modern building; it has been renovated to include radiators with gas heat and water closets with flushing toilets. But every room has high ceilings and arched Gothic windows, and the November wind is drafty. I can never get entirely warm here.

"You're a clever girl, Catherine. I trust you have noticed the divide within the Sisterhood at present," Sister Cora begins. "Some have grown tired of waiting, weary of the injustices against witches and women alike. Now that we've found you, they want outright war with the Brothers. The time is coming, they say, for us to take back our power, to strike using whatever means necessary. Have you heard that sort of talk?"

"I have." I've heard Alice give impassioned speeches in the sitting room after dinner.

"Then there are those of us who would bide our time. Who are afraid of what the human cost of such a war could be. I fall into the latter camp," Sister Cora admits. "I think waging war before we are ready could be disastrous."

I take a sip of my tea, which is delicious and spicy; I think it must have powdered ginger in it. "What would you have us do in the meantime?"

"Wait for you to come into your own. I have faith in Persephone and in this prophecy, Catherine, even if we don't fully understand it yet." Even if I haven't proved useful yet, she means. "I would gather intelligence. I have spies within the Brotherhood. One of them is a member of the Head Council. He'll be in line for succession after Covington, and he's working to see to it that those on our side are placed in positions of power. It won't happen overnight, but I think it's the best way."

"The safest, probably," I say. "Less chance of us all being murdered in our beds."

She smiles wryly, and I can see that, once, she must have been a very beautiful woman. It's still there in the curve of her jaw, the tilt of her head. "I am trying to prevent that, yes. The odds are stacked against us if it comes to outright war. There are thousands of Brothers and only a few hundred of us."

"Brother Covington could lead for another twenty years," I point out. "He's popular. Charming."

"We could see to it that he doesn't. Things are changing, Catherine. The general populace is becoming dissatisfied with the Brothers' heavy hand." I nod, remembering the boys throwing rocks at O'Shea and Helmsley. "But if we move too fast—if we lead by fear—well. I would hate to see us repeat the mistakes of the past."

I run a finger around the edge of my teacup. Her caution appeals to me. How often has Maura chided me for being too plodding and careful? "I'm in no hurry to lead a war, if that's what you're asking."

Her smile has more warmth in it now. "I'm glad to hear that, because I—"

The door bursts open, and Sister Gretchen clatters in, flushed and panting from her climb up the stairs. "Cora! Forgive the intrusion. Two members of the New London council have just turned up, requesting an audience with you. I've put them in the parlor."

Sister Cora grabs a leather-bound diary from the tea table and slips on her half-moon spectacles. "We had no appointment. Did they say what's the matter?"

Sister Gretchen shakes her head, thick gray curls bouncing. "No, but O'Shea doesn't seem like the patient sort."

"He's not. Odious creature. I wish they'd sent Brennan," Sister Cora mutters, bracing herself against the back of the chair as she stands. Pain flits across her face. "Blast."

Her blue eyes meet Sister Gretchen's, warm and hazel. They seem to have a whole conversation without words. Rilla told me that they're thick as thieves, these two, that they've been best friends since they were girls together in the convent school. If Mother and Zara were both still alive, would they be able to talk with their eyes, too?

Will Rilla and I, someday?

"Why don't you accompany us, Catherine?" Sister Cora asks. "A call like this, coming out of the blue—it's almost certain to be trouble. If not for us, then for others. But it's imperative that you stay quiet, no matter what they say. Can you do that?"

"Yes." But I can't help feeling nervous. What could the Brothers want at this hour? What is so important that it couldn't wait for morning?

"Let's go, then. It won't do to keep them waiting."

Sister Gretchen offers her arm, but Cora waves her off. She doesn't limp, but she walks gingerly, as though each movement causes her pain. Gretchen and I follow.

When we finally reach the front parlor, two Brothers are sitting side by side on the olive settee. This room is an austere affair, all stiff horsehair furniture with ornately carved arms and subdued dark hues. Dead headmistresses' portraits adorn the walls; heavy velvet curtains shroud us in darkness. Sister Cora meets with girls' parents and liaisons from the Brotherhood here.

It was here that I slapped Mrs. Corbett—*Sister* Gillian Corbett, my former neighbor and chaperone on the trip to New London—the day I arrived. She assured me she would look after my sisters in my absence; she said they could only benefit from being out from under my thumb. I lost my temper, and I slapped her right across her smug fat face. I smile at the memory, but it disappears when I see the grim looks on the Brothers' faces. They are familiar: Brother O'Shea is the same man who arrested Lavinia Anderson, and he's brought his hulking accomplice with him.

"Sister Cora," Brother O'Shea says, standing, "this is Brother Helmsley. And—Sister Gertrude, was it?"

"Gretchen," Cora corrects him. "And this is one of our most promising young novitiates, Sister Catherine."

I am taller than he is, but I don't dare look him in the eye. Instead I bow my head, fighting not to shiver. The room is freezing, the fire no doubt hastily lit when callers turned up.

"It is a relief to find a young woman dedicating herself to the Lord instead of wantonly parading herself through the city streets," O'Shea says. It's obvious that he does not recognize me, and for once I'm glad of the anonymity of the Sisterhood.

Brother O'Shea gestures toward the floor, and the three of us kneel. "The Lord bless you and keep you this and all the days of your life," he intones.

"Thanks be," we chorus, hauling ourselves back to our feet. And though it is our home, we do not sit until Brother O'Shea lowers himself back to the settee and gestures at us again. Then Sister Cora takes the brown silk chair by the fire, with Sister Gretchen on the round, tasseled ottoman next to her. I stand like a sentinel behind them, nerves stretched thin.

"As you may know, the National Council session has begun," Brother O'Shea says. As if we could forget. The city's been flooded with hundreds of Brothers, and Sister Cora warned us to be particularly careful of our conduct during their three-week meeting. "It is a time of reflection. We pray to the Lord to guide us, to teach us how to better control our weak and rebellious flock. Today we were blessed with his wisdom. Two new measures have been passed."

"Two?" Sister Cora gasps.

That's unheard of. Sometimes entire years and National Council meetings pass without new measures. I clasp my hands in front of me, twisting Mother's pearl ring round and round on my finger.

"When we heard the news from France, we realized measures had to be taken immediately to prevent the contagion from spreading," O'Shea says, crossing his feet at the ankles.

Contagion? I don't pay much attention to the news from overseas, but I don't remember hearing of a sickness.

Helmsley is silent, dwarfing the settee with his bulk. It would seem his purpose is to manhandle women and frighten children, not to speak.

Brother O'Shea pauses, perhaps for dramatic effect. I look at his fingers, spread on his knee: clean and uncallused, with long, neatly trimmed nails. Somehow I think of Finn's hands: freckled, splotched with ink, dirt beneath his nails from an honest day's work in the garden.

Is Finn in New London? New members always accompany Brother Ishida to the National Council meeting for their initiation ceremony.

He must be here, but he hasn't tried to see me.

Does he hate me?

He would have every right. He joined the Brotherhood to protect me and then I left him without an explanation.

But the notion of him giving up on me, on us, so easily— it stings.

"The French have given their women the right to vote," Brother O'Shea continues. "Perhaps it is to be expected, given their close ties with Arabia. But it's forced us to take stock. We must make certain that our women remain innocent of such worldly matters, focused on maintaining a cheerful home and raising good, Lord-fearing children. Our new measures are meant to remind women of their true purpose."

Oh, no. This will be worse than a plague.

"Of course." Sister Cora's head is bowed slightly, like a tulip in the rain. "We are here to help you in any way we can."

"I hope that your resolve will remain steadfast after you learn how the measures will affect the Sisterhood." Brother O'Shea clears his throat. Helmsley smiles and flexes his big hands. Is he hoping that we will rebel and that he'll get to arrest someone tonight?

My heart pounds in my chest. Is this some perverse sort of test?

"The first measure, effective immediately, forbids women from working outside the home." O'Shea puffs out his chest, obviously pleased.

I think of Marianne Belastra, whose bookshop kept her family afloat after Finn's father's death. Of Mrs. Kosmoski, the dressmaker in Chatham. Of widows like Lavinia Anderson, who will now need to rely on the Brothers' charity to feed their families. That's what the Brothers want, I suppose. Utter dependence.

"Are there provisions for widows?" Sister Gretchen asks. She's a widow herself. Childless. She returned to the Sisterhood after her husband's death.

Brother O'Shea shakes his head. "The sole exception is for nurses—for modesty's sake, you know. Now. The second measure, also effective immediately, forbids that girls should be taught to read. We cannot help those who already have such knowledge, of course, but in the future, we think it unnecessary and even dangerous. Girls can rely upon the knowledge of their fathers, their husbands, and the Brotherhood. They need not seek it elsewhere."

The room is shocked silent. There's no sound save the hissing of the gas lamps on either side of the mantel.

I look down at Sister Cora and Sister Gretchen, at their carefully blank faces.

I cannot imagine a life without books.

Without Father's stories of the ancient Greek gods and goddesses, without pirate stories and fairy tales and poems. Without the hope of another way, of freedom and adventure beyond what we have here and now. How dark life would be.

I think of the people I love, the ones I would trust with my own life. Maura. Tess. Finn. Marianne. Mad about books, all of them. What will this new decree do to them?

I find myself clenching my fists and force my fingers to relax. I mustn't look as though I want to start a brawl.

"You will need to recall your governesses," Brother O'Shea says.

"I understand." Sister Cora's voice is hushed, her shoulders rigid. "I will write them immediately. Is our school to remain open?"

"For the time being." His clipped voice and lemon face make it clear he doesn't approve. "There will be a bonfire in Richmond Square on Friday night, as there will be in each town in the coming days. We ask the faithful to bring books from their own libraries—fiction and fairy tales, that sort of thing—to burn."

My hand flies, horrified, to my mouth. Brother O'Shea's pale eyes follow it.

"Pardon me, sir," I wheeze, forcing a cough.

He stiffens on the settee, back ramrod-straight. "We trust we can count on the Sisters for a contribution."

"Oh, yes," Sister Cora says, shifting in the slippery silk chair. "You can always count on us."

"I'm glad to hear it." He leans forward, his eyes narrow as he looks at each of us in turn. "There's one more matter, and it's the most vital. We've discovered an oracle in Harwood Asylum."

I command my face not to betray a single emotion. Brenna Elliott. It has to be Brenna.

"An oracle?" Sister Cora echoes. "Are you quite sure?"

He nods. "We've been watching her for weeks now. It was little things at first. The storm we had, the identity of a girl who's been stealing trinkets from the others, a nurse's baby that died of the fever." I hardly imagine that was a little thing to the nurse. "The nurse accused her of cursing the baby, and that's when she came to our notice. Now she's saying that another oracle is rising—one who has the power to sway the hearts of the people back to the witches, for she's a powerful witch herself, cursed with mind-magic."

Silence swells and fills the room, relieved only by the crackle of the fire. "Do you mean . . . ?" Cora asks.

For a moment, fear rumples O'Shea's thin face. Then he swallows, Adam's apple bobbing, and it's gone. "Yes. This new oracle, on the brink of discovering her powers, is the prophesied witch. The one we've been hunting for a hundred years."

Oh. I go so still that I can feel the blood surging through my veins, feel the air move in and out of my lungs. I am a Cate statue made of flesh and bone and pounding heart.

He's talking about me.

But I haven't had any premonitions. Not yet. *On the brink of discovering her powers,* he said. Prophecies are frustratingly vague. I could start having visions ten minutes from now or tomorrow or next week or next year.

Fear chatters through me. I don't *want* to have visions. The responsibility of leading the Sisterhood is enough. Too much. I don't want the weight of the future on my shoulders, too.

"Obviously, we must flush this creature out of hiding," O'Shea says, and Helmsley pops his knuckles one by one, as though he relishes the bloodthirsty prospect. "There has never been an oracle who was also a witch, much less one capable of altering people's minds. There are always some whispers against us, but I fear the sort of frenzy she could whip the people into. She could use her magic to twist them against us. The future of New England rests on finding and containing her, Cora. Women's tongues may be less guarded around you and your novitiates. If you hear the slightest whisper—even the barest suspicion of mind-magic *or* of premonitions—you must report it to us."

"Y-yes, of course," Sister Cora stammers. Sister Gretchen helps her to her feet as Brother O'Shea stands.

My heart hammers through the ritual blessings.

When the Brothers arrested Brenna, they said she was delusional. That it was presumptuous to think a woman could do the work of the Lord. Now they believe in her visions?

Perhaps she's got it wrong. She *is* half mad.

Do all oracles go mad? The thought leaves me trembling.

When the Brothers take their leave, when the front door is shut firmly behind them, Sister Cora turns to me and puts her hands on my shoulders, her wrinkled face folding into an origami frown. "Have you had any visions? Premonitions of the future?"

I shake my head. "No."

"No sense that something is about to happen, no dreams that came true later?" she presses. "I know this must be frightening, but I need you tell me the truth, Catherine, so that we can protect you."

42

I gaze back at her solemnly. She's just my height—tall for a woman. "Never. I swear it."

Gretchen bustles back into the room from seeing the Brothers out. "Have your sisters?" Cora asks.

"Not to my knowledge." They would tell me, wouldn't they?

"It could have manifested in the time since you left Chatham," Cora muses. "This confuses everything. I wish we knew the exact wording of the prophecy. You know the oracle they spoke of, don't you? She's from Chatham."

"Brenna." I nod, remembering the last time I saw her—cowering in the gutter, her yellow dress splashed with mud. She screamed, and the Brothers' guards slapped her into silence.

"Does Brenna know what you are?" Sister Gretchen asks.

"That's difficult to say. If you're asking did I tell her, no. But she knows things without anyone telling her." I turn away, warming my hands before the fire.

What if Brenna reveals me to the Brothers?

"An oracle who's not of sound mind is the last thing we need," Sister Cora mutters, staring out the window at the ice-covered trees.

Sister Inez, the illusions teacher, strides into the room. Within the privacy of the convent, most of the other teachers wear color, but not her. She is always dressed in unrelieved, funereal black. "It would be easy enough to eliminate a threat like Brenna," she suggests.

Sister Sophia, the plump and pretty healing teacher, follows her. "She's just a girl, Inez, and a sick one at that. I hardly think assassination is called for."

Assassination? I gawk at them. They can't just *kill* Brenna!

Inez shrugs. Her brown hair is pulled back into a bun at the nape of her neck, and between that and her sharp cheekbones, her face looks perpetually pinched. "They'll have her watched night and day. It'd be easier than breaking her out of that place, and with an oracle, compelling her to keep her mouth shut might not work."

"Listening at the vent again, Inez?" Gretchen glares.

"I knew there would be trouble as soon as I heard the news from France," Inez says. "Who knows what this mad creature will tell them next? She's a danger to us all, and particularly to Miss Cahill. Controlling an oracle, having foreknowledge of the future, could be what helps us regain our power. We can't risk that over childish scruples."

Controlling an oracle. I frown at her choice of words. The Sisterhood does not—will not—*control* me. I'm no one's puppet, oracle or not.

"I have sources in Harwood. I'll have them keep a closer eye on Brenna." When Sister Cora speaks, they all quiet. "I think it's too soon to suggest such dire methods. We may be able to use Brenna to our benefit."

"They'll be arresting girls left and right now," Inez points out, "on any pretense they can. They won't take any chances, not if this oracle could swing public opinion our way."

I pluck at Sister Cora's gray sleeve, careful not to touch her bare skin. "If things are getting worse, Maura and Tess should be here, with us."

I bite my lip, praying that this is the right decision. Am I making a mistake or rectifying one?

Cora gestures at the others. "I'd like a moment alone with Catherine, please."

Inez frowns, but she follows Gretchen and Sophia out. Cora shuts the door behind them. This time, she reaches up and pulls the chain to close the copper vent high in the wall. She grins as it creaks shut, then turns to examine me with her bright blue eyes.

"I'll write to Elena immediately, summoning her and your sisters, but there's something else I think we need to do, as soon as possible." I take a deep breath—what more could she want from me?—but Cora barely pauses. "I think it's time you met your godmother."

My godmother, Zara Roth, is in Harwood Asylum. I don't remember her; she was arrested for possessing banned books when I was only a child. But she was a scholar who studied the oracles, and I daresay she knows more about them than anyone else living.

"But she's in Harwood," I point out. Because Sister Cora didn't intervene in her trial. My mother never forgave the Sisters for that.

Sister Cora sinks onto the settee with a groan. "Yes. I want you to go speak with her. Find out as much about the previous oracles as you can—how old they were when their visions began and how they first manifested. There were two oracles between the Great Temple fire and Brenna, and the Brothers caught both of them before we did. Zara will know how. We won't let that happen to you. We *will* protect you, Catherine."

"You're sending me to Harwood? On purpose?" I can't get

past that. The asylum is the stuff of nightmares. All my life I've had the threat of it hanging over my head.

"You wouldn't be alone," Sister Cora rushes to reassure me. "Sophia goes every week on a nursing mission. If there were any other way—I don't relish the thought of you in that place. But Zara is very stubborn. She won't speak to anyone else; she hasn't forgiven us for her imprisonment."

I sit on the slippery silk chair, which threatens to dump me onto the floor. "What makes you think she'll talk to me?"

Sister Cora smiles. "You're her goddaughter. She owes you that much."

"And suppose I owe you, for seeing to it that Maura and Tess are safe."

"I'll send for Maura and Tess regardless. This new prophecy—it does cast some doubt on which of you is the prophesied witch. It seems that your magic is the strongest, but if—*when*—one of you begins to manifest visions—well, that ought to answer the question for certain." Cora's blue eyes meet mine. "It's your choice, Cate, but I do think it would be wise to seek Zara's counsel. She may be able to help you."

I raise my chin, pushing past my fear. "You're right. It's past time I met my godmother."

CHAPTER
3

THE SKY IS THE COLOR OF ASH.

Flames throw hideous shadows over the crowd in Richmond Square. People are gathered, thousands of them: working men in jeans and patched jackets and slouchy felt hats; businessmen in tweed suits and crisp cravats; children playing. Vendors sell drumsticks, paper cones of hot roasted chestnuts, and mugs of cider, as though we're at a fair. Women cluster together and gossip as they bounce babies in their arms, or shout merrily at their children, or keep quiet and curl into their cloaks. The air has a bite to it now that the sun's gone down.

There may be others moving in secret, as the Sisters do. But no one will stand up to denounce the Brotherhood tonight. Alice has been full of brave talk since she heard the new edicts, but she won't perform magic in a crowd like this. Not with hundreds of Brothers and their guards filling the square. Not with the bonfire right here, ready and waiting for us.

This could too easily be a night in 1796, when bonfires were held all over New England. When they burnt women instead of books.

The thought is not new, but it sickens me just the same.

I've never seen so many Brothers gathered in one place. They crowd around the makeshift wooden stage like a flock of ravens. It sets my heart racing, fear tumbling through my veins, and I hate that they frighten me.

Sister Cora has positioned us in the middle of the crowd, among dozens of families. In front of me, a woman in a gray cloak croons a lullaby to a baby in a red woolen hat. Her little boy, dressed in a matching red scarf, darts away to join a friend. "Jimmy, don't go far!" she calls after him.

I've turned to Rilla to suggest we buy some cider when I see him.

Finn.

He's at the edge of the crowd, standing next to Brother Ishida.

He looks just the same, but not.

His hair: impossible as ever, thick and unruly. His cheeks and nose, dusted with brown-sugar freckles. His full, cherry lips. His chocolate eyes, sad behind wire-rimmed spectacles.

The long black cloak that falls to his feet and covers his wrists. The silver ring of the Brotherhood that catches the firelight as he gestures. Guilt crushes me. He's had too many responsibilities since his father's death, but this new heaviness in his bearing—this is my fault. Whatever he's done in the last few weeks, it weighs on him.

He joined the Brotherhood for me.

I drop my eyes to the dead grass at my feet. I'm suddenly warm, suffocating despite the brisk air; I claw at the ribbon that ties my hood, and it falls back, revealing blond hair wound in braids around my temples.

I want to cross the plaza and go to Finn, take his hand, and lead him far away from here. Take him somewhere private where I can tell him the truth: I love him, I will always love him, no matter what they force me to do.

Does he still love me? Can he ever forgive what I've done?

I raise my eyes again, and this time they collide with his. I stumble back, reaching, unthinking, for Rilla's arm. My feelings must be written plainly across my face, but I cannot read him. Does he miss me, even a little? This terrible longing, this urge to run across the grass and hurl myself into his arms—that can't be one-sided, can it?

"Finn," I breathe. His name on my lips is a sigh, a love song, a plea for forgiveness.

And he turns away.

We are separated by twenty yards and hundreds of people, but it still feels like a rejection.

"Cate?" My roommate stares up at me, her hazel eyes full of concern. How many times has she said my name? "Cate, are you all right?"

"Yes." The word breaks from my throat. I press my fingertips to the corners of my eyes, hiding the tears, holding my breath to try and keep them from coming.

A movement—a flash of pink—catches my eye. Sachi Ishida, my best friend from Chatham, and her half sister, Rory Elliott, are waving their handkerchiefs frantically to get my attention. I pull my hood back up to shadow my face, to hide the stupid traitorous tears that will come despite my best efforts. "Excuse me, Rilla. I see some girls I know."

I weave through the crowd, dodging children playing tag. Sachi and Rory have a prime spot at the back of the crowd beneath a red maple. There are a few pigtailed girls playing near the tree but no adults within earshot. I launch myself at Sachi, almost knocking her down with the force of my hug. It's not seemly, but I don't care. She squeezes me tight, the gray fur of her hood tickling my nose, and then Rory air-kisses my cheeks with brash smacking noises. If anyone had told me two months ago that I would consider these girls trusted friends, that I would greet them with such blinding delight, I'd have insisted they were mad.

"I'm so glad to see you! What are you doing in New London?" I demand.

"We might ask you the same question, *Sister*," Rory says.

Sachi's dark eyes rest on my face. "What possessed you to join the Sisterhood, Cate?"

"I don't know what you mean. I'm very happy here in New London," I evade, glancing over my shoulder. A little blond girl gets her feet tangled in the hoop and tumbles to the ground. Her Indo friend helps her up, dusting off the back of her navy cape.

"Liar." Rory isn't one to mince words. "You've been crying, plain as day."

"You don't have to tell us now," Sachi says, eyeing me sideways. "Father's here for the duration of the council meeting. Finn, too. I take it you've seen him? Did he speak to you?"

I shake my head, unable to speak past the lump that's reappeared in my throat.

"Oh, Cate, you look a mess." She tosses me her bright pink lace handkerchief.

"Has he"—I wipe my eyes, battle my pride, and lose—"has he said anything about me?"

Sachi frowns. "To me? No. But I'm hardly his confidante. Father thinks he's marvelous, you know. He's always going on about Finn, what a brilliant mind he has, how he put his own mother out of business and so on. But there were moments in the carriage—when Father was asleep and he thought no one was looking—Finn seemed miserable. Just like you do now," she says, touching my arm with her gloved hand. She's got new pink satin gloves with mother-of-pearl buttons, and Rory has matching red ones. They're utterly impractical in this cold, but pretty.

I don't want Finn miserable, but the thought is still cheering. I stuff Sachi's handkerchief in my pocket and try to pretend I'm not scanning the crowd for his face. "Truly?"

"Truly. But you aren't the only one with news." Sachi raises her cider in a toast, then clinks her mug against Rory's, ignoring her sour look. "I'm betrothed!"

That snags my attention. "To your cousin Renjiro?"

"Father wouldn't stand for anything else." Brother Ishida is head of the Chatham council. He has no notion that his daughters are witches—or that Sachi knows about Rory's paternity. Rory herself doesn't know. Sachi thinks it's safer that way, as Rory has a tendency toward heedlessness enhanced by her sherry habit.

"She can't marry him. He's a dreadful prig. That's where you come in, Cate." Rory gives me her rabbity smile. Save their dark, straight hair, she and Sachi look nothing alike. Rory is tall and voluptuous and always a little coarse-looking; Sachi is petite and dark-eyed and elegant. But they're both dressed in the latest fashions, with heeled calfskin boots and fur hoods and bright, gaudy lace dresses peeking out beneath. At a glance, one would assume they're vapid society girls—not the sort to make trouble.

That would be a grave mistake.

"Me?" I ask. "How?"

"I don't see how I can get out of it, unless—" Sachi's cheeks go as violently pink as her gloves. "I hoped you might put in a good word for me with the Sisters."

"The Sisters?" I echo stupidly. I glance over at them. From here it's hard to discern one figure cloaked in Sisterly black from another; I can't even pick out Rilla. It would be a boon for me to have a friend in New London—a true friend I could trust with all my secrets. And Sachi is a witch, though she doesn't know the Sisterhood's true purpose. She must be truly desperate to suggest posing as a nun for the rest of her life.

"Do you think they would take me? I'm not very religious, but Lord knows I'm good at pretending to be things I'm not," she sighs.

"I don't know," I say slowly, though my heart leaps at the

52

thought. "I could speak to Sister Cora for you. You, too, Rory?"

Rory lets out a raucous bark of laughter, tucking a strand of black hair beneath her hood. "Can you imagine *me* a nun? No, thank you."

"Do you really want to go home and marry Nils?" Sachi frowns. "You'll become his *property*. And you're twelve times cleverer than he is. You can't want—"

"I do," Rory interrupts. "I want to be a wife and a mother. I want to be a normal girl. I've never had that. I want my daughter to have that."

Sachi's hands clench around her mug. "But—if you go back to Chatham, we'll be separated."

"We were always going to be separated. You can come visit me at holidays." Rory smiles. "And I suppose I'll have to behave, since you won't be there to intervene with your father. I don't want to end up like Cousin Brenna."

"Father wouldn't send you to *Harwood*," Sachi insists, lowering her voice despite the cacophony of the crowd.

Rory raises her thick eyebrows. "You give him more credit than I do. I suspect he'd be glad to see the back of me."

I bite my tongue out of deference to Sachi, but I suspect Rory's right.

Rory's wide mouth is set as she lounges against the trunk of the maple, staring at the bonfire. "Old hypocrite. He had no right."

"We'll find another copy," Sachi promises, tucking Rory's arm through hers. "Perhaps, when you get home, you could ask Mrs. Belastra."

Rory shakes her off. "It won't be the same! It won't be mine."

"Who? What's happened?" I ask, perplexed. At the front of the square, guards emerge from the cathedral, escorting a broad-shouldered figure all in black, and I know that must be Covington. People begin to press eagerly toward the stage. They say Covington is a wonderful speaker; people travel for days to hear his sermons, though they're printed the next day in the *Sentinel* for anyone to read.

"Father wanted to contribute to the bonfire," Sachi explains. "He went through our things while we were out shopping yesterday and took some of our books. There was one that was very special to Rory."

"*Cassandra*," Rory says. Tess had that book when she was little. I thought it was creepy, myself—the adventures of a doll that comes to life while the child is sleeping. "I know that book by heart. There's a jam spot on page thirteen. Mama was in such good spirits, she wasn't even cross with me for it. We had a tea party with my dolls that afternoon."

"You and your mother had a tea party?" Sachi asks. Around us, children pick up their toys and return to their parents, fidgeting as they wait for the ceremony to begin.

"She wasn't always the way she is now." Rory blinks away tears, her shoulders hunched, hands shoved in the pockets of her cloak. "When I was little, she was sweet. She used to sew dresses for my dolls. We'd make up stories about the adventures they had while I was sleeping, like Cassandra."

I think back, trying to recall this version of Rory's mother. She must have been respectable once, but I can't remember it. I know her only as a strange shut-in, supposedly suffering from nerves, actually plagued by drink. It's a wonder she hasn't been arrested—or perhaps it's not. Perhaps Brother Ishida worries what secrets might come out if she were put on trial.

I know what it's like to miss a mother. I can't imagine having to miss her when she's right there.

Sachi loops her arm through Rory's, and we take a few steps toward the stage as a handsome, broad-shouldered man steps up onto it. He has sharp cheekbones and black hair peppered with gray at the temples, and somehow he makes the Brothers' standard black cloak look like a fine suit. I've never seen him before, but I know who he is. Everyone in New England knows who he is. Brother William Covington is the head of the National Council.

Now he stands above us all as the crowd sputters into silence. Fathers lift children up onto their shoulders for a better look. A dozen guards in their black and gold livery surround the platform. I lift my face respectfully toward the stage. Covington is speaking now, in a drawl rich as honey:

"Fiction cultivates the imagination in dangerous ways. It encourages our girls to play dangerous games of what-if, when the truth is, it does not matter what if. What matters is the here and now. What matters is the path the Lord has set out for you." Covington's eyes scan the crowd, and he gestures in a way that makes it seem as though he is speaking directly to me. "We must cultivate other qualities in our girls. We must raise them to be good, obedient daughters and humble, obedient wives. Our girls must be pure of heart, and meek of spirit, and chaste of virtue. If they have questions, if they have longings they do not understand, they must offer them up to the Lord—and to us, the Lord's vessels here on earth."

The sky is an inky blue now. The bonfire crackles and belches smoke, but the night air has grown cold. Across the street, Richmond Cathedral looms up, blotting out the stars. I shove my hands into my fur muff, trying to search the crowd for Finn while giving the appearance of listening to Covington.

"I have asked the faithful to bring fodder for our fire. I am pleased to see so many of you have brought books." People in the crowd wave their offerings in the air, delighted by his approval. "In a moment, I will ask you to step forward, but first—"

Two guards drag a woman forward. She is crying, struggling against them, her hands bound behind her. A third guard pulls a cart piled high with books. "This woman, Hannah Maclay," Brother Covington says, "has been dealing in forbidden books. Selling them right here in the streets of New London."

The crowd boos. People crane their necks to see around their neighbors; children dance forward and are yanked back by their mothers.

Finn's mother is—was, until very recently—a bookseller.

"She has been poisoning the minds of our women and children with the kind of tawdry romances and macabre tales that are popular overseas. She claims that these novels are a treasure rather than treason. I would like to show her—show all of you gathered here tonight—just how little they are worth."

Two of the guards gather up great handfuls of books and toss them into the fire. The pages begin to blacken and curl, the words inside rendered dead and useless. Hannah Maclay lurches away from the guard holding her, and he shoves her, and—

She falls, shrieking, right into the bonfire.

Her black cloak catches fire. Her long brown hair.

Good Lord, will they just let her burn? Will no one help her?

No one is moving. The crowd seems frozen. A few children begin to shriek, and their fathers, unprepared for this spectacle, set them hastily on their feet. I want to shriek, too.

My magic bristles, rising in my throat. I'm about to cast a silent animation spell to move her out of harm's way when I realize I won't be the one the Brothers blame. They'll assume she used magic to save herself. And if they think she's a witch, they might toss her right back into the fire.

I force the magic down and pray instead. Please don't let the guards be as heartless as they seem.

It is a long moment before they reach in and haul her out. She is flailing, screaming. They push her to the ground and throw a cloak over her, dousing the flames, hiding her from view. She goes quiet.

The crowd is silent. I look to the Sisterhood. This time I spot Rilla, her freckled hands clasped over her mouth in horror. In front of her, the woman with the baby in the red hat is cuddling him close, turned slightly away from the stage as

57

if to shield him from the sight. Her son is clutching at her skirts.

I look up at Brother Covington. Everyone is looking to him.

His handsome face is arranged in solemn lines. He shakes his head as the guards carry the woman away. Is she alive? She is so quiet. "A regrettable accident," he says. "Caused by her own disobedience."

That did not seem an accident. It seemed a carefully orchestrated statement. A warning.

Sachi and Rory are huddled close together, their hands clasped, faces ashen.

The ceremony continues as though nothing's amiss. As though we haven't just seen a woman set on fire, perhaps killed. Certainly burnt and scarred for life.

A row of Brothers moves forward, each holding a book or two in his hands. They toss them into the fire and nod as if performing a sacrament. It's silent as a church service.

Have Maura and Tess received Sister Cora's letter yet? Are they still in Chatham, being forced to witness a bonfire of their own tonight? I know they'll think it sacrilege; I know they'll want to intervene. Even Father will be hard-pressed to stand by and watch this.

The woman pushed into the fire could have so easily been Marianne Belastra.

"That woman wasn't hurting anyone," Rory hisses suddenly. "And neither is my book. This is ridiculous!"

Her father has moved to the front of the line. Her eyes are focused on the book in his hands—a slim book with a painting of a doll on it and pink letters that spell out the name *Cassandra*.

"He's got to follow the rules." Sachi's shoulders have gone tight with worry. "You know that. He doesn't believe in exceptions."

"Even for his own daughters?" A muscle jumps in Rory's jaw.

Daughters? I almost fall over with shock. Rory knows?

"Even then," Sachi says, her guilty eyes meeting mine. When did she tell Rory?

"Are you defending him?" Rory's voice rises, and around us, people begin to stare.

"Hush!" Sachi drags her backward, under the shelter of the maple, and I trail after them. "No. Of course not. I am on your side. I am *always* on your side, Rory."

Rory is trembling with anger. "I hate him," she spits, staring across the square as Brother Ishida drops *Cassandra* into the fire.

And the fire leaps higher, flames jumping twenty feet. The Brothers scramble backward to avoid the heat of the sudden inferno. Women in the crowd are screaming. People are beating sparks from their cloaks, stamping them out with boots, muttering in consternation.

"Witchery!" Brother Covington barks.

I turn to Sachi and Rory, and then I see it: the book winging its way through the smoky air, over the heads of the terrified crowd, over the heads of the Sisters, and straight toward us.

The bonfire is reflected in Rory's vacant brown eyes.

59

It's Rory. She's the one doing this. She's lost control.

"Rory," I whisper, trying to bring her back to herself. The book is almost upon us, and then—

Sachi stretches up on tiptoe and snatches it. She hugs it to her chest with both hands, arms clasped around it as though it's a precious, precious treasure.

Around us, the crowd draws away, erupting in cries of horror and fear. People point and gasp. "Witchery!" "Magic!" "Lord help us!" Out of the corner of my eye, I glimpse a rich girl in white fur fainting dead away. A thickset man with muttonchop whiskers and plaid pants catches her. I suppose most of these people have never seen true magic before. Two dirty-faced boys dash toward us, curious, before their mother screeches at them to stay back.

I throw a quick glance toward the Sisters and find everyone—Sister Cora, Inez, Alice, Rilla—staring not at Sachi or Rory, but at *me*. I flush. I shouldn't be here, shouldn't draw any attention to myself, but I can't slip away now; I can't just *leave* them like this.

"Sachi, no!" Rory tries to wrestle the book away from her sister, but Sachi shoves her, hard. Rory falls to the ground.

"Stay away from me," Sachi growls.

Good Lord, what has Rory done?

My mind spins helplessly. There's nothing I can do to fix this. The Brothers' guards are pushing through the crowd, almost upon us. Everyone saw Sachi do magic—or seem to do it.

Rory scrambles to her feet, mud on her chin, on her hands,

on her fine fur hood. I grab her arm and yank her away just as the guards reach us. A tall bearded man slams a rifle into Sachi's temple, and she crumples to the ground.

I wrap my arm around Rory, restraining her even as I appear to give comfort. Rory fights me, her nails sharp against my wrists.

"Let me go!" she cries, her breath hot against my ear. "I have to tell them it was me. Let me go!"

What good is Sachi's sacrifice if Rory gets arrested, too?

"No," I say, voice loud. "Stay away from her. She's a witch."

Then Brother Ishida is next to us, his face gray and frozen with shock. I feel almost sorry for him as he looks down at his daughter, lying unconscious at the feet of the guards in a flurry of pink lace and black wool and gray fur. There's a gash on her temple, blood trickling down into the dirt. I think nonsensically that I could heal it, if only I could touch her. But of course I couldn't. Not in front of all these people.

A handsome blond guard spits on her. "Damned witch."

"Should throw her into the fire, too," a dark-haired one says, pointing his rifle as though he's prepared to shoot her if she so much as twitches.

No. Please, Lord, no.

"Sachiko, a witch?" Brother Ishida murmurs, confused. "My daughter, a witch?"

An older guard picks Sachi up, hauling her over his shoulder like a sack of potatoes. "This girl is your daughter, sir? I'm sorry for your loss."

"Where—where are you taking her?" Brother Ishida asks.

"To the prison, to await trial. Though after a display like that, there isn't much need of a trial, is there?" The guard shakes his head. "Best to get her out of here, sir."

"No," Rory moans.

I grab her by the shoulders and shake her, hard. "Stop it. Stop it this instant! You have to pull yourself together."

Rory looks down at me, then buries her face in my hair, her voice soft in my ear. "Cate, please, please, don't let them take her away. She's all I have. Please."

And even though she's been a fool, my heart breaks for her.

"Brother Ishida." It's Finn, standing very close but not quite touching me. His voice is smooth, unfettered by emotion. I stare at him blankly, stupidly. "Sir, allow me to see Miss Elliott back to the inn for you. She's suffering from a great shock."

Brother Ishida doesn't even glance back at Rory. He has so little concern for her, even now. "Of course. Thank you, Belastra. I'll just . . ." At a loss for words, he strides after the guards.

We are alone now, the three of us on an island apart from the rest of the gawking crowd. Half of the people around us have fled to a safer distance, while the curiosity-seekers have pushed closer to watch the spectacle. Cheeks flaming, I pat Rory awkwardly on the back. Sister Cora will have my head for this.

Brother Covington says something about how evil will out itself, but the light of the Lord and the virtuous cannot be extinguished. He seems pleased by this awful display. The fire has settled. The ceremony begins anew. Sister Cora and Sister Inez lead a group of the convent girls forward with books from our library.

Covington's words seem to come at me from very far away. "We have seen tonight that witches are so eager to save their false idols they would even risk performing magic in a crowd of this size. Of course, this only proves the righteousness of our cause."

My arms are trembling, my legs unsteady. Rory seems suddenly, impossibly heavy.

"Give her to me," Finn says, taking her weight. "I'll see her home. You ought to join the rest of your order, Sister Catherine."

Oh. It's so strange, Finn calling me that. So formal.

My composure cracks, my eyes flying to his. "I—I—"

"Miss Elliott ought to be more restrained in her grief," he interrupts. "A lady should not show emotion in public. Your choice of companion is drawing attention to you in a way that is unbecoming to a Sister."

I gape at him, surprised by his coldness. After all that's happened, he can't offer a word of comfort? Rory isn't the only one in shock.

I gather myself, giving Rory's hand a quick squeeze. "I'll come to you when I can. Or you can call on me at the convent. You aren't alone, Rory. Do you hear me?"

Her tearstained face peeks at me from Finn's shoulder. "You aren't alone," I repeat, before making my way back across the grass toward the Sisters.

Rilla steps forward, grasping my hand. "Oh, Cate, how

awful. Did you know that girl very well? What on earth was she thinking? Lord, your hands are freezing. Drink some of my cider; it'll warm you up." She shoves a cup at me.

I take a sip, warmth burning down my throat. I inhale the bracing cinnamon scent of it before I hand it back to her. "Thank you."

"Oh, you look as though you're about to fall over. Here, lean on me," Rilla says, putting her arm around me and rubbing my back. She's a big sister, too; she's good at comfort. "Lord, this night has been just awful."

My eyes prick with tears at her kindness. I don't deserve it. I haven't been a good friend to her. I haven't been a good friend to anyone. I just saw Sachi beaten and arrested, and I stood there and did nothing to help.

What good is all my magic if I can't help the people I love?

I shove my hands in the pockets of my cloak, and my fingers brush a folded piece of paper. A piece of paper that was not there an hour ago, I'm certain of it. I tease it out of my pocket and glance down at it surreptitiously.

Cate, it says. And the handwriting is Finn's.

CHAPTER

4

THERE AREN'T ENOUGH CARRIAGES for all of us, so we walk back to the convent. It is a long way, and the night has grown bitterly cold. We walk in twos and threes along the cobbled sidewalks, hands shoved into fur muffs or cloak pockets. The mood is somber; even Rilla doesn't try to make idle chat. People stream past us: fathers carrying sleepy-eyed children and women with their gloved hands twined around their husbands' arms. A sour-smelling man jostles my shoulder without so much as an apology.

We cross from the government district into the market district. During the day, it's a madhouse of people rushing in and out of cheesemongers' and dressmakers' and butchers' shops, but now all the shops are shuttered. Candles flicker in the flats above the stores as shopkeepers arrive home from the bonfire. The foot traffic thins even more as we reach our own quiet neighborhood; most of the people who live in these fine houses have the means to travel by carriage. I trail my fingers along a neighbor's trellis of red roses, inhaling their sweet scent.

As we walk up the marble steps, I look longingly toward the window of my third-story room.

Sister Cora is waiting for us inside, her face lined with worry. She waits until everyone is gathered in the front hall, and then she holds up a hand for quiet. "What we were forced to witness tonight was horrible. I'm sorry you had to see it. But it serves as an important reminder that we must keep control of our magic. What happened to that young witch tonight could happen to any of us who lost our temper. With the Brothers searching for the new oracle, we must be particularly circumspect."

"That girl was a fool." Alice pulls off her cloak to reveal a black brocade dress with a velvet sash at the waist.

I flare. "That girl was my friend. *Is* my friend," I amend, horrified. Sachi isn't dead.

Alice folds her arms across her ample chest. "And by standing there while she was arrested, you drew attention to all of us. I'm surprised the guards didn't question you."

"I'm sure Catherine would have handled herself well if they had," Sister Cora says. She raises her voice again. "Be careful, girls, and do not lose hope. These dark times will not last forever."

With that, she turns and walks upstairs, a dark figure disappearing into the shadows. Girls hang their cloaks on pegs in the front hall and then scatter in all directions. Most hurry upstairs to their bedrooms; some wander into the library, though I can't imagine how they would study; some rush to the sitting room, eager to talk over the night's horrors. Rilla catches me as I put my hand on the carved wooden newel at the bottom of the stairs.

"Come have some cocoa," she urges. "You shouldn't be alone."

Being alone is what I want. But I did promise that I would try harder and be a better friend, didn't I? So I let her tow me into the student sitting room. There are two parlors in the convent, as befit the private and public facades of the Sisterhood. This is where we take tea at the close of classes each day, and where girls gather in the evenings to socialize. It's a cheerful room with blue gingham curtains at the windows, gas lamps aglow, and colorful hooked rugs underfoot. There's a piano, a chess set on a little tea table, a basket of knitting supplies, and a stack of fashion magazines.

Mei sinks into a blue plaid chair, and I take the ottoman at her feet. Rilla hurries to the kitchen to fetch cocoa. Alice and Violet take their usual seats on the plush pink settee, and a few other girls scatter on various chairs and poufs around the room. For a few minutes, the only sound is the crackle of logs in the fireplace.

"Mama has a stack of novels hidden in a secret compartment in her closet," Lucy Wheeler blurts out, shifting on the piano bench.

"My aunt teaches the old dances." Daisy Reed is a tall girl with skin like cocoa and a slow molasses drawl. "She holds lessons in her barn. Girls come and waltz with each other, and my uncle plays his fiddle for the reels. My grandmother taught Aunt Sadie, and my great-grandmother taught her."

Daisy's little sister, Rebekah, sitting next to Lucy, gnaws on a fingernail. "They keep it secret from Gramps 'cause he's on the town council."

Mei slips a hand into her pocket, drawing out her carved ivory mala beads. "My family still practices the religion from the old country. We speak Chinese at home. *And* we're immigrants, so that makes us suspicious right off the bat."

"My father commits treason every day." Violet van Buren is the coachman's daughter and Alice's bosom friend. "He'd be executed for certain."

"Stop it. You're acting like scared little ninnies, all of you. This is what they want." Alice sneers at us. "They want us frightened. Too scared to defy them."

"I've only got the one parent now. The notion of losing him—" Vi swallows. She's a pretty girl, with shining black hair and big plummy eyes that must have inspired her name.

Alice rolls her eyes. "You should be proud of your father! Most people are sheep."

Vi takes the pins out of her hair, laying them on the arm of the settee, running her fingers through the glossy strands. Anything to avoid Alice's eyes. "I *am* proud. It doesn't mean I don't worry."

"I wonder if more people are dissatisfied with the Brothers than we know." My voice is quiet, but every head in the room turns. "Those boys who hit Mei were aiming for the Brothers. I've never seen that before."

68

"I saw my folks yesterday," Mei says, bending to unlace her boots. "Baba's not the political sort, but he was *hollering* about that new measure against girls working. My sister Li turned sixteen a few weeks ago, and she got a job embroidering corsets right off—making good money, too. Baba hopes they'll let her keep on sewing from home, but if not—"

"It won't make a difference to anyone with money. Their wives and daughters don't go out to work," Alice says, her heels tapping out an impatient rhythm against the wooden floorboards.

I flush. Father started off as a poor teacher, but once he inherited his uncle's shipping business, he became a merchant like Alice's father, with enough money that my sisters and I would never have to seek employment to make ends meet. Finn used to worry that people would say I was lowering myself by marrying into his family. That I would grow to resent him for having to sew on my own buttons and cook my own suppers. That was one of the reasons he joined the Brothers—to be able to afford a wife.

My mind keeps returning to his note.

Meet me at the garden gate at midnight. I need to talk to you.

That was all it said.

"Papa hardly talks politics to me, but I'd wager he couldn't care less," Alice continues. "The Brothers might listen to someone like him—someone they respect—but they won't pay any mind to shopkeepers."

"But if enough people are angry—" I begin. I feel like a child sitting on the ottoman, with my knees halfway to my ears, so I stand.

"It won't change anything. *We* have to be the ones to change things. Why can't you see that?" Alice demands, throwing up her hands. "'These dark times won't last forever,' Sister Cora says—but they won't end without some help from us! We can't just sit here waiting for you to start having visions."

I flush. She has no idea what it's like to feel so utterly useless. "If there was something I could do to make them come, I would!"

"Would you?" Alice sneers, and my eyes fall guiltily to the blue rug.

"We've got to do *something,*" Lucy says. She's one of the youngest girls at the convent, only twelve, with ruddy cheeks and long caramel braids. "We can't just wait for them to lock up more girls or—or start setting them on fire!"

"See, even Piggy here understands that much," Alice snaps. Lucy is a plump girl, and even a child's harmless love for sweets is fodder for Alice's malicious tongue. "Don't fool yourself, Cate; these people don't give a fig for women's rights, only for putting food on their tables. The Brothers keep them frightened—perhaps we should, too. Perhaps that's the only way to keep them in line."

"Isn't that what got the Daughters of Persephone ousted in the first place?" I ask.

My words fall into silence. The hair on the nape of my neck prickles, and I turn slowly.

"Miss Cahill?" Sister Inez stands in the doorway. "A word, please?"

Her voice still carries a heavy Spanish accent, musical and distinctly at odds with the rest of her. I've heard rumors that she stole across the border from the Spanish territories to the south when she was just a girl, risking execution to come to New England and find other witches. It makes her sound quite romantic, but I pity the border guard who might encounter her. I'm fairly certain she could eviscerate men with those eyes.

"Yes, ma'am." I follow Inez down the hall. She marches through her shadowy classroom to the wide oak desk at the front and sits behind it, her back ramrod-straight.

"Times are dark for the Daughters of Persephone, Miss Cahill, and I suspect they will get darker before this is through. The Brothers reminded us tonight what they are capable of." She straightens a pile of student papers and sets them aside. I recognize Rilla's messy scrawl on top. "I daresay it's time for us to do the same. And for that, we need a leader. Some sad little waif drifting through the halls won't do. The girls here need you to be strong."

"I am strong." Irritation stiffens my spine, and I throw my shoulders back.

"Prove it." She touches the ivory brooch at her throat. As usual, she wears black bombazine from wrist to throat to ankles, without any ornament, save this brooch.

"I've done everything you've asked of me so far. If there's something more I need to do, tell me and I'll do that, too." I left everything, Finn. My sisters. My garden. I left everything

I love to come here, to protect them. What more of myself could I possibly give up?

"Mind-magic," Inez says softly. "It is our greatest weapon against our enemies. I want to see what you're truly capable of."

I hesitate, my eyes falling to the thick leather-bound dictionary at the corner of her desk. "You want me to do mind-magic on you?" I don't know anyone who would volunteer for that, and she doesn't seem the sort to relinquish control easily.

"No." Sister Inez's mouth twitches, as though I've suggested something absurd. "I want you to go into the parlor and compel as many girls as you can to come to me."

The gas lamp hisses on the corner of her desk. From this angle, I can see that the blue glass shade is thick with dust. Sister Inez doesn't strike me as the sort to care for anything ornamental; there are few personal touches in her classroom. No paintings or fresh flowers or pretty vases. "With such simple commands, there's very little risk to the subjects, if that's what concerns you," she says.

I bite my lip. Surely she wouldn't put her own students in danger unnecessarily, but—

"It feels wrong to me, to go into their minds without their consent," I explain. "Perhaps I haven't acted like it, but I do want to make friends here. How can I expect them to trust me if I do something like this?"

"If you do it properly, they'll never know," Sister Inez says. "You aren't here to make friends, Miss Cahill, and you are not their peer. You are the prophesied witch. They don't need to trust you, or even like you; they need to respect you. If they fear you a bit—well, so much the better."

Her words unsettle me. She may be right, but that's not the sort of leader I want to be.

"Why now?" I ask, taking a seat behind a desk in the first row.

Inez's brown eyes narrow, her thick brows drawing together in the middle. "Would you rather wait until some moment of danger and then find you're not capable of it? Your squeamishness on this matter disappoints me."

I fold my hands on the scarred wooden desktop. "I'm confident that I *could* do it, were it necessary. But I won't do it just to please you, against my own conscience. I'm not a hurdy-gurdy monkey, you know, performing magic on command."

Sister Inez looks at me in amazement, but I won't drop my eyes.

"Of course not," she says finally, restraightening the already-perfect stack of papers as though she needs something to do with her hands. "I apologize. I understand that this must be overwhelming. We don't even know if you're the prophesied witch, now that this oracle business has come up. But until we discover otherwise, we shall proceed as if you are. And if it's true—well, you may be called to lead sooner than you think."

"Because Sister Cora is dying."

"She's told you?" Inez looks momentarily thrown by this. "Yes. It will be a miracle if she lives until the New Year. And when she is gone, there will be those who look to you for leadership, despite your youth and your inexperience, simply

73

because you are the prophesied witch. I want you to know that when that time comes, when we lose Cora, you may count on me. You're just a girl, Miss Cahill. Difficult decisions—heartbreaking decisions—come with the position. I've been Cora's second-in-command for years. I can make those decisions with you—make them for you, if you like."

She rises and comes around the corner of her desk. "You come of age in March, but there isn't any rush. I'm happy to lead for as long as you like." She puts a cold, bony hand on my shoulder. "Do you understand what I'm saying?"

"Yes, ma'am." She's giving me an out—a tempting one. "Thank you."

"Good. I'll see you tomorrow in class, then."

I stand, recognizing that I've been dismissed. But I've got the eerie sensation that I've just been given a test, and I'm not certain whether I've passed or failed.

Two floors down, the grandfather clock chimes midnight. I glance at Rilla, curled on her side beneath her yellow quilt. She lets out a reassuring snore. I tiptoe across the room and ease the door open, holding my breath.

I cringe at every creak in the old wooden steps. Down in the kitchen, I pause to wrap my cloak around my shoulders, tugging the hood up over my long blond braids. The November wind whistles eerily in the chimney.

The cold inside the convent is nothing compared to the cold without. As soon as I step into the backyard, it bites at my nose and cheeks and fingertips. The water in the marble birdbath is frozen solid. I hurry past the fogged windows of

Sister Evelyn's conservatory, longing for the steamy warmth within.

The wind slices through my cloak, blowing my hood back and sending my hair whipping around my face. The half-moon throws shadows onto the slate path. It would only take one girl pressing her nose to the chilled windowpane of a garden-facing room, and I'd be discovered.

The garden stretches the entire width of a city block; a wrought-iron gate at the far end opens onto the lane behind the convent. I grip the freezing metal and drag it open. A tall figure darts around the corner.

For a minute, I grin foolishly. Then I rush toward him, heedless, wanting.

"*Why?*" His face is shadowed by his black hood, but I'd know that voice anywhere—only I've never heard it sound so furious with me.

I slam to a halt as though a glass pane separates us.

It was the last thing Finn said to me that day in church. The first thing he's asking now.

We're so close. Inches apart. I could reach out and—

"We had a plan. I went through with my part. I expected you to go through with yours. I expected you to announce our betrothal. What happened, Cate? Did you—" His hood blows off, revealing coppery hair that's unrulier than ever. His cheeks are red, and the tips of his ears. He takes a deep breath, fighting for control. "Have your feelings for me changed?"

"No!" I stare at him, shocked. Does he think me so fickle, so faithless?

"Then tell me why you would do this." His shoulders are stiff beneath his black cloak, and the way he looks at me—I can't believe I thought him cold *earlier*.

I'm meant to tell him we can't be together. Convince him that I don't want him. It would be safer for him to forget me, go back to Chatham, and find some other girl. I should make him hate me.

I've told a great many lies, but not this. I can't bring myself to do it.

"*Tell me.*" His voice is clipped, but his brown eyes search mine for answers. I'm tempted to spill everything. To let him comfort me, convince me, obliterate my fears with kisses.

The first time I kissed Finn, his lips hungry on mine, his hands gentle as feathers on my waist, all my good sense was lost in a flurry of wanting—and then there were feathers everywhere: crunching beneath my slippers, drifting over the forbidden books piled in the closet, stuck in his ridiculous messy hair.

Even now, magic sings through my skin, aroused by this mad mix of fear and guilt and love and shame swirling through me. Aroused by Finn's body, inches from mine. He's the only one who's ever made me feel this way, half wild with wanting.

"If I am the prophesied sister, I owe it to the other girls. The other—witches." Even though we're alone in the night garden, the wind roaring around us, my voice drops on the word.

"What about what you owe *me*? Or yourself, for that matter?" His shoulders slump. "This isn't like you, Cate. Being here in New London, with the Sisters—it isn't what you want—or what the girl I fell in love with wanted, anyway. Perhaps I misunderstood."

"No!" I blurt out, scalded by the doubt in his voice. "I'm still that girl."

"Then what changed? I heard about Brenna's prophecy. The Brothers are looking for you. They won't stop until—" His voice falters, but we both know how the sentence ends. *Until I'm dead.* "Or is that it? Have you been having visions? You should have told me; you could have trusted me with—"

"I know," I interrupt. "I haven't had any visions yet."

"What, then? Did they threaten your sisters?" His voice softens, but behind his spectacles, his eyes are impatient.

"No." By then they wanted me, not Maura or Tess. I begged them to take Maura—it was what she wanted, after all, and it would have gotten her away from Elena—and to leave me at home to look after Tess. They refused. Said a witch of my caliber belonged to the Sisterhood.

Remembering it, I shiver.

"Mother gave up the bookshop for us. That was her life's work. My father's dream. I joined the Brothers, even though they stand for everything I hate. I did that for you, and then you left as if—as if it was nothing!" Finn's voice rises, and he turns away from me, gripping the iron gate with his gloved fingers.

"I'm sorry." It doesn't feel like enough. I shove my hands in my pockets to keep from reaching out to him. "I hated leaving you like that. I thought there'd be a chance for me to explain. I never wanted to hurt you."

"You did. You are." His words are blunt as he turns to face me. "Explain now. You owe me that much."

I look past him at the staring black windows of the convent. "We shouldn't stand here in the open," I say, leading him away from the gate and farther into the garden. The boxwoods are covered in a lace of frost. We press into one shielded corner, where the air is crisp and green and quiet. It doesn't feel as though we're in the midst of a huge, thriving city. We could be anywhere.

I hate to tell him the truth—to take the burden of it from my shoulders and put it on his—but perhaps it's better for him to know what's at stake. How he puts himself in danger every time he comes near me. Then he can choose for himself whether it's worth the risk of loving me.

The fear of him deciding it *isn't* battles against my desire for him to be safe.

"It wasn't my sisters they threatened," I whisper.

"Your father?" he asks, and I shake my head.

The moment the realization hits him, his face crumples, his eyes closing behind his spectacles. He lets loose with a barrage of curses. "It was me."

"And they said they'd inform on your mother. Or Clara." Tears lodge in my throat, and my voice comes out a croak.

"Damn them," Finn mutters. He slams his palm against the high stone wall that separates the garden from the neighbors' lawn. "You should have told me. We could have figured it out together. Now we're both stuck here with half the town hunting you and the Brothers throwing booksellers into fires—I nearly stole a horse and rode home. I'm still tempted."

"That would only cast more suspicion on her," I point out. I step forward, my hand almost brushing his arm, almost feeling the warmth of him.

"I know that," he snaps, and I take a step back. "I can't quit the Brotherhood. Trust me, I've given it some thought."

"I'm sorry, Finn. I'm so sorry." I don't know what more to say.

He runs a hand through his hair. "I've missed you. I didn't understand why you left, and it nearly drove me mad. And things are getting worse at home. They—we—arrested two girls last month in Chatham. It's like that all through New England. Harwood's overflowing with innocents."

His voice is bitter. Lord knows what he's been forced to do. "Who was it?"

"Mina Coste, on grounds of immorality." Finn's forehead rumples, and it's all I can do not to reach out and smooth it with my fingers. Mina's the youngest daughter of the family who runs the boardinghouse in Chatham: a willowy, laughing girl with strawberry-blond hair. "Her father caught her sneaking out her bedroom window one night. She refused to say where she was going. He beat her, Cate, and Ishida practically congratulated him for it, and I just stood there. I had to just *stand* there!"

I clench my fists. I've never seen him like this. He's always chafed against the Brothers' restrictions, but this barely leashed fury is new. Guilt washes over me. "That must have been awful for you."

"It was a damn sight worse for her. I couldn't do anything!" His laugh is a snarled, unpleasant sound. "Then they caught Jennie Sauter with an old atlas. She's just an ignorant girl from an illiterate farm family, trying to educate herself about the world, and—"

He cuts himself off. "I suspect it will only get worse. Part of me wants to go home to protect Mother and Clara, and part of me wants to stay here, where I can look after you."

"Where we can look after each other," I correct, tilting toward him.

He smiles, and it makes his eyes go crinkly at the corners. Seeing it makes the knot in my chest unravel a bit. Perhaps he can forgive me after all. "I could use a bit of looking after. I really have been miserable without you."

"Me, too. I missed you terribly." I'm aware of his eyes on my mouth, of the air gone electric between us. "But you could still tell them you've changed your mind. I wouldn't blame you."

"It's treason to quit once you've gone through the initiation ceremony." Finn removes his right glove and holds up his hand, displaying the silver ring of office on his finger. "Besides, I think—hope—I can do more good by staying."

His earnestness is my undoing. I take a step forward, and Finn crushes me to him, his lips soft at my temple.

"Cate," he murmurs, and his voice is hoarse with wanting.

"I know." I stroke his stubbled jaw with one finger, then curl my hands around his waist. I rest my head against his shoulder, inhaling the scent of tea and ink, of Finn.

Happiness chokes me.

I didn't know if I would ever be able to do this again.

His hands are tangled in my hair, roaming over my back,

tracing the lines of my hips, as if he's reassuring himself it's really me and I'm really here, in his arms, safe and sound. His lips work their way from my temple to my cheekbone. I tilt my face up, eager for his kiss.

It does not disappoint.

For a few moments, my entire world consists of Finn—his mouth, his hands. Eventually, I pull away, burrowing my cold face into his neck. He shivers and wraps both arms around me. "Good Lord, you're freezing."

"I'm all right," I insist. But above us, the clock tower chimes half past.

"You ought to go in. What if someone notices you missing?"

"They won't. My roommate sleeps very soundly."

"The one with the short hair and freckles? She gave you her cider," he remembers, and I nod, ridiculously pleased that he was watching, as conscious of me as I was of him.

"She's very sweet." I pull back to look up at him. "How's Rory?"

"Hysterical. I gave her some whiskey and stayed with her until she nodded off."

"It was good of you to look after her." It's so very Finn to want to care for everyone, even a sobbing girl he barely knows. "It was Rory, you know, who did the magic. Not Sachi. She lost control."

I explain the truth of it—that they're sisters and witches—much to Finn's surprise. "Sachi will be sent to Harwood, won't she?" I ask.

Finn nods, his chocolate eyes sad. "There's no avoiding it. Not with that many witnesses." He's right, I know, but it breaks my heart to hear it. He twines his fingers through mine. "Do you think you can risk sneaking out like this again? Not two nights in a row, but—"

"The day after tomorrow?" I suggest.

"Sunday," he agrees. "It can't come soon enough. I—I love you, Cate."

It still feels like magic, hearing him say it. I touch my lips to his, a quick butterfly brush. "And I love you. You mustn't ever doubt it."

It's mad and dangerous, these midnight trysts. For both of us. The day after tomorrow feels an eon away—particularly with my trip to Harwood looming. But as I slip back toward the convent, I feel more determined than ever to use my magic to help change things.

It's as though a pale, sad, imitation Cate has been drifting through these halls the last month, and now, buoyed up by Finn's love and the promise of soon seeing my sisters, I am made solid.

My confidence lasts until I slip into the shadowy kitchen, bend to remove my boots, and find Sister Inez staring at me.

"Hello, Miss Cahill." She's perching on a high kitchen stool near the fireplace. Ashes glow a soft orange in the grate. "Your roommate woke and found you missing. She was worried that some terrible accident had befallen you—that you had been kidnapped, perhaps."

I let out a forced laugh. "Rilla reads too many novels. I couldn't sleep, so I went out for a walk in the garden."

"At midnight? In this weather?" Sister Inez lights a candle

and sets it between us on the oak table that serves as a kitchen workspace. "I'm not a fool. I saw you weren't alone."

I go still. Has she told anyone else? Should I erase her memory of seeing us together? I suppose I'd have to compel Rilla, too, to keep her from asking Inez any troublesome questions. My mind whirls.

"There's no need to do anything rash." Even now Inez is wearing her black uniform. Does she sleep in it? Her chestnut hair is braided into a long plait that reaches her waist, and though she must be near forty, there's only a little gray at her temples. "I've no intention of harming Brother Belastra."

I hang my cloak on the peg by the door, though I'm reluctant to take my eyes off her. It feels rather like turning my back on a poisonous snake.

She taps her long, bony fingers against the table, and the silver ring of the Sisterhood catches the candlelight. "I take it the two of you have made amends? He's forgiven you for your desertion?"

As though I ever wanted to desert him. I give a terse nod.

"And he knows what you are? Knows the truth of the Sisterhood? It won't help him if you lie to me," she adds sharply.

"He won't tell anyone—he's far more sympathetic to us than to the Brotherhood," I assure her. I'm still hovering just inside the door, my back against the wall where the cheery yellow paper is marred by gray soot.

"That's perfect." Inez smiles. "Brother Belastra is a clever young man, by all accounts. There's a position available as a clerk for one of the members of the Head Council, Brother

Denisof. If Belastra applied for it, I could see to it he would be successful. He would remain right here in New London—and think how helpful it would be for the Sisterhood to have such an ally."

Selfishly, I am tempted. In a few weeks, the National Council meetings will be over, and Finn and Brother Ishida will go back to Chatham. Who knows when we might see each other again.

"I'd ask that you keep this arrangement just between the three of us, of course. There would be no need for anyone else to know—not even Cora," Sister Inez says.

I sidle closer. Candlelight makes the copper pots glow against the brick wall behind the cookstove. "But she already has a spy on the Head Council, doesn't she?"

"She does." Inez's jaw clenches. "But if you and I work together, we would be quite formidable. Cora is content to let dozens more girls suffer, perhaps even die, at the Brothers' hands. She'll tell you that sacrifices must be made, that it could be years until we are able to share power with the Brothers—and even then, it will be *shared*." Sister Inez spits out the word. "If things go my way, we could be in power in a matter of months. You and Mr. Belastra could marry instead of sneaking around."

I lean forward, resting my palms against the trestle table. Sister Sophia has left the bread for our breakfast out to rise. "I've already declared my intention. I can't marry."

Inez leans forward on the other side of the table. "If the ruse of the Sisterhood were no longer necessary, you could do whatever you like."

Inez is using my feelings for Finn to manipulate me; I know that, and yet I'm not immune to it. Frankly, her arguments make sense. After what we saw tonight, perhaps they make more sense than Sister Cora's caution.

"Will you speak with him about it? Ask him to apply for that position?"

I hesitate. "What else would you need him to do?"

"Just apply, for now." Inez blows out the candle. "You're doing the right thing, Miss Cahill. Put your faith in me, and I'll see to it that we both get what we want."

CHAPTER

5

THE NEXT MORNING, SISTER GRETCHEN knocks on my door before breakfast. "We have a problem downstairs. Can you come with me?"

I drop my brush onto my unmade bed. It's amazing how much sunnier I feel, having reconciled with Finn. And if there's a chance that he could stay in New London and we could see each other often—

"Of course. What is it?"

Gretchen squints at me through the bright light pouring in through the yellow curtains. "There's a girl here begging to join the Sisterhood. Miss Elliott. Says she's a friend of yours?"

I grab a few pins from the dressing table, twisting my hair up as we go. "Rory," I say from between the hairpins in my mouth. Tess always reprimands me when I do this; she says one day I'll swallow one. I smile. She and Maura should be here soon—perhaps even tomorrow.

"Is she a likely candidate?" Sister Gretchen asks.

Is she a witch, Sister Gretchen means.

But, in Rory's case, is that enough?

"Yes and no," I say. Gretchen and I clatter down the stairs along with dozens of girls streaming toward their breakfasts. "She's a witch, but she's unstable."

Sister Gretchen blinks at me owlishly. "Weren't we all once?" She waves a hand at the formal sitting room. "She's in there, with Cora."

Sister Cora sits on the olive settee. Her face is pale, her blue eyes haloed with pained purple shadows. Rory is pacing before the cold, ash-filled grate. She whirls on me the moment I enter. Her eyes are red-rimmed, and her black hair is sliding out of its messy chignon. She's dressed with uncharacteristic modesty in a ruffled mint-green taffeta monstrosity.

"Cate! You have to help me." She snatches my wrist with cold fingers.

"What's the matter? Is it Sachi?" Her crime—Rory's crime—was shocking, but surely they would still hold a trial for her?

"It's my father." The word is venomous on Rory's tongue. "Now that she's been arrested, he can't see the back of me fast enough. He's sending me home. I'm to leave tomorrow morning."

I adjust a hairpin that's poking me. "Well, that's probably for the best. You don't want to spend any more time with him than you've got to."

"Do you honestly expect me to go home and marry Nils as though nothing's happened?" Rory rocks backward as though I've slapped her. "This is all my fault, Cate!"

I glare at her, stalking over to the window. The burgundy curtains are tied back with brown velvet bows, and I gaze out at the empty street, trying to control my temper. "Then don't make it worse. Sachi wanted you safe, and you can't do anything for her here. Go home and stay out of trouble."

Rory collapses onto the brown silk chair, burying her face in her hands. "I want to do better. *Be* better. And I believe I could, except then I think of how he's always looked down his nose at me, how he never thought I was good enough to be friends with Sachi, and—I get so angry I could smash everything in sight. Perhaps I could forgive him for the way he's treated me, if he was a good father to her, but he's completely renounced her! Said he no longer has a daughter."

When he had one staring right at him. Brother Ishida is a cruel man.

"I can't see him at church twice a week. I can't be in the same town!" Rory presses her fist to her mouth, her breath ragged. "You have to help me, Cate. Please? I can't go back to Chatham."

I glance sidelong at Sister Cora, but her face is impassive. I look up at the ceiling, searching for the right words, admiring the ornate cornices fashioned with grapevines and clusters of thick grapes. I've never noticed it before, but they do match the hideous purple and olive grape-themed wallpaper. I wonder if the original decorator of this room intended for people to want to escape it as soon as possible. "I understand that you're upset, Rory, but you mustn't do anything rash. Just last night, you said you wanted to be a mother more than anything. Has that changed?"

Rory eyes me steadily. "*Everything* has changed. I want to be the sister Sachi deserves. If—*when*—she gets out of that place, I want to be someone she can be proud of."

Oh. The fact that she doesn't deny what she's done, that she doesn't try to make excuses for it, makes me think better of her. I feel a stab of guilt for treating her so coldly, but I won't coddle her. If I am to vouch for her, I need to know she won't pose a risk to me and my sisters and the rest of the convent girls.

"Can we trust you not to lose control again?"

Rory and I both spin to look at Sister Cora, who has obviously figured out the truth of last night.

"The Sisterhood is a refuge for dozens of girls," she adds. "We can't have you jeopardizing us."

"A refuge for . . ." Rory repeats slowly, and I can practically see the gears in her mind turning. She looks from me to Cora and back again. "You're witches? All of you? But that's *perfect*! I'd make such an awful nun."

"But you have to be able to *pretend*," I point out.

Rory looks at me with eager puppy's eyes. "I'll be good, I swear it! I grew up with Sachi, didn't I? I know how to dissemble when I need to. I can do this, Cate. I know I can."

I look at Sister Cora. She hasn't moved, has barely blinked. It's impossible to deduce what she's thinking. "Let me speak to Sister Cora alone for a moment, Rory. You can wait in the hall."

Rory tugs at her awful green skirt. "I know what I've done,

and I'll never forgive myself for it. If I could take Sachi's place, I would, truly. But as I can't—I need to be near her. And away from my father. Give me this chance. Let me prove that I can be better, Cate, please."

I nod, and Rory plods out into the hall. Her bouncy, hip-swaying gait is gone; she walks head down, as though she's on her way to a prison sentence of her own.

When the door closes behind her, I sit next to Sister Cora on the settee. I want to be seen as her equal, not a supplicant student. I want a say in this.

"So Miss Elliott and the girl who was arrested last night are sisters?" she asks.

"Half sisters. Rory's a bastard."

"She's the one who did magic in the square? And she let her sister take the blame?" Cora's feathery eyebrows arch in disapproval.

"Rory would have stepped forward, too, but I stopped her. I couldn't see any good in them both getting arrested," I explain. "Rory hasn't had an easy life. She's got a lush for a mother and a sherry habit of her own. And that mad oracle—Brenna Elliott—that's her cousin."

"Interesting. Perhaps she could give us some insight into Brenna." Sister Cora's blue eyes rest on me. "You want to send her away?"

I stare back, lifting my chin. "On the contrary, I think we should take her in."

"Why?" Cora drums her fingers on the carved mahogany armrest. Almost a dozen silver rings line her hands. "You've just outlined a damning case against her."

"But we've got a duty to Rory. Isn't that why the Sisterhood exists, to take in witches like her and teach them to control their magic? Half the reason she's so reckless is because she doesn't want to be a witch; she doesn't know what to do with it. And the other half is because—because she's never felt like she belongs anywhere except with Sachi," I say, puzzling it out as I go. "We could help her."

Sister Cora rises, wincing, and reaches for her cane. "It's a risk."

"It is." Rory has her faults, but so do I. So do *my* sisters. And what Rory did was only a more public version of what Maura did after Elena betrayed her.

I frown, remembering Maura on the night before I left Chatham: a small hurricane of heartbreak, shattering everything in her path.

I would want someone to give my sister a second chance.

"She said she's betrothed," Sister Cora points out. "Breaking her intention could cause quite a stir."

I rise, too, gray skirts swaying. "Brother Winfield would be glad to get rid of her. We could use Sachi's arrest to explain her sudden religious devotion. The two of them have always been inseparable."

Cora purses her lips thoughtfully. Behind her, three former headmistresses stare at me accusingly from their gilt-edged frames. "You're certain this is what you want?"

I nod. "If we turn away the girls who need us most out of a desire to save our own skins, what good are we?"

Cora smiles. "Your affinity for healing—your decision on this matter—how swiftly you sent for your sisters, despite the potential danger to yourself—it all speaks very well of you."

I stop Cora as she hobbles toward the door, wanting to correct her on one point. "It wasn't a sacrifice, you know, sending for Maura and Tess. They would never hurt me."

Sister Cora's mouth twists in pity. "For your sake, I hope that's so, Catherine. I truly do."

The carriage jolts forward as it turns off the well-traveled road from New London and begins to wind up the hill toward Harwood Asylum for the Criminally Insane. It's begun to sleet; tiny drops of ice ping off the windows. I shove the curtain aside and press my face to the clouded glass, watching as the frozen countryside rattles past. Cows lie in the muddy pasture near a half-frozen pond. A moment later, Robert stops the carriage to let a farmer lead a herd of shaggy brown goats across the road. It's nice to be out of the city—or it would be, if I could forget our destination.

There are five of us crowded into the carriage: five wide black bombazine skirts, five pairs of hands shoved into identical black fur muffs, five pairs of black buttoned boots hovering over the hot water bottles on the carriage's chilly wooden floor. Our disguise is more important here than ever.

Sister Sophia pulls her hood up over her black curls, and the rest of us follow suit. We must be getting close now. Anxiety twists my stomach.

"Good Lord, I'm nervous," I blurt, then immediately blush. What kind of leader admits she's frightened?

But the other girls are nodding. Mei squeezes my arm, her dark eyes sympathetic. "First time I came here, I was scared half to death. Nothing to be ashamed of."

"It gets easier." Addie pushes her spectacles up her long nose. "At first I was furious at the way these girls are treated. But that doesn't help anything. Now I just try to do whatever I can to make it a little better for them."

Even shy Pearl, who hardly ever says a thing, smiles at me encouragingly. She has enormous buckteeth that she's very self-conscious of, and no wonder; Alice is forever making fun of them.

The three of them come here every week with Sister Sophia. I marvel at their quiet bravery. Don't they worry that someday they might not be allowed to leave?

When it comes right down to it, that's what frightens me most about this visit. Not the fear that Zara won't speak to me, or seeing the suffering of girls who, but for the Sisterhood's interference and Tess's mind-magic, could be me. No, I'm afraid that the moment we roll through the gates looming ahead of us, an alarm will peal, announcing the presence of a witch, and I will be stuck here forever.

It's mad, going to this place on purpose. I can't help the nameless, superstitious terror that sweeps through my veins, turning my entire body to ice.

Sister Sophia puts her warm hand over mine, and my nausea subsides. "Calm yourself, Cate," she murmurs. "You won't be able to help anyone if you're in such a state before you walk through the doors."

I feel such a coward. If Cora hadn't suggested that I talk to Zara, would I have volunteered to come on a nursing mission? Or would I have hidden behind being the prophesied witch, the one who mustn't be endangered, and let others go in my stead, even though my gift for healing has surpassed everyone else's? I've been practicing, and though healing leaves me weak and sick, it gives me satisfaction that no other magic ever has.

The carriage rolls to a halt before an enormous wrought-iron gate with HARWOOD ASYLUM spelled out on top. The high fence stretches away on both sides, topped with barbed wire.

Robert exchanges a few words with the guard. Peering out the window, I catch my first glimpse of the monster that lurks on the barren hillside. It's a menacing three-story building of weathered gray stone. Two wings stretch out to either side, and at either end, huge chimneys puff charcoal smoke into the pale sky. Iron bars cross most of the windows; some are bricked over entirely.

The carriage rolls to a halt. Robert hands us down one by one onto the icy carriageway. Inside my fur muff, my fingers are clenched into fists. The four of us trail Sister Sophia like frightened ducklings.

Before we can ring the bell, a white-aproned matron opens the door. She has gray hair that waves back from her wrinkled forehead, a bulbous nose, and flushed cheeks. "Sisters, bless you for coming."

"It is our duty to tend to the less fortunate," Sister Sophia says.

"Thanks be," the matron murmurs, ushering us in. "Come

in, come in, get out of the cold. The uncooperative ward first, as usual?"

We troop up two flights of stairs, hesitating outside a large door that shuts off the whole south wing. The matron takes a brass key from a chain around her neck and fits it into the lock. As she pushes the door open, I clasp my hands behind my back to still their trembling.

I don't know what I expect—a bedlam of voices, girls shouting and cursing? angry rants and desperate pleas for help?—but it's silent as a cemetery. The faces that swivel to stare at us are blank, their eyes devoid of emotion. It's positively chilling.

The room is cloaked in gloom, without benefit of candles or gas lamps. I wrinkle my nose at the unpleasant smell—a combination of chamber pot and harsh lye soap. Two long rows of beds march down to the far end of the room, where an unlit fireplace takes up most of the wall. I suppose fire would be too great a hazard here. I shiver into my cloak, grateful for its warmth.

The women here must be freezing. They wear thin white blouses and coarse brown skirts like the burlap sacks of flour at the general store. Some of them have rough woolen blankets wrapped around their shoulders. The girls themselves are thin and hollow-eyed, as though they don't get enough to eat, and unkempt, with snarled hair and dirty faces and stains on their blouses.

Two nurses sit just inside the door. They rise as we come in; the plump one groans as her knees creak. "Look, girls, the Sisters are here to pray with you before tea!"

The girls look at us, then they go back about their business without a shard of interest. Our arrival barely penetrates their fog.

Sister Sophia warned me that the patients are kept drugged with laudanum in their tea. It prevents the real witches from focusing enough to do any magic and keeps the others quiet and obedient.

I am used to seeing women quiet and obedient. But I've come to understand that more often than not, it's a facade. This is a different thing entirely. Fury cuts through me, rooting me in place. It's not enough that the Brothers have taken these women away from their families and their homes, condemned them to live out the rest of their lives in this miserable prison. They've also taken away their abilities to think and choose, their ability to *fight*.

"Sisters!" A beanpole of a girl tumbles forward, falling at Sister Sophia's feet. "I am very wicked. I fear I cannot be saved."

"Get up, child," Sister Sophia says. "You should pray to the Lord to help you."

The girl shakes her head, her blue eyes morose. Her skin looks sickly and yellow with jaundice. "He doesn't hear me. I'm too lost. I'm a wicked, wicked girl."

"The Lord hears all his children." Sister Sophia crouches, her plump face soft and sympathetic. "What's your name?"

The girl huddles on the floor, her dark braid hiding her face. "Stella. Oh, Sister, help me, please. The Lord comes to me in my dreams, and I beg him for forgiveness, but he never speaks."

"It's a hallucination from your medicine, you ninny," the skinny nurse barks. Beneath her frilly white cap, her black hair looks limp and greasy. "The Lord does not appear to wicked girls."

Sister Sophia rises, pulling Stella with her. "Come sit with me, Stella, and we will pray together."

"This is your first time here, ain't it?" The fat nurse notes my interest as Addie kneels at the bedside of a girl with bouncy cinnamon curls who lies on her back, eyes staring at the ceiling like a corpse. "That one was a wildcat when she came. Bit and scratched the matron. Wouldn't know it now, would you? Won't say boo to a goose!" She chuckles, and spittle hits my cheek. I resist the urge to wipe it away.

She gestures at the blond girl curtsying to Pearl. "That one says she's engaged to a prince! Still does her hair real nice, just in case he comes to call."

"They aren't permitted visitors, are they?"

At the end of the row, several other girls are curled up, sleeping, beneath threadbare brown blankets.

The nurse shakes her head, double chin wagging. "Oh, no, they're best kept away from normal folks. 'Specially the girls up here. They're the ones what fought us when they came in or what don't take their tea. They get extra medicine now. Gives a few of them right funny ideas, but keeps most of 'em quiet as mice."

I work to keep the horror off my face. Mei heads down the second row of beds, taking the hands of a beautiful brown-skinned Indo girl who is swaying back and forth to music only she can hear. As she turns to Mei, I see the bruise blackening her right eye and the cut on her cheekbone.

"What happened to that girl?"

"Oh, she's one of Brother Cabot's favorites. Doesn't usually put up such a fuss anymore."

"His . . . favorites?" I echo uncertainly.

"He likes the pretty ones." The nurse winks at me.

"Is that . . . common?" I ask, remembering lovely Mina Coste and Jennie Sauter and all the other girls from Chatham who have been sentenced here.

"Well, he ain't the only one who comes by for inspections regular-like. The matron before this one tried to put a stop to it, you know, and got sacked for her trouble. It's best not to get involved."

Someone claws at my wrist with sharp nails, and I jump.

"Sarah Mae," the nurse chides, and I look down into squinted green eyes. A freckled girl, no more than thirteen, stares up at me. The bottom of her skirt is muddy, and her cheek is smudged with dirt, her brown hair tangled with leaves. "Look at you. What were you doing on your morning constitutional?"

"Presiding over a funeral," she says. "Will you say a prayer with me, Sister?"

"Er—certainly, I'll—"

The nurse tuts. "Not in this shameful state, missy! Only good girls what brush their hair and behave get to speak to the nice Sister," she insists, hustling me down the row. "Loves animals, that one. Finds dead birds and buries them. Right creepy, it is."

98

There's a sudden clamor as the door opens and the matron reenters with a tea cart. "Teatime, girls!" she announces, smiling. "Line up!"

Several women bolt forward.

"They act like they're starving." But there doesn't seem to be any food on the cart.

The nurse shakes her frizzy gray head. "They get two meals a day—porridge for breakfast and a hot supper. What those girls want is their tea." I raise my eyebrows, and she cackles again. "Some of 'em get the shakes without it."

"I see." The girls each take a cup and hold it out to be filled—not poured from a teapot but ladled from a large, steaming soup tureen. Some of them cup their hands around the warmth and stare down at it for a moment first; others slurp greedily. The matron and the skinny dark-haired nurse watch as each girl drinks.

"Drink up, Mercedes," the matron chides, and a woman obediently tilts the cup to her mouth, her throat working.

"Some of 'em will try and give it away, or pour it into the chamber pot if we ain't careful," the nurse explains. "Sneaky things."

She goes on, gossiping about this patient and that, but I'm watching the girls at the end of the line. A few try to maneuver their way out of taking the tea, to no avail. One woman drops her cup on the floor, and the matron slaps her before handing her another. A tiny blonde holds the cup in her hands but refuses to drink, staring stonily as the matron exhorts her not to put up a fuss. Eventually, the matron nods at the skinny nurse, who pinches the girl's nose shut. When she gasps for air, the matron pours the tea down her throat. The girl gags and coughs—and swallows.

"It's time for us to move on to another ward," Sister Sophia calls from the doorway.

I look around the room, committing the misery to memory, and I make a promise. I will make things better for these girls. They will not spend the rest of their lives here—not if I can help it.

Out in the hall, Sister Sophia takes my elbow. "Are you all right?" she asks, and I nod. I wonder if I look as horrified as I feel. "Pearl and Addie and I will go to the infirmary on the first floor. Why don't you and Mei visit the second floor and then meet us downstairs? Mei will take the north wing, and you can take the south."

My mind spins with questions. Will I know Zara when I see her? Will she recognize me? She must have some of her wits about her; she wrote me a note earlier this fall, urging me to seek out my mother's diary. How drugged is she? Is her mind clear enough to help us, even if she's willing?

There is a nurse posted just inside the door to the south wing. She's a tall, broad woman bent over some knitting; she doesn't bother to leave her stool when she sees it's only me. "Most of the girls here are at work, Sister."

"Work?" I ask. "What sort of work are they capable of?"

"Ah, you must be a new one." The nurse smiles. She has an enormous red birthmark splotched over her right cheek. "This wing houses the patients who don't give us any trouble. Some of them help with the kitchen garden, some down in the kitchens or the laundry. All supervised, of course, but you know what they say—idle hands breed devilry."

"Of course." It's such a gloomy place; I don't know how anyone keeps from going mad here. The scratched wooden floorboards warp and waver beneath my boots, and the hallway is dark save the nurse's lamp, with moth-eaten curtains covering the windows and peeling paper on the walls. There are no paintings or plants to alleviate the sense of crumbling abandonment. A small dark shape—a mouse?—darts across the end of the hall, tiny nails scrabbling.

There are small windows looking into each cell, with tags bearing the patients' names. I walk down the hall, peering into mostly empty rooms. Halfway down the right-hand side, I finally see z. ROTH, marked in faded blue ink.

My godmother.

Inside, a tall woman sits in a wooden rocking chair facing the window. Her cloud of curly dark hair surprises me. Somehow I expected her to be a little redhead, like Mother.

I take a deep breath and push at the door. It groans as it swings open.

"Miss Roth? Zara Roth?"

"What do you want?" Zara's voice is a dreamy rasp. Her brown eyes are dazed, the pupils narrowed to pinpricks despite the gloom. "I'm not in the mood to pray today, Sister."

"I'm not—I didn't—" I panic as the door slams shut behind me and the lock clicks into place. The nurse will come. Sister Sophia won't leave me behind. But I have to fight the urge to pound on the door with both fists and scream to be let out. The room feels suffocatingly small, barely big enough for the narrow bed and chair. There is not a single personal touch: nothing cheery or welcoming, nothing beautiful.

How can Zara stand it? She's been in this place for ten years.

"Go away and leave me alone." My godmother must have been pretty once, but now she's gaunt: long limbs poke out from beneath her ragged hem and cuffs like a scarecrow's, her cheeks are hollow, and her hooked nose is a little too big for her thin face.

I hesitate. I wish I had Tess's talent for reading people. "It's Cate," I say, stepping closer. "Anna's daughter, Cate."

"Cate Cahill?" Zara's hand flies to the gold locket around her neck. She searches my face for a long time. "You don't look like Anna," she says, turning away as though that's that.

"Maura looks like Mother; I take after Father," I explain, pushing a strand of blond hair back into my chignon.

Zara squints at me. Closer, I can feel the draft from the iron-barred window; I can see the crow's-feet etched around her eyes and the gray threading through her hair. She is only thirty-seven, the same as Mother would be, but she looks older. "Brendan was never handsome. Anna was so beautiful, she could have done better for herself, but they were in love." She shakes her head. "Why are you trying to confuse me, talking about Anna? What do you want?"

I bite my lip. "I just want to talk to you. I'm studying at the convent school with the Sisters, and I wanted to meet my godmother."

"The Sisters? Ah. Cora's heard about the new oracle, then."

Her laugh is a rusty screech. "She needs me. I knew it would come to this, soon as I heard the nurses gossiping."

I don't know what I expected—for us to fall into a teary embrace? for her to lie and say how much I resemble my mother?—but it was not *this*.

"Damn her for using Anna's memory to get to me," Zara says, apparently accepting that I am who I say. She flips open the locket. Inside, there's a tintype of Mother from when she was young.

"Oh." Emotion knots my throat. It's been a month since I've seen my mother's face in a picture; I brought none with me to the convent. She does look like Maura, with her curls and big eyes and heart-shaped face.

"I loved her like a sister," Zara says sadly. Then she recoils, as if stung by a wasp. "Your sisters—are they both alive?"

"Of course. They're on their way to New London now. Sister Cora thought it best—safest—for us all to be at the convent," I explain, perching on her bed.

"Is that wise, do you think?" Zara seems more alert now. "Considering the prophecy?"

"The prophecy is wrong," I say flatly, crossing my arms over my chest.

Zara's smile softens her long, angular face. "You're a fighter, aren't you, Cate Cahill? Even when you were a child, you had a temper. Lord, you were such a ragamuffin. Always chasing that neighbor boy of yours." I frown. Paul isn't mine anymore. "You kept coming home with your knees all scraped up from tumbling out of trees. Anna was afraid you were going to break your fool neck."

"Not yet, fortunately."

Zara twists her chair to face me, her knees bumping against mine in the tiny space. "They'll hang you, you know. Or perhaps burn you alive," she says, her eyes darting toward the door, and my smile fades to horror. "If you're the oracle. There have been two others since the Great Temple. They kept them here and tortured the prophecies out of them. That's what they'll do with Brenna. But you—they won't let you live."

I try not to let her words rattle me, but they do. "Because I'm a witch?"

"There's never been an oracle with magic before. And mind-magic, at that." Zara leaps up and crosses the room to peer out the peephole, then returns to the chair, her voice dropping to a scratchy whisper. "*Is* it you? Is that why Cora sent you?"

"I don't know. I haven't had any visions. I was hoping perhaps you could tell me what to expect. What happened to the other two oracles?"

Zara chews at one fingernail thoughtfully. Her nails are all bitten short, her fingertips cracked and bleeding. "I would like to help you. For Anna's sake. But you're one of them now, and I can't forgive what they've done. Not just to me, though that's bad enough. Do you know how many girls pass through these doors? How many are beaten or used as the Brothers' playthings? And when they die—and so many do, you know, they stop eating and just will themselves to go—when they die, there aren't even proper rites. There's a communal grave over the hill. That's all that's waiting for us. *And Cora just lets it happen.*"

I want to echo the vow I made to myself upstairs: I will save these girls.

But I don't know how, or when. "She can't save everyone," I say softly.

Zara turns on me, her eyes furious, thin nostrils flaring. "Is that what she told you? She could have saved *me*!"

She stares out the window for a moment. The sleet has turned to snow, coating the hillside in sugary white. In the distance, I can see the red silo from a nearby farm—and beyond that, the white spire of a church. "I'm angry with Cora, but not fool enough to make you suffer for it. You will suffer enough, if you're the oracle," she says.

"I hope I am. I'd rather it be me than Maura or Tess." I take a deep breath. "Will you tell me about the other oracles? How did the Brothers find them?"

Zara doesn't need more prompting. "Marcela Salazar was only fourteen when she tried to warn her father that he would drown swimming in a nearby lake. After he died, they turned her over to the Brothers. It's a wonder she wasn't killed outright for a witch. They kept her upstairs under lock and key her whole life. She died at twenty-five in the typhoid outbreak of 1829."

"Not much of a life," I remark.

"Not as bad as Thomasina Abbott's." Zara looks at me solemnly, fiddling with the chain at her throat. As she speaks, words rushing out faster and faster, she rocks more violently in her chair. "When she was twelve, she tried to warn a neighbor about a house fire. The neighbor didn't listen, the house burnt down, and then they accused her of being a witch and sent her here. She refused to speak to the Brothers, but they could tell when she was having one of her spells, so they resorted to torture—cut off her fingers and broke her leg so badly it never healed right. Then she started speaking nonsense, and they couldn't figure out if she was mad or only pretending, so they tried all sorts of awful experiments on her. Drilled a hole in her skull to try and alleviate the insanity, but that killed her. That was three—no, four—years ago. Then they dissected her brain. The nurse said there was no abnormality to explain the madness or the visions."

My stomach twists, and I feel flushed and sick at the thought of my corpse being cut up for research. "Will"—my voice comes out a croak—"will I go mad?"

Zara's wild rocking stills so suddenly that her chair crashes back into the cement wall. "I don't know. You'll be better off than most, because you'll know what the visions are. They can be disorienting. Cause headaches and confusion. The others tried to prevent bad things from happening, and that put them in danger. The prophecies always come to pass."

We stare at each other in dismayed silence. I know Zara thinks she's telling me the truth, but I refuse to believe it.

"Zara?" The nurse with the birthmark knocks on the door and leans in. I look up, hoping she hasn't overheard anything she oughtn't, but she only looks exasperated. "You mustn't waste the young Sister's time telling your stories. She's needed down in the infirmary."

"I was just telling her about the Minotaur," Zara says, her voice dreamy again. "All the maidens lost in the labyrinth. They needed a champion to save them."

"She'll tell you those scandalous Greek stories all day if you let her. She was a governess once," the nurse says, clucking disapprovingly. She holds her knitting against her white apron, and now I can make out a child's blue stocking. For a grandson, perhaps? "Say good-bye now, Zara."

Zara gives me a wide, eerie smile. She's missing several teeth. "Good-bye, Sister Catherine. *Cave quid dicis, quando, et cui.*"

"There'll be none of that, now. You'll speak proper English like the rest of us, Zara, or you'll get no supper," the nurse scolds. She turns to me. "What did she say?"

"I've no idea," I lie.

Thanks to Father's insistence that we all be educated in Latin, I'm familiar with the phrase.

Beware of what you say, when, and to whom.

CHAPTER
6

THE HARWOOD INFIRMARY IS A HELLISH place. An oppressive wave of heat greets me, like opening an oven door. The fireplace burns hot at one end, and the room feels small and stifling. The heavy curtains are pulled shut; candles throw monstrous shadows onto the walls. A dozen patients doze and cry and cough on their narrow metal beds, and the air smells coppery, like blood.

In the corner, a girl cries out for her mother in her sleep. Another girl is coughing—horrible hacking noises that rack her thin body. Addie sits beside a skeletal old woman who sucks in each harsh, rasping breath as though it might be her last. Addie looks so young next to her, head bowed in prayer, her smooth brown hair pulled back at the nape of her neck. As I watch, she touches the woman's hand and the patient slips into a peaceful slumber.

I hesitate in the doorway, perspiration gathering at my spine. I don't want to go in. It reminds me too much of my mother's sickroom, of death and dying. Down the hall, two nurses chat and laugh, having abandoned their posts to the Sisters' capable hands.

Sister Sophia hurries forward. "There's a patient here who's beyond my skill. Would you sit with her for a minute and see if you can help?"

Sophia leads me toward a woman tossing and moaning on her bed. Purple shadows blossom beneath her eyes. As she clutches her swollen stomach, I have a sudden dreadful suspicion.

"Please," she begs, with tear-filled blue eyes, "please bring me my baby. I just want to see her. Just once, before you send her away."

I look to Sister Sophia, who gives the slightest shake of her head, confirming my guess. The baby is dead.

"She was crying and then she—stopped, and now they won't let me see her. Where is she?"

Sister Sophia gives me a little push in the woman's direction. I want to run away. What help can I be, in the face of such immense grief?

"Sister, please," the woman whispers, her bloodless lips parched and dry. I look back at Sister Sophia before I realize she's talking to *me*. I pour a glass of cloudy water from the pitcher on her nightstand and hold it to her mouth.

The woman takes a sip, then turns her head away. "I want my baby," she says, her voice fierce. She has pale hair that tumbles down over both shoulders.

"I'm sorry," I say, wondering what else this woman has suffered, why she is in this place. "I'm terribly sorry for your loss."

It is the wrong thing to say.

"No." Her eyes go wild, and she thrashes toward the side of the bed, determined to rise and find her child. "No! You're lying. I heard her cry."

I reach out and grab her thin wrist, tugging her back to her pillow before she can pitch herself onto the floor. "Stop. You're not well, ma'am. You'll hurt yourself."

My words are calm, but inside I'm reeling with horror. This woman is dreadfully sick. I could feel it the moment I touched her. It's a miracle that she and the baby aren't *both* dead.

"What do I care?" She snatches her arm away. "I'd rather die than live the rest of my life in this hell. At least I'd be with her. They said she was a girl. My only daughter!"

I seize on this new bit of information. "You have sons?"

She nods, wiping tears away with the backs of her hands. "Two of them."

"Then you must take care of yourself. They need their mother."

More tears leak from her eyes. "I'll never see them again. They'll grow up hating me for leaving them," she whimpers.

"No. You're their mother. They'll understand, when they're older." I wish I could promise her that she will leave this place, that she'll see her children again. But why would she believe me, dressed in the garb of the Sisters? And dare I promise such a thing?

"What do you know of it? Married to the Lord," she scoffs. "You'll never be a mother."

Oh. I'd like to be a mother, someday.

I think of this woman's sons. I picture them as two tow-headed little boys, lips wobbling as they hear of their mother's death. That is a grief I do know. I reach out and circle her wrist with my hand, and I wish she could go home to her little boys so they need not know how it feels to lose her. I wish that she could be healthy enough to fight, when the time comes.

The spell pours through me. It eviscerates me, turning my body inside out, twisting my stomach.

Oh, it hurts. It hurts. This is much worse than healing Mei.

I slump over the woman's bed, head spinning, but I try to keep the image of those two boys in my mind. I don't let go of her wrist. I can do this. I have to do this, for them.

"Cate." Sister Sophia's hand is on my shoulder, pulling me back, breaking my grip.

I look at the patient through bleary eyes. My head is pounding. She doesn't look any different, only puzzled at my almost swooning on top of her. Did the spell work? I can't tell without touching her again, and if I touch her again, I will faint.

Sister Sophia apologizes to the woman—something about how new I am to nursing and how I'm overcome at her sad loss—and then she's wrapping her arm around me, shepherding me out of the room and down the hall and out into the snow. I throw up on the grass beside the carriageway. She bundles me into the carriage and instructs me to lie down on the leather seat. Only then is it safe to ask the question pressing on me:

"Will she live?" Was it enough? Was *I* enough?

It stuns me, how desperately I want my spell to have worked.

Sister Sophia studies me. She's so sweet; it's easy to forget she has a powerful intellect, an understanding of anatomy and biology that would rival any male physician's. I've heard the other girls whisper that she once dissected a human corpse.

She reaches out and brushes my hair back from my face. The gesture is heartbreakingly maternal. "You felt a strong connection to her, didn't you?"

I nod and the carriage spins around me. "I know what it's like to lose a mother."

"I thought her case might resonate with you, given your history," Sister Sophia admits. "She'll recover. You couldn't feel that the spell was successful?"

"I was too focused on my intention, I think."

"That happens sometimes, when you want to heal someone very badly. It's difficult to strike the right balance. Our work requires empathy, but you must remain detached enough to feel whether the spell is working and when to stop. Attempting to heal someone whose injuries are beyond the scope of your gift will make you very ill."

The nausea and dizziness are subsiding a little. I swing my feet onto the wooden floorboards of the carriage and sit up.

"That woman would have died in that place, without

proper medical care," Sister Sophia continues, her brown eyes steady on mine. "You saved her life, Cate. That's work to be proud of."

"I—thank you." The notion of taking pride in my magic, in being a witch, feels wrong. But saving that woman didn't. It was painful and difficult, but right.

"Before the other girls join us—" Sister Sophia leans forward, bracing her elbows on the knees of her black skirt. "Your gift for healing is very strong. You could do a great deal of good with it. But there are things you ought to know. May I speak frankly?"

"Please."

"First, you must be careful of the work you perform in the hospital, or in any public place, or upon anyone who is unaware of your witchery. The nurses here don't care enough to be suspicious of us. But if we were to entirely heal a string of patients, it would call attention to our visits—to you, and to the entire Sisterhood."

Oh. I didn't think of the difference between giving momentary relief and completely healing someone, and how risky the latter could be.

"Good Lord, I didn't even—"

Sister Sophia puts out a hand. "No. It's incredible, what you're capable of. But there are those who would take advantage of it. They will want to ferret out the limits of your power, determine how you can use it on behalf of the Sisterhood. There *are* limits; we are not gods. We must respect that, or it can be dangerous to our well-being, both physically and spiritually."

I nod. "I understand."

"I'm not sure you do." Sister Sophia sighs. "Life and death are two sides of the same coin. Being able to feel a person's life flickering inside him—it can be seductive. There have been witches who used their healing for ill. Who have used it against their enemies."

"How would they use it for ill?" I'm puzzled. "Do you mean—can we *make* people sick? Could I give someone a headache, instead of taking it away?" She's never mentioned that in class.

I thought healing magic was good. Pure.

I should have known better. Magic is never simple.

Sister Sophia nods. "You cannot give someone pain out of nowhere, but you can greatly magnify it. I don't mean to frighten you. You are only beginning to understand the scope of your gift, Cate. What we can do—in the right hands, it's a blessing. Priests and physicians often speak of their work as a calling. I believe mine is, too. From the Lord or Persephone or someone else altogether, I don't know, but I'm grateful for it."

"Oh, I . . ." I trail off as Pearl opens the carriage door and the others climb in.

"I'm grateful to have four wonderful apprentices." Sister Sophia smiles at all of us. "The side effects of healing tend to discourage most girls from studying it seriously—not to mention the ridiculous notion that biology and anatomy are unladylike. It's nonsense."

She's off on her pet rant, but I'm lost in thought as the carriage begins to rattle back down the driveway. I've never thought of my magic as a blessing, only a curse. I thought perhaps healing would be different. Less complicated than mind-magic. A way to help people, to prove that the Brothers are wrong when they say all magic is wicked. But like any kind of power, it depends on the character of the person using it.

When I get home, the convent is abuzz with news of my sisters' arrival. I've missed afternoon tea; girls are studying in the library or clattering upstairs to their rooms. On their lips, I hear the whispers: *Prophecy. Maura and Tess. Cahill sisters.*

I rush to the sitting room, then stop dead on the threshold. They're here.

For the last month, it's what I've wanted more than any-thing—to see my sisters. But now that they're here, I feel a peculiar flutter of nerves. I'm not certain I'm the same Cate who left them at the church door a month ago. Have they changed, too, in my absence?

Maura holds court next to Alice on the pink love seat. She's gorgeous in an emerald gown that makes her eyes look green as spring grass. Her red hair is done up in a pompadour, held in place with jeweled combs; her feet are adorned with pink velvet slippers trimmed with green bows.

"I've always had strong intuition," she says, eyelashes flut-tering modestly. "I just *sense* things about people."

"What kind of things?" Vi asks, rapt. She's squeezed herself onto the settee on the other side of Alice, but her enormous lavender skirts poof out in front of her. Vi's thin like me and requires a bustle to enhance her figure.

"Oh, you know." Maura waves a languid hand. "What sort of things they might be capable of. Whether or not they're trustworthy. I wouldn't be surprised if I graduated to visions any day now."

Looking past her, I find Tess on an ottoman next to Rory, her pale hair in braids that wind around her head like mine. She's wearing a red plaid dress, and she looks flushed and rosy and healthy—if a bit skeptical of Maura's newfound psychic tendencies. When she sees me, she leaps up. I'd swear she's an inch taller than when I last saw her.

"Cate!" She hurls herself at me, and I catch her, squeezing her so tight she lets out a little squeak. She laughs and I laugh, too, at hearing it.

Maura rises and gives me a perfunctory hug. She smells sweet and citrusy, like lemon verbena. "*There* you are! We've been waiting for you for ages."

"I'm sorry I wasn't here when you arrived. I've missed you both so much," I say, eyeing Maura carefully. Is she still angry with me for leaving her behind?

I'm glad they're here. The Sisterhood isn't what I wanted for them, but it's not as evil as Mother made it out to be, either. And perhaps it shouldn't have been my decision alone. Seeing them here, taller and prettier and more grown-up than ever, it wallops me over the head: they aren't children anymore. They have the right to choose their own futures.

Maura turns back to her captive audience, clasping her hands to her heart theatrically. Everyone's eyes are on her, just the way she likes it. "It's been awful, cooped up all alone in the country."

Tess smacks Maura's arm. "You weren't alone, you goose. I was there!"

"Oh, you know what I mean." Maura's laugh is bright and bubbly. "Chatham is frightfully dull, and we've never known any other witches. Our mother was so strict, we were hardly ever allowed to practice. I want to learn everything I can about the Sisterhood and the history of magic. I envy you girls; I'm afraid I'm horribly behind for my age."

I stare at Maura, her forehead puckered with worry. She's never possessed a lack of confidence. But it's precisely the right tactic; Alice and Vi and their lackeys are already falling over themselves, offering to tutor her or help her in any way they can. I turn back to Tess. "I like your hair like that. And what have you been doing, growing when I've got my back turned? You're up to my chin now."

"I'm an absolute giant." Tess grins up at me. "Oh, Cate, I'm so glad to see you. I've missed you!"

"Not as much as I've missed you." I take in the other inhabitants of the room: Rebekah is sitting at the piano, with Lucy next to her, though they've abandoned their music. Mei is beating Rilla handily at chess. A few of Alice's lackeys are sprawled on the floor before the fire, flipping through magazines. But there are no teachers present. "Is Elena here, too?"

The name catches Maura's attention. "Naturally. She's with Sister Inez now. She and Paul escorted us."

"Paul McLeod? *My* Paul?" He's the last person I'd expect to chaperone my sisters.

"Is he yours?" Maura grins. "He's called on us several times since you left."

Tess pauses in her examination of the bookshelf, which contains a host of Gothic romances for pleasure reading. "He's been worried about you."

"Has he? He hardly mentions Cate to *me*," Maura teases, and I flush. The last time I saw her, she was heartbroken over Elena's betrayal. "Where have you been, anyway? No one would tell us."

I shiver, slumping against the blue-flowered wallpaper. "I was at Harwood."

"Why?" Maura gasps, all her bright artifice falling away. She sinks back onto the pink love seat, and Alice pats her sleeve sympathetically.

Tess huddles next to me, gray eyes worried. "Are you all right?"

I press my fingertips to my temples, massaging the headache that's sprung up. "I'm fine. I went on a nursing mission. Sister Cora wanted me to speak with Zara, since she studied the oracles."

"Zara's our godmother," Maura explains to the others, though in truth she is only my godmother. "She's a powerful witch and a brilliant scholar."

Alice leans forward eagerly, bracing her elbows on her knees. Her dress is a striking purple velvet today. "What did she tell you?"

My memory conjures up Zara: dark curls and dreamy eyes and gold locket. "She's a bit muddled from the laudanum, but I got her to tell me about the two other oracles before Brenna. The Brothers kept them in Harwood and tortured prophecies out of them."

"They tortured them?" Tess whispers, fiddling with her lace cuffs.

I nod. She and Maura and I stare at each other, united in our fear, and I decide to keep the other gruesome details to myself.

"Have you had visions? Is that why Sister Cora sent you?" Alice asks.

"No. Not yet," I say, and it feels as though the entire room heaves a sigh of disappointment. "I don't know why—Brenna's been having visions since she was at least fifteen, and Zara said the others were twelve and fourteen when the Brothers caught them."

"Perhaps you're a late bloomer," Alice says caustically, judging the way the black bombazine dress hangs on my thin frame.

I flush. I know the Sisters' uniform does me no favors. "Well, if it's going to happen, I wish it would happen already. It's like waiting for an ax to fall."

"We can always hope," Alice jests, her pink lips pursed.

Maura turns. "Don't you speak to my sister like that."

Alice gapes at her. "Pardon me?"

"You heard me." Maura's smile bares her teeth. "If Cate *is* the oracle, she's the most powerful witch in this room. She deserves your respect. Don't forget that."

Alice draws back, pressing into the corner of the love seat. It's the first time I've seen her cowed by anything, and I can't stop the smile that twitches over my face. I'd expected Maura to be furious with me, not defending me. I'd forgotten how fiercely loyal she can be.

"Making friends already, Maura?" Elena Robichaud slides past me into the room, her taffeta skirts rustling. Against her cream-colored dress, her dark skin practically glows. She's a very beautiful girl.

"I was just telling Cate how lost Tess and I would have been without you this last month," Maura says coolly, somehow managing to convey the exact opposite. I note the way her shoulders go tight, her smile brittle, at Elena's appearance.

Elena ignores her, patting her dark ringlets into place. If I didn't know better, I'd think she was nervous, too. "Hello, Cate."

I smile evenly, though I'd still like to throttle her for breaking my sister's heart. "Hello."

"Why don't you come help us unpack, Cate?" Maura stands and gives the girls her most charming smile as Elena, Tess, and I file out into the hall. "I'm so glad to finally be here. I hope we'll all be great friends."

"There's no doubt who's the beauty in that family," Vi says, her voice pitched loud enough for us all to hear.

"She's got gumption, I'll give her that," Alice agrees.

Tess slips her small hand into mine. "Don't pay them any mind."

"Oh, I never do." But their easy acceptance of Maura smarts. She's managed to earn their respect in five minutes, and I haven't done it in a month. I'm reminded, suddenly, of how people would stop on the street to coo over Maura when she was little, to tell Mother what a gorgeous child she was, give her lollipops and pet her red curls and ply her with questions she answered in her adorable lisp. I was the plain one with thin, straight hair that fell out of my braids no matter how tightly Mother wound them, and mud over my hems from running wild, and no interest in talking to strangers. Sometimes they gave me sweets, too—but it was always an afterthought.

People like Maura; they're drawn to her vivacity and beauty. They always have been. It wasn't so obvious when we were all shut up at home, but now I feel like an overlooked child again. Shouldn't I be past this?

Elena stops at the foot of the stairs. "That was quite a performance."

Maura gives her a steely glare. "I meant every word."

"Of course you did. You're very ambitious of late." Elena's smile is bitter, and I'm perplexed. Persuading the three of us to join the Sisterhood was always Elena's goal; it's what she was sent to Chatham to accomplish. She ought to be thrilled.

Maura raises one eyebrow. "You say it as though you disapprove."

"No. I'd just hate to see you lose basic kindness in your quest for popularity."

Maura chortles. "I hardly think you, of all people, have the right to lecture me on kindness."

She hurries upstairs, hips swaying, and Tess follows.

I hesitate, one hand on the banister. "I've never seen you and Maura argue like that."

Elena shrugs a shoulder. "She hasn't forgiven me."

I stand on the bottom step, looming above Elena. I'd forgotten how petite she is; she has that kind of presence. "You toyed with her to get to me. I don't blame her."

"I haven't forgiven myself, if that helps." Elena drops her gaze to the wooden floorboards. "Be careful, Cate. I'm not the only one she's still angry with."

"Cate! Come on!" Maura calls imperiously from the second-floor landing.

"You'd better go. She hates being kept waiting," Elena sighs.

"You're not coming with us?" The Elena I left a month ago would have been eager to insinuate herself into our every conversation.

"No. I'll let the three of you sort things out yourselves."

My sisters lead me to their room on the third floor. Maura ties back the heavy green curtains, staring out at the snow-covered garden. Tess is inching her trunk across the floor toward the bookshelf. She kneels and undoes a false satin lining beneath her dresses, revealing two dozen books. She pulls out a battered copy of *The Metamorphoses* first, hugging it to her.

"I could hardly leave them behind for the Brothers to burn," she says, catching my smile. She rifles through the rest and hands me *Arabella, Brave and True*. "This is for you, from Mrs. Belastra."

I thumb through my favorite childhood novel, touched that Marianne thought of me. I hope that someday I'll get to make amends with her, to show her how much I appreciated the sacrifices she made for Finn and me to be together, even if it didn't seem like it at the time. "How is Marianne?"

"Did you know they burnt most of her books?" Tess's gray eyes flash. "She smuggled a few out to customers like Father, but the rest of them—they built a bonfire right in the town square and threw them in by the wheelbarrow load. Brother Winfield even gave a speech about how important it is to guard our minds against the insidious sin of novels!"

"It must have killed Marianne to watch that." And her son wasn't there to comfort her. Guilt saws away at me.

"You could see the smoke for miles. We could smell it all the way at our house." Tess cuddles her book as though protecting its delicate ears from the fate of its friends. "Father was furious. *I* was furious."

"Speaking of Marianne," Maura says, turning from the window, "I can't believe Finn Belastra joined the Brotherhood. He doesn't seem the type."

She's staring right at me, obviously waiting for my answer. How much does she know? "He isn't."

"Everyone at home is saying that's why you joined the Sisterhood. Because Finn jilted you." Maura slides the jeweled combs from her hair and lays them on her dressing table. "Is it true?"

My hands land on my hips. "No. I joined the Sisterhood to protect the two of you, because Elena was threatening you. You know that."

"That's too bad," Maura sighs. "I was rather impressed. My big sister, having a scandalous love affair with the gardener! It was like something from one of my novels. You mean there was nothing between you? No stolen kisses out by the gazebo?"

"No. Well, yes. I mean, it's not what you think," I insist, flushed and flustered. "He didn't jilt me. He's not like that."

"Of course he is. You poor thing." Maura's reflection stares at me from the mirror. Tess is watching, too, her gray eyes bright with sympathy. "It must have been an awful shock. Betraying his own mother, then throwing you over. He was always ambitious, wasn't he? I remember him in Sunday school when we were little. Such a know-it-all."

"Maura!" Tess chides. "She doesn't want to talk about it. Stop needling her."

"I'm not needling. I'm comforting. Perhaps I'm not very good at it." Maura kneels and pulls a shimmering gold dress from one of her trunks. She looks up at me, her face sad, vulnerable. "I know what it's like to be toyed with. You could have come to me, Cate. Confided in me."

"That's not how it was with Finn and me," I protest. "It wasn't like you and Elena."

A mask slides over her face as she stands. "Of course not. I'm sure what you had was deeply profound—until he jilted you for Brother Ishida. At least now we know why you wouldn't marry Paul. Unhook me, Tess, will you?" Maura turns her back to us.

Drat. I've said the wrong thing. How do I always say the wrong thing with her?

Tess obligingly begins to unhook the row of buttons down the back of Maura's green gown. I close my eyes and pray for patience. "I wasn't in love with Paul. Didn't you once tell me I should only marry someone who made my heart pound?"

Maura steals a look at me in the mirror. "I wouldn't fret about Paul. He was surprised, certainly, but he seems to be getting along well enough without you."

"I'm glad to hear it," I say dryly. "So he's come back to New London?"

"Yes." Maura's voice is muffled as Tess pulls the dress over her head. "To take a job at Mr. Jones's architecture firm. He said there was nothing left for him in Chatham."

I shouldn't ask. She wants me to ask, and I'm loath to give her the satisfaction. But I can't resist my curiosity. "Downstairs, you said—you implied—did Paul come to call on *you?*"

"Don't sound so shocked!" Maura laughs. "I am adorable, you know."

"I do know." She's more beautiful than I am, more outgoing, and cleverer. She loves the city, just as Paul does, and she wants adventures. It's not the first time I've thought they might make a good match, but I'm still surprised. "It's just that the last time I saw him, he proposed to me, and the last time I saw you, you were—"

"The last time you saw me, I was a fool. My feelings for Elena were nothing but a two-minute infatuation for a teacher. I was lonely, and she flattered me, made me feel important. I was foolish enough to think it meant more than it did. I'm past that now." Maura's voice is clipped and angry; she doesn't *sound* entirely past it.

"Now you have feelings for Paul." I look at my sister, standing there utterly unself-consciously in her ivory corset and petticoats, red curls tumbling down her back, and I feel a strange splash of uncertainty, as though I'm looking at a stranger. Do I know her at all?

"You said I'd change my mind about marriage when I found the right man. Perhaps I have. And Paul was so hurt when you left. You didn't even say good-bye, much less give him an answer to his proposal. He deserves better than that."

He does, I don't deny that, but—

"He talked with you about it?" The notion makes me feel itchy and uncomfortable. He was always *my* friend. Maura was the pest, the tagalong little sister.

Maura nods. "He wanted answers. I couldn't tell him the truth about the Sisterhood, of course, so I let him think it *was* because of Finn Belastra. I'm afraid it makes you look rather pathetic."

Tess tugs the golden dress over Maura's shoulders. "I'm sure Cate had her reasons."

"Cate always has her reasons. But as she chooses not to share them with us, all we can do is speculate," Maura says airily, arranging the dress over her hips. "In any case, Paul said he'd come to see that we're all settled in. Perhaps I can persuade him to take me shopping. Tess, you could come along and chaperone. I'd ask you, Cate, but I'm afraid that might be awkward."

"No. I wouldn't want to stand in the way of your fun," I agree.

"That's very kind of you. I can't wait to see the city properly. Thank the Lord for Brenna Elliott and this new prophecy. I was afraid I'd spend the rest of my life wasting away in Chatham!" Maura sighs.

"Home isn't that bad," Tess says, tying a wide, brown velvet sash around Maura's waist.

"Oh, you know what I mean. This changes things. Elena says the Sisterhood isn't so certain of you anymore, Cate. The prophesied witch could be any of us."

"Don't, Maura." Tess looks on the verge of tears. "Stop trying to pick a fight. We'll find out soon enough which of us is the oracle, but for now we're all finally together again. Aren't you glad?"

Maura eyes me with trepidation, as though admitting she missed me will take something away from her. Perhaps it will.

"I'm sorry. I owe you both an apology." I take a deep breath. "Especially you, Maura. The decision for me to come here, and the two of you to stay home—it was a decision we should have made together. You're both old enough to have a say in what happens to you. You told me that, and I didn't listen. I—I'm not a very good listener, sometimes."

"Sometimes?" Maura scoffs, rolling her eyes to the shadowy ceiling.

"Maura!" Tess snaps.

I offer Maura my hand. She looks at me for a long moment, and then she takes it.

"Fine," she says. "I missed you, too."

CHAPTER
7

THE NEXT AFTERNOON DURING TEA, Tess grabs a plate of pumpkin scones. "The front parlor?" she suggests, heading for the door while I grab two cups of tea.

Maura tugs on one of Tess's braids as she passes the pink love seat. "Where are you going?"

"Cate and I were going to find a quiet place to catch up," Tess explains. "Do you want to come with us?"

Maura rolls her eyes. "Oh, no, I wouldn't want to intrude."

I add milk and sugar to Tess's tea the way she likes it, trying not to seem as though I'm eavesdropping. Tess sighs. "You wouldn't be intruding, Maura. I just haven't seen her in weeks; I want to hear all about everything."

"That's all right. I find the company here more

stimulating anyway," Maura says, turning back to Alice, and hurt flashes across Tess's face.

"Thanks," she mutters. I finish with the tea, and we walk in companionable silence to the front parlor and shut the door behind us.

"Tell me, how were things at home?" I ask.

Tess curls up on the stiff settee, her stocking feet tucked beneath her, munching on a scone. Cinnamon and nutmeg perfume the air. She gestures at the other scone on the plate. "You should eat something. You're too skinny."

I take matches from the tinderbox and light the gas lamps on either side of the mantel. It gives the illusion of warmth, at least. It's freezing in here without a fire, despite the hiss of heat through the radiator. "Are you avoiding my question?"

"No. Well, perhaps." Tess hands me the scone as I plop down next to her. "You're always fretting about us. Aren't I allowed to worry about you?"

"No." But I take a bite just to appease her. "There. Now tell me."

"Things weren't good." Tess sighs, retying the pink bow on her braid and avoiding my eyes. "After you left, Maura stayed in her room for almost a week. Then she and Elena got into a screaming match. Maura was—I've never heard her so angry. Even Father came to see what happened. Maura did mind-magic on him so he'd forget what he'd heard, and she was different after that. I caught her practicing on John and Mrs. O'Hare last week."

"What?" I yelp. The O'Hares have been our housekeeper and coachman since we were little; they're practically family.

"Yes." Tess raises miserable gray eyes to mine. "I don't think it was the first time, either. I don't know how often she'd done it before I caught her. She wouldn't tell."

"What did she have to say for herself?" I put my unfinished scone down.

Tess hunches her shoulders. "She didn't think she was doing anything wrong. She said she needed to work on compelling multiple subjects. I told her if she did it again, I'd never speak to her for the rest of my life." Unlike Maura, Tess isn't the sort to make empty threats. "She swore she wouldn't."

"Are the O'Hares all right?" I trace the carved pineapple on the arm of the settee.

"They seem to be. It's Maura I'm worried about. She's become *obsessed* with magic. The whole way here, whenever she wasn't flirting with Paul, she was asking Elena questions about the Sisterhood. It's as though she thinks she can be the prophesied sister if she tries hard enough." Tess bites her lip. "I don't think that's how prophecies work, though. I don't know what Maura will do if it's not her."

"Be even angrier? I thought we made a truce last night, but she's ignored me ever since." I kick off my slippers and curl my feet under me on the settee, mirroring Tess's position. "Do you hate it here?"

"No, it's grand. Very—homey." Tess glances around the dour parlor and rolls her eyes.

"I'm serious!" I protest. I can practically feel the headmistresses sneering at me from their portraits, disapproving of my show of emotion. It seems unfathomable that I could join them someday.

"I've only been here a day," Tess says. "I haven't formed an opinion yet."

"I couldn't bear it if you were angry with me, too." I smooth the ruffles at the bottom of my blue plaid dress. "I know you wanted to stay home with Father and—"

"I understand why you sent for us," Tess interrupts. "I think I'll like it. It's a little overwhelming, is all. I'm used to it being just us. It feels like everyone's always staring at me now."

Tess is wearing a new blue dress with pink and purple polka dots, and combined with the pink bows in her braids, the effect is sweet and girlish. It makes me want to look after her, mother her, and I have to remind myself of my promise not to treat her like a child.

"They're all curious about us because of the prophecy. You'll get used to it."

She nods. "Everyone seems nice. Almost everyone, anyway."

I freeze, anger buzzing through me, scone halfway to my mouth. "Has someone been unkind to you? Who?"

"Cate, you look as though you're about to brain someone with that scone." Tess giggles. I flush and put it back on the plate. "No one's been mean to me, but Alice and Vi aren't very nice to *you*."

I try to shrug it off. "Don't worry about that. I want you to make friends."

Tess scowls. "I couldn't be friends with anyone who doesn't like you, silly."

I give her a quick hug, touched by her sweetness. Obviously Maura doesn't feel the same way. She sat with Alice and Vi at supper last night and again at breakfast this morning.

Tess grins. "Guess what? Sister Gretchen offered to teach me German."

I grin back. "Mei's family speaks Chinese at home. I bet she would teach you."

"Chinese?" Tess shrieks, practically insane with joy. "Really?"

"Truly. Do you want to go ask her? I bet she's still playing chess with Addie." I blow out the lamps and Tess grabs the plate and her still-full teacup. She pauses by the table in the front hall.

"That's pretty," she says, pointing at the silver letter tray. It's topped with a fanciful letter rack in the shape of a lyre. As she reaches for it, her tea spills all over the table. "Oops!"

I grab up the lone, tea-stained letter, addressed to Sister Cora, and wave it in the air. "Go fetch a towel from the kitchen."

"Is the letter ruined?" Tess asks. "You'd better take it out of the envelope before it seeps through."

I frown at her. "And read Sister Cora's private post? I doubt she'd appreciate that." There's no return address; it must have been hand-delivered. What if it's something important, and we've just rendered it illegible? Tess scurries off, and I slip my fingernail beneath the red wax seal. It's marked with a letter B.

I don't have to read it, I decide. I'll just take it out of the envelope for safekeeping.

As it turns out, I needn't have worried. The letter is a little browned with tea at the bottom, but the six lines of text are all still perfectly legible—except the letters are arranged in strange combinations that don't make the slightest bit of sense to me.

Tess comes rushing back with a towel. "Did I ruin it?" she asks, biting her lip as she mops up the table. "Was it something important?"

"I don't know. I think it's in code." I wave the letter at her.

"Really?" She snatches it from me, forehead rumpled. She looks very like Father when he's puzzling over a translation. "It's a Caesar cipher," she says after a minute of squinting.

"Am I meant to know what that means?"

"It's a substitution cipher, where every letter is replaced by another letter. They say Caesar used three shifts to the right—replaced A with D, B with E, C with F, and so forth. This looks like it's a left shift of two instead, so . . ." Tess pauses. "A becomes Y, B becomes Z, C becomes A, and so on. That's good. Not as easy to break."

I'm gaping at her again, confounded by her cleverness. "But you just broke it in less than a minute."

She flushes. "I read a book of Father's on cryptography. You know I like puzzles and equations and all that. I wrote Mrs. O'Hare notes in code for a month afterward. She wasn't very good at reading them, though; I had to give her the key. Anyway, a normal person wouldn't figure it out so quickly. Or at all."

I laugh. Only Tess. "So you mean you can read this?"

"Yes." Her grin fades as she puzzles out the text. "It says *On high alert after the latest report from Harwood. Have arrested 8 girls in last 2 days*—I think that's right, or it'd be 6 girls in 0 days, which doesn't make sense—*without trial. Being kept under heavy guard in basement of National Council building and*"—Tess's voice falters, and I put my hand on her shoulder—"*tortured and starved. Would not be surprised if they simply disappear. Even under duress 6 swear they cannot prophesize. 2 have claimed they can but one is mad and one simple. The families are in an uproar. We may be able to use this to our advantage.*"

We're both silent for a moment. "Those poor girls," I say finally.

It's me the Brothers want, not them. Eight innocent girls are suffering while I'm safe in my bed at night.

Tess tosses the letter back onto the table and stares up at me. "How," she demands, "could this possibly be to anyone's advantage?"

"Sister Cora hopes people are getting sick of the Brothers, that they might be ready for new leadership soon. *Shared* leadership, between the Brothers and witches," I explain, pacing the front hall. "The worse the Brothers are, the better people might think of us."

Tess plants her hands on her hips, scowling. "So she'll just let those poor girls rot, in the hopes of inciting some kind of riot? That's not right. There must be something we can do."

I peer out the window beside the front door. A black brougham drives by in the street below, the horse's hooves loud in the silence. The red maples are shifting in the wind, waving their bare fingers. "I don't know what."

"I'm going to fetch Maura," Tess decides.

As she scurries off, I grab the letter from the table and head back into the front parlor to relight the gas lamps. Then

I sit on the silk chair by the fireplace, staring up at the grape-vine cornices and wishing for guidance.

Tess returns with Maura only a minute later. Maura is furious, her blue eyes snapping. "What does Cora mean to do, just let those poor girls be murdered? Who knows how many more the Brothers will snatch up!"

"What else can she do? She's protecting *us*," I point out.

Maura sinks onto the settee. She's wearing another new gown, sapphire with black pinstripes. "Alice says the war council is meeting right now to talk about possible courses of action."

"War council?" I ask as Tess sits next to Maura.

"The Sisters' war council. Alice told me all about it. Cate, you've been here a month, don't you know anything?" Maura sighs. "It's Sister Cora, of course, and Gretchen, Sophia, Johanna, Evelyn, and Inez. The six most senior members of the Sisterhood. They vote on anything important, but Alice says lately they've been deadlocked on everything because Inez and Cora are always at odds."

Alice says, Alice says. "How does Alice know everything?" I demand, peevish.

"She's a horrible snoop is how," Maura confesses, and I laugh. "But it's useful. She overheard Johanna and Inez talking about Brenna's latest prophecy, too. Brenna told the Brothers the other oracle is in New London now." She tucks a red curl behind her ear, preening a little.

"That must be 'the latest report from Harwood,'" I say, waving the letter. "It's got the Brothers in a tizzy, hunting for oracles everywhere."

Tess leans over and takes the letter from me, scanning it as though she's hoping she translated wrong. "This is all our fault."

"It's not our fault. It's Brenna's for not being able to keep her mouth shut," Maura argues. "What if her next prophecy leads them right to our doorstep? Gives them an exact location?"

I stare at the brown carpet. "Perhaps we could sneak Rory in to ask Brenna to keep quiet."

Tess bounces the letter against her polka-dotted knee. "The moment Brenna stops telling them her visions willingly, they'll torture them out of her. She's only safe as long as she's useful to them."

I grimace, imagining the Brothers cutting off Brenna's fingers. Breaking her legs.

Maura taps her black slipper against the floor. The look on her face is studied indifference. "It might be a mercy to end her suffering, then."

The room is silent for a minute. A wagon goes past outside; I can hear the rattle of the wheels and the clomp of the horses' hooves. Tess holds herself stiffly, her shoulders tight. "You want to kill her?" she says softly.

"I don't *want* to, but—what life does she have in that place?" Maura's mask of nonchalance slips, her blue eyes darting hopefully to mine. For a minute, she looks like my little sister again, with her heart-shaped face open and craving approval I can't give.

"It's still her life," I argue, remembering Sister Sophia's

conversation in the carriage yesterday. "It's not for us to play at being gods."

"They would torture her, and who knows what they'd get out of her in the process? It would be quick coming from one of us. Alice says Sister Sophia could do it just like that." Maura snaps her fingers.

Has Sophia done it before—killed at the Sisters' bidding? Was she trying to warn me that someday they might ask it of me? I feel sick at the prospect.

"Brenna isn't well," Tess says. Her face has gone pale. "Who knows what it does to a person, seeing the future? We've got to think of it like that—what if it was one of us shut up in there?"

"It might be one of us soon, if she doesn't keep her visions to herself." Maura picks up the gold-rimmed teacup she brought with her and takes a sip of tea. "Brenna was strange before. I daresay her madness is down to her being Brenna, not her being an oracle."

I grimace, remembering Thomasina Abbott. "It wouldn't kill you to show some compassion."

"We haven't the luxury of compassion at times like this." Maura sets her teacup back onto its saucer with a clatter. "Because of her, eight innocent girls are going to be murdered. How many lives do we risk every day we pardon her?"

"No, Maura. It's wrong. We aren't murderers." Tess's gray eyes are terribly serious.

"Maybe you're too young to understand the complexities of this," Maura ventures.

"Don't you dare." Tess jumps up, braids swinging. "I may be young, but that doesn't mean I'm a fool or that I don't have a right to my opinion."

I stand, too. "I agree with Tess."

"Of course you do!" Maura throws her hands up in the air.

"What's happening to those girls is wrong, and I hope Sister Cora and the war council can come up with a way to stop it." I glance down at the letter in Tess's hand, a little crumpled now from her tight grasp. "The note says this may actually be to our advantage, to help turn public opinion toward us. I hate thinking of it so callously, but perhaps we should wait and see what—"

"Wait and see, wait and see," Maura mimics. "You and Cora are a fine pair, aren't you? Lord, I hope I *am* the oracle, or the Sisterhood will never *do* anything! You'll just sit back and watch girls die without a care in the world!"

I step forward, chin leading the charge. "I do too care."

"You've got a poor way of showing it," Maura snaps, stomping from the room. She slams the door behind her.

Tess leans against the marble mantel, tears slipping silently down her cheeks. "I'm just angry," she explains, wiping them away with both hands. "I hate being patronized. And I don't like the way Maura's acting, so . . . superior. You know she's parroting all the things Sister Inez says, don't you?"

I nod. It's bad enough hearing Inez propose such a cold-hearted idea, but to hear it from Maura, who knows Brenna and grew up with her! When did Maura become a girl who could talk about assassination so calmly?

I'm meeting Finn tonight, but I haven't decided what to

do about Inez's suggestion that he spy for the Sisterhood. I don't entirely trust her, but I'm tired of secrets and lies and girls being hurt because we're too frightened to fight back. If Finn could get information about the Brotherhood's plans, could Inez use it to bring them down?

Inez is the sort of woman who might win a war, but at what cost?

Tess retreats to her room, but I make my way down to the sitting room to find Mei and ask about Chinese lessons. Maura, Alice, and Vi are chattering away on the love seat, and Maura glares at me when I come in. Lucy Wheeler is playing the piano, badly, while her friends Hope and Rebekah stand next to it, turning the pages for her and singing along to the old folk songs. Hope has a pretty, high soprano. Mei and Addie are gone, but Rory sits slumped in the corner in a blue plaid chair, listlessly flipping through a fashion magazine. She looks up when I come in. "Cate!"

"Rory. Did you post your letters today?"

She moved into the convent yesterday, with no objection from Brother Ishida. Cora offered to speak to him, but it wasn't necessary; I daresay he was glad to have her off his hands. Sister Cora wrote a letter to Mrs. Elliott, and Rory wrote one to Nils to break their betrothal. Tess and I helped with it last night after supper. It was a masterpiece, all about atoning for her blindness to the evil of her bosom friend and choosing devotion to the Lord over her earthly affection for Nils.

Rory nods. She looks more like herself today in a tiered

crimson dress with lace at the cuffs. "Nils won't have any trouble finding another girl. I've caught him looking at Emily Ruhl before."

I sink onto the fat blue ottoman at her feet. "Will you miss him?"

Rory shrugs. "I'll miss the idea of him. I'll miss having someone to kiss, someone to make me feel special," she says, blinking back tears. "You understand, I suppose. Sachi told me it was Finn you were kissing, not Paul McLeod."

The hair at the nape of my neck prickles, and I glance behind me. I expect to catch Maura and Alice gossiping about me, but instead I see Sister Inez lurking in the doorway. She turns her gaze to my sister. "Maura, may I have a word?"

Maura looks up eagerly. "Of course."

I frown, wondering what Inez wants with Maura, and then turn back to Rory. "Sachi told you all the secrets, didn't she?" She was the only person I'd confided in about Finn, right after she told me Rory was her sister.

Rory flushes. I've never seen her blush before; I didn't think her quite capable of it. She glances at the little girls singing at the piano, at Alice and Vi chatting on the settee.

"After I caught her kissing Elizabeth Evans," she whispers.

"Kissing—Elizabeth?" Elizabeth Evans is a shopgirl, tall and pretty, the niece of the Chatham chocolatier.

"Your face, Cate! I was shocked, too. Afraid for my virtue, naturally," Rory jokes, tossing her dark hair.

A giggle escapes me. Rory's relationship with Nils was hardly chaste. "Sachi explained that she didn't have designs on me, and then I was rather offended that she didn't! Why not? I'm an attractive girl." Rory rolls her eyes at herself. "She was afraid I'd try to compromise her in some mad scheme to prove I was desirable, so she finally told me we were sisters."

"And how did that go?"

Rory crosses her arms over her ample bosom. "I was angry she hadn't told me the truth sooner. I suppose she was afraid I'd run through the streets denouncing our dear papa or go on a sherry binge. I didn't, not at the time, but—" Rory's smile slides off her face. "As it turns out, I suppose she was right not to trust me with it."

I put my hand on her red sleeve. "I'm sorry."

Rory bites her lip, her brown eyes worried. "You won't think less of her, will you?"

"For kissing a girl, or for trusting you?" I frown at her. "The answer is no, either way."

"Elizabeth's half in love with her," Rory says. "It was fun to tease Sachi about it."

"Poor Elizabeth." I glance over my shoulder as Maura strides back into the room and takes her seat next to Alice. Would things be different between Maura and me if I'd accepted her infatuation with Elena with better grace? If I'd seen it as something to tease her about? The situations are different, of course; Elena was only toying with her. But I want Maura to have what I have with Finn, to be as happy as he makes me.

I steal a glance at the clock on the mantel. It's hours yet before I'll see him, and it feels like an age. He must have heard about the Brothers snatching those poor girls. Something ought to be done, but what? Surely he wouldn't agree with Maura that assassinating Brenna is the best solution.

"Do you think it would be impossible to break someone out of Harwood?" Rory asks suddenly.

Behind us, the piano music stops, but Hope and Rebekah keep singing.

"I think it would be very difficult."

Hope and then Rebekah trail into silence. I turn to see if Lucy's overheard us, but she's marching toward the door. A moment later, Hope and Rebekah follow her. I turn back to Rory, but she's standing, dropping the magazine on her empty seat. Her face is strange—emptied of all its usual vivacity.

"Rory?" I say, but she only saunters away, joining the strange procession.

I'm baffled until I see Vi rise from the love seat. Beside her, Maura is staring into the fire, her blue eyes blank. Scarcely a second later, Alice follows Vi out the door.

Get up. The thought imposes itself on me now, out of nowhere. My limbs flex, and I am about to stand when I feel the telltale prickle of Maura's compulsion.

No, I think. I place my boots flat on the floor and fold my hands neatly in my lap, fingers interlaced. I settle myself firmly on the blue cushion, feel the heat against my back from the fire. I close my eyes and breathe, resisting the urge to stand and walk toward the door.

The moment passes. I open my eyes to find my sister looming over me, grinning like a loon. "I got everyone except you. Six!" she crows.

My spine goes tight. I don't care to have anyone poking

about in my mind, not even my sister. My memories are *mine*; they're not for anyone to experiment with.

"Oh, don't be angry." Maura frowns. The room is empty now save the two of us. "Sister Inez asked me to."

"You went into their minds without their permission. They're supposed to be your *friends*." I stand, clasping my hands behind my back. "You don't see anything wrong in that?"

"I compelled them to walk into another room. It was nothing. No harm done," Maura insists. "Don't be such a killjoy, Cate."

I hear the telltale *tap, tap, tap* of Sister Inez's heels as she walks down the hall from her office. "Good work, Maura," she says.

Maura beams. "Six—that's rare, isn't it? That's *powerful*."

"It is," Sister Inez allows. But she turns her hawklike eyes on me. "Did you feel anything, Miss Cahill?"

"I did," I admit. "I wanted to get up and walk to the door—and I didn't, all at the same time. It was very strange."

"You felt the compulsion, but you were able to resist it." Sister Inez studies me like a bug beneath a microscope. "That's what happened the last time Maura tried to perform mind-magic on you, isn't it?"

I nod. I don't dare look at my sister, but I can practically feel her crumple.

"Well. Six subjects is still a tremendous achievement. So far, no other pupil here has been able to accomplish anything like it. I wish there were more of us capable of it; it could be of use to us when war breaks out." Sister Inez grants Maura

143

a rare smile, but her gaze flits back to me. "If Miss Cahill would take her own examination, I would be better able to judge which of you is more powerful."

"Compulsion isn't the only kind of magic that matters," I snap.

Fury flashes over Maura's face. My sister has been angry with me more times than I care to count. She's been scornful and dismissive and jealous. But she's never looked at me quite like this.

Like she *hates* me.

I'm not trying to demean Maura's accomplishment, truly. It's only that this focus on mind-magic frightens me. Why is Sister Inez so intent on it? What does she mean to do?

A shiver passes over me.

Just someone walking over my grave, Mrs. O'Hare would say.

CHAPTER
8

FINN IS WAITING FOR ME AT THE GARDEN gate at midnight, his cloak and hair dusted with snowflakes.

"Fancy meeting you here." He gives me a crooked grin and takes my hand, entwining his leather-gloved fingers with mine. His voice is cheery, his stride jaunty, despite the dreary weather. "You've forgotten your gloves again."

I'm not bold enough to tell him I didn't forget. I wanted to touch him with nothing between us.

"Let's go into the conservatory," I suggest, shivering, squinting against the wind's powdery gusts. My boots sink into six inches of snow as we wade across the garden. By the time we reach the octagonal glass building, the hems of my cloak, dress, and chemise are all coated with snow. I use a spell to unlock the door. I'd like to doff my cloak, but I'm already scandalously attired without corset or petticoats. Rilla only just fell asleep, and I was afraid to rouse her and her endless curiosity.

Inside, the steam pipes hiss beneath the floorboards. Warm air fogs the glass walls. Rows of feathery ferns and Sister Evelyn's prizewinning orchids fill the center of the room. In the back, lemon and orange trees are dotted with tiny bright fruits. It smells of damp earth and green, growing things, like an oasis of spring and hope in the midst of this dreary New England winter.

Finn pulls me into his arms, brushing a kiss over my cold lips. He tosses his gloves onto one of the tables and bends to examine a red phalaenopsis. I toy with the stem of a spindly white cattleya.

"This is beautiful. What's it called?" he asks. Gardening is one of the few subjects where my knowledge outweighs his.

I lead him down the aisle. "These are oncidiums—they're called dancing ladies, because they look like a lady's skirts. And these are the dendrobiums. They're a bit sturdier than the others, so Sister Evelyn lets me help with them."

Finn stands behind me, wrapping his arms around me. "You love it out here, don't you?"

I do. It's a relief to get away from the prying eyes and gossiping tongues inside the convent, but I always feel a bit guilty somehow, as though I'm being unfaithful to Mother's roses with these hothouse orchids.

"It's my favorite place in New London, especially now that it's too cold for proper gardening." I lean back into his embrace. "Have you had any time for your translations lately?"

"Hardly any. They keep us busy between council meetings and feasts and sermons. Ishida introduces me to everyone we pass as if I'm some sort of pet. It's revolting."

"Really? You seem rather cheery," I say, suspicious.

"Well, I'm happy to see you, of course. That and—I've got a plan." He spins me to face him. "I wasn't going to tell you until it was official, but I met this afternoon with Brother Szymborska, the head of the National Archives. I've applied for a job in their office, as a clerk, and I think I've got a good shot at it."

"You want to stay here, in New London?" I ask. Sister Inez's offer pounds like a drumbeat in my head.

"With you." He looks at me expectantly.

"That's grand. I'm so glad," I say, but my voice comes out flat. How can I ask it of him?

His smile fades. "You don't sound glad."

I turn, plucking a weed from a seedling. "You've always wanted to be a teacher. And what if something happens to your mother or Clara and you aren't there? I don't want you to wind up hating me for keeping you here."

"I won't. This isn't just for you, Cate." He smiles to soften the words. "In part, yes, I want to be near you. But teaching the Brothers' approved curriculum is hardly my dream. At the Archives, I won't be arresting innocent girls. I'll be registering and preserving books—the only extant copies in New England, in some cases."

He's already given up so much for me. How can I ask him to sacrifice this, too? I move on to the next plot. "That sounds perfect for you."

147

"For us, I thought." Finn circles my wrists with his hands, stopping my busyness. "If you don't want me staying in New London, you ought to just say so."

I whirl on him. "No! That's not it at all. *Of course* I want you nearby."

"You could have fooled me." He stares down at me. "Look, Cate. All of the Brothers' records are housed in the Archives. The local councils send reports of every arrest. If I worked at the Archives, I'd be privy to information that could prove useful to the Sisterhood."

"Are—are you saying you want to be a spy?" I burst into laughter.

Finn nods uncertainly. "Why is that so ridiculous?"

"It's not! Sister Inez caught me coming back inside the other night. She saw us together. Perhaps I should have compelled her to forget, but I didn't. She suggested that you might be able to help us. There's another position open, as a clerk for a member of the Head Council—a Brother Denisof—and Inez asked if you would apply for it."

Finn lounges against the table. "Well, I can see how information from the Head Council would be advantageous."

The Head Council includes Brother Covington and eleven of his closest advisers. Their meetings are shadowy, secretive affairs; no one knows where or when they'll be. Rumors abound about who the eleven advisers are, but no one will admit to it publicly for fear of becoming a target.

I shuck off my cloak, damp with melted snow. "It's awfully dangerous. If they caught you passing information—"

"I'd still be in less danger than you are," he points out, running a finger over my bare wrist.

My pulse jumps in response. "I was born into that. I haven't got a choice. Besides, it sounds like you could be happy at the Archives."

"I'd rather be useful. I know Denisof. Know *of* him, anyway. I'm not surprised he's on the Head Council." Despite the scruff of his beard, Finn's face looks suddenly boyish, vulnerable. "Whichever position I get—you wouldn't be unhappy to have me in New London?"

I shake my head. "Not at all. I want to see you as much as we can manage it." I twine my arms around his neck. He's got a headache; I can feel it whenever I touch him. "I haven't had a chance to tell you yet. I've become a very capable nurse. I can tell you've got a headache, for instance."

He pinches the bridge of his nose, grimacing. "It's Ishida. The man goes on and on."

I lean my forehead against his. I can see his headache: a red, throbbing haze that slowly subsides as I push against it with my magic. I would protect him from all the harm in the world if I could; a headache is nothing.

"Better now?" I ask, and he nods, looking astonished. I clutch at his shoulders as the world spins around me. "I can heal more serious injuries, too, but there are side effects. It makes me feel a bit—wobbly."

"Wobbly?" He steadies me with a hand on either side of my waist.

"I'm fine. A headache is very minor magic; loads of witches

could do that much. I saved a woman's life yesterday." I'm startled by my own boasting; I've never felt this way about magic before. I continue, in an impulsive rush: "It's getting easier, the more I practice. I'm the best in the convent, aside from Sister Sophia, and she's the healing teacher. I like it. I like helping people. At Harwood, I felt like—like I was doing something useful, something good."

"At Harwood?" Finn's voice rises. "You were at Harwood?"

I nod, pulling back so I can see his face better. His forehead is furrowed, his brown eyes grim behind his glasses. "I wasn't alone. Sister Sophia takes girls on a nursing mission once a week. And I got to meet my godmother, Zara. Did your mother ever mention her to you?"

"The Sisters let you go to Harwood?" He seems stuck on that.

"I was perfectly safe," I assure him. "Sister Cora—she's the headmistress here—asked me to go speak to Zara about the past oracles. There were two between the Great Temple Fire and Brenna."

"What happened to them?" he asks warily.

"It's a little unsettling," I confess. It's a relief to tell him about the torture and experiments and madness Thomasina suffered. I haven't wanted to worry Maura and Tess, but last night I dreamed of Brothers closing in on me with old-fashioned torches. Ishida was right at the front of the pack, cackling. It was dreadful.

I pray that it was just my fear and not a premonition.

"Good Lord." Finn's hands clutch at my waist. "How can

they torture girls like that and still claim to be men of the Lord?"

"If they're witches, no one cares." My voice breaks, and I lean my cheek against his shoulder. "Have you heard about the girls they're holding in the basement of the National Council building?"

Finn runs his hand over my hair. "I have. Nine of them now."

One more since Cora's report.

"I don't know what to do," I confess. "Maura and Tess are here now. Maura's blaming Sister Cora for not doing more to protect the girls, and Brenna for telling the Brothers the oracle's here in New London. She thinks we ought to assassinate Brenna before she can say anything else to implicate us."

"What do you think?" Finn asks, drawing back so he can see me.

I am so glad to have him here to talk to. With him, I don't feel guilty for not having all the answers yet. "I don't want to consider it. But if she knows it's one of us, she could lead them here. I don't know how to stop that. I don't know how to stop *any* of it."

Finn sets his jaw. "I'm half tempted to spirit you away from here right now. Some remote place where no one would ever find us. If I thought you'd go—"

I squeeze my eyes shut against the temptation. "I can't. I have to look after Maura and Tess. What if it's not me? What if it's actually one of them?"

"That would be a grand relief for me." Finn's voice dips

low. "You worry about what the prophecy means for them, but I worry about *you*, Cate. Someone's got to. You'd sacrifice yourself in a second to keep them safe. You'd sacrifice *us*."

His words hang there between us, a reminder that I already have.

"I don't know if I could do it again," I say truthfully. "I know being here is dangerous for you. I should send you away, but I don't want to give you up. It's selfish of me."

"Good. Be selfish." Finn's mouth claims mine in a searing kiss, and my mind empties of everything except his hands, his lips, his tongue.

He pulls away to shrug off his cloak. Beneath it, he's wearing a crisp white linen shirt, gray vest, and matching gray linen trousers. He looks fashionable. Handsome. But he doesn't look quite like my Finn, rumpled and awkward and scholarly.

I start with his hair, running my fingers through the thick strands. I slip my fingers beneath his collar, undoing the top button as my mouth moves to his throat. His hands clutch reflexively at my back, anchoring me against him. Without my heavy corset between us, the buttons of his vest press into my stomach.

I fumble with the top button of his vest and, when it comes undone, tug at the next one. Finn catches my earlobe between his teeth. "Are you undressing me?"

I shiver at his breath against my ear, achieving a third button. "Do you object?"

"No." His voice is a little hoarse as I remove his vest and toss it onto the floor along with his cloak. My arms wind around his neck again; the sinewy muscles of his shoulders bunch beneath my fingertips.

I wonder what he'd look like without this shirt on.

I wonder what he looks like with nothing on at all.

If I'd stayed in Chatham, refused the Sisters, would we be married by now and sharing a bed every night? I press tighter against him as his hands slip beneath my cloak, stroking my sides. I blush to think how much I want that.

Then the door slams open, and we spring apart.

Maura stands in the doorway, snow drifting in behind her. "I'd ask what you're doing, but that's fairly obvious," she snaps.

I pat my disheveled hair back into place, blushing furiously. Finn turns away, snatching up his vest.

"I couldn't sleep, so I was watching the snow. I saw you out my window—but this is worse than I imagined! What are you thinking, Cate? Anyone could have seen you!"

She needn't look so scandalized. "I'm fine, Maura. Go back to bed."

"You expect me to leave you here to carry on like this? With him?" Maura sputters, outraged, and I realize it's not my virtue she's concerned about. "Haven't you any sense at all? Any pride?"

Finn shoots me a wounded look as he struggles into his cloak. "You didn't tell your sisters?"

"I didn't tell anyone," I explain.

"I understand how this must look," he says, "but I assure you, Maura, I have only the most honorable intentions toward your sister."

"Well, my sister may be fool enough to believe that, but I'm not. Cate, he broke whatever vow he made to you. He's a *Brother* now!" The door bangs shut behind her as she stalks closer, pointing at the silver ring on his finger.

Finn whirls on Maura, the black cloak flaring out around him. How he can make a symbol I've hated all my life look almost dashing, I don't know.

I daresay he could make anything look dashing to me.

"I only joined the Brothers to help Cate. To be able to support a wife," he insists.

Maura laughs. "Please tell me you don't believe this nonsense, Cate. When he's ruined you, what then? Sisters are meant to be chaste; you'd be arrested if anyone found out! You're putting yourself in danger for a few kisses, and that puts all of us in danger. Don't you ever think of anyone but yourself?"

"Don't I—?" Finn is the one part of my life that is *mine,* and she wants to shame me for it? Dismiss it as meaningless? She is always so quick to assume the worst of me.

Anger and embarrassment clash inside me, and my magic rises, inextricably linked to my emotions. I send Maura flying back several paces, flinging her against the glass wall. Not hard enough to hurt her, but sudden enough to surprise her.

I've never used magic against her before, but I want her to know that I'm serious. "Shut up, Maura, and give us a chance to explain."

"What are you doing?" she shrieks. Her red hair is tumbling out of its loose braid; her boots are leaving puddles across the floor.

"He already knows I'm a witch. He knows everything. I would trust Finn with my life. More than that, I'd trust him with *yours*."

Maura gasps. "Are you mad? He could be a spy!"

Finn takes my hand in his. "I am a spy. For the Sisterhood."

"What?" Her blue eyes go wide.

I tug away from him. "Are you sure? What about the job at the Archives?"

"I'm sure," Finn says, running a hand through his hair. "I'll apply for the other position, if that's where I'll be most useful to the Sisterhood. What does Sister Inez need to know?"

"Sister Inez knows that you're seeing Finn? She *approves?*" Maura slumps back against the wall. The wet, blue cotton hem of her nightgown peeks out beneath her new black cloak.

"She thinks Finn could be a valuable ally," I explain.

"And you're in love with her," she says to Finn. All the fight has drained out of her. She looks very young suddenly, with wisps of red hair curling around her pale face. "You're willing to risk your life for her."

"Yes." Finn turns all his earnestness on Maura. It's impressive, as I know full well. "It's important to me to do something. Even before I fell in love with Cate, I disagreed with the Brothers' policies. I see it every day, how much contempt the men around me have for witches, how little regard for women. They talk of what they'd do to witches if they caught them, if there weren't laws in place to stop it." His face darkens. "If I don't do something to fight on the right side, what kind of man am I?"

He's a good man. Honorable. I stare at him, struck all over again by how very lucky I am.

Maura takes it all in. "You never said you were in love with him." Her voice is small, hurt.

I take a few steps toward her. "I should have told you from the beginning. I'm sorry."

Maura shakes her head, tears brimming in her blue eyes. "Everything comes so easily for you, Cate. It's not fair."

Without giving me time to respond—to argue against the obvious untruth of it—she picks up her skirts and hurries out the door into the snow.

I turn back to Finn, burying my face in my hands. I should have told her and Tess the truth about him yesterday. No matter how much Maura claims to be over Elena, it's obvious that she isn't. Not if seeing me happy affects her this way.

Finn puts a hand on my shoulder. "Should you go after her?"

"No. I'll try and talk to her tomorrow. She's had a— disappointment. Perhaps she's not as past it as she thought." How did everything become a competition between us? How does my relationship with Finn take anything away from her?

"Sometimes it's better to let them cool off," Finn agrees. "It might all be forgotten by tomorrow."

Somehow I doubt that. "Do you and Clara get into rows?"

Finn nods, his lips twitching. "Loads. She accuses me of being a bossy know-it-all, if you can imagine."

"Never." I laugh, taking his hand. "I want to discuss this spying a bit more. I'm not quite comfortable with—"

"What would you do if I forbade you to go back to Harwood?" he interrupts, raising his eyebrows at me.

"You would never forbid me anything," I say, wrinkling my nose. It's one of the things I love best about him.

"Rightly so. I need you to afford me the same respect," he says.

"Of course I *respect* you. Don't be silly. You're the cleverest person I know, except maybe Tess." I take a deep breath, straightening his vest. In his hurry to get it back on, he's done up the buttons crooked. "I'm just scared. I don't want to lose you."

"You won't. You have to let me take the same risks you take yourself, Cate." He pulls me into his arms, and this time I cling to him. Anxiety blooms through me, dark and dreadful.

I didn't think anything could compare with the fear of losing one of my sisters, but this cuts just as deep. What if I never get to hear the warm rustle of his laugh again, or talk through my problems with him, or kiss him?

The terrible notion of a world without Finn Belastra in it slices through me. I love him. I *knew* that. I mourned the marriage that wasn't; I worried he wouldn't forgive me or that I might not see him again for years. But I knew he was safe in Chatham; I could picture him going about his day, teaching in the boys' school, sitting through Brother Ishida's sermons, eating supper in his mother's flat. I could picture the geography of his life, even though I was no longer part of it. But the awful image of him, dead and pale like my mother, buried in a graveyard somewhere—it's more than I can bear.

I can't breathe, can't think past the sudden panic. I cannot lose him. I *cannot.*

"Cate." Finn tilts my chin up with one finger, and I kiss him. I kiss him as though I will break into a thousand tiny pieces if I don't; I kiss him as though my lips on his can protect him from any possible danger.

When he pulls away, there are tears gathering in my eyes. I tilt my head down so he won't see them.

"You have to go in," he says. "I'll see you soon. I promise."

I curl my little finger around his. The smallest brush of warm, freckled skin against mine.

I nod, and I pretend to believe him. But he can't make promises like that.

None of us can.

CHAPTER
9

THE NEXT AFTERNOON, ALICE AND MEI and I go out to deliver food to the poor. A cloud of discontent seems to have settled on each of the flats we visit. The mothers look drawn and worried, and though they don't dare utter a word of complaint, they wonder aloud how they can stretch these vegetables in soups. Daughters who worked as shopgirls last week glare at us over their sewing and pace like pent-up cats.

I feel a pang of guilt, knowing some of them may go to bed hungry by the end of the week. For all my worries, that's never been one of them. Is there more we could do to help? If we waged war against the Brothers, would these families be better off?

The men who are home don't hesitate to speak up. Fathers grumble about the extra burden the Brothers' new measures put on their pockets; aged grandfathers joke about having to return to work. I see more than one man stuff a newspaper beneath the sofa cushions when we enter, and I know it's not the sanctioned *New London Sentinel,* the Brothers' mouthpiece, that they've been reading. Part of me is afraid for them, but their complaints make me hopeful, too. Perhaps they're finally seeing the cruelty of the Brothers' whims.

"They've got plenty of money in their coffers, thanks to our tithes!" Mr. Brooke is usually jolly, despite the broken leg that keeps him home from his factory job—but not today. He sits in a sturdy blue armchair, leg propped on an ottoman, with his wooden crutches leaning in the corner behind him. He and his family occupy one half of a brownstone duplex just outside the market district. "I ain't suggesting girls should be prancing around the city, mind you, or working jobs what aren't decent. My Molly worked at the flower shop around the corner, you know. And if she flattered the men a little to get 'em to buy flowers for their wives, that's just good business, ain't it? She sold more flowers than any other girl."

"Papa, hush!" Molly's a pretty girl, with frightened cornflower-blue eyes. "Are you trying to get me arrested?"

"We won't say anything," I promise her, and her knitting needles flash to work again.

Mr. Brooke frowns. "I didn't mean anything by it. Molly's a good girl."

"Course she is." Mei grins. Alice just sniffs, as usual.

There's talk of more disappeared girls, too—girls the Brothers suspect of being the oracle. The Chen sisters whisper about their friend's cousin across the city. They say the

Brothers heard neighbors gossiping about a strange dream she had, then took her away and told her family to forget her. As if it's as easy as that.

By my count, it's up to ten girls now.

All afternoon, we walk a fine line between sympathizing with the families we visit and criticizing the Brotherhood. After we visit the last house and pile back into the carriage, I turn to Mei. "Do you think it's like this all over the city?"

Mei nods. "My brother says people have been talking about a protest."

"That's never happened before, has it?" Would I have known, tucked away in Chatham?

"Not since the Daughters of Persephone were in power," Mei says. "And we all know how that turned out."

We're nearly home when the carriage slams to a halt. Mei slides right onto the floor. I imagine Robert's had to yank on the reins to avoid plowing into the back of a wagon, and I pity the horses' poor mouths and think no more of it, until—

"Look!" Alice points out the window with a shaking finger. The street is lined with black carriages bearing the Brothers' gold seal. My heart races. I count six of them, which means at least two dozen Brothers. Why bring so many, unless there's trouble?

There's got to be trouble.

Maura and Tess are inside.

Some small, sensible voice points out that I ought to run in the opposite direction. That if I *am* the oracle and the Brothers find me, it could make everything ten times worse.

At best, they'll torture me until I give them prophecies. At worst, they will burn me in Richmond Square with everyone I love watching.

I know this; I've heard it plainly from the mouths of people I trust; but I cannot turn my back on my sisters if they are in danger.

And it's not only Maura and Tess who worry me. Somehow, over the last week or two, the convent has worked its way beneath my skin. I can't pinpoint the moment it happened, but it has come to feel like a second home, and the girls there a second family. Rilla, Addie, Daisy, Sister Sophia, little Lucy Wheeler—they all know me better than my own father, and I wouldn't see harm done to any of them. Not if I can help it.

I throw open the carriage door, gather my skirts, and jump down onto the cobblestones.

Alice and Mei follow. Robert runs toward the convent ahead of us, and I can't blame him for abandoning his charges; he must be mad with worry for Vi's safety. We hurry after him, racing up the convent steps.

The front hall is crawling with Brothers. One perches on the first-floor landing, holding a sheet of parchment and calling out names in a high, nasal voice. Girls are lined up down the hallway; they are being led one by one into classrooms and the front parlor. It's easy to spot Maura, resplendent in a sunny yellow gown with a red cummerbund, but I can't find Tess.

A fat Brother with a thatch of blond hair and small, piggy

eyes catches my arm as I push past him. "You there, wait a minute. Who are you?"

I bow my head, trying to slow my breathing from my mad dash. To act unconcerned, as though there's nothing to fear. "Catherine Cahill, sir."

He consults a list. Peering over his elbow, I see that it's a roster of students, with a line through some of the names. "We've already called your name. They said you were out delivering rations by the river."

"Yes, sir. I just got back." What's all this about? Where is Tess?

"Come with me," he says. Girls scurry out of his way as he lumbers down the hallway and gestures into the illusions classroom. "In there."

Three Brothers stand against the chalkboard; the oldest sits at Sister Inez's desk with a pen in his hand and blank parchment before him. I stand with my eyes cast down demurely, hands clasped in front of me.

"Name?" one of them barks.

"Catherine Cahill, sir." I hear the scribe taking down my answer as I stare at the shining wooden floorboards of Sister Inez's classroom. Someone must have waxed them since class yesterday. The room still smells faintly of lemons.

"What brought you to the Sisterhood, Miss Cahill?"

"I hoped to be of service to the poor and the sick. To do charitable work in the name of the Lord." Pure of heart, meek of spirit, and chaste of virtue. That is what I must appear. They won't hurt me if I answer their questions correctly.

"Do you find such work pleasant?" he snarls.

Pleasant? What answer do they want? I think of the Harwood infirmary, of the girls in the uncooperative ward, and barely suppress a shudder. "No, sir, but there but for the grace of the Lord am I. It makes me grateful for my own blessings."

Pen scratches across parchment again. Is he only writing down my answer, or something more? "What is the most important virtue for a young lady, Miss Cahill?" another voice asks.

"Obedience." That answer has been drilled into us since we were children.

"Very good. Have you ever had any premonitions, Miss Cahill? A very strong hunch, perhaps, of something about to happen? A dream that later came true? Look at us when you make your answer."

That's why they are here, then. Oracle hunting.

I look up at them with shocked eyes. "No, sir. Never."

"Have you heard any of the girls here claim such a thing?"

I do not even blink. "No, sir."

"What would you think of a girl who did?"

"I would think her very wicked and presumptuous, sir. We must put our faith in the Lord to guide us, and not think it the work of weak and sinful mortals like ourselves," I explain. My eyes fall to the blue glass lamp on Sister Inez's desk. She's dusted it.

The whiskered old man at the desk puts down his pen and gives me a smile. "Very good, Miss Cahill. You are dismissed." He does not waste time with the ritual blessings, only makes a shooing gesture with his hand.

"Thank you, sir." I hurry back into the hallway, eager to find my sisters.

Maura stands with Vi in front of the library. "They're still questioning Tess," she says, her shoulders tight with worry. "She's been in there a long time."

I grab Maura's hand, fighting back the fear that swamps me. "I'm sure she's fine."

"Of course." But Maura squeezes my fingers in hers, last night's argument forgotten.

The Brothers' questions weren't difficult. If I managed to keep my temper and answer appropriately, I daresay Tess won't have any trouble. But as the minutes tick by, my mind seeks potential disasters. She's in a library. What if they ask her about the moral insidiousness of novels? What if they question her stance on book-burning? Will she be able to lie convincingly?

The library door bangs open, and two Brothers stride out, dragging a small blond figure between them. "We're taking this girl with us for further questioning."

Maura's grip tightens until I feel as though the bones in my palm will crack. My heart plummets before I recognize Lucy's friend, Hope Ashby.

We press back against the walls. Sister Cora steps out of the front parlor. "May I ask on what grounds?"

"She did not answer the questions to our satisfaction. We believe she may be an oracle or have knowledge of one."

My pulse races. Hope is twelve and terrified. What if they torture her? She cannot be expected to keep quiet. Sister Cora's got to do something to stop them from taking her.

"Sister Cora, please! Help me," Hope begs.

"If you are innocent, you will be back with us soon enough." Sister Cora's face is a sick gray and her smile is false. She must know we won't see Hope again.

I see my horror reflected on the faces of all the girls around me. Sister Cora cannot—will not—save us. Part of me hopes that in her place, I would do more. Fight harder. But the pragmatic part knows she is sacrificing Hope to protect the rest of us.

The Brothers begin to shuffle out the door, evidently content now that they've made an arrest. The man who's been calling out names on the steps stuffs his papers in a black leather satchel and clears his throat. "Let this be a lesson. No one is exempt. Wickedness can worm its way into even the youngest, most innocent souls, and we will root it out and punish it wheresoever we find it." He bows to Sister Cora. "Thank you for your compliance, Sister. We will be back soon to conduct another search."

The Brothers file out, taking Hope with them. Tess emerges from the library, her arm wrapped around a sobbing Lucy. When she sees me, her face crumples, and she lets go of Lucy to throw her arms around my waist.

"They took Hope!" she sobs.

Maura's creamy complexion looks sickly. "Thank the Lord it wasn't you."

"It *should* be me," Tess whimpers, burying her face in my shoulder. "Hope doesn't know anything about anything! She just *froze* when they questioned her. Oh, Cate, it was awful!"

"I know," I murmur. I pat her shoulder and look to Maura, but she's already turned away, hips swaying as she makes her way down the hall toward Alice.

Behind her, Sister Cora is leaning heavily against the newel post at the bottom of the stairs. Now she slumps to the floor in a dead faint.

"Carry her into the parlor, and I'll see to her there," Sister Sophia instructs. "She shouldn't be doing magic, as ill as she is."

"What did she do?" I hear Maura ask, glancing down at our fallen headmistress scornfully. "She certainly didn't help Hope."

"Miss Ashby can't reveal what she can't remember," Sister Inez says simply. She claps her hands twice, and everyone crowds into the front hall. "Girls, I do not mean to alarm you, but perhaps this is the time for alarm. This is the first raid the Brothers have conducted here, but it will not be the last. We must be vigilant. If you possess any banned books, please see to it that they are concealed by magic whenever they are not in use. The Sisterhood is obviously no longer above suspicion."

The next morning, I'm heading down to the library with an armful of anatomy books filled with diagrams of the human body. Despite our protestations that our healing is magic, Sister Sophia is determined that we learn the science, too. Our current task is memorizing the two hundred–odd bones of the human body. And while I'm a bit preoccupied right now with the Brothers rounding up supposed oracles and Finn applying for a job that could get him killed, I'm not willing to look a dunce in front of the other girls.

I'm dawdling down the stairs to the first floor when I pass Tess going up. I smile at her, but she seems lost in thought. Nothing unusual in that. But then her slipper catches in the hem of her peach brocade dress, and she stumbles, books spilling out of her arms. She catches herself on her hands and knees just before her face mashes into the wooden railing.

"Are you all right?" I gasp. She's always been apt to run into things while her mind's preoccupied, but she doesn't normally fall *up* stairs.

She gazes up at me—no, *through* me, her gray eyes unfocused.

"Tess?" I hold out a hand to help her up, but she doesn't move to take it.

"I'm fine." She picks herself up.

She doesn't look fine. She's gone pale; her smile is forced, and she's not looking me in the eye.

I lean down and pick up her books—two thick, dog-eared tomes of the history of witchcraft. "Did you hurt yourself?"

"I said I'm fine, didn't I? Have you gone deaf?" She claps a hand over her mouth.

I bite my lip. "I'm sorry. I didn't mean to badger you."

"It's not you." The way she's looking at me now, though, it's as if she's never seen me before, as if she's studying me. Weighing me.

"There's something I need to tell you," she says finally. Evidently I've passed muster. "Can we go to your room?"

"Of course." My stomach twists as I lead her upstairs. What has her sounding so dire?

Sunlight billows into my bedroom through the gap in Rilla's curtains, slanting across the colorful hooked rugs, glinting in the mirror over our dressing table. I usher Tess inside and shut the door.

"Rilla's at botany for another hour, so we shouldn't be interrupted." I feel a tiny stab of jealousy, wishing I had time in my schedule for botany. My roommate barely knows the difference between tulips and roses, or peonies and ranunculus.

Tess sits at the foot of my bed, knees pressed to her chest. I kick off my slippers and sit at the other end, facing her, my long legs stretched out between us. I want to ply her with questions, but I bite my tongue. I know from experience that Tess will speak when she's ready and not a moment before.

"There's no easy way to say it. Will you promise to listen, and not interrupt?"

I twist Mother's ring on my finger. "I promise."

Tess props her pointy chin on her knees and gazes at me, her face scrunched up just like Father's. "I've been having visions. I wasn't sure at first. It started—well, I think it started some time ago, but I didn't realize what it was. When it happens, I feel light-headed, and sometimes I lose sight of where I am. I've got a half dozen bruises from knocking into things. For a while, I thought I was hallucinating, that it was a fever, or some kind of fit. But then the things I saw started coming true. The bonfire, with the Brothers burning piles of books. The Dolamores moving away after Gabrielle was arrested. Little Adam Collier falling through the ice on their pond. Our barn cat having kittens—three white as snow, one black. How could I see those things before they happened? How could I know?"

My baby sister's voice is calm as she explains how she has logically deduced that she is a seer.

"Those are just a few examples. I've had a dozen visions, and so far seven have come to pass, that I can tell." Tess's gray eyes are intent on mine. "It didn't happen very often at first, but now—I've had two just this week. I think—Cate, I think *I'm* the new oracle."

I struggle to keep the panic off my face. I mustn't frighten her.

"Have you told anyone else?" I whisper.

Tess shakes her head. Her hair is down today, in two long blond braids. "No. I don't want—" She gulps, and her voice quavers just a little. "I don't want people to think I'm mad."

My composure shatters. I dive across the bed, wrapping her in a fierce hug. Her skin smells like vanilla and spices. "No one would think that. You're the sanest person I know. Look how calm you are. I'd be hiding under the bed if it were me."

Tess burrows her face in my shoulder, and I rub her back in circles, the way I used to when she woke sobbing from nightmares.

"Brenna went mad," she mumbles against my neck.

I pull back and look down into her worried little face. "You are not Brenna Elliott."

"She's the only other person I know who has visions."

Her worry breaks my heart. It was the first thing I feared,

too. How long has she been fretting about it? It's too heavy a burden for her to manage on her own. "Brenna wasn't so bad before she went to Harwood. That won't happen to you."

"If the Brothers knew—if anyone else found out—"

"They won't." My voice is sharp. "You're a witch, Tess, and a powerful one. You can do mind-magic. If someone suspects, you can protect yourself."

Even Mother would approve of that.

"The Brothers are killing all those girls because they're looking for me," Tess whispers. "They took Hope away yesterday, and—and Maura wants to kill Brenna, and it's all my fault."

"No." I put my hands on her shoulders and look her right in the eye. "It is not your fault. It's—it's all dreadful, but it's not down to you."

Tess fiddles with the golden locket around her neck. "It's so strange, Cate. Like a flash of memory, except I see something that hasn't happened yet. It's as clear as a photograph. On the stairs, just now, I saw Sister Evelyn slip on ice and break her arm. I don't know when it will happen—today or tomorrow, or February or next year. But I know it will."

Sister Evelyn teaches botany and history, and she's the oldest person I've ever seen. Her skin is a wrinkled brown like a chestnut, and she has hair like wispy cotton and a pair of half-moon spectacles. She looks as though a strong wind could blow her away, but she still manages to care for her prizewinning orchids out in the conservatory.

I pull the pins from my hair, just for something to do with my hands. "Have you seen anything about us?" She hesitates, and I panic. "What did you see? If you don't tell me, I'll only imagine the worst."

Tess flushes. "You and Finn Belastra. You were kissing. It was dark. You were in a pink dress with roses all over it. It's the one Elena just brought for you; I helped her pick out the fabric, after I saw you in it. You looked pretty."

"Oh." I blush, too.

"You've been meeting him in secret, haven't you?" Tess asks. There is no judgment in her voice, and it occurs to me how lucky we are it's *Tess* having these visions. In the wrong person, this ability would be terrifying. If it were Maura— well. I'm glad it's Tess. "Is he some sort of spy? He can't really believe in the Brotherhood. He's not that sort."

"Did you see that, too?" I lean forward, eager.

Tess looks at me as though I'm very dim. She must be feeling better. "No. That's common sense. I can't see any other reason he would shut down the bookshop, unless it was to help you somehow. He loves books." She gives me a tiny, owlish smile. "He must love you more."

"Is that all you've seen about me, or you or Maura?"

"I saw us opening Sister Cora's letter yesterday. That's why I spilled my tea on it," she confesses. She picks up one of the books she was carrying. "I've been reading about the oracles since I got here. I need to find out if their visions always come true, or if sometimes the details change. If I see bad things, can I prevent them from happening? I felt so awful when Adam Collier fell through the ice. His father found him in time, and he's fine, but—it could have been terrible."

"That wouldn't be your fault."

Tess skewers me with a glance. "It's nice of you to say that, but you wouldn't feel that way if it were you, would you?"

I lean back against the brass headboard, my hair loose over my shoulders now. She doesn't need me to make false assurances. This isn't the problem of a child; I can't keep treating her like one. "No, likely not. I'm glad you told me. Thank you for trusting me with it."

Tess nods, tracing circles on the red leather cover with her fingertip. "I think you're the only person I should tell, for now. I feel dreadful keeping it from Maura." She takes a deep, jagged breath. "I'm afraid she'd be angry with me if she found out. She wants to be the prophesied witch so much. But it feels too big to keep all to myself. I—I'm scared, Cate."

So am I.

CHAPTER
10

SISTER INEZ KEEPS ME AFTER CLASS the next afternoon. I plod slowly to her desk, dreading the reprimand I'm about to receive. Today's lesson was on glamouring ourselves to look like specific Brothers. Rilla was marvelous, spooking us all with her eerie impersonation of Covington. Maura transformed herself into Brother Ishida for most of class. But though I kept a very distinct image of O'Shea in my head, I couldn't maintain the illusion for more than two minutes at a time. The result—my chocolate brocade dress with his long, thin face and bald head—was deserving of Alice and Maura's snickering, and this lecture, too.

Truth be told, I can't stop worrying about Tess. I never relished the notion of being the prophesied witch, but I hate that the burden has fallen on her small shoulders instead. It will be four years yet before she comes of age and leads the Sisterhood, but in the meantime, she will want to be involved in Inez's governance—and I can't help wondering how Inez will react to that. Tess is young, but she's always had very strong opinions; she won't be anyone's puppet. Will Inez be willing to take her feelings under advisement, or will she—like Maura—wave off Tess's opinions as those of an immature child?

I'm proud of Tess for keeping her head, despite her fear. She really is the smartest and best of the three of us.

"We have a problem, Miss Cahill," Sister Inez says now. Her voice is hard, clipped, and I realize that this is more serious than my performance today.

"We do?" I ask.

"Brother Belastra has applied to be Denisof's clerk, but it seems that someone is standing in his way. In *our* way."

"Who?" Finn isn't beholden to anyone except his mother. Has something happened in Chatham? I remember Hannah Maclay and shiver.

"Brother Ishida is reluctant to give up his new recruit," Inez says. As she speaks, she casts illusions over the books on her shelves, transforming them from magical textbooks into respectable Spanish primers. The twelve hand mirrors that showed our Brotherly reflections become a dozen small easels displaying innocent watercolors. "He claims Belastra should serve the Chatham council for a full year before he begins elsewhere. Denisof is of much higher standing, but clerks are a dime a dozen; he won't choose Belastra if it will make a fuss."

Blast. Of all the people to stand in our way, it has to be Ishida. I *hate* that man. "What should we do?"

"How much do you want Brother Belastra to remain in New London?" Inez asks.

My eyes meet hers. "Very much." Perhaps I ought to let him go, see this as a sign that he would be safer at home, but the thought of him going back to Chatham is devastating.

"You know Ishida. Call on him. Compel him to let Belastra go." Inez leans over the desk toward me like a long black shadow. "Can you do that?"

My mouth curves into a smile. Truth be told, it would not trouble me to use mind-magic on Ishida. "I can."

"Excellent. Time is of the essence, Miss Cahill." There's a sense of barely leashed impatience in her as she taps her skinny fingers against the desk. "Tell Belastra that his first order of business will be to discover the time and location of the next Head Council meeting."

"I'll take care of it today," I promise.

This time I don't ask any questions.

I can't find Rory anywhere—not in the third-floor room she shares with Daisy or in the sitting room or in the kitchen. The library is an unlikely place for her, but I check there, too. Sister Gretchen sits behind her desk, reading a German novel and watching over a dozen studying girls.

"Have you seen Rory?" I whisper.

"Cora sent for her a few minutes ago," Gretchen says.

Oh, no. I take the steps two at a time. What has Rory done to warrant a disciplinary meeting already? She promised me she'd behave! She's seemed fine—a little subdued, perhaps, but I haven't smelled sherry on her once or heard her making inappropriate jokes—though, honestly, I've been preoccupied. Perhaps I should have been looking after her more. She must be lonely and half mad with worry for Sachi.

Sachi. I've hardly thought of her lately, in all the bustle of my sisters arriving. What sort of place are they holding her in? What must she be going through, waiting for her trial, knowing how likely it is she'll be sentenced to Harwood for the rest of her life?

I burst into Sister Cora's sitting room in a panic. "Whatever she's done, she's sorry," I announce breathlessly. "Please don't dismiss her."

"Catherine," Sister Cora says, "what on earth are you talking about?"

"Me, I think." Rory's sitting in one of the green-flowered chairs by the window, in a tomato-red dress with enormous puffed sleeves and a daring décolletage. She looks more courtesan than nun. "She thinks I've been misbehaving. Reasonable assumption, really, but I've been a model student, Cate. No flirting with men on the sidewalks."

Sister Cora chuckles. Sister Sophia must have been to see her recently; she looks hale and hearty in a purple gown with silver fringe. "It's not a disciplinary meeting. I wanted to speak with her about her cousin Brenna."

"Oh. Well." I hover in the doorway awkwardly. "I'm sorry for doubting you, Rory."

"You're forgiven. It's quite nice, really, the way you came flying to my rescue."

Sister Cora beckons me in. "Now that you're here, you

may as well join us. Victoria was just giving me a bit of background on Brenna." She waves a hand, and the high-backed desk chair slides across the room to rest opposite her and Rory.

Rory nods, the red feather in her hair wagging. "We grew up together, in and out of each other's houses a dozen times a day. Brenna's father and my stepfather, Jack, were brothers." Rory's brown eyes dance, remembering, but then the light in them dims. "When my mother—fell ill, Brenna's family kept her from visiting so much."

"How did you find out about her prophecies?" Cora asks.

"Brenna came to us the day before Jack died. She told him not to go Newburgh—not to go anywhere he couldn't walk. He laughed it off. And then on the way back from Newburgh, his horse spooked and the carriage crashed into a tree. Just like Brenna said it would. The day after the funeral, her father sent her to Harwood."

So Brenna tried to stop it. She must have known how dangerous it was to speak of having visions, but she tried to warn him anyway, and look what thanks she got for her troubles.

No one can find out what Tess is.

"She's always been a bit odd, but it was Harwood that turned her mind," Rory says, her full lips pursed, and I know that she must be thinking of Sachi. Of whether that place will break her sister, just as it did her cousin.

"Was it Harwood, or was it her prophecies? Do oracles often go mad?" I'm frightened to ask, but I need to know. Have there been others besides Brenna and Thomasina?

"She's not the first," Sister Cora sighs. "But Brenna's visions aren't the cause of her illness—or at least they're not the *only* cause. I daresay you girls ought to know the truth of it, especially you, Cate."

Rory and I exchange mystified glances.

"We tried to intervene at Brenna's first trial. When I heard she was an oracle, I wanted her safe at the Sisterhood. Witch or no, it was the best place for her." Sister Cora's voice is kind, as though they were doing Brenna a favor. "As she wasn't a witch, however, we gave Brenna the choice. She refused to come to New London with us. She was frightened; she wanted to stay in Chatham. Honestly, I didn't think it would be long before she was arrested again."

"So *you* sent her to Harwood?" Rory shoots to her feet, incensed.

Sister Cora holds up a silencing hand. "That wasn't our original intention. I meant to erase her memory of the conversation and our presence there. I'd brought a student with me who was capable of mind-magic; I thought it beneficial for her to witness a trial. I allowed her to compel Brenna. Unfortunately, it all went wrong. Understand—this is a risk we take, each and every time we perform mind-magic. Brenna's not been the same since."

Alice must be the one who ruined Brenna.

Brenna's creepy chatter makes sense, suddenly. *Holes in my head. The crows put them there. They came to my trial. The Brothers left me alone with them. I was so frightened. I thought they would peck out my eyes, but they only took my memories.*

I'm so horrified I can hardly think straight. *This is why*

Mother preached against mind-magic, why it mustn't ever be used casually.

At the same time, a tiny part of me is *relieved*. Brenna's madness isn't because of her visions. That's one less thing for Tess to fret about.

There are tears in Rory's brown eyes. "You broke her. You let a student practice on her, you broke her, and then you abandoned her!"

"Victoria, I understand this is difficult for you. Please, sit down, so we can discuss it," Cora says. "Brenna wasn't well. Harwood was the best place for her."

"Harwood isn't a place anyone goes to get *better*," I object. Cora must know that.

"That's a lie. You were afraid she would give you away," Rory accuses, looming over us. She's as tall as I am, but voluptuous in all the places I'm not. Her eyes narrow. "You sent her there to rot, thinking no one would pay any mind to the ravings of a madwoman. But now they are paying attention, and you—I've heard the rumors. The war council met to discuss killing her!" Tears run down Rory's face, and she's trembling like a snowflake on the November wind.

"I'm sorry." Sister Cora spreads her hands wide, shaking her snowy head. "I would like to promise you that no harm will come to Brenna from the Sisterhood, but I cannot. My first duty is to protect our girls, especially the next oracle. I can only tell you that, for now, we intend Brenna no injury."

I wince. Lord, what a dreadful decision to make.

I'm glad I'm not the one who has to make it.

Will it be Tess soon? If Tess argued against killing Brenna

but Inez argued for it, whose vote would win out? Would Tess *have* a vote, as the future headmistress? I am helping Inez, and yet it strikes me that if I were the oracle and had to let her rule in my stead for a matter of years instead of months, I would not be entirely comfortable with the arrangement.

"Can't promise? *Won't,* you mean. If it were Cate, you'd move heaven and earth to get her free," Rory says bitterly. "But my cousin—my sister—they're expendable!"

She stomps toward the door, her words reminding me of Zara's warnings about Cora. Then she's flailing, sliding back toward us. She collapses awkwardly into her chair, as if pushed by an invisible hand.

Sister Cora rises. There's no sign of her pain today; her movements are graceful and strong. "You should thank Persephone it is not Cate. Do you know what could happen if it were? The prophecy says very clearly that if she falls into the hands of the Brothers, it could cause a second Terror." Glaring down at Rory, her tall body clad in purple, Cora still looks like a fierce old queen. "Brenna wouldn't be the only one imprisoned. We'd all be locked up, or worse. Burnt in our beds at night like the witches in the Great Temple, or in town squares throughout New England. Beheaded in front of our families—and our families beheaded, too, as sympathizers, if they tried to interfere. Weighted down with stones and thrown into rivers to drown. Is that what you want?"

"Of course not! I just want my family back!" Rory shouts.

"Rory. Let's go to my room and talk," I suggest, pulling her away. I need to get her out of here before she loses control.

Frankly, I think she has a point. Sister Cora had a duty to Brenna, and she failed her.

"You can't fix this, Cate." Out in the hallway, Rory grips her satin skirt in both fists as she sinks against the wall. I pull her into the alcove of the third-floor window seat. We settle onto the soft cushions, staring out at the slush falling from the gray sky.

"I can't fix Brenna," I admit. "And I can't stop Sachi from being sent to Harwood. I wish I could make it right, but I don't know how."

Rory sniffles. "I want to go to her trial."

"I'm not sure that's a good idea." Rory's been learning to control her magic and her temper, but under those circumstances—well, who wouldn't be tested?

Rory frowns. "I'm not asking you for permission, Cate. She needs to see a friendly face." There's a touch of iron in her voice.

"Well, then I'll go with you; you mustn't go alone," I decide, crossing my ankles. "But first, we need to find out when the trial *is.* Your father would know that, wouldn't he? Even if he's not planning to attend?"

"I doubt he'll be able to stay away. Maybe he'll even testify against her." Rory reaches up and adjusts her feather, which has blown askew in the draft from the window. "The way he's acting now would break her heart."

My lips twitch into a smile. There is one thing I can do for Rory. "How would you like a chance to tell him what you think of him? *Without* being arrested for insubordination?"

Rory squints at me. "How is that possible?"

"It just so happens that I've got an errand to run that involves your father and compulsion," I confess. "Would you like to come with me?"

She grins. "I'd have to be mad to pass that up."

The cobbled sidewalks are covered in a thick, slippery layer of ice, and it's treacherous going. Perhaps we should have waited for the carriage to be free after all. Freezing rain pelts down, stinging my exposed nose and cheeks. Above us, the sky is a stormy gray just the color of Tess's eyes.

Rory pauses before a four-story brick hotel. A doorman in black livery ushers us inside, where our cloaks drip onto the white marble floor. Rory leads the way to the second floor, where she hammers on a heavy oak door. The hallway around us is papered in rich gold, with ornate crown moldings. I feel like a sodden mess in this elegant place, but hopefully the Sisterhood's cloaks afford us at least a little respectability. It's a long, nervous moment before Brother Ishida opens the door, dressed in black trousers and a gray collared shirt. It's strange to see him without his black cloak of office. It makes him look more like a man, a father, than a priest.

"Miss Elliott." He nods brusquely, not quite meeting her eyes. "Ah, and Sister Catherine. Good day."

Now that the moment is here, Rory seems to have lost all her bravado. She stares at her father wordlessly.

"May we come in, sir?" I ask. "We'd like to speak with you."

"Certainly." He steps back, bowing. My hand flies to my cheek. The cut has healed, and he won't remember slapping me for my insubordination. Tess saw to that. But I'll never forget it, nor the ravings that accompanied it. He said if it were up to him, he'd resurrect the burnings.

The memory strengthens my resolve.

"How can I help you?" Brother Ishida forgoes the usual ceremony, gesturing for us to sit on the green sofa. His sitting room is grand: full of velvet sofas and chairs, heavy gold damask drapes with a leafy print, and shining rosewood tea tables with curved legs like serpents' heads. A brown and gold Oriental rug stretches across the wooden floor, and gas lamps with gold fixtures give off a bright, steady glow despite the gloom outside.

"Have you had any news of Sachi?" I ask.

"She's in prison, awaiting her trial, as she ought to be," Brother Ishida says flatly, taking the chair opposite us.

"As she ought to be?" Rory echoes.

"Indeed." He turns black marble eyes on her. "She is a *witch*. She deserves whatever punishment the New London council deems appropriate."

"Do you know when her trial is?" I ask.

"Saturday," he says.

"Have you been to see her?" Rory asks. "Is she well?"

Brother Ishida taps his fingers on the dragon's head carved into the arm of his chair. "I have not, nor will I."

I expected it, but I'm still taken aback by his coldness.

"It's that easy for you to cut her out of your heart, just like that?" Rory snaps her fingers.

Brother Ishida eyes her with distaste. "It was not easy, but it is the Lord's will. The moment Sachiko first did magic, she erased herself from our family and from all good society. She is a blot on the Ishida name, and I will not—"

"But she's still your daughter," Rory says, her voice low and tense. "Isn't there anything you could do for her? To help her?"

"Do not interrupt me." Brother Ishida tugs at his collar with fleshy fingers. "There is nothing I could do, even if I were moved to intercede. And I am not. I have erased Sachiko's name from our book of Scriptures. I no longer have a daughter."

Rory gives a strangled laugh. "Yes, you do."

A strand of black hair falls over Ishida's forehead as he shakes his head. "No. I have cast Sachiko out. That is my duty to—"

"I don't mean Sachi," Rory says softly. "Me. I'm your daughter."

Brother Ishida freezes, his eyes darting to me. "That's ludicrous."

"It's not. You gave my mother money to keep her quiet." Rory lifts her chin. "I'm your daughter."

Brother Ishida rises, his face flushed with anger. He turns to me, not Rory. "Lydia Elliott is a common slut. She could have consorted with half a dozen men. Sister Catherine, I beg you not to listen to this nonsense."

"Is it nonsense?" I ask, my hands clasped in my lap. "There have been—rumors, to the contrary."

"That's nothing but malicious gossip!" He turns on Rory,

the vein in his forehead bulging. "How dare you come here and prey on a father's grief? What a scheming, manipulative girl you are. Perhaps you knew of my daughter's witchery—even encouraged it, thinking you could make a place for yourself in my home. As if the likes of *you* could ever replace my Sachiko! You were never worthy of her friendship. Perhaps you're the one who taught her such wicked ways!"

Rory doesn't flinch, though he's shouting practically into her face. "If she gets witchery from anyone, it's you. Your grandmother was a witch."

Brother Ishida grabs her arm and hauls her to her feet. His grip must be bruising. "That is nonsense. I forbid you to repeat it."

"What does it matter?" Rory snaps. "Sachi will be sent to Harwood. You won't have any grandchildren. Your bloodline is dead—unless you've got another bastard somewhere."

Brother Ishida slaps her across the face, sending Rory tumbling across the sofa. Her head almost lands in my lap. She's not little, like Sachi. He must have hit her hard.

"How dare you speak to me like that!" he roars, spittle flying from his mouth. "I should have you arrested for your impertinence."

Rory's hand flies to her cheek. "You don't have an ounce of fatherly feeling, do you?"

I stand. "Rory is a novitiate of the Sisterhood now. I'll thank you not to lay your hands on her again." A little thrill goes through me at being so audacious.

"I beg your pardon?" Brother Ishida looks flabbergasted.

It's not uncommon for men to take their fists to their wives and daughters. The Brotherhood preaches that women should submit to the authority of their fathers and then their husbands.

"You should beg Rory's pardon," I snap. She's still lying there on her back, looking a trifle dazed. "Is there anything else you'd like to say to your father, Rory?"

She doesn't need me to ask twice. She struggles to her feet, her black cloak askew, her red dress peeking out. Her scarlet slippers are ruined from charging through the slush and salt. Her dark hair is mussed, the red feather sodden and askew. But she's beautiful, standing there, squaring off against the man who's never acknowledged her as his.

"You disgust me," she says clearly. Brother Ishida recoils, shock and fury warring on his face. "You play at being a paragon of morality, but what kind of man commits adultery? What kind of father abandons his children? You're nothing but a lying hypocrite."

"How dare you speak to me like that!" Brother Ishida shouts, lunging toward her. Rory dodges around the sofa.

The mind-magic comes easily this time. Power whirls through me, skipping out my fingertips. My focus is scalpel-sharp and unhindered by any sense of guilt whatsoever. I command him to forget this scene, and to let Finn Belastra stay in New London where he can better serve the Brotherhood's aims.

The resulting exhaustion is nothing compared to the nausea of healing. I brush it aside, eyeing Brother Ishida carefully.

He crashes into one of the tea tables, knocking it over with a clatter, and then he stops. Confusion passes over his face as he turns to look at Rory and me. "Girls? What was I saying? I'm sorry, I had a bit of a dizzy spell."

"Are you all right, sir?" I try to keep the triumph from my voice.

"Yes, yes." He nods, leaning down to right the table.

"We were just leaving, after offering our condolences about Sachi. We are so sorry for your loss, and if our visit upset you," I say, though the words taste like mud in my mouth. "We ought to be getting back to the Sisterhood for our supper."

"Very well. Thank you for coming, girls. I'm sorry your faith in Sachiko was misplaced. So was mine. The Lord would have us cast her out, you know."

I take Rory's hand. "We know."

In the hallway, Rory collapses against the gold wallpaper, both hands covering her face. "Thank you," she whispers.

"I'm sorry it was necessary. You deserve a better father."

"Jack was always good to me," Rory says. "I'm glad I have his name and not that monster's."

"I hope Sachi never knows the things he said about her."

"She won't hear it from me." Rory's face crumples. "We have to help her, Cate. I can't let her spend the rest of her life in Harwood. Her mother won't ever go against him; I'm all the family she's got now."

"She has me, too," I insist. "And the whole Sisterhood, if I've anything to say about it."

There's a little cut on Rory's cheek from her father's ring. I call up my magic again and touch her cheek, lightly, with my fingertips. "Hold still."

Rory grabs my arm when I sway. "You're marvelous, Cate Cahill, do you know that? I—I never thought you liked me much. Most people don't. They only put up with me for Sachi's sake."

Oh. It's true that I only befriended Rory because that was Sachi's prerequisite—and her fierce "love me, love my sister" attitude kept me from criticizing Rory aloud. I have judged her silently, though—for her loud ways, her daring dresses, her drunken mother, her impulsiveness. She's had a horrible time of it, but instead of putting myself in her shoes, I've condemned her for seeking comfort in a few nips of sherry, in the arms of that lug-headed Nils Winfield. And, worst of all, I never gave her credit for being sensitive enough to notice.

Shame coats me like ice.

"I do like you," I insist, realizing that it's true. "You're brave enough to say what you think. You're loyal, even when it's not easy, like with Brenna. And you don't give a fig what anyone thinks of you."

Rory glows under my praise. "That last is a lie. But thank you. No one's ever taken up for me like this before except my sister."

I grin at her dizzily. "You can repay me. Do you know where Finn's room is?"

"It's right there." Rory gestures to the door across from us. "Why?"

"Will you stand guard for me? Cough if someone else comes into the hall. I want to leave him a note."

"Now, this sort of mischief I can handle," Rory says, taking up position at the end of the hall. Fondness envelops me. Bless her for not asking questions or judging me for slipping into a man's hotel room.

I put my hand over the gold doorknob, commanding it to unlock. He doesn't have a grand sitting room, only a bedroom with a little desk in the corner. I hurry over to it. There are a few books stacked on top. A black cloak is draped over the back of the desk chair; a pair of boots is lined up neatly before the fireplace. Behind me, the four-poster bed is unmade, rumpled sheets twisting out from beneath the thick green duvet.

I think of Finn coming back to this room, shedding his heavy winter clothes, slipping into bed. Does he lie awake at night thinking of me, the way I do him?

I blush and turn back to the desk. I'm here for a purpose; I haven't got time to moon around wondering how he looks in his sleep. There's a fountain pen on the desk atop a stack of parchment paper. He's begun a letter to his mother. I can't help scanning the first few lines:

I've applied for a clerk's position here in New London. I hope you will understand. I will miss you and Clara, of course, but my heart is in the city at present, and in addition, I think I might be able to do some good work here, work I think you would approve . . .

My heart is in the city—does he mean me? His heart? I can't help a foolish smile at that. I grab the fountain pen and pull a blank sheet of paper from beneath the letter.

Meet me for a walk at four tomorrow in Richmond Square Gardens. I miss you.

I hesitate, biting at the tip of the pen, and then add: *Love, C.*

CHAPTER
11

I'M IN MY ROOM THE FOLLOWING afternoon when Maura knocks on the open door.

"Sister dearest," she trills from the doorway, glorious in a cream-colored brocade embroidered with shimmering blue leaves. She must have half a dozen new dresses. I look down at my own gray gown with red piping. I felt pretty five minutes ago, but now I'm the drab little dove compared to her bluebird. "Could I have a word? In private?" She smiles pointedly at Rilla, who's lying on her stomach on her yellow quilt, reading a romance novel.

"I'll just run down to the kitchen for some cocoa," Rilla says, jumping up, leaving her novel open on her bed. "Would you like some, Cate?"

"No, thank you. I'm going out; I've got an errand to run."

Maura smiles as Rilla bounces off. "A rendezvous with your dashing spy?"

I yank her into the room and shut the door. "Hush!"

"Oh, I'm not going to spill your secret," she says, twirling a red curl around her finger. "I hope he tells you something useful, though. He's got to start earning his keep."

Fear washes over me. Earning her silence, she means? "Maura, you do realize no one else can know about this."

"I haven't told a soul. Ooh, these are pretty." Maura snatches up a pair of pearl earbobs from my dresser and slides them on. "I've got plans of my own this afternoon. Special tutoring with Sister Inez."

I sit on the edge of my bed, reaching for my boots. "Practicing mind-magic on your friends again?" I want to stuff the words back into my mouth the second they escape. The last thing I want is to irritate her more.

"Judgmental, aren't we?" Maura arches her eyebrows at my waspish tone. "I didn't see you complaining when Sister Cora erased Hope's memory."

I slide on heeled black boots. "That was to protect us, not for fun."

"What part of this do you suppose is fun for me? Letting the Brothers storm in here and interrogate us? Watching an innocent little girl get arrested, knowing they're going to let her rot in a cellar somewhere?" Maura stalks around the room, stepping over the slippers and stockings Rilla's dropped helter-skelter. "We're not safe here anymore. They could seize any of us at any moment."

"I know that."

"They've arrested at least thirteen girls now, counting Hope. Sister Cora's ill. We need a strong leader, not all this uncertainty." Maura plops down on Rilla's rumpled yellow quilt. "I want you to take the test."

"No." I lean down and tie my laces.

Maura groans. "Why are you being so selfish? If you would take the test, we'd find out which of us is the most powerful and we could start planning accordingly. If it's me, I'd like to work with Sister Inez to start *doing* things."

"It only tests one kind of magic," I point out, straightening. What is it that she's so eager to do, besides murdering Brenna?

"The most important kind." Maura narrows her blue eyes at me. "Is that why you're so reluctant? Are you afraid it will confirm that *I'm* the prophesied witch?"

"That's ridiculous," I say flatly. I'm thinking of Tess, wishing that I could tell Maura the truth, but as soon as it's out of my mouth, I realize I've misspoken again. How do I always manage to say the exact wrong thing to her?

"It is *not* ridiculous!" Maura slams her hands down on either side of her, making Rilla's bed quiver. "You've never wanted this as much as I have. I've been working ten times as hard as you—not just at magic, but to win these girls' respect. Do you think I like spending so much time with that little snob Alice Auclair?"

I gape at her. "Yes?"

"No! Good Lord, don't you know me at all?" Maura demands, springing up. "She's popular because everyone's scared of her. I'm trying to curry favor so that she and all her friends will support Inez and me. When it comes time for war, we'll need everyone working together, not split down the middle like they are now. I'm working night and day to earn my place here, which is more than I can say for you. But the Sisters are still stuck on the notion that you're the prophesied one, even though you haven't had any visions yet."

I focus on the row of blue buttons marching up her bodice instead of looking her in the eye. "Neither have you."

"*I will*," Maura says, her voice fierce. "I'm not going to spend the rest of my life standing by while girls are hunted down. Take the test, Cate."

I stand, temper simmering. "I said no, and I meant it. I already know I can do mind-magic. I'm not going to practice just to show off. And I'm certainly not going to break my friends' trust—or my family's—by practicing on them!"

Maura leans against my dresser, hurt flashing across her face. "I see someone's been tattling. Tess or Elena?"

"It doesn't matter. I can't believe you did that to the O'Hares!"

Maura clenches her ruffled cream skirt in her fist. I have the unsettling feeling that she'd like to crush me instead of that pretty brocade. "You're as much of a snob as Alice, thinking you're better than everyone else."

"That's not true! I never said I was a better witch than you."

Maura stalks toward the door. "No, you just think you're a better person. And it's not true. The only reason Cora favors you is because she hates Inez. If my birthday were first, it would be me. That's all it is, Cate, so don't go around thinking you're anything extraordinary."

She slams the door behind her, and I sink down onto my bed, head in my hands. Is she right? Have Cora's pretty compliments only been flattery, because I'm a better alternative than Inez?

I remind myself that it doesn't really matter now anyway.

I can't reveal Tess's secret before she's ready, but this constant competition with Maura is wearying. It feels like everyone in the convent is watching, waiting to see which of us will be the prophesied sister. None of the teachers have admitted that Sister Cora is dying, but everyone knows she's ill; it's an open secret. It feels as though everyone is waiting for her to die, and for Inez to take charge and make things happen. But what is Inez planning—and how is my sister wrapped up in it?

I stand and search through my mahogany jewelry box for another pair of earbobs, since Maura took the pearls. Perhaps it's madness, meeting Finn in the middle of the afternoon in broad daylight. But he'll be dressed as a Brother, and as long as we're careful to keep a proper distance, no one's likely to suspect him of any wrongdoing.

There's a cursory knock at the door, and Tess pokes her head in. "There you are. Are you going out?" She peers at the garnets in my hand, lowering her voice. "Are you meeting Finn?"

"How did you know?" I demand, slipping them on.

"You've done your hair." Tess points at the braids wound

prettily around the crown of my head. "You've got to stop looking at me as though I'm going to spontaneously burst into fire at any moment, or people are going to start suspecting something. You're the least sneaky girl I know. Can I come with you?"

"To meet Finn?" I ask uncertainly.

"Yes, silly." Tess grabs my spare pair of brown boots from the corner by the armoire and steps into them. "I just want to meet him. I mean, I've met him in the shop dozens of times, but not when I knew you *loved* him. I should get to know him a bit, shouldn't I, if he's to be my brother someday?"

"We're not betrothed anymore." My voice is brusque, though it hurts me to say it. "I gave his ring back before I left Chatham."

Tess loops her arm around my waist. "You're still betrothed in your hearts."

I can't help smiling. "When did you become such a little romantic? Have you been reading Maura's novels?"

Tess bends down to buckle the boots, flushing. "Don't judge. Some of them are quite entertaining."

Oh, she is growing up. Dreaming of a beau of her own, perhaps. When I was twelve, I thought I'd grow up to be Catherine McLeod; I assumed it the way I knew grass was green and the sky was blue. Was there a boy in Chatham Tess thought handsome?

"You won't tell Finn, will you? About my visions?" Her gray eyes are serious again. "I don't want anyone to know yet. No one but you."

"Then I won't."

I won't lose Tess by making the same mistakes I made with Maura. I'm going to do things differently with her—and that means listening to what she wants and respecting it, not bullying or bossing.

Even if it means that Maura seems farther away every day.

Richmond Square Gardens are next to the cathedral, directly across the street from the barren square where the bonfire was held. The public park is hardly the lovely green oasis it must be in spring or summer, but it's still a colorful escape from the brick and stone of the city. The red maples are holding on to autumn, stretching their leafy fingers toward the weak sun. Beneath them, witch hazel flaunts its spidery yellow flowers while the rosebushes sleep. All around us, there's the sound of dripping water, ice melting after yesterday's storm. Today is positively balmy in comparison.

All the paths are muddy, trampled messes. At the far end of the park, a little boy jumps delightedly into a puddle with both feet. I spot Finn sitting on a marble bench by the duck pond. In the spring I daresay it would be crowded with children feeding the birds and splashing in the shallow water while their mothers scold, but today there are only a few mottled ducks floating placidly on the brown water.

He hasn't seen us yet. I take the rare chance to watch him unobserved. He's leaning over a book, reading as he waits. His thick brown hair stands up as if he's already run his hands through it half a dozen times, and there's stubble on his chin as though he forgot to shave the last morning or two.

Just then, he looks up and sees us—sees me—and his gap-toothed grin is enormous. He stands, poking his spectacles up with his index finger and tucking the book into his pocket.

I want to run to him, hurl myself into his arms, but Sister Catherine picks her way carefully down the path.

"You know my sister, Tess. She wanted to come and meet you properly. Tess, this is Finn." My stomach twists as it occurs to me that these are my two favorite people in the world, and I want them to adore one another.

"Good day, Brother Belastra," Tess says shyly, her hands stuffed in her cloak pockets.

"Finn," he corrects her. "Please. It's good to see you again, Tess."

"Thank you for meeting us." I'm so used to us sneaking around, meeting in secret places—in his mother's bookshop, our garden at home, the Sisters' conservatory. I feel oddly shy and formal, with Tess here and the whole world watching.

"I was glad to." He takes a step closer, lowering his voice. "I heard the Brothers raided the convent. I thought you would be safe there. I thought that was the entire *point.*"

"There isn't anywhere safe anymore." I stare past him at the carefree ducks, remembering the terror in Hope's voice. "Have you heard anything about the girls they've arrested?"

"One of them died yesterday—the simpleminded one. They tortured her. I daresay the others won't last long. They're interrogating them night and day, refusing them food or water or sleep." Tess inches closer to me, and Finn's cherry mouth tilts into a frown. "I'm sorry—did you know the girl they took from the convent?"

"She was Tess's friend." I fight the urge to put my arm around her, knowing it will embarrass her. She's gnawing on her bottom lip with her two pearly front teeth, a bad habit she gets from me and a sure sign of distress, so I change the subject. "Was it difficult to get away?"

Finn shrugs. "Ishida gave me leave to skip the council sessions to meet with my new boss. Denisof will assume I've been in the sessions all afternoon. They'll never miss me."

I grin. "Does that mean you got the position?"

"I had word this morning." His brown eyes are earnest behind his spectacles, but he bows theatrically, lightening the mood. "What's my assignment, milady?"

"Find out when the next Head Council meeting is, and where." I run a hand along the back of the bench, tracing the curves with my fingertip. "I hate asking this of you."

"I volunteered, remember? And I'm eager to do it, so stop apologizing, Cate."

My heart thrills at just this: the sound of my name on his tongue.

"Besides, it's hardly a swashbuckling adventure." He looks faintly disappointed, and my lips twitch at his urge to play the hero. I'm glad it's not more dangerous; after all, this isn't one of his books. "Denisof's a member; I imagine he'll have me clear his schedule. What's Inez planning?"

"I don't know," I confess. "She's been teaching us how to glamour ourselves as Brothers. Perhaps she's going to kidnap one of the Head Council members before the meeting and put one of us in his place to find out what their plans are. Has Brenna said anything new?"

Finn takes off his cloak and spreads it across the damp bench. I sit perhaps a *tad* closer than is strictly proper, my hip almost brushing his gray trousers. He's dressed in his fine Brotherhood clothes today: gray vest, white shirtsleeves, black boots speckled with mud. Tess plops down on the other side of me.

"Er—yes, actually." He clears his throat. "She's predicted that one of the Brothers' own will betray them by siding with the witches."

"What?" I shriek, rocketing to my feet, almost tripping over the cobblestones lining the path.

"Shhh." Finn grabs my wrist and tugs me back down. "She didn't give any specifics. There's nothing to identify me."

I take a deep breath. I stood up for Brenna, but if her prophesying keeps putting the people I love in greater danger, what can I do? Are Inez and Maura right?

"This is entirely too dangerous now," I begin. "I don't want—"

"It's not up to you. It's my decision. I've heard some rumblings about the Sisterhood, too," Finn continues. His freckled hand lies on his knee, inches away from mine. He has a smudge of black ink on his forefinger.

"What kind of rumblings?" Tess demands, craning around me to see him.

"The strictest members of the council wanted to close the convent school. They were outvoted. The vote to forbid women's education wasn't unanimous, you know—at least a third of the council was against it. As a concession to them, the convent school was permitted to stay open."

"As though fifty educated girls make such a difference," Tess snaps, bouncing her fists against her thighs.

"O'Shea's faction argues that they do. He claims that any stronghold of feminine learning is a bastion of wickedness. A source of potential rebellion."

I give a mischievous grin. "Well, he's not wrong in that."

"His faction believes there should be no exceptions, no exemptions, and that the Brotherhood should have more control over the daily workings of the Sisterhood. I wouldn't be surprised if that's on the agenda for the Head Council meeting."

I laugh in disbelief. "How? What do they mean to do, move a man in to run the place?"

Finn adjusts his glasses again. "That's *exactly* what they mean to do. O'Shea thinks a Brother ought to be made headmaster. That if the girls there must be educated, a man ought to oversee the curriculum."

I utter a few very unladylike words. "We'd have to modify his memory every other day! He'd turn into a vegetable."

"Or we'd have to study nothing more taxing than watercolors and Scriptures and French," Tess huffs.

"Not French. Now that French ladies have the vote, it's been forbidden, lest our impressionable girls find the language a gateway to immorality." Finn's mouth twitches as though he wants to laugh. "Brennan, another member of the Head Council, is opposing O'Shea. He's a good sort. Has three daughters of his own, which I daresay makes a difference."

"I find it hard to believe that *any* member of the

Brotherhood is a good sort," I grumble. Finn flinches, shifting his weight on the bench, and I wish I could stuff the words back down my throat. What is wrong with me today? "I'm sorry. I didn't mean you, obviously. I know you don't want to be there."

"I can't be the first man who joined to protect his family." Finn stares down at the engraved silver ring on his right ring finger. "It's easier to stay silent than to have your values questioned—your dedication to the Brothers and to the Lord himself."

"That's cowardice. If there are as many as you say, they could change things by speaking up!" I hiss. A few yards away, two pigtailed girls play with dolls on a bench while their mother pushes a pram around the duck pond.

"Then I'm a coward myself. I was there the day the new measures were debated. I didn't have a vote yet, but I could have argued against them. Perhaps I could have made a difference." Finn's voice is rich with self-loathing.

"No. You couldn't risk calling attention to yourself! That's different," I insist, putting my hand over his. I don't even think of who might see us—I only want to comfort him, to atone for my reckless words.

Finn slides his hand away. "It's not. These men are husbands and fathers and brothers, too. I believe there will come a time when they *do* speak up."

"That's grand, but how bad will things have to get for us before they rouse themselves?" I shift away from him on the cold marble. "What will it take? The Brothers are murdering innocent girls as we speak!"

"And what are you doing about it?" The question feels like a slap—an echo of all of Maura's criticisms. "You're powerful, Cate. The Sisterhood together must be incredibly strong, and yet you're just—biding your time. I'm not blaming you, but—"

"It sounds as if you are. What are we meant to do without giving ourselves away?" I demand. "It's not as simple as just speaking up. Not for women."

Finn frowns. "I know that. I don't want you putting yourself at risk, Lord knows—but if everyone felt that way, how would we ever move forward?"

We stare at each other in melancholy quiet. It's our first—not fight, not exactly. But the first time we've seen something big so differently. *Is* it up to me to act? It is so much easier to put the blame solely on the Brothers' hateful policies. I know he has a point, logically; I know the Brotherhood cannot consist entirely of hateful, smarmy hypocrites like Brother Ishida who would deny their own daughters. But I can't reconcile that logic with the fear I've felt for them my entire life.

Is that how most people feel about witches?

Tess stands, head cocked. "What's all that noise?"

I've been so preoccupied with our argument I hadn't even noticed, but now I hear the shouts coming from Richmond Square, the steady roar of voices chanting in unison.

I can't make out the words, but whenever a crowd assembles, it's rarely good for girls like us.

Tess is already hurrying down the muddy path toward the front of the park.

"Tess, wait!" I cry, chasing after her. I'm practically running, my boots sliding in the mud, hardly conscious of Finn scrambling after me. Once I get past the trees, I can see the crowd gathered in Richmond Square, spilling over into the cobbled street that runs in front of the cathedral itself, pressing up against its wide marble steps. It's not dozens of people shouting. It's *hundreds*. Maybe thousands.

There are more people assembled here than I've ever seen in my life.

Are they burning more than books this time?

Tess has stopped, wide-eyed, at the very edge of the crowd.

"Let our women work! Let our women work!" The people chant it, over and over. Some hold brightly painted wooden signs proclaiming LET OUR WOMEN WORK and WOMEN'S WAGES HELP FEED FAMILIES and OUR FAMILIES ARE HUNGRY. The crowd is mostly working-class: men in patched trousers or the new blue jeans, shirtsleeves rolled up to their elbows, wearing caps and muddy work boots. Some of them sling mugs of cider in the air as they shout. There are a few women in the crowd, shouting alongside their husbands: "Let us work!"

Dozens of people clutch printed pamphlets. A passing man crumples one in his fist and drops it, and I snatch it as it flutters toward the ground. There's a cartoon of two thin, big-eyed children with empty plates looking pleadingly at their mother, who sits knitting in her rocker. In the next panel, two fat men in dark cloaks gorge themselves on a rich feast of ham hocks and chicken legs and cake. The caption says simply *Let Our Women Work! Come to Richmond Square*

and protest the Brothers' new measure against women's em-
ployment. Our families go hungry while our women sit idle.

"I don't think we ought to be here," Finn says over my shoulder.

"I've never seen a protest before," I breathe. "This is splendid!"

"I'm not certain there's ever *been* a protest before. Not against the Brotherhood, anyhow," Tess says. Her gray eyes meet mine, and I know what we're both thinking. There were protests against the Daughters of Persephone. I've read about them. That was how it started.

A burly man with a slouchy corduroy cap approaches us. "Come to join us, Brother?"

"We were just leaving," Finn insists, grabbing my elbow.

The man hands him a leaflet. "Stay. You should see what people think of your new laws."

"It's not my law. I believe in women's right to work," Finn declares.

"Voted against it, did you?" Finn hesitates, and the burly man laughs. "And why would you? You sit back and get rich off our tithes, while our families starve. Easy enough to think about morals when you're well-fed."

A square-jawed, olive-skinned man with a red flannel shirt saunters up. "Not so sure this one's moral, Ted. Carrying on with two girls bold as brass. Hypocrites, the lot of them."

"Keep a civil tongue in your head. These ladies are novitiates of the Sisterhood." Finn pulls Tess behind him.

"Those convent girls are no better than the Brothers. Never done an honest day's work in your life, I bet," the dark-haired man drawls. He has the same Spanish accent as Sister Inez.

I'm surprised by my own outrage. "We do. We nurse the sick at the hospital. We take food to those who need it."

"But you don't go without, do you? You still go to sleep at night with full bellies on your fine feather pillows," Ted points out.

"We don't want your charity," the Spaniard says. "We want to do for ourselves."

I eye them both distastefully. "You hardly look like you're starving."

The dark-haired man laughs and grabs my arm, pulling me away from Finn. "Feisty one, aren't you? I doubt he approves of that," he says, nodding at Finn. "I could show you a good time, Sister."

His breath smells of liquor, and now I understand why Finn was wary. This protest is a powder keg ripe for violence, heightened by alcohol and the hot sunshine and a mob mentality. I plant my feet as much as I can in the sodden ground. If this oaf thinks he can manhandle me, he's sorely mistaken. "Take your hands off me. I'm not going anywhere with you."

"Come on, just have a look around with me. I betcha I'm more fun than he is. You ever had whiskey?" He fumbles in his pocket for a flask, and his dark eyes rake over me. "You ever been kissed, Sister?"

Oh, this is too much. I slap him across the face.

His friend laughs. "She showed you, Marco!"

Flushing red, Marco rubs his cheek and glares at me. "Uppity chit."

Finn steps toward us, eyes snapping. "Is this how you show your respect for women?"

Marco grins. "You're right. My quarrel's with *you*."

He shoves Finn, who staggers back and bumps into Tess. She slips, falling to the ground. The mud is thick here—it splashes across her cloak and spatters her face. Finn comes up swinging, but the dark-haired man twists away easily and lands a punch. Finn reels back.

"Stop it! You should be ashamed of yourself," I spit, helping Tess to her feet. "Look what you've done. Does hurting a child make you feel manly?"

Marco advances on me again, but this time he stumbles, tripping spectacularly over his own feet and sprawling in the mud.

Tess. I can hardly disapprove—I don't suppose a subtle bit of magic's much worse than public brawling. I flex my fingers, which are still tingling from slapping him.

"Come on, Marco, you're foxed. This isn't the kind of trouble we're after," Ted says, hustling his friend away into the crowd.

Finn takes my arm and Tess's, hauling us speedily in the opposite direction. "Splendid protest, is it?" He glares at me. "Come on, I'll see you home."

I open my mouth to argue that he shouldn't be seen anywhere near the convent, but he gives me such a murderous look that I don't dare utter another word.

We pause when we reach the market district, a few blocks away from the city center.

"Here," Tess says, handing Finn her handkerchief. Blood is trickling from his nose, and his cheek is already swelling. It looks painful.

Finn pauses and rips off his cloak, instructing us to do the same. "If the rest of the city's in this mood, we'll be safer this way."

It is strange, walking down the city streets uncloaked, my hair uncovered. I haven't risked it since I was a little girl. In any case, no one challenges us. That's strange, too. I couldn't walk the length of Church Street at home without someone greeting me or inquiring after Father. In the length of one block here we encounter two fine ladies leaving a dress-maker's, a maid trailing after them carrying several new gowns; a mother dragging three squalling, sticky-faced boys out of a candy shop; a man standing outside a butcher's hawking fresh cuts of meat while a pig's head stares at us un-nervingly from the picture window; and another man carry-ing four hatboxes stacked up to his chin, who jostles me and sends me tripping into Tess. No one smiles or wishes us good day. No one looks askance at us for not wearing our cloaks, either. They're all intent upon their own business.

We walk in silence punctuated by the creaking of wagon wheels and the clip-clop of horseshoes, the shouts of *Sentinel* newspaper boys and vendors hawking flowers and roasted chestnuts and savory meat pies. It's the end of the workday, and the streets are crowded. I press close to Finn, my arm brushing his, and keep Tess ahead of me where I can see her. As we pass into the residential neighborhood near the convent, the houses get bigger and the noise falls away, until there are only a few passing phaetons and the sound of water rushing down the gutters.

Finn stops a block away from the convent. "May I have a moment?" I ask Tess.

She nods. "Thank you for defending our honor, Finn."

"Fat lot of good I was," Finn mutters.

"You were brilliant," Tess insists, touching his arm. Then she steps a discreet distance away, fussing with the holly that grows over the neighbor's gate.

"I'm sorry I didn't listen when you said we should leave. Are you terribly angry with me?" I reach out and touch his cheek, wincing in sympathy.

Finn shakes his head, not quite meeting my eyes. "It was hardly the first time I've been beaten in a fight, but I hate that you saw it."

Oh. I always think of Finn as so certain of himself, so confident and clever. But the boy I knew growing up was altogether different—a pompous know-it-all, tall but skinny as a string bean, and prone to getting his arse kicked in the school yard.

"I don't think any less of you. In fact, if we were somewhere a bit more private, I'd show you how very much I think of you," I flirt, and his lips twitch in a reluctant smile. "Brawling isn't the only way to be brave. Joining the Brotherhood for me and spying for us—that's brave."

"I want to be able to protect you," he mutters.

"I can protect myself." I squeeze his hand, concentrating

on his injuries. It takes only a moment to heal them. This time I don't even feel dizzy.

Finn examines his cheek with his fingertips, confirming that it's no longer swollen. "You didn't have to do that," he mutters.

"It's easy enough." I'm hardly going to let him go around bruised and bleeding just to salvage his pride.

He shoves the stained handkerchief into his pocket, scuffing his boot against the sidewalk. "I wish there were more I could do to keep you safe. I want to be your husband, Cate. Sneaking around like this—"

"I know." A stray tabby cat is rubbing against Tess's ankles, and she's bending to pet it, cooing endearments. *This* is the girl the Brothers are so terrified of? "It's not what I want, either. Whatever Inez is planning, it's got to work."

CHAPTER
12

THE SIMMERING TENSION WITHIN THE
convent comes to a head the next afternoon during
history of witchery. Sister Sophia is teaching in
place of ancient Sister Evelyn, who took a tumble
down the front porch steps and broke her arm, just
as Tess predicted. Most of our classes are based on
magical skill rather than age, but history of witchery
is an exception; it's made up of twelve of the oldest
convent girls. We sit at our desks—narrow wooden
benches with slanted, scarred desktops attached—
in neat rows of four by four, with the back row
empty.

Sister Sophia is reading us passages about the
Brotherhood's increasingly restrictive measures in
the early 1800s, back when they first outlawed the-
ater and public dances. It seems silly to focus on

things that happened nearly a hundred years ago when we could be talking about the protest yesterday or all the girls being snatched up. Hardly anyone is paying attention. The fire in the hearth is burning hot enough to make the room feel close and drowsy. In front of me, studious Pearl copies down notes on her slate, but Alexa's blond head is nodding and Maud and Eugenia are passing notes. To my left, Rilla's drawing hearts on her slate with her pencil.

To my right, Mei is counting her ivory mala beads and worrying about her sisters. Her brother Yang came to the convent last night with the disquieting news that Li and Hua had snuck out to the protest and were among the two hundred people arrested by the Brothers' guards. There isn't enough room for them in the New London prison, so they're being held like cattle in a warehouse along the river.

"Baba went to see them, and the guards gave him a talking-to for raising right troublesome girls," Mei told us last night. "He thinks they'll hold the men a few days, to teach 'em a lesson, and put the women on trial for public indecency."

Nothing good can come from that. I glance over at Mei, whose mouth is moving in a silent mantra as she thumbs the beads draped over her middle finger.

There are heavy footsteps in the hall, and Sister Gretchen appears in the doorway. "Pardon me, Sophia. I hate to interrupt, but Cora's asking for you."

Sister Sophia snaps the book shut with a loud crack that startles Alexa awake and jostles everyone else out of their stupors. "Girls, you're dismissed."

Sister Cora must be in great pain to call her away from class.

"Is Sister Cora dying?" Daisy asks Sister Sophia. I twist to face her, noticing that she and Rory have been playing a game of Birds, Beasts, and Fishes on her slate. Rory hasn't guessed many letters, and the sight of the half-drawn man dangling from a hangman's noose gives me a chill even in the hot classroom.

"Not today," Sister Sophia says briskly. "If she were, there would be nothing I could do for her."

I catch at the yellow silk of her sleeve as she passes down the aisle. "Can I help?"

She pats my shoulder with a distracted smile. "No, dear, but it's good of you to ask."

She and Sister Gretchen take their leave, whispering. Even though we've been dismissed, we all stay in our seats, shaken. It's the first time any of the teachers have admitted publicly that Sister Cora is dying.

"I saw her in the hall this morning when I was running an errand for Sister Gretchen," Daisy says in her slow drawl, wiping the game off her slate with a rag. "She looked dreadful. Could barely walk."

Rilla sets her pencil aside. "I was helping in the kitchen at breakfast, and Sister Gretchen said Cora can't keep anything down but broth and tea. It won't be very long now, I expect. My grandmother was like that, at the end."

Maura saunters to the front of the room, pushes aside the stack of books on Sister Evelyn's desk, and perches right on top. "We ought to make Sister Inez the head *now*, so we can get on with things instead of just waiting for Cora to die. With the Brothers all caught up in oracle hunting and the protest, it's the perfect time to strike."

Mei flinches and stuffs the beads back into the pocket of her orange gown. "It's a *dangerous* time, with so many Brothers in town for the National Council meeting. Sister Cora says we should be extra careful."

"Sister Cora's too old and too cautious. We need someone with guts to lead us," Maura says, swinging her feet like a child. She's wearing heeled brown slippers with gold tassels on the toes. "There have been a dozen girls arrested and held without trial as potential oracles. If we could break them out of the National Council building, think what a splash that would make! The Brothers would be furious."

"That's impossible," Eugenia blurts. She hazards a glance over her shoulder at Alice and flushes, fiddling nervously with her brown chignon. "The National Council building is an absolute fortress. Brother Covington has a grand apartment inside, and the Brothers' guards patrol constantly."

I feel a second of déjà vu: Rory, in the sitting room, asking me, *Do you think it would be impossible to break someone out of Harwood?*

For once, I don't stop to think things through. "If we're thinking of staging a jailbreak," I say slowly, my eyes on Rory, "what about Harwood?"

Rory's slate falls from her hand and clatters to the ground. "Really?" she gasps.

Maura folds her arms over her cream-colored bodice. "The girls there aren't in imminent danger."

"That's where the oracle is, though." I drum my fingers against the wooden desktop. "Brenna's the one who's putting everyone else in danger, including us. If we could get Brenna out—"

"And Sachi!" Rory interrupts, bending to pick up her cracked slate.

"We already know how to get in. Cate and Pearl and I go every week on nursing missions," Mei adds. "The question would be how to get them *out*."

"Why, Cate Cahill." Alice narrows her blue eyes at me, lips pursed. "You might actually have a few good ideas in that head of yours after all. If we're risking our necks to save girls, they might as well be witches, and where are there more potential witches than Harwood? Besides here, of course."

"If we broke them out somehow—say, if Harwood were to catch fire—we *would* have better numbers when the war starts," Maura muses, caught in the rising tide of enthusiasm.

"Catch fire?" I shake my head. "The women there are *drugged*. If there were a fire, how many of them would be burnt alive in their beds?"

"It doesn't have to be a fire," Alice snaps, rolling her eyes. "We just need something to send the nurses into a tizzy, so they'll call the fire brigade, so the gate will be left open and they won't notice if a few girls escape in all the fuss. We could see to it that your sister got out, Rory."

"What about Lucy Wheeler's sister? She's in there too, but she's not a witch," Daisy says, her dark brow furrowed.

"I think we ought to limit it to witches," Alice insists. "We can't save everyone."

"That's cruel." Mei swipes her bangs out of her eyes. "I'll tell you right now, if Li and Hua are sentenced there, I won't let them rot just because they aren't witches. They're still my sisters."

Maud waves her hand in the air as if for permission to speak, and I nod at her. She's a short girl with red hair—not Maura's pretty curls but straight, carroty red—and more freckles than I've ever seen on a person in my life. "My cousin Caroline's there," she says. "She's not a witch, though; she was arrested for having an affair with one of the Brothers on our town council. He was already married, but he didn't get in any trouble at all."

"That's how it always goes," Rory says bitterly, tugging on the pink lace at her cuffs.

"I'm with Alice on this. There are hundreds of girls there. We can't bring them all back to the Sisterhood. Even if they were grateful at first for saving them, who says they'll keep our secrets?" Maura smooths her cream-colored skirt. "We have to put the Sisterhood first."

"And you're friends with the architect on the Harwood construction, aren't you?" Alice gives Maura a calculating smile. "A little flirting, and I bet you could find out how to pull this off. We'll glamour ourselves to look like construction men, and then we'll create some sort of distraction, and in the midst of all the fuss, we'll sneak the witches out."

I have a sudden suspicion of what job brought Paul back to New London. His firm must be overseeing the

217

construction on Harwood. Curious that Maura never mentioned that. I bite my lip. How did she and Alice get to be in charge so quickly? It was my idea, and now they're the ones making decisions about who will be saved and doling out instructions?

Rilla shakes her head, brown curls bouncing. "I think Mei's right. If only *some* of the girls escape, won't the Brothers retaliate against the rest? If conditions there are already as bad as you say—"

"They are," Mei and Pearl chorus.

"I won't leave Caroline behind to be punished," Maud says stubbornly.

"Oh, fine, we can rescue your stupid cousin. But we can't worry about *everyone*. There are some risks in waging war," Alice says. And though I know she's right, and Sister Cora herself would agree, it doesn't sit well with me.

I stand. "I've been to Harwood and seen the conditions there. It's awful. I say we keep thinking until we can figure out a way to get all the girls out, witches or no."

Mei pauses in her mantra. "I agree with Cate."

"Me, too," chorus Rilla and Maud and Daisy and Pearl.

"But you won't take too long, thinking? We won't let them languish there forever?" Rory presses.

I know she's thinking of Sachi, of the trial that will be held tomorrow. "No, of course not. There's got to be a way."

"I'm disappointed in you all." Maura glowers at me. "I knew Cate wouldn't really go through with it, but I didn't think you'd all fall in line with her like scared little ducks. We can *make* this work, I know it. If one of the nurses sees some-thing she shouldn't, Alice and I will just compel her."

"That's not the point," I argue, hopping up on my desktop.

"And what if there's more than one witness?" Vi speaks up for the first time, scooting her desk away from Alice's with a sharp screeching noise. "What if your glamours fail and you expose all of us? You can't bully your way through this."

"What's that supposed to mean?" Alice snaps, toying with one of her onyx earbobs. "Maura's marvelous at compulsion, and I'll be there to help her."

"What if you can't? If it comes out that the Sisterhood is a nest of witches, what would happen to all of us? To my father?"

"Don't be a fool," Alice snaps. "Your father could tell ev-eryone he was compelled, that he didn't know anything about our magic. I could erase his memory so he wouldn't even be lying."

Vi slams her slate down on her desk, so hard it cracks right in two. Half the girls in the room jump in their seats. "The devil you will!"

"Vi!" Alice gasps, her ears flushing bright red.

"No! Mind-magic's not a toy, for all you strut around boasting of it. I won't have you ruining his mind like you did that poor girl last year."

Alice's hand flies to her bosom. If I thought she had a heart in there, I'd feel sorry for her. "How dare you!"

Vi glowers at her best friend, defiant. "You would under-stand if your father meant any more to you than his purse strings."

Alice slips out from behind her desk and stomps over to Maura, in high dudgeon. "Well, now I see who my *true* friends are."

"This is too important to wait. If we had more witches with mind-magic, we could protect ourselves," Maura insists, refusing to acknowledge that she's lost the crowd. "We wouldn't have to wait for the Brothers to come and take us away one by one. We could go after them."

"How?" Violet gives an unladylike snort. "You can't go compelling every Brother you meet on the street."

I'm surprised Alice's glare doesn't turn her right to stone. "Why not? It's a sight better than sitting here waiting for that mad oracle to give us away. We ought to be doing *something*, and I for one am glad to have someone around"—she eyes Maura—"who isn't such a yellow-livered scaredy-cat."

"It's not cowardly to think things through instead of rushing into something," I argue, setting my jaw.

"Maybe you just want to delay attacking the Brothers. Maybe you have more sympathy for them than you want to let on, because of your beau," Alice scoffs, and my heart falls. Did Maura tell her I've still been seeing Finn? "It's pathetic, taking up for man who jilted you."

"You had a beau who was a Brother?" Next to me, Rilla gasps. "You never said!"

"You always do this, Alice," Vi complains. "You mock everyone who doesn't agree with you. The rest of us are allowed to have opinions, you know."

"You're just jealous because we'd have no use for you in this. You can't do mind-magic, and your illusions are terrible.

If your father hadn't offered to be the coachman without pay, it wouldn't have been worth it to save you!" Alice shouts, her pretty face red.

"Is that so?" Vi narrows her eyes, and suddenly Alice's green dress is crawling with spiders. *Hundreds* of spiders.

It's an illusion—a terrifying one, if you're frightened of spiders. Judging by the way Alice is shrieking and dancing around, she is. "Get them off! Get them off!"

Maura goes to Alice, brushing a few spiders onto the floor. They scuttle away with surprising speed, and several of the girls draw their feet onto their chairs, screeching. Daisy tosses a book at a particularly large spider, flattening it.

"Calm yourself. They're not real. You can't fight back if you can't focus," Maura tells Alice.

"They shouldn't be fighting in the first place," I say, but with Maura's coaching, Alice seems to have recovered her wits. She vanishes the spiders.

"Illusions? Let's see," Vi says, and then Alice is growing, taller than I am, tall as the bookshelves that line the back wall. Two curved horns like a ram's poke through her golden hair, and her skin goes a gruesome olive-green, like a storybook monster's.

Rilla bursts into giggles. Pearl covers her mouth with a hand. Even Eugenia and Maud, who usually defer to Alice, are hard-pressed not to smile.

Alice screams and runs to the gilt-edged mirror over the fireplace, bending and twisting so that her face is low enough to see. She screams again when she catches a bit of her reflection.

"Vi, that's enough," I reprimand, rising from my desk.

"No, it isn't," Vi argues, giving Alice a pig snout. Behind me, Rory laughs so hard she snorts. "She gives herself such airs. She's not even the best witch here."

"Neither are you. Don't get above yourself," Maura snaps, and Vi's shoulders buck and bow, her black hair graying, perfect skin wrinkling, mouth puckering around missing teeth, until she's a crone. The girls gasp, horrified, while Alice cackles. Even I take a step back, startled by the vividness of the illusion.

"Maura," I groan, "you're not helping."

Maura smirks at me. "Break it—if you can."

I want to—not only because I'm on Vi's side in this, but because Maura's thrown it down like a challenge, and I've never been one to turn away from a challenge. I reach for my magic and find it hovering, ready, stirred up by my mingled fear and anger. But I hesitate. If I can't break Maura's illusion, she'll never let me forget it. And if I can, if I show her up in front of a dozen witnesses—will she ever forgive me?

"What did you *do* to me?" Vi demands, her fingers exploring her wizened face.

"Made you as ugly on the outside as you are on the inside," Alice taunts.

"Enough!" I bark. I focus on Vi first, knowing Maura's illusion will be the more difficult to crack. As always in times of stress, I revert to casting aloud. "*Acclaro!*"

It's not easy. When I tap the illusion with my magic, it resists, stubborn. I push, and it wavers. Maura is watching me, a self-satisfied look on her pretty face. I shove, and the spell breaks, returning Vi to her elegant sixteen-year-old self.

"What about me?" Alice stomps toward me, enormous and angry, knocking desks aside in her wake. "You can't just leave me like this!"

Maura waves a hand, and Alice shrinks to her normal size, horns disappearing, skin lightening.

Mei looks anxiously toward the hall. "Sister Inez'll have a fit if she catches us."

"It was only a bit of fun. Don't be such a killjoy," Maura snaps.

Alice combs her fingers through her mussed golden hair, sniffing. "Vi started it."

"You provoked her," I point out.

"Who are you to tell me what to do? You're not a teacher, you—"

I cast silently, and she clutches at her throat, glaring, mute.

"I'm the strongest witch in this room, that's who." The words are out of my mouth before I can stop them. Maura flinches as though I've struck her, but Rilla and Mei twist in their chairs to grin at me. "Things are getting worse. The Brothers came here, to our home, where we're supposed to be safe, and took Hope away from us. I know you're angry about it. I'm angry, too. But we've got to stick together. We can't start fighting each other, and we can't go off on mad schemes without thinking them through and giving everyone a chance to weigh in."

"What a pretty speech." Sister Inez strides to the front of

the room, her heels ringing out with every step. "But may I remind you, you're not in charge here yet, Miss Cahill."

Neither are you, I think, and my suspicion of her hardens into something colder.

"Release your spell on Miss Auclair."

I comply, swallowing a smile, lowering my eyes so she can't see the triumph in them. If Inez has to ask me to do it, that means the spell is too strong for her to break. "I didn't mean to overreach. You weren't here," I say.

It's as close to an apology as she's likely to get.

"You're not to do magic on each other without a teacher present, as you all well know," Sister Inez says. "As you can't occupy yourselves properly, I'm assigning you three pages in your copybooks on the National Council's progressively restrictive measures over the last fifty years. Perhaps you'd like to get started on that now, before I make it five."

The girls scatter. "That was spectacular," Rilla whispers, bouncing along next to me.

"The look on Alice's face when you shut her up was brilliant," Rory adds.

Pearl gives me a smile so big it shows her teeth.

"Pardon me. I'd like to speak with my sister for a moment." Maura grabs my elbow and tows me across the hall into the empty literature classroom.

"How dare you," she spits, whirling on me as she slams the door.

I collapse into a desk. All that spellwork in quick succession has left me exhausted, and frankly I'm in no mood to fight with her. "How dare I what? Disagree with you and Alice? She might be a harpy, but she thinks you really like her, you know."

"You just can't stand that I'm more popular than you!"

Oh, not this again. "I don't care if you have a hundred new friends. It's the quality of them that concerns me. You haven't shown the best judgment in the past."

"You *would* throw that in my face." Maura's cheeks go pink. "Elena did care for me. She admitted it later. She lied to pacify *you* and get *you* to the Sisterhood, and to please her stupid precious Sister Cora."

"I'm sorry," I say truthfully. "I'm sorry she hurt you and that I was part of the reason why. But I don't like the way you were acting in there. Lately it's as though you're a different person, Maura. Like you'll do anything to prove yourself to Sister Inez."

"Maybe I *want* to be a different person! I'm tired of being one of the Cahill girls—the silly romantic one, the pretty one, the one who needs looking after because she might do something rash." Maura throws up her hands, exasperated. "What earthly good is being *pretty* if I don't have any say in anything?"

I clench my jaw, stung despite myself. "I wouldn't know. *You've* always been the pretty one."

My sister paces up and down the aisles, weaving around the desks. "You did everything you could to discredit my ideas in there. And if that's not bad enough, you went and said you're the strongest witch in the room as though it's a proven fact! I want to lead the Sisterhood when I come of age. *You* want marriage and babies and a pretty little house with a garden. Why are you fighting me for this?"

Because I don't trust her to be careful with people the way she should. Because I'm starting to suspect that the only person I trust to lead the Sisterhood for Tess until she comes of age is *me*.

"Perhaps I could do both," I say, my eyes falling to the scuffed wooden floor.

"You're so damned selfish!" Maura shouts. She closes her eyes, struggling for control. "You won't even take the mind-magic test. How will you govern without using compulsion?"

I think of Brother Ishida. Should I tell her about that? No, she'll only throw it in my face that I did it because of Finn, as if I'm some love-muddled fool. "I can use it when I have to."

"Could you? Or would you hem and haw about it until the time was past? Alice and I came up with an idea to get those girls out of Harwood, and because it wasn't *your* idea and it doesn't fit with your fine principles, you swayed everyone against it!"

"I wasn't the only one who had doubts," I protest, shivering. This room hasn't been used today and the hearth is full of cold ashes.

Maura groans, throwing up her hands again. She's already taken to wearing a thin silver ring on her right ring finger. Though it isn't engraved with the Sisters' motto yet, it's a clear sign of her commitment. "If Brenna gets anyone else killed while you're *thinking,* that will be on your head."

I rise to my feet. "You haven't been to Harwood, Maura.

You haven't seen what it's like. If I do this, I'm going to do it right."

"*If* you do this," Maura mocks, leaning so close I can smell the lemon verbena she wears. "You're too chicken to actually *do* anything, Cate. That's the problem with you."

"I will save them." I plant my hands on my hips, linking my thumbs through the blue sash at my waist. "Just wait and see."

"*You* wait. Soon Cora will be dead and Inez will be in charge. She's going to make me her second-in-command, not you. She's just using you to get information from Finn."

I grab her arm, whirling her around, my fingers pressing into the cream taffeta at her wrist. "Can you trust her any more than Elena? Do you honestly think if she succeeds Cora and deposes the Brotherhood, she'll just step aside when you're ready to lead?"

Maura gapes at me. "Inez believes in me."

I shake my head. "*I* believe in you! I believe that you're smarter than this."

Anger flashes over Maura's face, thinning her lips and narrowing her eyes, and then I'm flying backward a dozen feet. My back slams against the chalkboard, hard, and I slide onto the floor like a rag doll tossed by a giant. My gray skirts pool around me.

My sister looms over me, blue eyes glittering. "I intend to lead the Sisterhood, Cate. I'll thank you not to get in my way. I'm done playing nice."

I wince, struggling to my feet, clutching my elbow where it smacked into the chalk tray. That will leave a bruise. "That's what you've been doing, humiliating me by telling everyone how I've been jilted, and how stupid I am, and what a *coward*? Trying to show me up at every turn?"

My sister rubs a hand over her heart-shaped face. "This would all be easier without you here," she says simply, unsettlingly, and a shiver crawls up my spine.

Oh.

"What do you mean?" I whisper, heart pounding.

She backs away, moving to stand by Sister Gretchen's desk. "You make me lose my temper and say stupid hurtful things I don't mean, and—I can't forget how you made Elena turn on me. She takes up for you, you know. She says she cares for me, but she thinks *you'd* be the better leader." Maura gives a harsh laugh, and my eyes fly to hers. "If it weren't for you, I would have everything I want."

I've made mistakes, certainly. Perhaps I've been thoughtless, stubborn, but I was never unkind on purpose. I love Maura. I would do anything for her.

"I don't want to fight you, Cate, truly," she says. "But I'm not going to back down."

"Neither am I." I can't. Not when the future of the Sisterhood and all the girls at Harwood is at stake.

I look at my sister, and even though she's right here in front of me, in the very same room, she feels oceans away.

I don't know how to reach her anymore.

Sister Sophia comes to fetch me during supper, drawing the stares of all the other girls.

"I'm sorry to interrupt your dinner, Cate," she says, touching my shoulder. "Cora's asked for you."

The conversation at our table stutters and stops. Whispers dance through the dining room.

"Of course," I say, folding my napkin and placing it on the table. Things must be truly dire if Sophia can no longer help.

"Should I bring the rest of your dinner up to your room?" Tess asks. She sits with Lucy and Rebekah and the younger girls at breakfast, but we always eat supper together.

"No, thank you." I glance regretfully at the roasted sweet potatoes, butternut squash, and chicken on my plate. I won't want it after a healing session, and it's better not to do this with a full stomach.

There are five long oak tables in the dining room—four for students and one for teachers. After her fight with Alice this afternoon, Vi made a great show of sitting at our table tonight. Maud came with her, though she keeps looking anxiously toward Alice's table.

I do, too. I catch Maura glaring at me and look away, fast.

She's angry with me, and jealous. She'll get past that. It's the way of sisters; it's hardly the first time that a rivalry has sprung up between us.

But this feels more important than who Tess crawled to first, or who goes to town with Mother, or whose turn it is for a new gown. This goes right to the heart of who we are, what we were made for.

Maura has never made any bones about being cleverer, prettier, more ambitious and interesting and talented than me. I used to ignore the stings.

I used to think she was right.

I stand up and walk away from the table, head held high,

ignoring the whispers. I'm the one Sister Cora is asking for; I'm the only one who can do this. That's got to count for something.

Sophia shows me into Cora's sitting room, then flutters like a bright moth in the doorway. I take the flowered chair angled next to Cora's. There's a steaming pot of tea on the table between us. She's already poured a cup for herself, and now she pours one for me.

"You may go, Sophia. Thank you," she says.

Sophia slips out of the room, leaving us shrouded in shadows. The gas lamp on Cora's desk throws a small circle of light that doesn't quite reach us.

"Sophia said you'd offered to heal me, Catherine." Cora's wearing a cornflower-blue dressing gown with a white blanket draped across her lap. Her hair falls in a long plait over her right shoulder. "I thank you for it. Even a few hours to think more clearly would help."

Panic bubbles through me. "I haven't found the limit of my healing yet. Perhaps—"

Cora shakes her head. "Don't push yourself past your limit for my sake. I've made my peace with dying, insofar as any woman can. All I hope for is a few hours without such pain, to get my affairs in order." She sets her cup down and holds out her hand, palm facing up. It's all very businesslike: ticktock, no time to waste.

I clasp her hand, soft and still warm from her tea. My magic shudders back at the sickness in her.

I grip her hand harder and think of how we need Sister Cora.

I am not ready to lead. Tess is not ready to lead.

She needs time. *We* need time.

I cast, and the pain is immediate and blinding.

I gasp, curling into myself, my stomach twisting. My head swims; I feel hot and sick. But I keep pushing against the sickness in her. I think of girls—stuck-up ones like Alice, ambitious ones like Maura, sweet ones like Lucy, desperate ones like Rory. Sister Cora saves half a dozen girls each year from the Brothers. That is reason enough to fight for her, isn't it?

It's more than enough.

It feels like knives in my stomach, in my head.

It's worse than the sharp awfulness of falling off the pigpen fence and twisting my ankle. Worse than any physical pain I've ever felt.

My vision blurs, darkness at the edges, but I hang on. I can feel the magic working, can feel the sickness slinking away, shrinking, receding into its dark hiding places.

Eventually I say it out loud: a gasp, a spell, a sob. She cannot die. Not yet.

The magic leaps from my body into hers, leaving me empty, sick, wrung out. My spine feels like an insubstantial, rubbery thing. I slump sideways, my hand slipping from hers. I stop fighting.

I wake up with my head lolling on the tea table. The first thing I see is a cup of tea. The second is Sister Cora's silver rings catching the lamplight as she waves a vial of sharp smelling salts beneath my nose. I want to complain at the awful, pungent scent, but I'm afraid that if I open my mouth I'll be ill, so I clamp my jaw shut and sit up in my chair.

Cora is kneeling next to me. Her cheeks have some color in them now. "Are you all right?" she asks.

I nod, holding up a hand, waiting for the wave of nausea to pass.

"That was extraordinary," she says, rising. Her bare feet peek out beneath her blue hem. "I feel almost like my old self."

I mustn't give her false hope. Perhaps she can't tell, but—

"I'm sorry, I couldn't—"

"Don't you dare apologize. You gave me precisely what I asked for, and—don't let this go to your head, but I feel ten times better than after Sophia's been to see me. I feel like I did two months ago." Cora picks up the white blanket lying at her feet and folds it. "What you did was absolutely selfless."

If I didn't feel as though I'd been run over by a team of horses, I'd laugh. No one else has accused me of selflessness lately. Quite the opposite.

She hangs the blanket neatly over the back of her chair, then hands me my cup of tea. "This was made with grated ginger to help soothe your stomach. Sophia's been brewing it for me."

I feel too sick for subterfuge. "I couldn't save you. I don't think I can save anyone."

Sister Cora laughs her loud, raucous laugh. It makes her seem young and full of life, when she is neither. "That is precisely why it should be you, Catherine."

"Maura's the one who wants it," I admit. "She's willing to do whatever it takes. I'm sure you've heard she compelled six girls."

"I'd back you against your sister any day," Cora says, sitting down, and a tiny part of me, new and greenly sprouting, thrills at her words. "If she were leading the Sisterhood, would she be able to put her own feelings aside and do what was best for our girls? Or would she be ruled by her emotions? By her pride?"

I lean my head against the soft green and white satin of the chair, thinking of all the accusations Maura hurled at me this afternoon. "I want to help. But what if it's not enough? If *I'm* not enough?" I close my eyes, embarrassed by how pathetic I must sound. What if I am too plodding and careful; what if something awful happens because I didn't get Brenna out in time?

I can hear the smile in Sister Cora's voice. "Everyone worries about that. I doubt myself every single day. That's where faith comes in. We must trust in the prophecy and in the rightness of our cause."

"That's a great deal of trust," I say doubtfully, watching the flame flicker through the etched glass shade on her desk. "The prophecy says one of us will die before the turn of the century, too. I can't place my faith in that. I prefer to believe we have some hand in our fates, that our choices matter as much as our stars."

Cora leans forward in her chair. "Of course our choices matter, Catherine. They define us. You came here against your will, to protect your sisters and that young man of yours. That speaks to your selflessness, just as your healing does."

"I don't understand," I admit, squinting at her.

Sister Cora puts her hand on my knee. She moves more freely now, as though every gesture no longer pains her. "I want you to trust *yourself.*"

As though it's as simple as that.

"Even if you are not the prophesied one, Catherine, I would still choose you as my successor," she says softly. "Inez is too ruthless, Maura too much like her, and Teresa too young. If the Sisters rise to power again, we must not repeat the mistakes of our past. We need a woman with scruples."

I stare down into my tea. Am I mad to consider this? To stand up against Maura and Inez, to lead now that I don't have to? Would it be so terrible to allow Inez control until Tess comes of age? *Yes,* my conscience says. What would Inez do with four years? Would she truly give up the Sisterhood after such a long taste of power, or would she find a way around it?

"But I still want to marry Finn," I confess. "To have a family. I know it's horrible and selfish, but I don't *want* to give up my life for everyone else's."

Sister Cora smiles. "You may not have to. If things go our way—why, you could work openly as a nurse, and raise your own family, and help lead the Sisters. You wouldn't have to choose."

I imagine spending my days in a garden of my own, chasing freckled little girls with Finn's unruly hair and my penchant for climbing trees. I picture us all snuggled onto a sofa in the evenings, while Finn reads us pirate stories. My daughters might be witches, but if the Sisterhood ruled New England, they wouldn't have to live in fear of detection. They could learn to wield their magic wisely instead of in fear and shame.

It could be a blessing, not a curse.

Perhaps that is a gift I could give them.

CHAPTER
13

THE NEXT MORNING, TESS HAS ANOTHER vision.

She and Mei and I are in the front parlor. I'm lounging on the thin brown carpet before the fire, reading Tess's copy of *The Metamorphoses*. I've heard all the stories from Father, but I wanted to read it myself since it's Finn's favorite. Tess is leaning forward on the settee, picking up her tea, repeating a Chinese pronunciation, when her gray eyes go blank. She drops the cup onto the table, and it rolls onto the floor, spilling tea everywhere. It puddles on the table and drips down onto her leafy green skirts.

"Tess?" Tossing my book aside, I scramble across the carpet toward her.

Mei springs into action, sopping up the tea with her faded yellow handkerchief. Tess sits there, staring at nothing, until Mei shakes her arm. "Tess?"

"I'm sorry," she gasps, coming back to herself. "I felt faint for a moment."

Mei lays a hand on Tess's brow. "You don't feel feverish."

I pick up the chipped cup, searching for a reasonable subterfuge. "Is it your monthly affliction?"

Tess flushes bright red. "Perhaps," she squeaks.

"Do you want to go upstairs and lie down? I'll bring you a hot water bottle for your back," I suggest.

"Go on. I'll clean things up here," Mei offers.

"Thank you." I toss her my own handkerchief, then lead Tess into the hall.

We're quiet until we reach the bedroom she and Maura share, down the hall from mine. Maura's stockings are scattered everywhere, and a lacy blue petticoat is draped over the stool at the dressing table. Tess has taken the bed by the window and hung the curtains Mrs. O'Hare sewed for her years ago. There's a daguerreotype of Mother and Father on the sill, and her one-eyed teddy bear, Cyclops, occupies a place of honor on her pillow.

"I'm fine," she insists as soon as we shut the door. "You needn't fuss."

"It was another vision, wasn't it?" She's pressing her fingertips to her temples.

"Yes. Unhook me?" My fingers make quick work of the row of buttons at her back while I wait for her to elaborate. Tess only sighs as she pulls off the tea-soaked gown. "I can feel you staring at me, you know."

I try to ignore my raging curiosity. Her reluctance doesn't

necessarily portend something awful; she's going to be privy to loads of people's secrets, and possibly it's just none of my business. After all, I wouldn't want her going around telling everyone that she saw Finn and me kissing.

Tess will be thirteen in another month. Under Elena's tutelage, she's grown into a proper young lady who wears a corset and petticoats and her hair up. When she pulls her red plaid dress over her head, I see the new curves of her hips and breasts. She'll be voluptuous like Maura and Mother instead of skinny like me.

"I want to go with you to Harwood on Monday and see Zara," she says.

I fasten the buttons she can't reach and tie the black cummerbund at her waist. "I don't want you setting foot in that place."

She spins around to face me. "I thought you weren't going to boss me anymore?"

I did say that, didn't I? Old habits are hard to break. "All right. We'll ask Sister Sophia. But you have to promise to stay with me the whole time. And you've got to steel yourself for it. You're too important to the Sisterhood—and to me—to risk anything rash, no matter how much you want to help the girls there."

"I promise to stay with you. I just want to ask Zara about the other oracles—whether the rest of them went mad like Brenna. Zara didn't write about that in her book, but perhaps—"

Tess wasn't as comforted as I'd hoped by the truth about

Brenna. I sigh, tucking a wisp of blond hair back into her bun. "Brenna would be right as rain if it weren't for Alice."

Tess sits heavily on her bed, rumpling the green quilt. "She *could* be—we can't really know. She was odd before that."

"Odd isn't mad," I remind her, wishing I could forget about Thomasina, hoping Zara will have more discretion in front of Tess. "You'll be fine."

"Will I?" She grabs Cyclops and nestles her cheek against his furry head. "I hope so, Cate. I don't want to lose my mind. I *like* being clever. I want to keep learning Chinese, and Sister Gretchen promised to teach me German and cryptography properly, once Sister Cora—well, once she isn't so busy tending to her. Sister Sophia is going to show me how to make her Christmas pudding. And there are dozens of books in the library I haven't read, and someday when I run out of stories to read, perhaps I'll write my own. There's so much I want to do yet."

Her fear shatters me. "You *will*. There's plenty of time to do all those things."

"Is there?" She hugs Cyclops tighter. "It's already December. In a month it will be 1897, and the prophecy says one of us won't live until the turn of the century. That's only three years. Maybe less."

I grab her elbow, and she lets out a little yelp as I turn her roughly toward me. "Teresa Elizabeth Cahill, you listen to me. Nothing is going to happen to you. You aren't going to go mad, and you aren't going to be murdered. No one is going to harm you while there is breath left in my body, do you understand me?"

"Ouch, Cate, let me go," she whines.

"No. This is important. I won't have you give up. I don't care what happened to the other oracles, and I don't care what that blasted prophecy says. You are going to live a long, happy life. You're going to learn Chinese and bake a dozen Christmas puddings and get married and have babies—or not, whichever you want—and write that book of yours. Is that clear?"

"Yes, fine. Now will you stop lecturing me?" Tess rubs her elbow.

"I'm sorry. I didn't mean to raise my voice." I take a deep breath, struggling for control. "It's only that—Tess, I have to believe we aren't just puppets to Persephone or the Lord or the Brothers. That the choices we make *matter*."

"We've got to be brave, even if we're frightened some-times." Her eyes crinkle at the corners like Father's, and I hope she is taking my words to heart.

"Especially when we're frightened. I think the point is forging on anyway, even when we don't see how we can get through it. I'm scared about Finn and you and Maura all the time." I pick up her tea-stained dress from the floor and drape it over the dressing table. "Er—I don't know if she mentioned it, but Maura and I had an awful row yesterday."

Tess leans back against the brass headboard. "I heard."

I resist the urge to ask her what Maura said about me; I don't want to put her in the middle, especially when she and Maura are rooming together.

"I suggested we might be able to organize a jailbreak at Harwood." I dip a clean handkerchief in the pitcher of water by Tess's bed, then scrub at the brown splotches of tea on her dress. "It would solve our Brenna problem. Maura and Alice jumped on the idea, but they only want to free the witches, and that doesn't seem right to me."

Tess gives a grim little nod. "I agree."

"I think we ought to try and free everyone, but I don't know how. The girls are kept too drugged to organize a mutiny." I wring the dress out into the empty basin. "I'm so afraid we'll make things worse for them. But maybe Maura has a point—maybe it's better to risk it than to do nothing."

Tess steeples her fingers together, thoughtful. "Is that why she was angry?"

I twist the dress in my hands. "Not really. She wants me to step aside and let her lead the Sisterhood. Her and Inez."

"Is that what *you* want?" Tess traces the red squares on her plaid skirt. "Perhaps it isn't fair, letting everyone think you're the oracle, letting Maura be angry with you. I'm only delaying the inevitable. Maybe I ought to tell everyone it's me."

I sit next to her. "Are you ready for that? It's a tremendous responsibility, Tess, and once you say it—well, you can't unsay it. I don't mind shouldering the burden a little while longer."

"I *wish* I felt ready, but I don't. I don't know if I ever will." She sighs, and it's a heavy-hearted sound for a girl her age. "There's something else that troubles me about telling. If Inez knows she has four years till I come of age, who knows what she might try?"

"Whereas if she thinks she might have to turn power over

to me in a few months, it may keep her from doing anything rash," I suggest.

It doesn't escape me that I am in Inez's debt because she knows about Finn. I hope he finds the information she wants soon so we'll be free of her. Or will it go on and on? Will she demand something else next? Worries unspool through my mind. If she does, I'll compel her to forget about him; I'll have to.

Tess leans against me. "I don't trust her. That's not a premonition, just a feeling I have."

"I have the same feeling, but I don't know what to do about it." I slide my arm around her shoulders. "Should I pretend to be the oracle? You could tell me your visions, and I could pretend they were mine."

Tess giggles, knocking her blond head against my chin. "We could never pull that off. It would get too complicated, and you're a terrible liar."

I pull away. "I am not! Maybe to you, but—"

Tess swats my knee. "No, you really are. You think you're convincing, but you aren't. It would never work. We'll have to keep thinking."

More thinking, not doing. It nettles at me now; everything seems to come back to needing time, but that's in scarce supply.

"Don't look like that. We'll figure it out." Tess smiles up at me. "Together, I think we can manage just about anything."

I'm meant to be leaving for Sachi's trial, but I can't find Tess. I wanted to tell her I've secured Sister Sophia's permission for her to come to Harwood on Monday. But she's not in her bedroom or the library or the kitchen. I dart into the sitting room, where Mei and Pearl are playing a game of chess.

"Have either of you seen Tess?"

Mei's hair falls in a straight, shining black curtain to her waist. "She popped in half an hour ago and asked whether there'd been any word of my sisters. Seemed worried about 'em, with the snow coming."

I glance out the windows. "It isn't snowing now."

"Looks like it could any minute," Pearl says, huddling into her soft lavender shawl.

"It must be bitter cold down there. I gave Yang blankets to take to them. Families are allowed to visit twice a day, to bring them food, so Baba goes in the morning and Yang goes in the afternoon." Mei slides her queen across the board, and Pearl groans. "I wish there were more I could do, but it's not safe to go down there by myself. I was just telling Tess, it's a bad neighborhood down by the docks. Pickpockets and all sorts of rough people."

A sudden suspicion prickles my spine. "Tess was asking about that neighborhood?"

"Sure. Where the warehouse is, and what it's like down there." Mei captures another of Pearl's knights. "She's a right curious little thing. I guess she hasn't seen much of New London yet, has she?"

"No." I suspect she's out remedying that right now. I excuse myself and run into the front parlor, where Sister Sophia and Rory are waiting for me. Blast. I promised Rory I would go to the trial with her, but this is an emergency. "I can't—I'm sorry, something else has come up—will you go, and tell me what happens?"

Rory gapes at me. "It's Sachi's trial, Cate. What could be more important than this?"

"I'll tell you when we get back. Trust me, Rory, please. You know I wouldn't miss it unless I had to." I wrestle on my cloak and am out the front door and heading down the steps when a familiar laugh catches my attention. It's Maura, jumping down from a black phaeton, and for a moment, my heart lifts, hoping Tess is with her and my suspicions are unfounded.

"Thank you!" Maura giggles, and as the man sets her gently on the carriage block, I recognize my childhood best friend. I feel a pang of homesickness as I look at Paul. He seems just the same: square jaw, strong shoulders, sun-streaked blond hair that flops over his tanned forehead.

"Maura!" I shout, hurrying toward them. My heart drops when I see it's Alice sitting in the back of the carriage, not Tess.

"Cate!" Maura's radiant despite her plain black cloak—and not the studied gaiety she's adopted since she's been at the convent; she's really beaming. "We've had such an exciting morning. Paul was kind enough to take us shopping and treat us to lunch at a little café. It was just how I imagined life in the city would be—like something from a novel!"

"Hello, Cate," Paul says. "Or am I to call you Sister Catherine now?"

He moves to take my hand and then stops, as if uncertain whether such liberties are permitted with members of the

Sisterhood. Or perhaps it's just me he's uncertain of. The last time I spoke to him, I told him I'd consider his proposal of marriage. I let him kiss me. I kissed him back. I lied.

"You can still call me Cate," I say, offering an awkward smile. "It's good to see you again. I trust you're well?"

"Yes, indeed." Paul turns to catch Alice. "The Harwood addition is an important job for us, you know, a contract with the National Council. If they like our work, they may turn to us when they need an addition to Richmond Cathedral or a new National Archives. Jones made me the overseer on-site to ensure things go smoothly."

"I bet you're marvelous at that," Maura coos. She's standing very close to Paul, her head cocked up at him as though she hangs on every word. "You've become so—authoritative."

"That's grand," I say flatly. I hate to be rude, but I haven't time for this; I've got to go find Tess, and every minute we stand here chatting, she's getting farther ahead of me.

"How have you been, Cate?" The black horse fidgets in its harness, its hot breath fogging the air, and Paul reaches up to pat its neck.

"Fine. Glad to have Maura and Tess here now. Thank you for escorting them; it was very *neighborly* of you." I hate the way my voice stresses it. I have no right to feel uncomfortable about his attentions toward Maura. "If you'll all excuse me, I was just on my way out; I'm in a bit of a hurry."

"You can't go out alone," Alice reminds me.

"I'm catching up with Tess," I explain, praying she'll leave it at that.

"I'll come with you and tell you all about our day," Maura suggests. She turns to Paul, her hand toying with one earring in a way that somehow makes her look nervous and shy. Where did she learn these charming tricks? "Thank you again for a lovely lunch, Paul. I hope you'll call on us again soon."

I don't wait for him to make a reply, just rush off down the gray, blustery street. Maura has to practically trot to catch up with me. "That was rude. Why are you in such a rush? Are we really having a secret rendezvous with our spy?"

"He's not *your* anything," I snap. I want to order her back to the convent, but if Tess is in trouble, I might need Maura's help.

"Are you sure I can't give you a lift in the carriage?" Paul shouts.

"No, thank you! The wind is very—bracing!" I shout back.

"It's freezing," Maura complains, stuffing her hands into her black fur muff, snuggling her face into the warm lining of her cloak. "He's sweet to offer, isn't he? You should have seen the café he took us to for lunch. It was so elegant. Business must be booming for him to afford that plus his phaeton. Those little gigs are all the rage now, Alice says. Ugh, would you slow down? I can't keep up. Where are we going, anyhow?"

I whirl on her. "I am going down to the docks to stop Tess from liberating the Richmond Square prisoners. I'd welcome your help, if you can stop throwing Paul in my face for two minutes."

Maura stops in front of a neighbor's brick mansion. There are yellow roses climbing over the wrought-iron fence. "What? Why would she try to do that?"

A combination of my inspirational speech and her vision, I suspect.

But I can't tell Maura that.

I grab Maura's arm and pull her along. "I don't know, but I hope we can stop her if we hurry."

Did Tess foresee herself freeing the prisoners? Or did she see something dreadful happen to them, and this is her pigheaded way of trying to stop it because I told her we should fight our destinies, that it was better to try and fail than do nothing?

We're silent as we hurry through the well-to-do residential neighborhood. A few more phaetons pass us, carrying men and girls going for an afternoon drive, with a mother or sister or maid in the back seat serving as chaperone. Like Paul, they've got the leather hoods drawn up to protect their delicate passengers from the wind. We turn onto North Church Street, heading away from the great spire of Richmond Cathedral.

A block later, Maura clutches at my arm. "Cate, look!" she whispers.

On our right there's a blackened, burnt-out shell of a building. The brick facade still stands, but the roof and trim are darkened with soot, and the windows are all missing. It obviously used to be a shop of some kind, but now I can see clear through the big picture window to the building behind it. I wonder what it was until I see the sign dangling from a post out front.

"It was a bookstore," I say grimly. I can't help remembering the shuttered door of Belastras' bookshop on the day I left Chatham, the sign that read PERMANENTLY CLOSED.

Better that, at Marianne's choice, than this.

I doubt this fire was an accident.

Maura stalks ahead of me, her boots clopping angrily against the sidewalk like a horse's hooves. We pass through a small corner of the market district: a flower shop selling bouquets of roses, a haberdashery, an apothecary, and a cobbler's with a window full of fine leather boots. When a lady in a white fur hood comes out of the teashop, the bracing scent of bergamot washes over me. The last shop in the row is a toy store, and the windows are a child's dream come true, full of tin soldiers, rag dolls, spinning tops, puzzles, skipping ropes, and a great gorgeous dollhouse.

"Oh," Maura breathes, pausing for a second before the plate glass. Then she looks over her shoulder at me and blushes, plainly embarrassed to be caught mooning over such childish things. I feel a tug of affection toward her. She's still my little sister, trying so desperately to seem grown-up.

"Do you really like Paul?" I ask quietly. "Or were you just trying to get information from him?"

We turn onto a street full of red brick duplexes. The sidewalks here aren't as well-kept, but there are children laughing and playing with marbles.

"It had nothing to do with that," Maura insists. "He asked me to go for a ride in his new carriage, and I thought it would be fun, so I said yes."

"That was all?" I press.

Maura smirks. "Well, I thought it might annoy you. That was an added bonus. Look, you can do whatever you want about"—she lowers her voice—"Harwood. I've got more important things to worry me."

"All right," I say doubtfully.

"It's true." She turns her face into her cloak for warmth; her words are muffled when they reach me. "Just—stay out of my way, and I'll stay out of yours."

The street is sloping down toward the river now, and ahead of us I can see the mast of a tall ship. The buildings around us have grown more derelict. Ramshackle tenements crowd close together on overgrown lots. Rags are stuffed into cracked windowpanes to keep the cold out, but it doesn't stop the babble of voices from reaching the street. Wagons rumble past, laden with goods from the warehouses. A group of boys is playing stickball in a muddy park filled with debris. A man sits jabbering to himself on a park bench, surrounded by pigeons. I've delivered food to a tenement near the warehouse in question, so I'm passing familiar with this part of the city, but without Robert and the carriage, I don't feel safe here.

The sky is the heavy white of imminent snow, and the wind roars in my ears. As we get closer to the wharves without any sight of Tess, my worry grows. So many awful things could befall her in this neighborhood, not all of them to do with magic.

There's one long brick warehouse with half a dozen guards posted outside, and no one going in or out. "That must be it," I say, jerking my head in its direction. I pull Maura into the shadowy, garbage-filled alley between two buildings. "Should we disguise ourselves?"

"That's a good idea," Maura agrees. In the blink of an eye, she's transformed into a girl with dark curls and pouty lips and a patched red cloak.

I hesitate, breathing in the briny stink of rotting fish. "I haven't been able to hold those illusions."

"I'll do it for you," she offers, and I arch my eyebrows. "Oh, for Persephone's sake, I'm not going to let you get arrested. Certainly not before we can help Tess. She's my sister, too."

I examine a loose wisp of my hair and find it a dark brown that matches hers. My cloak is rough gray wool, and I'm wearing scuffed, muddy work boots. "Thank you," I say, leading the way toward the building.

It feels good to be working with Maura again, instead of against her.

One of the guards steps forward to bar my way. He's not much older than we are, with a fuzzy brown mustache lying like a caterpillar on his upper lip. "What's your business here?"

"We came to see our father. He's one of the prisoners?" I lower my eyes, trying to sound as meek as possible.

"Sorry, miss. Visiting isn't for another hour."

"Can't we wait inside, out of the cold?" Maura glances up from beneath dark lashes, shivering as she pulls her threadbare cloak tighter.

The guard softens, his eyes lingering on her face. She couldn't help making herself pretty. "All right. Just go straight inside. There are a few others waiting over by the fire. But don't approach the prisoner until you have leave, understand? Don't try to give him food or blankets until the guards say so. It will only get him in trouble."

"Thank you, sir," we chorus.

Just inside the cavernous space, half a dozen women warm their hands around a fire in a barrel. Most of them carry baskets of food for the prisoners, and I realize too late that we should have brought some provisions for our make-believe father. I blink against the smoke that stings my eyes. It takes me a minute to recognize Tess on the far side of the huddle, her blond hair tucked inside an unfamiliar blue hood. I make a beeline for her, and she looks bewildered by the two strange women advancing on her, glowering, until I hiss that it's us. "What are you doing here?"

"Visiting Father, same as you two. I brought him this," she says loudly, holding out a moth-eaten red blanket.

"It was mad of you to rush out alone like that. This is no place for a little girl," Maura exclaims, towing her aside.

Three more guards cluster in a corner, smoking their pipes. A few of the women around the fire—mothers of the prison-ers? wives?—eye us with curiosity, but most are chatting in low voices, stamping their feet to keep warm. If Yang is com-ing, he isn't here yet; no men are waiting besides the guards.

To our right is a row of holding pens, each closed off by a heavy sliding metal gate, padlocked shut. I can't see the pris-oners, but I can hear the low murmur of voices—and I can smell them. The odors of unwashed bodies and human waste waft toward us, nauseating even from several yards away. I wonder how the prisoners can stand it. How long do the Brothers intend to keep them here? It's already been two days. With this cold, people must be getting sick. And what about those whose families aren't bringing food? Are they being left to starve?

I shake off the sympathy. My business is getting Tess out of here safely.

"What were you thinking?" I demand in a furious whisper.

"Look at this place! They're not cattle," Tess hisses, her jaw set. She eyes the meat hooks hanging from the ceiling, the blood spattered on the cold concrete floor. "This isn't a warehouse, it's an abattoir, and it's not a fit place to keep *people*. I want to help them. I can do this. I know I can."

"Why do you even care?" Maura shoves her hands in her pockets. "They don't care about us. If we were the ones locked up, they'd throw away the key. Or worse."

Tess's cheeks and nose are red from the cold. "You don't know that."

"I do. You're being naïve if you think otherwise," Maura insists, tossing her brown curls.

"Cate?" Tess reaches out a hand. "Even if it's true, we should be better than that. We should help them because we can, because it's right. And if we don't, they're going to put them all on the prison ship."

"Where did you hear that?" Maura asks, glancing at the plump gray-haired woman nearest us.

"One of the guards said so. We can stop it, but we have to do it *now*. Before the storm gets worse." Tess points toward the high windows, at the fat snowflakes swirling in through the broken glass.

I suspect Tess is strong enough to manage this on her

own, but I take her hand anyway, letting her draw magic from me. She stares down the empty expanse of concrete toward the holding pens.

With a crack, each padlock drops to the floor. Scarcely a second later, the gates fly up, one by one, in a series of great crashes. The prisoners are screaming, shouting, flooding down the passageway toward us. A tall black man is the first out, followed by two burly blond men who look like brothers.

"Who opened the doors?" one of the blond men asks. His face is smudged with dirt.

"It was magic!" cries a thin girl with fuzzy black braids, rushing toward the prisoners. "Papa! It was magic!"

"What the devil? Stop right there! Stop!" one of the guards shouts, ineffectually waving his pistol. The crowd flows toward him, ignoring the warning shot he fires into the air.

"The witches are helping us!" someone shouts.

"Danny! Danny, where are you?" The stout old woman pushes past us.

The guards from outside stream in, and shots are fired, but most of the guards take in their odds, turn tail, and run. The prisoners tackle those who are left. Two guards are already being shoved down the hall toward the holding pens. Most of the prisoners are out now. A tall, thin man with dark hair half carries a limping old man.

"Oh, dear," Tess says as two prisoners kick a guard huddled on the floor. "I didn't mean—should we help?"

I grab her arm. "No. We've done enough."

"What about Mei's sisters? Should we see that they're all right?" she asks.

"We need to go. I bet those guards ran to get help." Maura slips toward the exit, and I drag Tess after her. Mei's sisters can find their own way out.

The bulk of the crowd is running up the street, shouting and making much of their sudden freedom. Maura leads us in the opposite direction, around the warehouse and along the creaking wooden docks. We stop between the gangplanks of two huge vessels—a schooner called the *Lizzie Mae* unloading coal and a great three-masted, iron-hulled ship swarming with sailors. There's so much banging and clanging, so much activity onboard, that no one will overhear us. Maura's hair goes red again, her cloak black, and I see my own windswept hair turn blond as she releases her illusions.

"We did it!" Tess says, launching herself at me with such force she almost knocks me over. "I knew we could. What did I tell you—we make a marvelous team!"

Maura stops walking and stares down at the sluggish gray river. "The two of you are a team?"

"I mean—the *three* of us always make a marvelous team, when we work together, don't we?" Tess babbles, flushing, her eyes falling guiltily to her feet. "That's why we can't let all of this Sisterhood business come between us."

"It already has," Maura says softly. There's a funny expression on her face. "I used to try to win you over, you know. I'd brush your hair out and braid it like you were my little doll and sing you songs and tell you fairy stories. But then Cate would come in from the garden, and you'd go running to *her*. It's always been her you've gone to, for everything, every bruise and bad dream."

"That's not true." Tess reaches out, catching at the snow-covered sleeve of Maura's cloak. "I've been confiding in Cate more lately, yes, but that's only because you've been so distant. Like you didn't want anything to do with us. I know Elena broke your heart, Maura, but ever since then, you've been so cold."

"You think *I'm* cold?" Maura shakes her off. "Cate's the one who couldn't care less about those girls being murdered! I suggested trying to break in and rescue them, and she discarded the idea, the way she rejects anything she doesn't think of first! All she cares about is saving her own skin—hers and Finn's. Do you know she's still seeing Brother Belastra?"

The wind picks up. Behind Maura, the water in the river begins to churn, the great ship nearest us rocking as if tossed in a tempest. The men on the deck shout, running to secure their cargo. Is it just the snowstorm, or is Maura losing her temper?

"This isn't about Cate," Tess says firmly, taking a cautious step backward. "This is about you and me. Our relationship as sisters."

"It's *always* about Cate," Maura disagrees, her black cloak rippling in the sudden squall. "She insinuates herself into everything! We don't even know which one of us is the oracle yet, but you've already made up your mind, haven't you? If it were up to you, you'd have Cate lead the Sisterhood."

Tess squares her shoulders. "I don't like Sister Inez. I don't trust her. So, yes, I think Cate's the best choice."

Maura looks stunned, as though she's been slapped.

"What about me? Don't you trust me?" She gives a hysterical little laugh. Tears are gathering in her blue eyes. "Let me guess: you think I'm reckless. 'Too easily ruled by my emotions,' Elena said. As though feeling things deeply—wanting more for myself and girls like us—is so terrible!"

A heavy crate falls overboard with a tremendous splash. On the gangway, there's a spate of cursing from the sailors.

"Maura, let's go home and talk about this there," Tess suggests.

"Cate won't win this war, you know," Maura insists. The snow is falling faster and faster now, obscuring the ships farther away. The dock is slippery beneath my heeled boots. "You'll need soldiers like me and Inez. People willing to do what needs to be done."

"We're not at war," I snap. "And it's a good thing, because the Brothers outnumber us a hundred to one."

"But we're a hundred times more powerful." Her smile is chilling as she gazes out over the harbor. "You want to free a few witches? That's not enough. We need to show people what we're really capable of. That's why we're going to ruin the Head Council."

"Ruin them how?" Tess asks, and my stomach sinks.

"We're going to erase their minds, the way the Daughters of Persephone did with their enemies. They won't remember their own names once we're finished with them." My sister's voice is vicious. "They'll stop murdering innocent girls, and we'll remind people what witches can do."

This is why Inez wanted Finn to spy. So she could start a war.

"She would expose us like that? We're not ready, Maura!" Tess's face is pale.

Maura swipes her hair out of her eyes. "No one will connect it with the Sisterhood. They'll only know witches were responsible."

"This won't stop the Brothers from murdering innocent girls. Don't you see, they'll crack down twice as hard!" I protest. "Inez can't do this. Cora isn't even dead yet, and once she is, Inez will only be regent until one of us comes of age."

"*It will be me,*" Maura insists. "Why can't you let me have this one thing?"

"It doesn't work like that, Maura. We can't just decide that it's you. It's up to Persephone," Tess says, stepping closer, hands outstretched like Maura's a wild animal.

"Even if you could, you wouldn't choose me, would you?" Maura's lip wobbles. "No one ever does."

Tess puts a hand on her arm. "Maura, I love you."

Maura shakes her off. "Get away from me!"

Tess skids backward—farther than Maura's push warrants. Her feet slip on the snowy dock. She teeters for a moment on the very edge, windmilling her arms above the freezing river. She screams.

I grab her, pulling her back toward me. She throws both arms around my waist, clinging like a child, her whole body trembling.

Tears are streaming down Maura's face now. "I didn't mean—"

"You could have killed me," Tess says, stunned. "I can't swim. You *know* I can't swim."

She's always been frightened of the water; she would never even wade in the pond with me. Mrs. O'Hare teases that Mother must have dropped her in the sink when she was a baby.

"I can't—when I'm upset, I can't control it," Maura says. "I told you to stay away from me, I—just let me alone, both of you! I don't need you. I don't need anyone!"

And with that, she's gone, running away down the snowy street. I hug Tess close and watch her go.

CHAPTER
14

"WE HAVE TO STOP INEZ."

I pick my way carefully up the snowy front steps of the convent. "I know."

Tess's nose is red from the cold and from crying. "People have had a hundred years to forget what the Daughters of Persephone did, and now she'll make us into bogeymen again. It will ruin any chance we have for sharing power."

"Maybe that's what she wants—to make it so we'll have to go to war." I shiver into my cloak. "Lord knows what the Brothers will do in response."

Tess sighs. "At least we saved the prisoners. We changed things, Cate! I saw them all being loaded onto the prison ship in the snow, and now they're free. That means—"

"We can change the prophecy," I realize, a grin nearly splitting my face in half.

"Maura might be angry with us now, but she'll get past it. Who knows? Perhaps in the oracle's vision, I *did* fall into the river today, and I drowned," Tess says, kicking the snow off her boots. "But you saved me. You can't know how much better this makes me feel. If I can change the things I see—if it's not all set in stone—that changes *everything*."

She wrenches open the heavy front door, and we hang up our wet cloaks and slide off our boots. The front parlor door is ajar, light spilling out, but I don't hear any voices. Putting my finger to my lips, I tiptoe over in stocking feet and peer in.

"Finn?" I gasp. He's standing before the fire in his gray vest and white shirtsleeves, hands clasped behind his back. "What are you doing here?"

Finn whirls around, smiling. "There you are! I worried when you weren't at the trial. Rory said there was some emergency."

I forgot all about Sachi's trial. Rory is perched on the settee, dabbing at her eyes with her pink lace handkerchief.

"Was it Harwood?" I ask.

Rory nods, swiping at another tear. "It was awful. The things they said about her—and she looked so frightened."

"We'll find a way to get her out of there, I promise." I turn to Finn, distracted. "You can't call on me here. It's too dangerous."

He moves aside, ushering Tess to stand front of the fire. "I was worried. And I got the information Inez wanted about the next Head Council meeting. It's going to be—"

"Hush!" I pull the door shut behind me, then cross the room, reach up, and pull the copper grate shut, too, for good measure. I don't want anyone eavesdropping. Finn stares at me, stunned. "Whatever you found out, you can't tell anyone. Don't even tell me. I don't want her compelling it out of me. I don't know if she *could,* but I wouldn't put it past her to try."

Finn pales beneath his freckles. "Who?"

I take his warm hand in my two icy ones. "Inez. She's not what I thought. We can't trust her."

Finn's curses would make the dockworkers blush. "It's too late. I've already told her."

"No." I look at Tess, who leans against the mantel and closes her gray eyes in dismay, and then I sink onto the brown silk chair.

"I asked the girl who answered the door if I could see you. She brought Inez, and Inez guessed who I was straight off. She said you'd gone out for a bit but I was welcome to wait for you in here, and she asked whether I'd been able to find out anything yet. I had, so—I told her. Dammit!" Finn puts a hand on my bare shoulder. "I thought that was what you wanted! What's changed?"

"I was wrong," I whisper. Stupid and trusting and so very wrong. "She wants to destroy them. Go into their minds and ruin them, like the witches used to do. The entire Head Council."

Finn's hand clenches on my collarbone. "She can't do that."

"Why not?" Rory stands up, crumpling her handkerchief

in her fist. It's the first time I've seen her in Sisterly black. "If you'd been at Sachi's trial today, Cate, if you'd seen how frightened she was—we've got to fight back. We've got to do *something*."

"Not this. It's wrong. It's murder, or as good as," Tess snaps, tucking her damp blond hair behind her ears. "And it will only make things worse!"

"It's unconscionable," Finn agrees, eyes snapping. "And she used me to do it."

"Both of us." I stand, folding myself into his arms. "I'm so sorry I involved you in it."

"I won't lie to you, my new boss is no prize. Most of the Head Council are power-hungry bastards. But look at Sean Brennan; he's a good man. And even the ones who aren't— Tess is right; it's akin to murder. The Brothers will strike back twice as hard to prove they're still in control. For this—" Finn swallows hard. "They might resurrect the burnings. There are men who would vote for it. They're just waiting for a reason, and this would give them one. What in the hell is Inez thinking?"

Tess's hands fly to her mouth, as though she's trying not to be sick. "It'll be a second Terror. They won't know it was Inez and Maura, but they'll find *someone* to blame. Just like those girls they arrested as oracles." She turns to me. "We can't let them do it, Cate!"

"Harwood!" Rory shouts. We all turn to stare at her. "People won't know the Sisters are responsible. They'll only know it's witchery. And if they want to punish witches, or women in general—"

"The girls at Harwood are the easiest target," I finish.

Rory's breath comes fast. "We have to get them out. Sachi and Brenna. *Now.*"

I extricate myself from Finn. "When is the meeting?"

"Wednesday night," he says.

It's Saturday. That's only four days. Not much time to engineer a jailbreak.

I cannot afford to panic. There isn't any time to waste.

"First I'm going to talk to Inez, and see if there's any possibility of changing her mind. With or without magic." I turn to Finn. I don't want him anywhere near Inez, lest she use him as a bargaining chip against me. "You've got to leave. Right now."

"Wait," Finn says, raking his hands through his already-messy hair. "What's this about rescuing Sachi and Brenna?"

"Not just them." I smooth my peach-colored skirt. "All the girls at Harwood. We've got four days to contrive a way to get them out."

He doesn't try to argue with me, to tell me that it's mad or impossible. He just takes my hand. "What can I do to help?"

My mind races. "You said they keep all kinds of files in the Archives. Would they have files on the girls in Harwood?" It would help to know which of the patients are witches, especially ones accused of mind-magic. If Inez is going to start a war, we'll need to be able to fight back.

"I'll find out. Tomorrow I've got to be at services all day, but Monday I'll pay a call on Brother Szymborska and do some snooping."

"That would be grand. Meet me Monday night at the

usual spot?" I ask. Finn nods, his gaze darting to my mouth, and I want to kiss him, but not in front of Rory and Tess. I squeeze his hand instead. "Be careful."

His brow furrows as he slides on the cloak of the Brotherhood. "You, too."

A few minutes later, I storm into Sister Inez's classroom. She's grading papers in the midafternoon gloom. When she hears me, she looks up, a sharp, wolfish smile flitting over her face. "Your sister can't keep her mouth shut, can she? That girl needs to learn to control her temper."

I stop before her heavy oak desk. "I would have found out eventually."

"Fortunately, it wasn't until after I had the information I needed from Brother Belastra." She stresses the word *Brother* just a tad, and my temper rises, pulling my magic with it. Perhaps I shouldn't bother with arguing; perhaps I ought to compel her to forget the time and location of the Head Council meeting now. It would be rectifying a mistake, because I should have compelled her in the first place, the night she caught me sneaking out to see Finn.

I don't know if my mind-magic is strong enough, but I'm willing to find out. I lean over the desk, narrowing my eyes at her.

"Before you go to the trouble of compelling me, I ought to warn you that I've already taken precautions." Inez clicks her tongue against her teeth reprovingly. "How do you ever tell a lie, child? You're as transparent as glass."

I am not a child. I clench my hands into fists at her

condescension. "What kind of precautions? How do I know you aren't lying to me again?"

"I never lied to you about my intentions," she points out, maddeningly.

She's right. She said she wanted war; I didn't ask questions. I wanted Finn to stay in New London, and having him spy for the Sisterhood was a noble reason, far less selfish than asking him to give up his job and his family to stay near me.

"I've just posted a letter to a dear friend. She's married a member of the Brotherhood, but she remains loyal to her former Sisters. I told her that I am in danger and gave very clear instructions: if she doesn't hear about the success of my plan, she will post another letter for me. One that explains the Sisterhood is a coven of witches and that Brother Finn Belastra has known the truth of it all along. I daresay Brother Belastra wouldn't fare well under charges of treason."

The smug expression on her face makes me want to slap her. I lean over her desk. "You're bluffing. You would never write all that down."

"Perhaps. Or perhaps I wrote it all in code. You can't know for sure." Inez taps her pen against the desktop in a steady, maddening rhythm.

I narrow my eyes at her, focusing all my anger into my magic. *Tell me who she is.*

"I can feel that, Miss Cahill." Inez's dark brows slant down, almost touching in the middle. "I'm very good at compulsion myself, you know. I daresay we're on the same level—though of course it's hard to know. Feel free to keep trying, but you'll only exhaust yourself. I've been training myself for years to be impervious to it."

"I won't let you do this," I hiss. A muscle in my right eye begins to twitch.

"I don't see how you can stop me." She leans back in her wooden chair. "Not without sacrificing every girl in this convent—or starting an outright war between the Brotherhood and the Sisterhood."

Magic simmers beneath my skin, twitching my fingertips. I fight down the frustration, crossing my arms over my ruffled peach bodice. "What do you hope to accomplish? You have to know this will cause a new Terror."

Inez fingers the brooch at her throat. "We're already halfway there, Miss Cahill. I will not stand by and do nothing while we are persecuted. I've spent the last twenty years watching Cora cower and cater to them. She's content to let change come at a snail's pace. I'm simply speeding things up."

My mouth falls open. "You *want* a new Terror. You want the Brothers to do their worst, so we look good in comparison! Don't you care about all the girls they'll hurt in the meantime? What about the girls at Harwood?" I remember the beautiful, bruised Indo girl in the uncooperative ward, and little Sarah Mae, who buries birds in the courtyard, and the girl who thinks she's engaged to a prince. They will be the ones to bear the brunt of this.

"There are casualties in every war."

I press my knuckles into my stinging eyes. How can she speak of it so callously? "There must be some witches there. You'd give them up?"

"Cora's already given up on those girls." Inez shrugs a black-clad shoulder. "Your sister told me about your ill-advised plan to free them. I don't think they're worth the trouble. I have bigger fish to fry."

I don't. Those girls are not expendable. Not to me.

I throw my hands up in the air in a show of defeat and stalk toward the door.

"Don't do anything foolish, Miss Cahill," Inez warns. "Or someone you love will wind up hurt."

I go to Cora. Insist on seeing her. After a moment of studying me, Gretchen gives in, perhaps sensing my desperation. I don't imagine I hide it well.

"Just a few minutes," she agrees, opening the door to Cora's bedroom and taking up her sentry position outside.

Cora lies propped up on pillows in her four-poster bed, her eyes sunken in shadows. She looks a decade older than she did just yesterday. Is this all the time my healing bought her?

I saw death in my mother's face, and seeing it now makes me feel twelve and frightened all over again. It makes me want to promise any number of reckless, impulsive things if only she will stay. *I'll listen and be a proper young lady, and I won't fight with Maura. I'll do anything.* I am older now and know better, but the way it hits me, this childish urge to bargain death away, is so visceral. It hunches my shoulders and roots my feet to the hooked brown rug on the threshold.

"Catherine," Cora says, through cracked and bloodless lips. Her shining white hair cascades down over her shoulders. The green coverlet is pulled up to her breast. "What is it?"

"I—I just wanted to see you," I lie.

"Time to say our good-byes," Cora says.

I pull the green and white flowered chair close to her bed. Everything in me wants to protest that she may yet rally, that perhaps this isn't the end. But that is the selfish thing, and a lie to boot. I bite back the words. She is in pain, and she has made her peace with going, and I must let her.

"Inez won't wait. My body will hardly be cold before she takes the Sisterhood, Cate."

It's the first time she's ever called me by my nickname.

If this is our good-bye, I owe it to Cora to help settle her mind, not the other way around. "I'm going to fight her for it."

"Good girl." Cora smiles. "Gretchen knows where my papers are hidden, and how to contact Brennan and our spies. She's known all my secrets since I was a girl. I trust her implicitly. She'll be a great help to you, as she has been to me."

My mind races. "Brennan—that's your man on the Head Council?"

Cora nods. "A good sort. Has daughters of his own and educates them in secret. You can trust him."

But I can't go to him and warn him not to attend the council meeting. He would want to know why, and if he is a good man—and I trust Finn and Cora that he is—he would try to stop it. Even an anonymous letter would raise suspicion that might cancel the meeting and risk our exposure.

"Who else among the staff?" I ask.

"Sophia, but she doesn't always have the stomach to do what must be done. The rest of them have allied themselves with Inez, except for Elena," Sister Cora muses, twirling her ring of office around her finger. It's loose from all the weight she's lost, wrapped in string to keep it from falling off entirely. It's the only one she wears now, and it's strange seeing her hands unlined with silver. "You might ask her for counsel. She's a very canny girl, you know, and I wouldn't have sent her to Chatham unless I trusted her."

I wonder how much Cora knows about what happened between Elena and Maura. Ugh. I make a face. I hardly relish the notion of being civil to Elena, much less asking her for favors.

There's a sudden hoarse, choking sound, and I leap up in alarm, worried that this is it—that Cora is dying now, here, right in front of me—until I realize she is *laughing*.

"What a lemon face," she wheezes. "Like I told you to eat a worm."

"Are you—can I help you?" I ask as she struggles for breath. Her hand next to mine is paper-white and stark with blue veins, and it looks small and naked without all her rings. Unthinkingly, I put my hand over it.

Her pain almost swallows me, its razor teeth nipping and tearing, and I snatch my hand back, chastened. "How do you bear it?"

She manages a few deep, full breaths, sinking back against her pillows. "You can't heal me, and I won't have you wasting your strength," she snaps, folding her hands across her chest. She closes her eyes for a moment, and without their vibrant blue, she looks dead already.

I find that I will miss her.

"I am sorry we didn't get a chance to know each other better, Cate," she says. "I'm tired now. Sophia insists on drugging my tea, though I told her I don't want it. Will you send Gretchen in? And pull the curtains, please. The light makes my head ache."

"Of course." I undo the tasseled gold ties that hold the emerald curtains back.

"May Persephone watch over you." Sister Cora's voice is softer now, already slurred with sleep. I turn back to her, my eyes adjusting to the dim room. "I have faith that you will do what is necessary, when it comes down to it."

"Thank you." Knowing Cora, that's the highest compliment she could give. She's shaped her life around it.

That night after supper, there's a commotion in the hall. I peer out my bedroom door and see Maura dragging her trunk down the hall. Her quilt and pillows are stacked neatly on top.

Tess is following her. "Maura, this isn't necessary."

Three doors down from me, Vi emerges from the room she and Alice share. She's carrying a brown valise, with a handful of dresses draped over her other arm.

Alice leans out the doorway. "Mustn't forget Bunny," she sneers, tossing a tattered stuffed rabbit at Vi. "I know you can't sleep without him."

Flushing, Vi catches it. "Shut up, Alice."

I look down the hall to Tess. "What's going on?"

Vi hears me and whirls around. "I can't stand living with this shrew one second longer, and as Maura seems to *enjoy* her company—"

Maura straightens, an icy smile on her lips. "It will be a relief to room with someone my own age."

Tess stops in her tracks, all her apology fading to anger. "Well, perhaps it will be a relief to me to live with someone who hasn't tried to *drown* me lately!"

"I didn't do that on purpose, and you know it!" Maura huffs, shoving the trunk another foot.

Tess plants her hands on her hips. "Well, perhaps you ought to learn to control your temper. You wonder why people don't trust you!"

Alice appears at her door again. This time she tosses a lacy lavender petticoat down the hall. "Well, *I'll* be glad to room with someone of my own station. Imagine me being friends with a coachman's daughter! Just think of all the nice presents I gave you. All my *charity* was wasted."

"Charity!" Vi shrieks. She bends to snatch up the petticoat, and her dresses tumble to the green carpet. Tess darts past Maura to help her gather them up. Vi reaches into her valise and pulls out a pair of black satin gloves with purple buttons. She pelts them at Alice, who shrinks back against the wall. "Here! Take these back. I don't want them anymore. I wouldn't put up with you for one more day—not for all the diamonds in the world!"

"Girls!" Sister Johanna, the mathematics and natural sciences teacher, storms down the hall. "What on earth is going on? Sister Cora is very ill. She doesn't need all this screeching."

Maura shoves her trunk past Vi and Tess. "Sorry, Sister," she says sweetly. "Vi and I are switching rooms. We'll be finished in just a minute."

"Don't do anything you'll regret, Maura, please," Tess says, and I think she's talking about more than just their room.

Maura straightens, flipping a red curl away from her face. "You don't need to worry about me anymore, Tess. I'm none of your concern."

CHAPTER
15

WE ARE HALFWAY THROUGH OUR breakfast when the doorbell sounds. Sister Sophia slides a plate of steaming hotcakes onto our table and hurries away to answer it. Around the room, breakfast pauses. Is it the Brothers? Who else would be calling at such an early hour? Lucy and Rebekah are dueling with butter knives, practicing their animation; the knives clatter to the table as they drop their spells. Girls transform their textbooks into Scriptures. Color slowly leeches from the room as we attire ourselves in drab, Sisterly dresses. Next to me, Rory's dress goes from a bright mandarin orange cascading with lace to a somber black wool. Transformation accomplished, she takes a hotcake and slathers it in butter. I push my plate aside.

"Mei?" Sister Sophia appears in the doorway.

"Your brother's here to see you. He's waiting in the front parlor."

"I bet it's news about Li and Hua." Mei pushes her chair back, her round face worried. "Cate, will you come with me?"

"Of course." The chatter around the table picks up again, the room flooding with pink and violet and sapphire as girls release their glamours. Rilla drowns her hotcake in maple syrup.

I hide a smile, locking eyes with Tess. Mei will be relieved to hear that her sisters are home, safe and sound. It's one bright spot in an otherwise dreadful day.

Only—I can tell from the minute we see Yang standing before the cold fireplace in his patched brown coat that something is wrong. This isn't the merry, mischievous brother whose clever pranks Mei loves to recount. His full mouth tilts down at the corners, and his dark eyes dart anxiously away from hers. Whatever news he's got, he doesn't relish the telling of it.

Mei stops dead beside me, clenching my hand so tightly the bones crunch. She doesn't bother with introductions. "What is it?"

"Li and Hua were recaptured this morning." Yang swallows, his Adam's apple bobbing. "The guards came for them before dawn."

"Recaptured?" Mei blinks at him. "I—I don't understand."

My stomach plummets. "Where did they take them?" I hope against hope that they'll stand trial and be sent to Harwood. If it's Harwood, I can save them. If it's Harwood, we still changed Tess's vision.

"The prison ship," Yang says, confirming my fears. "They broke out of prison yesterday. Or—someone broke them out. Witches, they said. All the prisoners escaped, except for two that were killed by the guards. We were going to send the girls to Cousin Ling, but Mama wanted them to get a good night's sleep first. They were packing their things when the guards came. An hour later, and they would have been gone." He pounds a fist into his palm.

Mei presses her hand to her mouth. "There won't be a trial?"

"No. The guards said we were lucky they weren't arresting the whole lot of us for harboring fugitives." Yang shakes his head, his shaggy black hair falling over his forehead. "They had a whole wagon full of prisoners out front. They were rearresting anyone they found at home, I guess. Hopefully, most of them were smart enough to hide out somewhere else."

Mei sinks into the silk chair, her dress a sunny yellow against the ugly brown. I'd told her earlier that she looked like a daffodil. Now she'll probably always associate the pretty dress with this dreadful news. I can tell she's trying not to cry, but her lip wobbles.

"I may never see them again," she says softly.

"Don't think like that." I kneel next to her.

"Aw, Mei," Yang says, putting his hand on her shoulder.

She shrugs him off. "At least you got to say good-bye!"

"Did they say how long the sentence will be?" I ask.

Yang gulps. "Five years."

I stare down at the ugly brown rug, wondering if they

would have been released had we not interfered. Instead of preventing her vision, did Tess and I make it happen?

"At least it's not Harwood," he offers. "They have a chance, this way."

Mei stands, squaring her shoulders, throwing off her despair in one quick movement. "They'll make it through this. We've got to have faith."

"In who, the Lord? The Brothers?" Yang scoffs.

"In Li and Hua. They're strong girls. Smart. They'll look out for each other." Mei puts her hand on her brother's arm. "You're the oldest one at home now that Li's gone. You have to watch out for the little ones and help Baba in the shop. And you mustn't do anything rash, understand?"

Yang nods. He's only fifteen himself. "I won't."

"Good. Get on home now," Mei says, giving him a quick hug. "Be careful."

"I will," he says, shuffling off, face red. His pant legs and coat are still dripping from the long walk here through the snow.

Mei waves to him, shivering, from the open doorway. Vi's father, Robert, is shoveling a path down the front steps. The sky is still a heavy gray, and snowflakes are still falling, but they're the fat ones that mean the storm is tapering off. We watch until Yang disappears down the street, and then Mei walks back into the parlor, plops down onto the settee, and looks at me with utter despair.

"I should go home," she says.

"I'm sure everyone would understand if you want to be with your family for a few days." I crouch to light the fire.

"I mean for good. If I left, perhaps I could get work from someone on the quiet. I'm not the seamstress Li is, but I could try. Or I could look after the little ones so Mama could work," Mei says.

I sprawl onto the hearth, rearranging the logs with the poker. "You'll be seventeen in a few weeks. You'd have to find a husband right quick."

Mei kicks off her red slippers and tucks her feet beneath her. "Baba has friends whose sons want Chinese wives. Their families might pay a dowry for me. I'm not doing any good here. How long will it be before the Brothers shut the convent school down entirely?"

"I'd be sad to see you go," I admit, thrusting the poker into the fire again. A log crashes down with a shower of sparks. Selfishly, I hope she'll stay and help me with the Harwood plan. My stomach tightens just thinking of it. It's down to three days now. Elena's been away this week, visiting family across town, but she was at breakfast. I'll have to go to her and beg for help, loathe as I am to do it.

There's a timid knock on the door, and Tess peers in at us. She's smiling, expecting news of the jailbreak. "What happened to your sisters, Mei?"

I wave her away, nerves jangling. She's going to be devastated. "I'll tell you later, Tess."

Her smile falters. "No. Tell me now."

Mei props her chin on her knees. "They escaped yesterday, but they were recaptured this morning."

"No." Tess's gray eyes go enormous. "How?"

"The guards were going house to house, rearresting all the

prisoners, Yang said. They're all being sentenced to five years on the prison ship."

"No. Oh, no. This is all my fault." Tess sinks right to the floor, her gray taffeta skirts puddling around her.

"*Tess*," I warn, jumping up to pull the door closed behind her, "don't be silly. You had nothing to do with this!"

"I thought I changed it," Tess mutters, tears gathering in her eyes. "I thought it worked. They were free. Cate, this means—"

"I know," I interrupt, kneeling next to her. We no longer have an example of a vision that hasn't come to pass, a prophecy that was proven false.

I can't think about that now. I shove it to the back of my mind, filing it away for later. Right now I have to help Tess through this. She's so clever, and she's been so careful, surely she won't—

"I'm sorry. I am so sorry," she says to Mei.

Sometimes I forget she's also twelve.

Mei isn't stupid. "Yang said witches released the prisoners yesterday. That was you? Is that why you were asking me all the questions about where they were being kept?"

Tess nods, and I want to clap a hand over her mouth to keep her from talking about prophecies, but I daresay that would be suspicious in itself. "I was only trying to help. It was freezing in there, and they were cold and hungry, and it was an old *slaughterhouse*." She sniffles. "What if I made it happen?"

I let out a little laugh. "Tess, you're not making any sense. You couldn't have known." I stand, trying to pull her to her feet, but she doesn't budge. "You're upset. Let me take you upstairs."

She stares across the room, gazing out the frosty window. "The sky was gray like this, with big fat snowflakes. Just like when a snowstorm starts—or ends, perhaps. I saw the sky yesterday, and I thought, *Now. This is my chance. I can change things.* I was arrogant."

I glance nervously at Mei. "Come on, Tess. Let's go upstairs."

"I failed them." Tess buries her face in her hands.

Mei is staring at us both. She gets up, and I think she's going to storm away, but instead she stands on tiptoe and pulls the copper grate shut. Even then, she comes and crouches on the floor with us.

"Tess, *you're* the oracle?" she whispers.

Tess raises her tearstained face. "Please forgive me."

"No one knows, Mei," I warn. "Not even Maura. *No one.*"

"I won't tell. I swear it." Mei is looking at Tess with sudden reverence, like she's a god instead of a girl. Like she hasn't seen Tess spill tea all over herself or beaten her at chess or teased her over awful Chinese pronunciations. "I thought perhaps—yesterday, when you went all funny during our lesson—"

"I'm sorry." Tess is sobbing, her whole body trembling. "I wanted to save them. I never thought the Brothers would have recorded all their names and where they lived."

"Shhh. Shhh, we know." I look to Mei, praying that she'll help Tess forgive herself. "Yesterday at breakfast, when she had that dizzy spell—she had a vision of the prisoners being put onto the ship. She wanted to stop it."

Mei puts a tentative hand on Tess's knee. "I bet some of

them got away. Yang said if the guards had come an hour later, Li and Hua would have been gone to our cousin's. I bet a lot of the prisoners weren't home or gave false addresses, or something."

"I couldn't change it. It was always going to happen like this." Tess wipes away tears with the backs of both hands. "The books say the oracles are infallible, but there's never been a witch who was an oracle before, so I thought—but I was wrong. No matter how many awful things I see, I'll never be able to stop them."

I look helplessly at Mei. This isn't as simple as a bruise to kiss, a tangled lace to straighten, or a missing necklace to find. This is a waking nightmare, and I don't know how to fix it.

"You were brave to try," Mei says. "That's all we can do, isn't it?"

"Can you ever forgive me?" Tess's voice is small.

"Nothing to forgive." Mei pats her again. "And you needn't worry—your secret's safe with me."

We talk a bit, until Tess is sufficiently calm, and then I take her upstairs and see her snuggled back into bed with Cyclops and one of Maura's romance novels. Strange bedfellows, but both seem to comfort her, and it serves to remind me again that she is a strange mix of woman and child, carrying a burden far too heavy for her.

I've got to do everything I can to help her. Even if it means making a deal with the devil.

"Come in," Elena says when I knock at her door. Her bedroom is smaller than the double rooms students share, but big enough for a canopy bed draped in gauzy pink and a settee covered in soft yellow chintz. There's a satchel lying open on the bed, as though she was just unpacking.

She gestures for me to sit on the settee. "How was your trip?" I ask.

"You noticed I was gone? I'm flattered, Cate." Elena sits at her dressing table. "I was visiting my aunt on the other side of town. Inez told me to go off and clear my head, with the understanding that I'd return cured of any romantic feelings for a student."

I gasp at her frankness. "Romantic feelings for a—for Maura, you mean?"

"For a clever girl, you can be utterly obtuse about people." Elena's words are mild, without bite, but I bristle anyway. She has that effect on me.

"Well, you did say—"

"That she misunderstood my feelings. That I didn't return her affections. That kissing her was a mistake," Elena recites. She rubs a weary hand over her face. "I am well aware of what I said. I *lied*."

I wince. "Why?"

"Because I was foolish and ambitious, and I thought I could forget my feelings for her." Elena sighs. "My purpose in that house was to procure you for the Sisterhood, not to dally with your sister. And you said quite plainly that you would not cooperate with me, ever, unless I told her I'd only been using her. Lying seemed—prudent at the time."

It's true, then. Maura's heartbreak was my fault. "I never dreamed you actually cared for her."

"Why?" Elena's dark eyes snap at me. "She's beautiful, you know. And bright and fierce, and that *smile* of hers—who could help but fall in love with her?"

"You threatened her and Tess, repeatedly!"

"They were the only leverage we had over you until we discovered your romance with the gardener." Elena waves a hand dismissively, and anger flares through me. "I tried to make amends, you know. Or perhaps you don't. Your sister is many things, but quick to forgive a slight? She's better at holding grudges than anyone I've ever met."

"True." I feel an odd, unexpected sympathy for Elena. "Perhaps, in time—"

"I don't think so." Elena shrugs, but her voice cracks just a little. "Perhaps she could get beyond me lying to her, making her think I didn't care, even humiliating her in front of you and Tess. But choosing you over her? I don't think she'll ever forgive that."

I look at her—really look. Elena's got the most marvelous game face of anyone I've ever met. But her long, elegant fingers are twisting together as she fiddles with the pink lace at her wrist. Her black curls are disheveled from the wind moaning outside the windows, and she hasn't bothered to put on earbobs or line her fingers with rings. By her own high standards, she looks half a mess.

"At any rate," she says, looking back at me just as curiously, "I doubt you're here to discuss my relationship with your sister."

"No." I jiggle my leg nervously and then cross my ankles. I loathe this. "I need your help."

Elena smiles. "Why the change of heart?"

I force myself not to take the words back. This is no time to be petty. I need someone who understands the workings of the Sisterhood better than I do, and Gretchen is too pre-occupied. "Cora says I can trust you."

I explain Inez's plan to attend the Head Council meeting and destroy their minds. Elena listens, her full lips pursed, then says, "I don't see how we can put a stop to it, either. And the repercussions are sure to be dreadful."

"It's hard to know what the Brothers might do in response, but I'm hoping we can mitigate a little of the damage," I suggest, tapping my fingers against the yellow arm of the settee. "The first place the Brothers will strike back is at Harwood. But if we can break all the girls out of Harwood the same night as the Head Council meeting, and bring some of the ones who are witches back to the convent, we'll save them *and* increase our numbers. There's just one problem. I know how to get in, but not how to get them all *out*."

Elena tosses her hair, some of her insouciance returning. "The biggest problem is that the girls are drugged, isn't it? They can't help themselves once you free them or access their own magic."

"Exactly."

"Paul McLeod is working at Harwood, isn't he, on the new construction?" she asks, and I nod. "Maura's been flirting with him to provoke you—and me, I expect, which has worked rather nicely. But she's also been plying him with questions. I daresay you could use the same tactic."

I make a face. "You want me to flirt with Paul to gather information?"

"I wouldn't be so crass—not when we both know your heart lies elsewhere." Elena smirks, and I glare at her. "But if you were to call at his office—I daresay they aren't working out on the site in this weather. And they would have floor plans for Harwood there. Who knows what you could find that might be helpful?"

"Won't Paul suspect me, once he hears about a mutiny at the asylum?" Elena stares at me, as though the answer to *that* is obvious, and I shift uncomfortably on the settee. "No. He's my oldest friend, I couldn't—"

"You could," Elena interrupts, smoothing her pink skirts. "If it's to save hundreds of girls' lives, you could. You *will*."

She's right.

"When is your next nursing trip to Harwood?" she asks.

I gulp. "Tomorrow afternoon. We usually go on Saturdays, but I wanted to attend Sachi's trial, and Sophia said she'd go with me."

"Then you ought to pay a call on Mr. McLeod tomorrow morning. And we'll need to figure out which of the girls in Harwood are actually witches. There must be records somewhere. The ones with mind-magic ought to be our priority, I think, in terms of who to bring back to the convent; they'll be the most use to us as things get more dangerous." Elena frowns, tapping one smooth nail against her lips.

"Finn says there are all kinds of records in the National Archives. He's going to see what he can find," I say cautiously, waiting for Elena to make some jest about him being a gardener again.

"I can't come with you tomorrow—I've got hardly any healing magic to speak of; it would raise suspicion—but I'll come on the mission itself," she says. I can practically see the wheels of her mind turning. "In the meantime, I'll start talking to some of the other governesses and teachers. Most of them are in Inez's pockets, but there are some I think will want to help us. I don't think we ought to give them too many details—well, we haven't *got* too many details yet, but the more people who know, the more likely it is to get out and get fouled up. I don't think Inez will bother trying to stop you—it will serve her well enough to have more witches—but she's hard to predict."

"Thank you." I peer at her curiously. "When Maura finds out that you helped me, she's going to be furious."

"I know." It's strange, after all her subterfuge, to hear Elena be so straightforward. "If there was anyone else who could help you, I'd let them. I would have refused Cora, dying or no. But there isn't anyone else, and she pointed out—rightly, I think—that if Inez gets power, she'll use Maura and then discard her."

"Maura trusts her. She says Inez believes in her." My voice is bitter.

"I'm afraid for her," Elena confesses, her brown eyes meeting mine.

I take a deep breath. "I'm afraid *of* her."

CHAPTER
16

"CATE?" PAUL STRIDES OUT OF HIS OFFICE, looking utterly flabbergasted to find *me* waiting in the small, elegant front room at Jones & Sons.

"Hello." I offer up a shy smile. "Do you have time for a chat?"

His green eyes light up, and I hate myself a little.

This is for the Sisterhood, I remind myself. For the innocent girls imprisoned in Harwood.

"I always have time for you," he says, ushering me down the carpeted hall and into a small room dominated by a shining mahogany desk piled high with architectural designs curling up at the edges. He hangs my cloak on a cast-iron coatrack in the corner, then folds himself behind the desk in a tall brown leather chair. I sit in the other, luxuriating in the buttery feel of the armrests beneath my palms.

The smell reminds me of the barn at home, of playing hide-and-seek with Paul when we were children. It puts me at ease.

"Is something wrong?" he asks. He looks terribly professional in his gray jacket and vest, with a green cravat wrapped around his throat. I daresay he knows it matches his eyes. Paul has never been immune to his own charms.

"No. Well—yes. I owe you an apology," I say quietly.

"Yes." He leans back in his chair and gazes at me, waiting. He has the body of a sportsman—tall, with broad shoulders and a square jaw—but the fine, detailed sketches on his desktop remind me that there's more to him than that. He's a man with ambition, who's secured a good place for himself in a booming profession in a booming city; a man who appreciates the fine things in life, as his new phaeton and handsome clothes suggest.

Paul will make someone a fine husband. Someone who can love him as he deserves.

"I don't regret my decision," I say. I want to be clear about that. "But it all happened very suddenly, and I'm sorry that I didn't have an opportunity to tell you—to give you an answer first. Your friendship—it means a great deal to me, and you deserved better."

My eyes falter, and then I see it—on the wall beside the door hang several framed diagrams of a large building. Are they copies of the plans for Harwood? It would make sense to display his first real project of importance.

Paul rubs a hand over his clean-shaven jaw thoughtfully;

it's a habit left over from the beard that's no longer there. "What are you doing here, Cate? In New London, I mean? You hated the thought of living in the city when I proposed it, and you've never been the religious sort."

"I felt a calling?" It comes out a question, rather than a deep conviction.

"To the Lord?" Paul raises his eyebrows. "I understand that your sisters want to continue their education, and given the new measure, this is the only way. But you've never been the scholarly sort."

Paul has always known how to read me; it makes it difficult to lie to him. What will have the ring of truth to it, but not involve the prophecy or my duty to the Sisterhood? I should have thought this part through more. Of course he wants explanations, just as Finn did. The difference is that Finn knows I'm a witch, and Paul does not.

"I want to be a nurse," I explain, twisting, pointing at the diagram on the wall. "I've been going to Harwood, you know, with Sister Sophia. We tend to the patients and provide spiritual guidance."

"You, a nurse?" Paul chokes with laughter. "You'd tell a man with a broken leg to stop his whining and walk it off. You hate the sickroom."

"I hated my mother's sickroom," I correct him, bristling and trying not to. He can't be expected to know what an exceptionally good nurse I am, thanks to my gift for healing. "I spent a great deal of time there, though. I can do some good this way."

Paul leans forward, planting his elbows on the desk,

crumpling some of the drawings. "Look, is this about Belastra? Because he joined the Brotherhood? It can't be coincidence that you announced your intention the next day. I know you had feelings for him, but you can't—"

"He had nothing to do with it," I lie. My eyes dart to the tilted wooden drawing table by the window and the high stool before it.

"You had other choices," Paul insists.

"No." I know him well enough to know where this argument is headed. I need to forestall it, before he embarrasses us both and makes me say things that will only hurt him. "I didn't."

"You did." He clenches his jaw and straightens the wrinkled drawings. "When you got up on that dais, I expected you to announce your betrothal to him. I prepared myself for it. I never imagined this. You could have had the grace to tell me I wasn't even an *option*."

I deserve that.

I bow my head, eyes on the rich red carpet instead of him. "I'm sorry. I don't know what else to say. I didn't tell anyone about my decision—not even Maura and Tess."

"Maura was devastated." He levels me with a disapproving look. "When she didn't show up at church the next week, I called on them. Tess said the only thing ill about her was her temper. But I daresay I know how she felt, being left behind."

And she made the most of that, didn't she?

Lord, I'm a hypocrite. How can I judge her with one breath and manipulate him with the next?

"Could I—?" I clear my throat, giving a little shiver for

good effect. "Could I possibly have a cup of tea? It's freezing out there."

"Of course." Paul forces a smile, unfolding his long legs from beneath the desk. "Where are my manners? Excuse me."

He's hardly gone before I leap out of the chair to examine the diagrams hanging on the wall. It *is* Harwood; the exterior is recognizable even from the side, with covered walkways connecting the new wing to the old on the first and second floors. Moving over to the interior sketches, I trace the doorways with my fingertips, wondering whether these could provide exits unsecured by guards. If it's only a matter of breaking locks, that should be simple enough; I'm counting on magic, not keys, to help us there.

"Cate?" I jump at the sound of my name. I was so entranced by the floor plans that I didn't even hear Paul come back in. "I asked our clerk to put the kettle on. I see you've found the Harwood plans. Impressive, aren't they?" He grins.

"Very." I tap the infirmary with my forefinger. "I've been to this ward, on nursing missions. I've seen the conditions. They're horrible. Everything's so cramped and dirty. The whole place looks as though it could crumble around their ears at any moment."

"Well, the existing structure was built shortly after the Brothers took power. The addition will be much more modern and comfortable. There will be security features, of course—bars on all the windows, doors that lock from the outside, that sort of thing. But there will be plenty of windows, and a nice courtyard for the patients to take constitutionals.

See?" He points at the space between the old and new buildings. "And there will be a sitting room on each floor where the women can gather to play chess or knit in the evenings."

As if they would ever be trusted with knitting needles! As though the girls aren't too drugged to manage a game of chess! I gawk at him, surprised by his willful naïveté. He must know the truth of how it is, and to ignore it—well, I thought better of him.

I ought to flatter him. Ask questions. Try to gather as much information as I can, because who knows what may help us? But even as my eyes rove over rooms marked *matron's office* (on the bottom floor, in the wing opposite the infirmary) and *isolation—maximum security* (on the top floor, in the wing opposite the uncooperatives), I find myself glowering.

"I think it's wrong, the way they're treated," I blurt out.

Paul squints at me with a quizzical expression. "They're witches, Cate. It could be worse."

Oh. For all his mother's piety, Paul never spoke of joining the Brotherhood. He never minded the dozens of small ways I disobeyed them, and I suppose he never knew about the big ways. Still, I hoped if he ever discovered the truth, he would accept me for what I am.

Now, his obliviousness makes me wonder. For the first time, despite all the lovely memories between us, I don't feel entirely safe with him.

"It's Jones's first big contract. How would I look if I refused to work on a project for the Brothers? And frankly, I wouldn't refuse. This is good for business, and if I intend to make partner someday—Jones hasn't any sons of his own to continue the firm, only a nephew he isn't fond of, you know . . ."

This isn't the same boy I played tag in the blueberry fields and pirates in the pond with. But perhaps I'm not the Cate he remembers, either.

I smile at him, trying to remember the coy way Maura looked up beneath her thick eyelashes. But my own lashes are spindly and blond, and I feel stupid. "You're right, of course. Forgive me. I suppose working with the girls in the infirmary makes me feel a little sorry for them."

"You should be more careful what you say. If it were anyone other than me, that kind of talk could get you in trouble." Paul puts his hand on my shoulder. He smells of pencil shavings and slate. "What would the Sisters think?"

"They preach compassion for the less fortunate. But you're right, we mustn't lose perspective on why those girls are there." *Because the Brothers are merciless.* I turn back to the floor plans. "Will the infirmary be moved into the new building?"

"No, the kitchens and infirmary will all stay put in the old wing, see?" Paul traces a line along the first floor with one tanned forefinger.

"What's that little room there?" I ask as his finger moves over an unmarked space next to the kitchen.

"Just a storage room," he says, shrugging. "It's where they keep medicines and the laudanum for the girls. The matron said they had trouble with some nurses sneaking the stuff for themselves, so now she keeps it locked up tight. And across here will be the covered walkway to the first floor of the addition, where the new laundry will be, and . . ."

He goes on, but I've stopped listening. I'd assumed the laudanum would be kept in the kitchens, where any number of cooks would be working, and it would be impossible to slip in unnoticed.

This changes *everything*.

My mind whirrs and clanks, and I'm half surprised smoke doesn't come out my ears as I plot. I want to dash out into the snow right now; I've got to talk to Sister Sophia. But I spend another twenty minutes there, admiring the drawings for the splendid new house Jones is letting him take the lead on, sipping tea in the big leather chair, listening to Paul hold forth about the Harwood project. I try to hide my horror at the fact the Brothers are building an addition in the first place. How many more girls are they planning to lock up?

Those girls' lives are more important than the success of Jones's business, and the fact that Paul can't or won't see it has changed things between us. He is the same man he was a month ago when he kissed me—same blond hair and broad shoulders and toothy grin—but I can't help looking at him differently.

I fell in love with Finn partly because he was suspicious of the Brothers, because he questioned their teachings even before he knew I was a witch. Perhaps it isn't fair to compare them, when Finn grew up with a clever bluestocking for a mother and Paul's was so deeply devout. But I do compare, and I know in my heart I could never have married a man who finds no fault in Harwood Asylum.

I feel less guilty about the mind-magic than I expected.

He is yammering on about construction deadlines when I narrow my eyes at him and compel him to forget we ever discussed Harwood or looked at the floor plans together. He hesitates, mid-sentence, and his tea spills a little when he sets it down on the blue saucer.

"I ought to be going. Thank you for seeing me," I say, rising.

He leaps up to help me into my cloak. His eyes have lost some of their spark; his face doesn't have the same bright, animated elasticity it did a minute ago. "Thank you for coming."

Does he remember my apology?

"Good-bye." Somehow I can't meet his eyes.

"Good-bye, Cate," Paul says, and there's something in his voice, something resigned and final and sad, that makes me suspect he will remember that much, at least.

When I get back to the convent, I hurry to Sister Sophia's classroom. She's just finished her anatomy class, which I skipped in order to call on Paul. Mei is the only student left, rolling up a few diagrams of the human musculature and internal organs.

"There you are, Cate. Where were you this morning?" Sophia asks, pushing Bones the skeleton back into the wooden armoire.

"I've been downtown to see my friend Paul, who's working

on the Harwood addition. There's something I need to tell you." I explain Inez's plan to Sophia.

"Why didn't you come to me right away?" She abandons Bones, her red lips pursed.

"I suppose I felt guilty. I should have seen what she was up to sooner," I confess.

"That's not your fault." Sophia plants her hands on her wide hips. "She knows how to exploit people's weaknesses to get what she wants. It's why so many of the teachers go along with her. Most of them are in her debt for one thing or another."

"Are you?" I ask. If she is, I ought to know it now.

Sophia turns away. "Not anymore."

Mei and I exchange mystified looks. "Well, now that you know, I'm hoping you'll help us." I explain what we mean to do at Harwood, and as I talk, I examine the little wooden cabinet hanging on the wall. There are two dozen clear glass bottles and tins filled with dried herbs and natural remedies of Sophia's. She must have *something*. "Do you know what powdered opium looks like? I need herbs that could pass for it."

"I presume you'd need quite a bit of them, if you mean to substitute them for the opium in the laudanum." Sister Sophia crosses to her windowsill, where four potted herbs soak up the weak December sunlight. She fingers one leafy stalk thoughtfully, gazing out at the backyard and the conservatory's fogged windows. "Rose petal powder would work. The texture wouldn't be right, and the scent would be a dead giveaway, of course. But we've got dying roses in spades, and you'd cast a glamour over it anyway."

I turn to Mei, noting the dark shadows under her brown eyes, the tired lines at her mouth. "Are you still planning to come to Harwood this afternoon?" I ask, and she nods, tucking the diagrams in the armoire beside Bones. "Good. I'll need a lookout while I break into their storeroom."

Mei gives me a sad smile. "Happy to help. If it had gone differently, Li and Hua might be in there."

Sister Sophia stares at me. "You mean to do this *today*? The patients may be able to access their magic within a few days, but they'll be in poor shape. Most of them are addicted to the opium; ridding their bodies of it completely will take weeks. They'll be weak and sick in the meantime, and that doesn't even take into account the psychological effects of—"

"We haven't got weeks," I interrupt. "We have to break them out by Wednesday night, or it will be too late."

Striding over to the blackboard, Sophia snatches up a piece of chalk and writes in foot-high letters: BEGINNER HEALING CLASS CANCELED. "Come on, then. You, too, Mei. I've got an extra pair of gloves in the kitchen."

After lunch, I draw Elena aside to explain the mechanics of the new plan. As we whisper, her dark head bent close to my blond one, I see Maura stop in the dining room doorway, shock playing over her pretty features. After a moment, she turns away, but I can tell by the set of her shoulders that she's dismayed to see us looking so cozy. It's no more than

I predicted, of course, but I still feel a pang of guilt. I brief Elena as quickly as I can, thank her for obtaining promises of help from two governesses, and hurry upstairs to change into my Sisterly black.

A few minutes later, I'm sitting in the carriage with Sophia, Addie, and Mei as we wait for Pearl to join us.

"Scoot over. I'm coming with you," Tess declares, clambering in the open door. She shoves me over so that I'm practically sitting in Mei's lap. Mei barely notices, her lips moving silently in a mantra as she worries her mala beads.

"You are most certainly not!" I shout, half rising from my seat.

"Calm down, Cate," Sophia says, and I flop back onto the leather seat. "I gave her permission. We'll tell the nurses she's a new student with an interest in nursing. They'll be charmed."

Tess flips her braids over her shoulder. "I am particularly adorable today."

I eye her suspiciously. The rest of us are dressed in our grim bombazine, but she's bright and girlish in a simple tulip-pink dress with full skirts and creamy lace at the throat and cuffs, tied with a wide black sash at the waist. She looks a pretty little doll, not a powerful young witch. It's as much a charade as our Sisterly black.

"Don't give me that look," she says, pinching me. "I can be every bit as stubborn as you. I only want to meet Zara; I won't make any trouble. And you *said* I could, before."

"Before I knew about today's extra mission," I hiss, patting the leather satchel next to me, filled with a dozen little stoppered bottles, themselves filled with ground-up rose petals and an herb stimulant Sister Sophia concocted to help counteract the girls' withdrawal. "You're infuriating."

"Then I should remind you of yourself," Tess jokes.

Mei sighs, her fingers still moving over the beads. "You two make me miss my sisters."

"Are you certain you feel up to this? We would all understand if you weren't," Sister Sophia says gently.

"No, I might as well be useful. I'll only fret otherwise." Mei gives a woeful excuse for a smile, and I hug her tight. I am lucky to have a friend like her who would put aside her own heartache to take on such a dangerous task.

But even as my heart breaks for her, I wonder what the continued infallibility of the oracles means for *us*.

"I'm nervous," Tess confesses as we hurry toward Zara's room. "What if she doesn't like me?"

"Everyone likes you. You're terribly likable." The matron and the nurses clucked over her from the instant she got out of the carriage, telling her what a grand selfless girl she is to be interested in such difficult work. And she was wonderful with the uncooperatives, even when we discovered a girl we knew among them. Mina Coste didn't seem to recognize us, though she attended services with us all our lives. Her brown eyes were lifeless, her strawberry-blond curls in knots. All this because she snuck out to meet a boy?

How many times have I risked the same punishment to

see Finn? And I will again tonight. I've just been luckier than Mina.

I take a deep breath, quelling my own nerves as we push open Zara's door. She slouches in her chair, frizzy head bowed, staring out at the snowy hillside or dozing. I don't know what to expect. Her distant memory seems unclouded by the laudanum, but will she remember our meeting last week?

"Zara?"

She startles awake, her brown eyes wild. "Who is it? What do you want?"

"It's me, Cate," I say softly. "Anna's Cate? And look—I've brought Tess."

"Hello," Tess says, smiling bashfully. "I'm so glad to meet you."

Zara stands, turning to me accusingly. "She's just a child. Why would you let her come to a place like this? Anna wouldn't approve."

"I didn't *let* her do anything. She's got a mind of her own," I point out.

But the criticism stings. Would Mother approve of how I've handled things of late?

"I insisted on coming. I've read your book," Tess says. "Marianne gave it to us."

"My book?" Zara sinks back down into her chair, her belligerence draining away. "She saved it?"

"Yes. There are a few illegible parts because of the water damage. It rained before she could rescue it from the roof where you hid it." Tess fiddles with the black bow at her waist. "But I was able to read most of it."

"I thought it was lost." Zara's dark eyes brim with tears as she begins to rock. "I thought I was stuck here forever for *nothing*."

"You aren't. Not for nothing, and not forever." I perch on the edge of the narrow bed, setting the satchel down on the floor. Tess comes with me. "We're going to get you out of here. Soon, even. Wednesday night."

Zara shakes her head. There's a splash of tea on the collar of her white blouse. "No. That's impossible. Cora will never allow it. I'll die here."

I frown. "Cora's dying."

Zara's bony hand flies to her lips. "Cora?" she repeats, struggling to focus on me.

"Cate," Tess chides, knocking her shoulder into mine, "you shouldn't be so blunt."

"I've suffered worse." Zara rocks faster. "You truly think you can get us out of here?"

"I've got to. You're all sitting ducks if I don't." I explain what Inez means to do.

"I told you, didn't I?" Zara slams her palms onto the arms of her chair with a sharp cracking sound. "I told you she'd stand back and let us all be killed if it suited her purposes!"

"Yes, well." My eyes dart toward the door, hoping the nurse with the strawberry birthmark is so involved in her knitting that she won't investigate the noise. "Unfortunately, you were right. I was hoping you'd help us spread the word to the other patients—especially the other witches. Will there be a chance to do that?"

"I can try." Zara stares at the peephole. "They haven't taken us out for our constitutionals because of the snow, but perhaps tomorrow—or while I'm in line to use the water closet. I don't know who are witches and who aren't, though. Not for certain. We don't dare talk about magic here."

Hopefully, Finn's found the Harwood records at the Archives, then.

"That's all right," I say. "We're going to get everyone out, witches or no. Don't say it will be Wednesday. Just tell them we'll pull the fire bell, and that will be the signal that we're here and they should get ready to leave."

Mei had come up with the idea for sounding the alarm this morning while we were pounding roses into a powder with a mortar and pestle. She was here once when a new patient got hold of a nurse's matches and set her bed on fire.

"I can try, but half of them won't remember. The laudanum plays strange tricks on the memory." Zara lowers her voice to a husky whisper. "I've been here long enough to grow used to the dosage. I play at being more afflicted than I am, but I still have some of my wits about me. On bad days, it takes a damnable amount of willpower not to beg for more. Can't blame the ones who do."

"I've got a plan for that, too." I've just finished explaining what Mei and I intend to do when Tess slumps backward onto the bed, eyelashes fluttering. Her head knocks into the cement wall.

"Tess? Tess!" I cry, gathering her limp weight into my arms.

"Shhh!" Zara warns, going to the door and peering out.

"Tess?" I give her a little shake. Of all times for her to have a vision. I've never seen one take hold of her so strongly.

Tess opens her eyes, staring at me groggily. Her breath catches. "Oh, Cate." She pulls away from me, both hands pressed to her mouth as though she's trying not to be sick. Closing her eyes, she takes several deep breaths. Her heart-shaped face—like Maura's, like Mother's—has gone pale.

Zara stands with her back to the door, blocking the peephole.

"Are you all right?" I ask, touching Tess's knee.

Tess nods, but her gray eyes look haunted. "It will work. I saw it. Sister Sophia was driving a wagon full of girls. I recognized some of them from the uncooperative ward. It was near dawn, I think; the sky was pink, and they were driving down a long carriageway toward a strange house. It was pink, too, with turrets and a widow's walk, and it was by the sea. I could hear the waves and the gulls; I could even smell the salt water. It was so peculiar." She puts a hand to her temple, and now I feel the red haze of her headache flaring.

"I—I know that house. I've been there." Zara's voice comes out a rasp, and she clears her throat. "There was a network of scholars who sympathized with the Daughters of Persephone. They came under the Brothers' suspicions often enough that they had need of safe houses. That was one of them."

"Could you tell us where it is?" I ask.

A grin stretches ghoulishly across Zara's thin face. "I can

do better than that. If you've got anything to write on, I'll draw you a map."

Tess produces a folded piece of paper and a stub of a pencil and gives them to Zara, her hands shaking.

"Let me fix your headache," I say, and she nods, leaning back against the wall, snuggling into her gray cloak. For a moment, the only sound in the room is the scratching of Zara's pencil as she marks out the map.

After Cora and my work in the infirmary, healing Tess's headache is nothing. I only feel a moment's dizziness. I'm more worried about her. She gives a little sigh when her headache disappears, but her face is still pinched with worry. If she saw our success, why is she so upset? The existence of a possible safe house is a boon; we can only hide a few girls in the convent, and I've been fretting about what will happen to the others after they leave Harwood.

Thank the Lord her vision came upon her now and not fifteen minutes ago. We would have been in the middle of the uncooperative ward, with dozens of witnesses. She's in no state to cast spells, and my mind-magic alone wouldn't have been enough.

Bringing her here was mad.

"Here." Zara hands us the map. Her pupils are normal now; the shock seems to have focused her. "It's a full night's drive, but it's the closest of the three safe houses we had. A married couple ran the place—John and Helen Grayson. And there was a password. It may have changed, but it used to be *corruptio optimi pessima.*"

"The corruption of the best is the worst," Tess translates.

Zara nods. She's gazing at Tess with fascination, as though she's an angel come to earth. "You—*you're* the oracle." She ducks her head and gives a shy little laugh. "I—oh, I've so many questions for you. I hoped that someday—I've never spoken with an oracle who wasn't touched by madness."

Tess bites her lip. "Were they all mad?"

"Brenna, and Thomasina before her. I don't know how Marcela might have turned out; she only lived to twenty-five." Tess flinches, and Zara puts out a hand toward her. "I'm sorry. I don't mean to frighten—"

"No. I want to know *everything*. That's why I came." Tess tucks her feet under her on the bed, then smooths her pink skirts around her. "Your book was very helpful. I read it twice, when the visions first began. It made me feel less alone," she confides, and Zara's smile could melt the snow on the hillside.

Tess needs more mothering—more guidance—than I can provide.

"I know the Sisterhood has been awful to you, Zara," I begin, haltingly, my hands knotted together in my lap. "I would understand if you wanted to go to one of the safe houses or somewhere else entirely. But I would like it very much if you'd come back to the convent with us. You'd be a great help to Tess—and to me."

Next to me, Tess is perfectly still, as though she's holding her breath.

Zara looks at me for a long moment, her dark eyes

searching. Then her hand goes to the gold locket at her throat. "You're Anna's girls. If you can get me out of here, I'll come."

Tess bursts into tears and hurls herself at Zara.

"Thank you," I say fervently.

Zara opens her arms. "Thank *you,*" she says, in a voice choked with emotion. I think of how easily Tess expresses her affection—the way we hug and swat and pinch, braid each other's hair and tie each other's sashes—and I wonder how long it's been since Zara's had that, the simple comfort of human touch.

Zara smiles at me over Tess's shoulder. "You're strong girls. Clever. I wish Anna were here to see it. She would be proud."

"Would she?" I stare at the ugly cement wall. "Sometimes I think she'd want us as far away from all this as we could get. Mother hated her magic."

Zara shakes her head as Tess settles back next to me on the scratchy brown blanket. "Not always. Not when we were girls. We loved being witches then. But Anna used her magic in a way she regretted, and it soured her. She came to think of her gift as poison."

I clench my hands tighter to hide their trembling. Here, finally, may be my chance for answers. "What did the Sisters make her do?"

Zara hesitates, glancing out the window. There's nothing to see but gray sky and white snow and the farmer's red silo over the hill. "This was your mother's secret to tell, not mine."

"But she didn't tell it," I say, tapping my boot impatiently. "There's so much she never told us. I can't forget the way she looked at me when she realized I could do mind-magic. She was *horrified*."

Zara leans forward, patched elbows propped on sharp knees, like a puppet all made of right angles. "Not at you, Cate. She was ashamed of *herself*. The magic that broke your mother's heart wasn't something the Sisters made her do. It was something she chose."

Tess and I shift closer to each other on the bed.

"You should know that she loved your father very much," Zara begins. "I remember when they met—Brendan was just a poor classics student, but Anna didn't care. She was so happy. So eager to become a wife and mother and leave the convent behind. She was always a bit of a romantic."

I nod. I remember the way my parents laughed together, the way they walked through the gardens hand in hand when Mother was well enough. Before she died, Father could be downright merry.

"She never told him about the magic, though." It seems such a large omission. Too big a lie for a marriage to survive.

"That," Zara says, "is where you are wrong."

But Father doesn't know about our magic. He's never once indicated—and Mother's instructions were very clear: we were to keep the magic a secret from everyone, including Father. If he knew about her magic—

My faith in him is shaky at best, but he never would have betrayed her.

Which means *she*—

Tess arrives at the same conclusion, a second before me. She jumps to her feet. "She erased his memory, didn't she?"

Outrage floods through me. Why deprive us of a father who could protect us, who would know what we are and love us anyway?

"For his own safety, and for yours," Zara says softly. "He would have done anything for Anna. When I came under suspicion, she was worried she would be next—and that if she were arrested, Brendan would do something desperate to protect her. Then both of your parents would have been gone."

"They might as well be," I mutter. Father's always away on business, and even when he's home, he's not present in any way that matters.

"No. If you'd been orphaned, the Sisters would have taken you in, even if your powers hadn't manifested yet. Because of the prophecy, they might have separated you. That wasn't what your mother wanted. She wanted you to have a normal childhood, together, no matter what your destiny."

Destiny. The word sounds so grand, and yet it promises such a horrible fate. One of us will not live to see the twentieth century. One of us will murder another.

"She came to regret it—keeping your father from knowing you. From knowing *her.* Once she erased Brendan's memory, she had to keep up the pretense. She was afraid of what it would mean to him if he found out."

Oh, Lord. Ever since I became a witch, I've resented him, thought of him as someone to fool and scorn, instead of someone who would love and protect us. It's difficult to accept; I'm so accustomed to thinking of him as weak.

"I knew it," Tess cries, pearly teeth bared. "He has his faults, Lord knows—I share most of them. But Mother's reasons never made sense to me."

Tess was only nine when Mother died and Father's business trips began to get longer and longer. She used to mope when he left, fretting that he would be in a carriage accident, or robbed by highwaymen, or come down with influenza in the city with no one to look after him. She has always depended on him—*wanted* to depend on him—far more than Maura or me.

I stare at the scuffed wooden floor. It feels like treachery even to think it, much less say it, but I have to. For Tess. "I loved Mother, but I think she was wrong in this."

Tess nods. "Father said he'll come to New London for Christmas, to celebrate the feast with us. I want to tell him the truth. I *insist.*"

I look at Tess: her pointy chin set, her hands in loose fists by her sides, her entire stance prepared for an argument. She is not the sort to insist on much. She wants peace and quiet and libraries full of books, and the right to read them.

I stand up. "All right, then."

"He deserves to know us. *We* deserve for him to know us, and—wait. Did you agree with me?" She throws her arms around me, bumping her head right into my chin. "Really? You won't fight me on it?"

I extricate myself, massaging my chin. "Really, truly. I'll even help you tell him."

"Thank you. Oh, you're the very *best* sister." Tess hesitates, bouncing back onto the narrow bed. "Do you think he'll be very hurt that we've kept it a secret so long?"

I love that Tess does not doubt Father for a second. She has perfect faith in his ability to accept three witchy daughters; she's worried only for his feelings, not her own.

I tuck a strand of hair back up into my simple chignon. "I don't know. I hope he'll understand that we were following Mother's wishes. I wonder that she didn't tell him the truth when she knew she was dying."

The truth is, Mother kept loads of secrets. If Zara hadn't written me, who knows whether I would have ever looked for her diary. We could have been utterly oblivious to the prophecy, pawns in the Sisterhood's manipulations.

"She was wrong to do it, but she did it because she wanted to keep us safe. That should count for something. She wasn't perfect, but she loved us, Cate."

"She did her best," I admit. As will I. I promised her I'd look after Maura and Tess, and perhaps they're not children anymore, but that doesn't mean I'll ever stop wanting to keep them safe and happy. "Will you do me a favor in return, Tess? Will you stay here with Zara while I go take care of a few things?"

Zara's gone quiet, staring dreamily out the window. She

comes back to herself now, touching the locket again. "Where are you going?"

"Tess isn't the only oracle we know. I mean to pay the other one a visit, and see whether she can tell me anything useful."

CHAPTER
17

HEART HAMMERING, I SCURRY UP TO the south wing of the third floor, where Paul's floor plans showed *isolation—maximum security.* There's a nurse sitting on a stool just inside the door, a thickset woman with gray curls and a double chin, reading Scriptures by light of a candle.

"What are you doing, Sister?" she asks. "No one's to be in here."

I gather my magic and arrow in on the blue shadows beneath her eyes, the droop of her shoulders. *Sleep,* I compel her. *You're exhausted. Forget you saw me.*

In a moment, her head is propped against the plaster wall, her soft snores filling the empty hallway, her book open on her ample bosom.

I find that I am not overly troubled by performing mind-magic on her. Zara's confession about

Mother has lightened my conscience considerably. We've all got to do what we think best, when it comes down to it, and hope that those who love us won't judge us too harshly.

I pick up the nurse's candle and head down the hall, wet boots squeaking against the tile floor. The other wings are grim and depressing places, but this one is positively desolate. There are no windows and only two gas lamps, one at each end of the corridor. Two buckets squat in the middle of the hall, catching water from a leak in the roof.

I hear faint scuffling inside one room and peer in the narrow window. There's a girl pacing back and forth, her white blouse stark in the darkness. She runs to the door when she sees the light, and I recognize the wild features and blond hair of the tiny girl who tried to refuse her tea last week. She hisses, scratching at the door like a cat. The sound is strangely muted; I wonder why until I glimpse the walls, which look to be made of cloth. The girl yowls, and I back away hastily.

Brenna ought to be very nearby.

I squint into the next cell—empty. Across the hall, though, there is a name tag. Neat handwriting spells out *B. Elliott*. I suppose, unlike the other patients rotated in and out depending on their behavior, Brenna has taken up permanent residence in this isolated place.

I squint through the tiny window beneath Brenna's name. It's hard to see in the darkness, but I finally glimpse a figure hunched in the corner. The small room seems empty except for a mattress and a few blankets lying tangled on the floor. Even the window's been bricked over and covered in that pale cloth.

Agito, I think, and the pins of the lock slide open.

Brenna jumps at the sound. I tense, readying a silencing spell. But when I push open the door and slip inside, my candle casting wavering shadows, Brenna just stares at me with her eerie blue eyes.

"Brenna, it's me. It's Cate Cahill, come to visit you."

"You look like one of the crows," Brenna says, pressing back against the soft wall. Her white blouse is buttoned crooked, and her coarse-looking brown skirt pools around her bare feet. "Did they send you to break me again?"

"No. No, that was—" How do I tell her that ruining her mind was an accident? "I'm so sorry you're broken, Brenna. I wish I could help."

"You can't. No one can. They're going to kill me." Brenna keens softly, rocking back and forth behind her knotted chestnut hair. "It's a very strange thing, knowing your own fate, Cate. Oh. Fate. Cate. That rhymes." She giggles.

"Er, yes." I'm whispering, though no one can possibly hear us. "Do you—Brenna, everything you see, does it all come true? Always?"

Brenna nods. "Oh, yes. I don't make it happen. You understand that." She rushes at me, grasping at my cloak. She's gotten even thinner in the month since she came here. She looks half starved, and there is a bruise shadowing one of her cheeks. "You do understand, don't you? Please. I tried. I tried with Jack, and with Grandfather, but no one believes me. They never listen."

"I understand." I reach out to pat her shoulder, and she

jumps, frightening both of us. I fight the urge to recoil. She's only a sad, broken girl. I take a deep breath, steeling myself. "Have you seen anything about my future?"

"Ah, that's why you've come." Brenna buries her head in her bony fingers. One blue eye peeks out at me from a gap. "I have."

"Will you tell me? I'd like to know."

Brenna shakes her head, her snarled hair lashing against me. "No, I don't think you would."

I swallow hard. "Please."

"Ask the little one downstairs. She knows," Brenna says. "She wants to change it."

Fear turns my legs to jelly. Does Brenna know that Tess is the oracle? Can she sense her, somehow?

"Who do you mean?" I demand.

"The other one. The little oracle." Brenna frowns, combing her tangled hair with her fingers. "I don't want them to have her. I don't see—why is she here? We *mustn't* let them have her. If they knew about her, they'd keep her here and make her tell all her secrets. I'm lonely, but not so lonely I'd wish that for the little one."

"You mustn't tell them, Brenna. They mustn't find out about her."

"No. Not from me. I'll lock it up and throw away the key." Brenna giggles, mimes turning a key in front of her mouth and throwing it over her shoulder.

It is hardly reassuring to have one's secrets kept by a madwoman.

"I don't want them to keep you here, either. What if—

314

what if I took you away?" I whisper, coming closer. "What if I took you somewhere safe? You and me and the little oracle. Rory's there, too."

Brenna puts her face right up against mine. "Rory? Uncle Jack's Rory?"

"Yes. We'd look after you. You'd be safe."

She wrinkles her brow, as if she can't quite understand that, and turns away, running her hand over the cloth walls. "They'll still kill me, in the end. But—yes. I think I would like to see Rory again."

"I'll come back for you soon. Just a few more days. You mustn't tell anyone that, either."

"I should like to meet the little one," Brenna muses. "She's not broken, like me. Not yet."

A shiver of fear works its way down my spine. "No. I'll protect her."

Brenna shakes her head. "You can't protect them both, Cate. That's *your* fate."

What does she mean? That someday, I'll have to choose between Maura and Tess? I want to ask, but I'm afraid the answers might break me.

I back away until the doorknob jabs into my hip. "I have to go. I'll come back for you, Brenna. I promise."

The look in Brenna's blue eyes hurts my heart—as though she is very used to people promising her things and not following through. She nods behind her curtain of snarled hair. "Good-bye, Cate."

Lord, I hope I can keep my word. Brenna is sick and sad, and she deserves better than this. They all do.

Out in the hallway, I droop against the wall like a wilted sunflower. The nurse snores, and water from the leaky roof plinks into the two tin pails.

I don't want to admit the truth, even to myself. I don't want to be the kind of girl who would consider such a possibility, who could weigh one life against another so callously. I will not let leading the Sisterhood turn me into Inez, or even Cora. I will stay true to myself.

But the facts present themselves on an endless loop in my head.

Brenna knows about Tess.

Brenna is mad. She can't be expected to keep secrets indefinitely.

Tess isn't just my little sister anymore. She's the oracle who could win this war for us.

Which means—

If I can't break Brenna out of here, I'm going to have to kill her.

I arrive at the infirmary doors at half past three, just as we agreed. I peek inside. Sister Sophia is speaking with the two nurses; her job is to keep them occupied. Addie sits beside the same coughing girl as last week. The skeletal old woman is gone, her bed empty, and I wonder whether she died. The mother I healed is missing, too—moved upstairs, I hope, and not into the mass grave Zara described. I vow to myself that none of these women will end up there.

Mei catches my eye and hurries out. "Ready?"

I nod, and we walk down the empty hallway. To our left is the kitchen. It smells sweet and sour, rotten meat mixed with fresh-baked bread, and I hold my breath until we are well past the door. I hear the clang of metal as someone washes pots and pans. A high, pretty voice rises in one of the old songs and then abruptly cuts off.

Heels clip toward the door, and Mei and I turn, making for the infirmary. We pause as a scullery maid storms out of the kitchen, towing a bedraggled brunette in her wake. The girl's face is flushed from the steam, her hair limp, and she still wears a wet white apron tied around her waist.

"How many times have I got to tell you, Livvy? No singing!" the scullery maid lectures. "Now I've got to step away from my tea just to escort you back to your room!"

"I'm sorry. It just popped out, on accident," Livvy says. When her brown eyes meet mine, I expect hers to drop—but instead she stares back curiously. "Good day, Sisters."

"Come along, girl, I haven't got all day," the maid grumbles.

We wait until they've pushed through the doors at the opposite end of the hall, Livvy still gawking over her shoulder at us while the maid drags her along by the wrist. Mei and I hurry past the kitchen to the locked storage room beyond.

"Cough if anyone comes. I'll try and be quick about it," I promise. The lock clicks open at my command, and I slip inside.

Blast. It's so dark I can barely see my hand in front of me. I pull out the extra candle and two matches I liberated from the sleeping nurse upstairs. My hand shakes so much that the first match burns down to my fingers, and I've got to blow it out before I can light the candle.

On the second try, the candle catches. I'm in a small room with stone walls and a dirt floor. Moisture drips along the cracks between floor and wall. In the corner, something dark scurries down into a privy hole. This must have once been a cell.

I scan the wooden shelves. On the bottom are some surgical implements: a large saw, a few knives, and some wickedly sharp scalpels. I imagine they're locked up in here to prevent the patients from turning them on the nurses—or the nurses from fencing them. Small brown bottles marked CHLOROFORM rest on a higher shelf. Bottles of whiskey and sherry line the lower shelves, along with small bottles marked OPIUM POWDER, big sacks of sugar, and tins of cinnamon: all the ingredients for the laudanum mixture.

One by one, I open the bottles and dump the opium powder down into the privy hole, thankful for its existence even as I shiver at the sound of claws scrabbling far below. I set the satchel onto a low shelf and carefully unwrap the white linen. Inside are the bottles filled with Sister Sophia's concoction.

"Cate," Mei says from outside the door. "Everything all right?"

"Just another minute!" I mutter.

I pour Sophia's mixture into each of the bottles. When I'm finished, I restopper all of them and put them back. I try to mask the rose scent and re-create the bitter smell of the opium with a glamour. With luck the matron or cook or whoever mixes the laudanum for the girls' tea won't taste it herself.

In three swift movements, I shove Sophia's empty bottles back into their linen nest, pull the satchel onto my shoulder, and blow out the candle.

Mei is pacing outside the door. I almost collide with her. Her nose is red from the cold, and her hands are shoved into her fur muff.

"Oh, thank heavens," she says, just as the door at the opposite end of the hall begins to open.

I drag her across the hallway in one giant leap, pushing through the billowing white sheet that hangs over the construction entrance. We huddle together in the cold of the courtyard, our boots sinking into a snowdrift. Above us, wooden beams sketch out the roof of the covered walkway that will lead to the new laundries. Head cocked, I listen to the maid's boots clomp down the hall and the kitchen door swing shut.

"That was close," Mei whispers, her breath warm on my ear.

I peek around the sheet to find the hallway empty again. "Tell Sister Sophia we're ready to leave. I'll fetch Tess."

A few moments later, I push into Zara's room, keeping one foot wedged behind me in the doorway. Tess is still sitting on the bed, her knees touching Zara's, their curly heads bent close together.

"Time to go," I announce.

"Already?" Tess's eyes are rimmed in red as though she's been crying.

It seems an age instead of only two hours since we arrived. Personally, I cannot leave the place soon enough. "Did you have a good talk?" What has Zara said to upset her?

"Oh, yes." Tess holds up two folded pieces of paper, which she quickly transforms into a pair of hairpins. "Zara drew us maps to all *three* safe houses and gave me the passwords."

"That's brilliant." I give Zara a quick smile. "Come on, Tess. We mustn't keep the others waiting. You'll have all the time in the world soon."

Tess throws her arms around Zara's neck, squeezing her tight. "I am very glad I got to meet you."

"Good-bye, Tess. Thank you. For everything," Zara says, patting her back. There are tears in her brown eyes, too. "I'll see you soon, Cate."

I shiver into my cloak. Between Mother's secrets, Brenna's creepy chatter, and sneaking into the storage room, it's already been a very long, fraught day. And the most dangerous part is yet to come.

"Cate? Are you awake?" Rilla whispers across our moonlit bedroom later that night.

There's no point in lying to her; I've been tossing and turning for the last hour, waiting impatiently for my meeting with Finn. "Yes. I'm sorry if I'm keeping you up."

I can see Rilla prop herself up on her elbows. "It's all right. Are you sneaking out again?" She hesitates. "I noticed you missing the other night, but I didn't say anything to anyone this time. I didn't want to get you in any trouble. But I do worry. It's not safe for you to be wandering around alone at night."

"I haven't been alone." It's past time I told her the truth. I lean over and light the candle on the dressing table. "I'm sorry for worrying you. I've been meeting someone. My beau—the one Alice mentioned in class the other day? His name's Finn."

Rilla sits against her brass headboard, pert nose wrinkling as she yawns, looking for all the world like a sleepy kitten. "But—I thought Alice said he was a Brother? And that he jilted you?"

I sit cross-legged, wrapping my soft blue quilt around my shoulders. "We were engaged before the Sisterhood forced me to come here. I suppose I jilted *him*, really, though I never wanted to. He's amazing, Rilla. He knows I'm a witch; he knows everything, and joined the Brotherhood to protect me." I give her an impulsive grin. "I wish you could meet him."

"Me, too." Rilla grins back, scratching her nose with one gloved hand. Alice has been tormenting her about how "common" freckles are, so she's been trying to lighten them with lemon juice, and she's taken to wearing gloves and hand cream to bed every night. "So you've been meeting for secret midnight rendezvous? How scandalous!"

"Well, there's more than just kissing involved," I point out, blushing. "Tonight we're going to sneak into the Archives and look at the records of the girls at Harwood."

I explain the Harwood plan to her, and Rilla listens. For all her chatter and bounce, she can be very attentive. "That sounds brilliant, Cate," she says when I'm finished. "Only—you said yourself that Sister Sophia does her nursing missions in the afternoons, not the evenings. What if the matron gets suspicious, or the guard won't let you inside in the first place?"

I frown. "Elena and I will compel them."

"It seems like an unnecessary risk." Rilla shivers, pulling her yellow quilt up to her chin. "Why don't you glamour yourselves as Brothers? Then the first hint that something is wrong will be when you pull the alarm. It would be a cinch to pull off. Far easier than mind-magic."

"Not for me," I sigh. Outside, the wind whistles through the bare trees. "I can't seem to get the hang of it."

Rilla squints at me through the shadows. "I could manage glamours for both of us. And they would only need to last until we've got the nurses locked up, right?"

"Right. But if something goes wrong, it will be awfully dangerous," I point out. I don't want her thinking this is one of her novels. "We *could* use a witch of your caliber, though. Are you sure?"

"Cate. As far as I'm concerned, we're not just roommates. You're my *sister.*" She gives me her sunny smile, but her hazel eyes are serious. "Now, tell me more about the marvelous Finn. How did you meet him?"

I laugh. "Well, I've known him forever, but I didn't really notice him until a few months ago, when we quite literally ran into each other in my garden. You see, Father hired him as our gardener . . ."

"You want to do *what?*" Finn yelps an hour later. His glasses are fogged from the steam of his breath, but I can imagine the disapproval in his eyes.

I shove through the wrought-iron gate that leads from the convent garden into the street behind it. "I suspect you heard me properly the first time."

"If I did, you're mad." He swipes a hand through his messy hair. "Why can't you just ask the girls if they're capable of mind-magic?"

"Because it's bound to be bedlam during the jailbreak. And who knows *what* they're aware of, what state they're in, after being drugged for such a long time? They may not trust us. Please don't argue with me on this." I lay my hand, covered in a black satin glove, on his arm.

He scuffs one heavy black boot through the snow. "Why can't I go and get the files for you?"

I frown at him. We're wasting precious time arguing. "You said there are hundreds of files. I'm not confident we can find the ones we want with both of us looking, much less just you."

"I read very fast," Finn says huffily.

"I'm certain you do." I roll my eyes at the snowy cobblestones. The last thing I want is to offend his scholarly pride. "But what if you're caught sneaking around Szymborska's office in the middle of the night with forbidden files? I doubt the guards would look very highly on that. I could compel them to forget. I can protect us."

Finn bends down and draws the pistol from his boot. "So can I."

"Not like that, you can't!" I bury my face in my hands, exasperated. "I'm not going to let you *shoot* someone just to prove how brave you are. I am going to the Archives tonight, whether you come with me or not. But I would very much appreciate your help."

"Fine." Finn sighs, setting off through the snow. "You're the most *infuriating* girl."

I grin, reaching for his hand. "You know, that's not even the first time today I've been called that."

"I don't doubt it." He squeezes my hand and then drops it. "We should be careful. Never know who might be up and about."

I squint at the gas streetlamp above us, and its flame wavers and goes out, plunging the street into shadows. Ahead of us, the next one extinguishes, and then the next. I grab Finn's hand. "Better?"

"Much," he says, voice low and admiring. He brushes his lips over mine. "Now, run through the plan for Wednesday night once more?"

I start, but the moment I get to *glamouring ourselves and the carriage,* Finn stops me. "I'll borrow Denisof's carriage. It will be easy enough while he's at the council meeting, and it will have the Brothers' seal, so that's one less illusion you have to worry about."

The city is quiet around us. No wagons rumble past at this late hour; the sidewalks are empty. Without the gas lamps, I can make out the stars in the night sky. "I can't let you steal a carriage for us. What if one of us crashes it, or—?"

"Borrow," Finn interrupts. "And I'll drive it myself, because I'm coming with you. The rest of you will have to play at being Brothers, but I'm the real thing." He gestures at his black cloak, his voice bitter.

I laugh to lighten his mood. "I'd try to dissuade you, but I suspect it'd be impossible. I'd never let *you* do something so mad on your own."

"Exactly," he says emphatically. "We're a team now. Where you go, I go."

"I suppose I can live with that." I grin, slipping a hand into my pocket and drawing out a small packet of herbs. "I have another task for you. You said Sean Brennan is a good man, and it turns out your judgment was right; he's been Sister Cora's spy on the Head Council for years now. Is there any chance you could engineer a meeting with him Wednesday morning? Fetch a cup of tea for him, perhaps? The herbs in here will make him sick, but only temporarily. Long enough that he'll have to miss the Head Council meeting."

"Brilliant." Finn takes the packet from me and tucks it in his own cloak pocket.

I run my thumb over his palm. "You're quite dashing in the role of spy, Mr. Belastra."

It feels terribly daring to hold his hand out in the open like this. We pass a cheese shop and a furrier's and two cafés, but everything in the market district is shuttered for the night; all the windows are dark. The city usually feels so alien to me, so big and noisy and foreboding, but tonight it feels intimate and abandoned and deceptively safe. Like it belongs just to us.

The National Archives are beautiful.

"It's like a temple," I breathe, holding my candle aloft. "A temple for books."

I've never seen anything like it. High above us, the vaulted wooden ceiling disappears into the shadows. A dozen trestle tables, piled high with books ready for cataloging, fill the center of the room. Bookshelves jammed with thousands more books line every wall. And a spiral staircase leads up to the balcony, which is filled with yet *more* rows of bookshelves. Crystal chandeliers catch the moonlight spilling in through the high arched windows.

"It's beautiful," I say. Beautiful doesn't feel like *enough*. There's something of the divine in this room, something that makes me go hushed and reverent. Standing here in this palace of books, I feel humbled, the same way I do when lightning flashes across the sky during an enormous, pounding thunderstorm.

Tess would love this beyond all reason. Bookstores are her church, and this is a cathedral.

"In other countries, they have libraries like this in all the cities," Finn says. "Anyone can borrow any book they like."

"I didn't know there *were* so many books," I confess, spinning around. I walk to the nearest shelf, lifting my candle to peer at them all.

Finn reaches out, fingers tripping over a row of dark spines. "They keep the ones sanctioned by the Brothers down here: translations of Scriptures, approved histories of New England, philosophical treatises, language texts, dictionaries, science and natural histories. But upstairs there's everything." He gives me a playful, wicked grin. "Everything they don't want us reading: mythology, plays, novels. Come, I want to show you something."

The guards just patrolled the main library; we waited until their lanterns passed to leave our hiding spot in the bushes outside. "Do we have time?" I ask.

"You'll want to see this," Finn promises.

I pick up my pink skirts and lead the way up the narrow, curving steps. I trip once, and Finn rights me, his hands gentle on my waist. His lips brush my neck, just above the pearl buttons that run up the back of my bodice, and my heart races.

Upstairs, I set the flickering candle on a low, wheeled cart filled with books. I lean over the balcony, admiring the beautiful room below. Finn braces his hands on the railing on either side of me. His mouth weaves a warm trail down the side of my throat, across the bare shivery skin of my collarbone, to the pale arch of my shoulder. I lean back against him. My entire body suddenly feels flushed and full of wanting.

"Cate," he sighs, and I turn to face him.

I'm wearing the new winter gown Elena had made up for me—the one Tess saw us together in. He loops one finger through the pink satin sash at my waist and tugs me against him.

"You, in the moonlight, in this library, in this dress—" His eyes rove over me, from my frothy pink skirts embroidered with dark pink roses, past the swell of my breasts, up to the creamy skin of my neck. My breath comes fast as his gaze lingers on my lips. He's barely touching me, but it feels as though he's already undressed me with his eyes.

"It's the most beautiful thing. Like a dream." His voice is hoarse and full of wonder.

"Then it's my dream, too," I confess as I claim his lips with mine.

It's a long, slow delight of a kiss. We melt into each other, soft pink chiffon and gray cotton and hands and lips and— oh, I could stay here like this until the sun came up. I could stay here like this forever.

When we finally part, I lay my head on his shoulder, my arms still twined around his waist. My mouth is a little swollen, chin tender from the sandpaper brush of his stubble, and my hair is falling down around my shoulders.

Finn clears his throat. "This isn't actually what I brought you up here for," he says, though he doesn't look displeased by the delay. He takes my hand, leading me across the balcony, heading right for a particular shelf, and hands me a book.

"*Arabella, Brave and True!*" I beam up at him, taking the novel carefully in both hands. The red cover is cracking, the pages yellowed and ripped. "This looks old."

"A first edition, printed in 1821." He gently opens the cover, pointing to a spidery swoop of handwriting on the title page. "Look, she signed her name."

"Who, Arabella?" I joke, bringing the page closer. Beneath the printed letters that read CARTER A. JENNING, the signature spells out clearly: *Catherine Amelia Jenning.*

I gasp, tracing the imprint of her pen.

"A woman, and a Catherine, no less." Finn's crooked smile is enormous.

"This is *marvelous.*" I wrap my free arm around him, hugging him tight. "Thank you for showing me."

"I'm glad you like it. Just think—someday, if the Sisterhood wins this war—we could make this into a proper library." Finn's voice is hushed. "We could have more of all the forbidden books printed to replace the ones the Brothers burnt. Then we could invite people in to borrow them and take them home and read them, the way they're meant to be read, without fear."

I slide the book reluctantly back onto its shelf. "I wish I could bring Tess here."

"Perhaps someday you will." Finn glances at his pocket watch and picks up the candle from the traveling cart. "We should hurry. I expect they'll be coming back through soon."

"And you know where the files are?" The Archives are much larger than I'd imagined.

"In a locked cabinet in Brother Szymborska's office. I saw them and filched the key yesterday while paying a brief call. Spilled a mug of tea on him, and in the hurry to clean it up— well, I daresay he's got a dozen keys on that ring, at least. He hasn't missed this one yet," Finn says. He looks so proud of his derring-do that I won't tell him I could have unlocked the cabinet without a key.

At the end of the balcony, a small door leads to a hallway lined with offices. Finn enters the last office on the right, which is dominated by a heavy desk and a row of matching wooden cabinets. Only one has a brass lock. He fits it with a small, tarnished skeleton key.

"Here we are," he announces, rummaging through the towering stack of papers. "Right on top, there's a file on Brenna Elliott." He places it on top of the desk and flips it open. "Predictions she's made so far, reports on her erratic behavior from the nurses. Looks like they sent someone to

Chatham last week to speak with her parents and the council about her history. Interviewed Ishida as well. He didn't mention that to me."

I grab a sheaf of paper and a fountain pen from Szymborska's desk and shove them at Finn. "Here. Write down any of her predictions that seem useful."

Finn nods, peering into the drawer again. "Looks like the Harwood files are alphabetical, but there are a few on top marked High Security. Those might be what you're looking for."

I glance out through the parted red damask curtains. The moon is lower in the sky, glinting off the white marble spire of Richmond Cathedral. Down the street, I can spot the imposing gray stone of the National Council building. How much time has passed since we left the convent? The walk itself took at least half an hour.

The first dozen files are for girls who have tried to escape by climbing the fence or stealing away in supply wagons. Two summers ago, a woman stole the matron's pistol and shot a nurse. Last year, a sixteen-year-old girl named Parvati Kapoor tried to strangle a visiting Brother Cabot with his own cravat, and when that failed, she tried to compel him to blind himself with the letter opener in the matron's desk. He came to with the instrument pointed at his own eye.

This girl seems like a good candidate for the Sisterhood, mind-magic or no.

"I've written them all down. Eleven prophecies since they started watching Brenna," Finn says, and I realize she's roughly on par with Tess. I hand him a stack of folios.

We make frustratingly slow progress. There are dozens of girls sentenced to Harwood for ridiculous reasons, like refusing to marry old men the Brothers betrothed them to or being caught in compromising positions with men who subsequently refused to marry *them*. There's a girl named Clementine who was arrested six months ago for turning her sister's hair blue, and the file says a silencing spell intended for the sister backfired on her, so she hasn't spoken since before her trial.

While I feel compassion for these girls—and loads of curiosity about some of them, like Clementine—I'm looking for clear evidence of mind-magic. My frustration grows as I flip through the files, nearing the section at the bottom marked DECEASED. The records are hardly surefire proof of a witch's capabilities. Zara, for instance, was never accused of compulsion, though I know she's capable of it; her crime was possessing books on witchery.

Eventually I find one more candidate: Olivia Price, accused of bewitching a member of the Brotherhood who tried to arrest her for possessing banned musical instruments and materials. This must be the brunette Mei and I ran into this afternoon, Livvy—the one who was reprimanded for singing in the kitchen.

Out the window, the sky is fading from inky, star-studded black to indigo. I'm about to give up when Finn crows beneath his breath.

"Did you find something?"

"Cordelia Alexander," he announces, waving a file triumphantly.

"What was she accused of?"

He sobers. "Irreparably damaging her older brother's mind. She was only twelve when it happened. She was playing dress-up with her mother's diamonds and lost one, and she tried to compel him not to tell. Her parents turned her in."

"Good Lord." I clap a hand over my mouth. "How awful."

Finn cocks his head. "Shh," he says, blowing out the candle. "Someone's coming."

I hear jingling keys and loud male voices. Finn bends down, and I think he's picking up the folios from the desk, but he reaches for his boot instead.

"What are you doing?" I hiss, pushing the cabinet closed.

"The pistol," he whispers.

"They have guns, too, I imagine. No one's getting shot if I can help it. Get under the desk." I snatch up the candle in one hand and the pile of folios in the other. "Perhaps they'll just peek in—if not, I can take care of them."

Finn shoves the leather chair aside and crawls beneath the desk. I squeeze in next to him, curling myself as small as possible.

"I think it was this one where I saw the light," one voice growls as footsteps hesitate outside.

Stupid. I should have drawn the curtains first thing.

"It was probably just the moon off the glass," another guard argues.

"Best check to be sure," the first insists. Light slides across the room as the door creaks open, and I hold my breath, heart hammering.

There are only two of them. Should I compel them to leave now?

Maura's right. My caution is going to get someone hurt.

Finn's hand finds mine in the darkness.

"Nothing. I told you." The second man chuckles. "Who'd be wandering around here in the dead of night? Even old Szymborska's not that mad about his books."

The door creaks closed, leaving us in silence and shadows.

We wait a long moment, listening as the footsteps recede back down the hall, and then I unfold myself and climb out. Finn follows, stretching his lanky body.

"That was a near miss. I was ready to do something utterly rash. Thank the Lord for your cool head," he says, looking at me admiringly. But I'm shaken by the close call.

"Do you really believe this will work?" I blurt. "Do you believe we can save them?"

Finn doesn't need to ask what I mean. He leans forward, his lips brushing mine. Behind his spectacles, his brown eyes are very serious. "I believe in *you*, Cate Cahill, and in us together. I'm here to help whenever you need me. No matter how mad the scheme, or what the risk. Don't you know that by now?"

CHAPTER
18

TUESDAY PASSES IN A BLUR. I LOSE focus and shatter a plate in animations, I can't maintain my glamours for more than two minutes together in illusions, and I mistake my *maxilla* for my *patella* in anatomy. I'm exhausted; I crept back into the convent at dawn and slept for all of two hours before breakfast, and I can't think of anything but the Harwood mutiny. The freedom of hundreds of girls seems to hinge on all the details falling perfectly into place. I pray that Inez is busy enough with her own scheme that she won't try to interfere with ours.

I've obtained promises of help from Sophia, Mei, Rory, and Rilla, and Elena's been spreading the word to everyone she thinks will support us. During afternoon tea, she stands next to the sideboard in a shimmering green silk gown that glows against her brown skin, and she pulls teachers and students aside to whisper with them.

I'm heading upstairs to take a nap when she catches at my sleeve. "I think we ought to have a meeting tonight for everyone who wants to help, so they all understand what's involved. Honestly, though, I think we'll be turning girls away for lack of transportation. We want to leave as much room as we can for the actual patients."

"That many girls have expressed interest?" I gasp, looking down into her pretty face.

"Everyone I approached." Elena picks up a cranberry scone from the platter. "Harwood's the specter that's been hanging over all our heads, Cate. The notion that we could rescue the girls who've been unlucky enough to land there— it's lit a match under everyone. Made us all feel hopeful again. And with Cora on her deathbed and the Brothers arresting all those girls, that's what everyone needs most right now. Truth be told, as your former governess, I'm—rather proud of you."

My gaze falls on Maura, sitting across the room on the pink love seat with Alice. Her blue eyes meet mine and narrow to a glare. "Not everyone's so delighted with me," I say, tilting my head in Maura's direction.

Elena turns, flushing scarlet as her gaze collides with Maura's. She turns back to me hastily. "Well, we expected that, didn't we?"

I did. I just didn't know it would hurt so much, having Maura here in the same room, not speaking to me. She's been avoiding Tess and me ever since our fight by the river. I daresay seeing me whispering with Elena hasn't helped matters. But Elena's become a powerful ally, and I can't give her up just to soothe Maura's temper.

She'll get over it, won't she? She's got to.

When Tess and I enter Elena's room just as the clock downstairs strikes eleven, I'm shocked.

The room is *packed*. Girls sit elbow to elbow on Elena's bed, rumpling her pink duvet, and sprawl across the wooden floor. Three governesses lounge on the yellow settee. Sister Sophia sits on the padded bench at Elena's dressing table, flanked by skinny Sister Edith, the art teacher, and shocking Sister Mélisande, who teaches French and wears trousers. As I take neither class, I hardly know either of them; I didn't expect to find them here. There are surprises among the convent girls, too. Eugenia and Maud both sit next to Vi on the bed.

All my friends are here: Rory and Rilla and Daisy, Mei and Addie and Pearl, Lucy and Rebekah. Tess squeezes my hand and joins the younger girls on the floor.

Elena comes to stand next to me. The convent girls are all dressed in their nightgowns, including me, but Elena still wears her pretty green frock. She claps her hands together. "Good evening," she says, and everyone stops chattering and stares at us.

Perspiration pools at the base of my neck, beneath my hair, and I don't know what to do with my hands. My ivory nightgown hasn't got pockets, so I clasp them behind my back.

"Thank you all for coming," Elena says. Though it's late, none of the girls look the least bit sleepy. "I've spoken to many of you over the last few days, but I just want to say this again now, here, in front of everyone. I believe freeing the Harwood patients is the right thing to do at this time. But we'll need your help tomorrow to carry it off. Cate, can you explain?"

I tell my audience the scheme we've worked out. Elena, Rory, Rilla and I will go first, in Finn's carriage, disguised as a contingent of Brothers. We need several volunteers to follow us in the Sisters' two carriages, free the patients from their locked rooms, and help guide them. We plan to split the prisoners into four groups: Brenna Elliott and known witches, who will accompany us back to the convent, and a wagon full of patients to be sent to each of Zara's three safe houses. Sophia saw two construction wagons in the courtyard at Harwood, and we intend to commandeer those. We still need one more wagon, plus volunteers to drive to the safe houses and stay long enough to see the patients settled.

"I'll drive one of the wagons," Sister Sophia offers, and my eyes meet Tess's. I'd be willing to bet Sophia will end up driving girls to the safe house by the ocean, just as Tess saw in her vision.

Maud raises her hand, and I nod at her to speak. She tosses her carroty hair. "Genie's father's got a wagon he uses to make deliveries," she says, elbowing her friend.

Eugenia scowls, tugging the cuffs of her blue nightgown down over her skinny wrists. "I'm not *stealing* from my father."

"We'll bring it back eventually," Maud argues.

337

"What if he loses customers because he misses deliveries?" Eugenia's voice is hoarse, as though she's getting a cold. "What if he's implicated in this somehow?"

"Come on, Genie, everyone's got to pitch in." Vi bounces on Elena's thick feather mattress. "I'll drive one of the carriages."

"You know how to drive a carriage?" Maud gapes.

"My father's a coachman." Vi rolls her eyes. "Course I do."

"You intend to help *all* the girls, not just the witches?" Sister Mélisande asks.

"Of course. We won't leave anyone behind," I assure her.

She tosses her short mop of dark hair. "Then I will help, too. I will drive another of the wagons."

"And we'll take the third together," two of the governesses offer.

Lucy Wheeler waves her hand wildly from her spot next to the radiator. "Bekah and I want to help!"

I smile down at them. "You're very brave to offer. I thank you for it. But I think perhaps we ought to limit this mission to girls fourteen and up. It's going to be very dangerous."

Lucy's brown eyes go wide. "But my sister—I've got to see her—"

"You will. We'll bring Grace here," I tell her.

Lucy claps a hand to her heart. "Here? But she's not a witch!"

"She's your sister. After what she's been through, she belongs here, with you," I say firmly. "Does anyone besides Lucy and Rory have relatives in Harwood? Maud, your cousin is there, right? Caroline, was it?"

"Yes." Maud grins.

It turns out that Sister Edith's niece is a patient there, too, and we agree to bring her and Caroline back with us.

"What about me? I can come, can't I?" Tess frowns up at me from her spot on the flowered rug.

"You are twelve, aren't you?" I point out. I've been avoiding this for days.

Her thin face flushes as she toys with the end of one blond braid. "Yes, but—"

"No. You're a brilliant witch—and so are you, Lucy, and you, Rebekah—and I daresay you'd all be an asset, and I shall regret not having you there. But I won't risk your safety," I explain. "Please don't fight me on this."

"I think Cate is right," Sister Sophia says gently.

"We need to fit into three carriages coming back," Elena decides. "Fifteen seems like the right number. What do you think, Cate?"

"Er—yes," I agree, still flabbergasted that she's asking for my approval. "We'll need a pair to cover each wing of the asylum, plus several waiting in the front hall to guide the patients. I imagine some of them will just run, and I can't blame them—but we should remind them that the Brothers may hunt them down again if they go home." We don't want a repeat of our mistake with the Richmond Square prisoners.

"You'll need us. Pearl and I are more familiar with Harwood than anybody." Addie pokes her drooping spectacles up on her nose. Next to her, quiet Pearl bobs her head in agreement.

In the end, we have almost twice as many volunteers as

we need. We settle on Elena and the two governesses who offered to drive a wagon; Sisters Sophia and Edith and Mélisande; Rory, who will look after Brenna; Rilla, who's brilliant with illusions; Addie and Pearl and Mei, who are all familiar with Harwood's layout; and Vi, Daisy, Maud, and me. Elena dismisses the rest of the girls, and the Harwood team stays to discuss details and divvy up our posts.

I nab Tess by the elbow. "You understand, don't you?"

She nods. "I didn't think you'd let me go, honestly. I hoped I was wrong, but—"

"We still need your help. You've got to stay and tell us more about the safe houses."

Eugenia taps me on the shoulder. "May I speak to you for a minute, privately?" she asks.

"Of course." I assume she has some concern about commandeering her father's delivery wagon, and I can't say I blame her for it. I trail her out into the hall, and we watch as girls tiptoe back to their rooms, careful not to wake their sleeping neighbors. At the far end of the hall, the door to Sister Cora's rooms is shut tight. Sophia said she could go any moment now. I close my eyes and say a silent prayer that it will be quick and peaceful.

When the last girl disappears downstairs, Eugenia turns to me.

"Since when are you and Elena such bosom friends?" she hisses.

"I—what?"

Her mouth stretches like a storybook monster's, and I

back away. Eugenia's straight brown braids turn a vibrant red, her brown eyes become a piercing blue, and her spotty complexion turns into my sister's smooth skin.

"Maura." I stare at her, horrified, bumping against the green floral wallpaper. "What did you do with Eugenia?"

"Oh, Genie's fine." Maura waves a hand, unconcerned. "I did a freezing spell on her and shoved her in her armoire. I'll let her out in a few minutes. I'm glad I came to your stupid meeting and found out what you and Elena have been up to. Look at all those ninnies, just falling over themselves to impress you!"

"They're not trying to impress me; they're doing what's right," I point out.

"You're so sanctimonious, it's sickening." Maura crosses her arms over her ruffled blue nightgown. "I can't believe you're working with her. I thought you hated her!"

I bite my lip. "She cares about you, you know. She's sorry for hurting you."

Maura stares down at the wooden floorboards. "Not enough to be on my side in this."

"Two people can disagree and still care for each other," I point out.

"Like you and Tess care about me?" Maura shakes her head, red curls flying. "No. I'm alone in this. I ought to be used to it by now, I suppose; I'm *always* alone."

"That's not true," I snap, planting my hands on my hips. "Stop feeling sorry for yourself."

"You wouldn't understand. People just flock to you,"

Maura accuses, and I gape at her, remembering how many times I've jealously thought the exact same thing about *her*. "Is Finn involved in this?"

"He is," I say, warily. "Why? Looking for more information to blackmail me with?"

"You shouldn't let him. This is your fight, not his." Maura's blue eyes meet mine solemnly. "He shouldn't have any part of it."

"Well, he insisted, and I'm trying not to forbid people things these days. It never seems to turn out well." I give her a small smile. "Look, I know you're angry with Tess and me, but this is bigger than just us. These girls need our help. If you and Inez succeed tomorrow night, you don't know what the Brothers will do to them."

"Neither do you," Maura points out, fidgeting with the white lace at her sleeve.

"I know it'll be awful. The Brothers will make examples of them—torture them or kill them. I can't just stand by and let that happen." I look at her imploringly. Even now, part of me hopes that she'll see reason, that she'll join us instead of Inez. "Whatever the Brothers do to retaliate, it will be on your head, Maura. Yours and Inez's. Can you live with that?"

Maura stares at me. "It's their choice how they respond. If they resurrect the burnings, it will show people how awful they really are. The Brothers are our enemies, Cate. We can't work together. The sooner you realize that, the better off you'll be."

Harwood Asylum squats like a dark monster on the hillside, blotting out the stars. The barred windows of the upper levels are sinister and shadowy; only a few gas lamps glow in the front hall and the nurses' first-floor sitting room. Fear twists my stomach as the carriage sways up the snowy gravel drive to the guardhouse. Elena, Rilla, Rory, and I have not said a single word to one another since we left the convent. The snow muffles the horses' hooves; our tense silence is relieved only by soft creaking as they shift in their leather harnesses.

After an interminable wait, the guard calls out, voice sharp with authority, and Finn responds, low and calm and self-assured. Across from me, Elena's black boots tap out an incessant, impatient beat against the floorboards, and she leans forward as though poised to perform magic at a moment's notice. Rory bounces on the leather seat like a child. But Finn's new ring of office and the Brotherhood's seal on the carriage must carry weight even at this late hour. The next sound is the screech of the gates swinging open.

I am here of my own volition, and yet I cannot help the irrational fear that swamps me again, the nightmare vision of the gates clanging shut and trapping us inside.

The carriage stops halfway through. I open the door and lean out.

"What's the matter, sir?" the guard asks.

Leave the gate open. Don't stop anyone who tries to come or go, I command, and he sways back into the guardhouse with a shambling, drunken gait.

Our carriage rolls up the hill, coming to a halt outside the wide front doors. I jump to the ground, taking a moment to trace the hard new angles of my face and—strangest of all—

the brown whiskers covering my cheeks. Rilla's illusion is still in place.

The matron opens the door. This one is fat and jolly-looking, with blond sausage curls and red chipmunk cheeks. "Good evening, sirs," she says. "I'm Mrs. Harris, the night matron. Can I help you?"

"Yes, we'd like to—" My voice comes out high and effeminate, and I cough.

"We're here to carry out an inspection of the oracle. Covington's orders," Elena says, in a husky voice that matches her now-considerable girth.

"The oracle?" The matron's pale eyebrows shoot up to her hairline.

Finn steps forward. "Brother Robbins," he lies, bowing officiously. Elena's glamoured him, too, so that no one will be able to give a proper description of him. "Good evening, ma'am."

"I wasn't told to expect anyone, sir. It's very late. Most of our patients are abed by now."

I frown. I'd rather bluff our way in, if we can, and save the mind-magic for later. "We've been busy day and night with the annual meeting, but Covington wants us to take a look at her before we leave town. We've been trained in psychological disorders."

Finn steps forward, lowering his voice as if to shelter us from unpleasant truths. "I understand the Brothers who were here earlier lost their temper with the patient for being uncooperative."

Mrs. Harris gives Finn an uneasy look. "She's bad off. Begging your pardon, sir, but it seems harsh for men of the Lord to handle a woman that way."

I shiver, imagining Brenna bloodied and beaten. When Finn met us on the street behind the convent, he told me that she refused to cooperate today and had been punished accordingly. What have they done to her, for Mrs. Harris to risk speaking up against it?

"You forget yourself. That girl is a damned witch," Finn snaps, his voice harder than I have ever heard it. "She is a detriment and a danger to New England, and it is only by our *mercy* that—"

"Forgive me. I didn't mean to cast aspersions on your judgment, sir." The matron looks at him with fear in her pale eyes. Finn gestures to the ground, and she kneels before him, knees cracking as she settles on the cold stone steps.

Finn lays a hand on her frilly white cap. "Lord bless you and keep you this and all the days of your life."

I take a step back, horrified, at the Brothers' words coming out of his mouth.

Oh, he must loathe this. I loathe watching it. It's not him, not my Finn at all.

"Thanks be," she murmurs, head bowed.

"We clear our minds and open our hearts to the Lord."

The rest of us join in on the refrain: "We clear our minds and open our hearts to the Lord."

"Get up." Finn gives her a scornful look. "And do not doubt your betters again."

"Yes, sir. Please. Come in, sir." She ushers us inside. "Miss Elliott is on the third floor, in the isolation wing. There's a nurse outside her door."

Finn's boots ring out against the warped wooden floorboards as he strides across the empty front hall.

The matron ducks behind her desk. "Wait!" she calls out, and I freeze, terror coursing through my veins, certain she's seen through the entire charade and is pulling out her pistol.

She only holds up a candle. "Here, sir, take this. It'll be pitch-dark upstairs. Patients aren't permitted fire, you know. Can be downright eerie up there."

"Thank you." I take the candle, and the matron lights it for me.

We scurry up the shadowy stairs. When we step into the isolation wing, the night nurse is peering into Brenna's cell. She whirls on us when she hears our footsteps.

Her mind feels easy, pliant. I compel her to go help in the uncooperative ward, on the instructions of Mrs. Harris, and erase her memory of ever having seen us. She walks away from her post without a word of resistance. It's terribly simple, and I don't even feel exhausted afterward.

My magic has gotten much stronger since I've arrived in New London. This spell would have incapacitated me before, and now it's nothing.

The cell that held the little blond girl is empty now. I wonder if she's been sent back to the uncooperative ward.

"Make sure there aren't any other girls in this wing. I'll get Brenna and then we'll pull the alarm," I say. Rilla releases my illusion, and I use my magic to unlock Brenna's door and slip inside. She's curled up in her nest of blankets on the floor, wearing the same white blouse and brown skirt as before. But now one of her eyes is blackened, her lip cut and bloodied.

"You came back," she says, peering at me with her good eye.

"I said I would, didn't I? So here I am."

Brenna struggles to her feet. "I had a vision today, but I wouldn't tell." She holds her left arm close to her body, like a wounded bird.

"They hit you for it." I don't know why I'm surprised. It's what they did to Thomasina. It's what they would do to Tess.

"They said I was insubordinate." Brenna holds out her left hand, and I gasp when I see the way her pinky and ring fingers are bent at odd, unnatural angles.

"Rory's here. She'll take you downstairs in a bit, and Sister Sophia can heal you." I pause. "What you saw—did it have anything to do with my sisters? Or me?"

Brenna fidgets with her long, chestnut braid. "I told you before, remember? I remember. We were in the graveyard." She lowers her voice. "Sacrifice."

"Like leaving Finn?" I ask, hopefully. "That turned out all right."

"The worst sacrifices are yet to come. Three sacrifices. And—" Brenna cocks her head at me, the candlelight casting shadows over her wasted face. "You'll bring death."

To whom? I drop my eyes to the floor.

"I told you that you wouldn't like to know." Brenna eyes me sadly. "Is it time? We ought to go. The war is about to start."

I freeze in the midst of opening the door. "War?"

"It will start tonight," Brenna says.

My pulse races. I think of Tess, playing chess with her friends in the sitting room, and of Sister Gretchen, keeping vigil over the dying Cora. What if it's all gone wrong at the Head Council meeting, and Maura's been captured, and we've all been exposed?

No. I can't think about that. I have to see this through.

"We're going to ring the fire bell in a minute. Don't be scared—it's just to get all the nurses in one place. Rory will stay with you, and then you'll go get her sister. You remember Sachi?"

"Three sisters," Brenna muses. "One brings healing and death. One brings ruin. The strongest will bring peace, but it will require a sacrifice. That's what the prophecy says."

The hair on my nape rises at the word *death*. I cannot stop my limbs from trembling, my teeth from chattering.

I flee, spooked, without another word to Brenna. Rory swings in the door behind me, and I hear the cousins chattering, happy at their reunion.

In the hallway, I take deep breaths. I can do this. I only have to get them out, and then we will go home and face whatever comes next. There will be no murder and no sacrifice tonight.

Elena pulls the fire bell, which lets out a series of piercing clangs. The alarm runs on ancient ropes and pulleys throughout the asylum; soon we hear its echo from downstairs. Rilla recreates my glamour, and she and Finn and Elena and I hurry out into the hallway. The two uncooperative ward nurses and the isolation wing nurse are already halfway down the stairs, and I wonder what they would do if there were a real fire. Would they let the patients out or leave them here to burn? On the second-floor landing, Mrs. Harris and the rest of the nurses are all gathered.

"I'm so sorry to interrupt your examination, sir," she says to Finn, obviously having identified him as our leader. "We hope it's only a false alarm, but it wouldn't be the first time one of the girls got hold of matches and tried to burn the place down."

Elena slips her hand into mine, offering me her power. I take a deep breath. Ten subjects. Even together, can we manage so many? But this isn't the time for hesitation.

Follow us into the uncooperative ward, I command. *That's where the fire is.*

All ten of them turn and rush upstairs.

"Oh, dear," Mrs. Harris says, her double chins wagging. "Those girls would burn us all in our beds if we gave them half a chance. What have they done now?"

I sway going up the stairs, dizzy from the magic, and have to hang on to the railing for dear life. Finn notices and falls behind me, making sure I don't tumble back down, ready to catch me as always.

"I'm fine," I whisper, and he brushes a hand against the small of my back.

Mrs. Harris takes the brass key from around her neck and unlocks the door to the south wing. They all rush in and then stop abruptly, faced not with a cloud of smoke but with dozens of unusually alert prisoners stampeding toward the door, which Finn holds open.

"What are you doing? Shut the door, before they get out!" Mrs. Harris scolds Finn.

"That's what we want," Finn confesses. "They've been trapped here long enough."

"You're not real Brothers, are you?" one of the nurses demands, her dark eyes terrified.

"No." Elena turns to the patients. "Don't be frightened; we're witches, and we're here to help you escape. This is your chance."

"The witches are here! The witches have come for us!" the patients shout, pushing and shoving each other in their frenzied excitement.

Zara has obviously spread the word of our escape.

"Lord save us." One of the nurses kneels, while the rest form a befuddled huddle.

"Bless you. Thank you," some of the patients mumble, but most are understandably intent on escaping this room that has served as their cage. I grin as I spot little Sarah Mae skipping past. A few women still lie curled in their beds, but other patients help them up.

Elena rips the key from around Mrs. Harris's neck, breaking the chain.

"What are you doing?" Mrs. Harris yelps, her hand flying to her wrinkled neck.

"You won't be needing these anymore," Elena says, and

another key flies out of a nurse's pocket and into her waiting hand.

"It's your turn to be shut up in here now!" One of the patients shrieks, shoving a nurse to the ground as she passes. "We ought to set the whole place on fire!"

"No—no—don't let them have us," one of the nurses begs, scrambling for the door.

Finn blocks her way. "No one is setting anyone on fire, but you're staying in here."

"Don't worry. We're taking them with us." Elena turns to me. "Why don't you go make sure everything's going smoothly?"

Dozens of girls stream out the door and downstairs. Waiting my turn, I bump into the beautiful Indo girl I noticed on my first visit. *One of Brother Cabot's favorites,* the nurse said, and something clicks in my memory. Parvati Kapoor was accused of doing mind-magic on a Brother Cabot, trying to get him to blind himself with the matron's letter opener.

"Pardon me. Are you Miss Kapoor?" I ask.

Parvati nods, her brown eyes fearful. "Are you really a witch? Where are you taking us?"

"*I* am taking you." As Rilla comes out into the hall, she lets both of our Brotherly illusions fade, revealing us as a tiny brunette in orange brocade and a tall blond in a gray dress with a cornflower-blue sash. Parvati gawks at us. "We have a safe place in the city, where there are dozens of other witches. You can come with us if you like, or there will be wagons going to other safe houses."

Parvati smiles slowly. "I'd like to come with you, I think. I want to learn how to use my magic. How to protect myself."

I leave her with Rory and Brenna and Rilla and join the flood of girls downstairs. At the second-floor landing, I pass Mélisande, Vi, and Daisy fighting the current on their way up. I'm relieved to see that the other carriages have arrived safely.

"Sophia and some of the others are trying to organize girls at the front door. Some of the patients are just running off, though," Mélisande reports.

"That was bound to happen, I suppose. I can't blame them for not trusting anyone," I say, though I worry they'll only get recaptured. Vi breaks off to go into the south wing, and I follow her.

To my surprise, patients already fill the hallway. I spot Zara moving from door to door, letting the women out of their cells.

"Zara!" I call, and she rushes toward me. "How did you get out of your room?"

She grins in a way that transforms her angular face into beauty. "My magic's back."

We work together, opening the doors, while Vi starts at the opposite end. Most of the patients on this floor are older women who have proven themselves cooperative and who have been granted the "privilege" of working in the laundries or kitchens. Some, bent and gray-haired, sprint toward the door like girls half their age.

"Olivia," Zara says as she unlocks the room of the curious

brunette from the kitchen, "this is my goddaughter, the one I told you about. Cate, this is Livvy. She's a witch."

"Zara told me all about the Sisterhood," Livvy says. "She said I could come with you."

"Cate!" Mélisande lopes down the hall in her trousers, her boots clapping against the floorboards. "Elena says there's a nurse missing."

I bite my lip. I was counting on the fact that they'd all followed some sort of procedure for the fire bell, and we had them all locked up in the uncooperative ward. If one escapes—well, Harwood is desolate enough that she'd have to walk quite a ways to find help. But we were hoping that no one would notice anything amiss until tomorrow morning, when the day nurses report for work. By then all the patients will be far away.

"Is Elena sure?" I ask.

Mélisande nods. "We've got to try and find her."

Blast. "Did anyone check the matron's office? If I were trying to hide, I'd go down to the first floor—somewhere without patients running amok. Zara, can you help Vi finish up here?"

Zara shakes her head, black curls flying. "I'll come with you. Livvy, can you help manage this wing? See to it that everyone's out and help them all downstairs."

Livvy nods, and the three of us hurry down to the first floor. The front hall is bedlam. Edith is shouting out names, and half a dozen of the convent girls are trying to stop patients at the front door to give them instructions. As I watch, several women push right past them. In their haste to flee, some are none too gentle; Maud's already holding a handkerchief to her bloody nose. Brenna, Sachi, and Rory are standing with Parvati and a thinner, taller version of Lucy Wheeler who must be her sister Grace.

I spare a smile as I turn into the south wing. It's working.

Mélisande investigates the nurses' sitting room, but it's empty. Zara and I peer into the matron's office. Thinking of my own subterfuge, I'm careful to check beneath the desk. But the room is silent and still. Zara follows along at my elbow, so close she trips over my skirt once. We look into the dining hall and the water closet, but there's no one left.

"No one's here except the mice," Mélisande decides.

I catch only the smallest movement—a flutter of white out of the corner of my eye. The sheet hanging over the construction exit ripples, as if blown by a sudden gust of wind.

There's a loud crack, and Mélisande cries out and stumbles back.

The gun fires again.

Zara is so close she knocks into my elbow when the bullet pierces her.

Intransito, I think, and the nurse is frozen. She falls through the sheet, ripping it down around her like a child pretending to be a ghost. The gun clatters to the floor, and the nurse smashes down face-first with a thud. She's a tall woman with a red birthmark on her cheek—I've seen her before.

Mélisande pushes herself up, eyes scrunched in pain,

hand clamped over her shoulder. Scarlet seeps between her fingers.

But Zara—Zara is lying still at my feet. A red patch blooms over the stomach of her white blouse.

I kneel next to her. "Zara?"

"Cate." Her voice is threadbare, husky, as though it hurts to speak. "I'm sorry."

"Why should you be sorry? You didn't ask to get shot."

Zara presses one hand against her stomach. Blood bubbles up.

She reaches for the locket at her throat and grimaces. "I don't think I'll be coming back to the convent, Cate."

I shake my head. "Don't be silly. Of course you will. I'll heal you."

Zara's face twists in alarm, her eyes fastened on something behind me. She gives a hoarse cry. I twist around, nerves jangling, but it's only Finn.

"It's all right," I say. "He's with us."

"A—Brother?"

"A spy for the Sisterhood," I clarify as Finn kneels next to me. "Zara, this is Finn Belastra, my fiancé. Finn, this is my godmother."

Zara's lips quirk upward. "Marianne's boy."

"Yes, ma'am." Finn swears beneath his breath as he looks at Zara.

"And you'll look after Cate?"

He manages a crooked grin. "We look after each other."

"Good," Zara says emphatically, before a coughing fit

overtakes her. Finn takes a handkerchief from his pocket. It's white, embroidered with the letter *B*. He hands it to me; I pass it to Zara; she presses it to her mouth. Even in the flickering candlelight, I can see that it comes away stained with blood.

I turn to Finn, taking comfort from his presence.

"I'm going to heal her, but I'll need your help to carry her out of here," I explain. Over his shoulder, I can see Sophia helping Mélisande to her feet.

"What should we do with the nurse?" Finn asks, his face grim.

"Take her upstairs with the others. Tell Elena to erase her memory—but leave her frozen like that," I say, vengeful, as I look down at Zara. The hall smells coppery, like old pennies. Like blood.

I touch her hand, tentatively, and then flinch away as her pain bites through me. Zara is in agony. Like Sister Cora, she feels closer to death than life.

Can I do this? I may not be able to walk out myself afterward.

Zara raises her head, her voice barely audible. "I don't want you to heal me, Cate. You can't, and trying will only make you ill."

I frown. "How do you know what I'm capable of?"

"Tess," Zara whispers. "Her vision in my room. She saw this, too."

That's why she was so upset. Why she cried and hugged Zara when they said their good-byes, as if she'd never see her again.

She knew she wouldn't.

No. I shake my head so hard my hair flies loose from its braid. "I won't give up on you. I won't just *leave* you like this for the Brothers to find." It could take hours for her to lose consciousness. If they find her, they'll torture her for information. She has to know that.

"There's only one thing you can do for me, Cate." She covers my hand with her own, her golden skin sticky with blood. Her pain cuts through me, piercing.

"I don't understand," I confess, leaning down. My blond hair touches her cheek. Does she want us to take her to the Sisterhood? I don't think she would survive the jostling of the journey; I daresay it would be excruciating. "What can I do? Tell me."

"Healing and death. You can do both. Two sides of the same coin."

I yank my arm away. "No!"

"I'm dying anyway. Help me do it quickly, without suffering. Without them here to take pleasure in my pain. Let me have this last bit of dignity."

Is this what I would want, in her place?

I barely have to think about it. Yes. I wouldn't want to give the Brotherhood the satisfaction of seeing my death. I wouldn't want to linger, in pain.

I close my eyes to shut her out, but she won't let me. "I want to see Anna again. I'll tell her—what a brave girl you are," she wheezes.

You'll bring death.

The prophecies always come true.

I lean down low, resting my forehead against Zara's, letting her pain touch me, envelop me, until I can feel the full, excruciating extent of her injuries. I can feel her fluid-filled lungs shudder as she struggles to breathe, and the agony of the gunshot wound, and the steady, sluggish beat of her heart as it battles to keep beating.

Instead of pushing the darkness away, I welcome it, letting it cover us in a blanket of icy, enveloping black. I think of Zara at peace. Free from pain. Altogether free.

Her heart thumps twice more, then stops.

Without the noisy sound of her breath, the room is perfectly still.

I lean down, closing Zara's staring brown eyes.

I was the one to close Mother's eyes, too. They were very blue. Like Maura's.

I lift Zara's limp head, unclasping the locket from around her neck. The golden chain pools in my shaking hands.

A killer's hands, now.

Healing and death.

The prophecies are never false.

CHAPTER
19

I STUMBLE OUT INTO THE HALL. Patients are still flowing down the steps and out the doors, and Sister Edith and Maud are still directing them. Finn and Elena are waiting for me, leaning against the dirty plaster walls.

When Finn's kind brown eyes meet mine, I begin to cry.

"Zara's dead. I—I killed her."

"Cate." Finn reaches for me. "Her injuries were—severe. You couldn't save her, but that doesn't mean you killed her."

"No, I did. She asked me to." The aftermath hits me, and I slide down the wall. Elena shoves a tin pail at me, and I heave the contents of my stomach into it. Then I slump back against the cold wall, too ill to even be embarrassed. How can killing feel just like healing?

Finn and Elena hold a whispered argument that I barely hear. My mind is reeling because Zara is dead. Zara cannot study the oracles or tell us stories about our mother as a schoolgirl. She's gone, forever, and I did that.

Elena kneels next to me, her pink skirts puddling on the floor. "Cate, how much of your magic did you use up?"

"I don't know. I've never killed anyone before." I close my eyes to shut her out.

Elena grabs my chin. "Try to do magic. Try anything. Turn my dress red."

I try to summon up my magic, but it feels like a burnt-out match. It sparks, smokes, but doesn't catch. I shake my head. "I can't."

She stands and turns to Finn. "All right, you win. She's no use to anyone like this. Take her home."

Then Sachi is here, leaning down to me. It's strange to see her like this, without her gaudy dresses, in the ugly white blouse and rough brown skirt, her hair in one long black braid down her back. She must be cold. Why isn't she wearing the cloak we brought for her? I hold my aching head between both palms.

Rory leans down on my other side. She looks worried. I thought she'd be delighted to have Sachi free. "Sachi and I aren't coming back to the convent tonight. We're going to drive the wagon Mélisande was supposed to take. But we'll be back soon. Will you be all right?"

"Cate." Sachi snaps her fingers in front of my face, but it seems as though she's very far away, beyond a screen of black dots.

"She's going to faint," Brenna says, but it doesn't take an oracle to know that.

I hardly remember leaving the asylum.

Finn carried me, I think.

Now I am in the carriage, curled on the leather seat beneath an itchy woolen blanket, staring out at the rain blurring the streets of New London.

I cannot stop shaking. I cannot let go the feel of Zara's hot, dry skin, or the smell of blood on her breath, or the sight of her blind brown eyes staring at me.

The carriage stops before the convent. Finn ties the horses and comes around to help us down. Brenna shuns his arm, jumping to the carriage block and then splashing down onto the sidewalk like a child. She is free. At least I did that much.

Finn helps me down to the sidewalk and then wraps his arm around me. I'm shivering. I've been shivering since I touched Zara. I can't seem to stop.

The convent door bangs open, a rectangle of golden light piercing the darkness. Maura rushes headlong down the steps toward me. She hasn't bothered to put on her cloak; she's wearing a bright blue dress.

"We did it!" she crows. "All eleven of them who showed up. One man was sick and missed the meeting, but the rest don't even remember their own names."

Finn turns to her, his brown eyes fierce. "And you're *proud* of that?"

"Yes!" she cries, defiant. "I wouldn't expect *you* to understand."

"I understand that there's no going back from what you did tonight. They only want a reason to resurrect the burnings. Are you ready for that?" Finn demands.

"Yes," Maura snaps. "Cora is dead, and Inez is head of the Sisterhood now. We don't intend to work with the Brothers anymore. You should go."

"The hell I will." His voice is harsh, and his grip on me is tight. "I love your sister, Maura, and that isn't going to change, so you and Inez may as well get used to having me around. I'm certainly not leaving her like this."

Maura peers at me. "What's the matter with her? I assumed everything was a success, since Brenna's here. Did something go wrong?"

"Zara's dead. I killed her." My voice comes out quiet. "The nurse shot her—she would have died anyway, eventually, but I—I made it go faster."

Maura steps closer. "You *what?*"

I reach into my pocket, fingering Zara's golden necklace, as I look to Finn. "I never wanted this. I thought healing was *good* magic. But Zara *asked* me to. It was doing her a kindness, wasn't it, to keep her from suffering? It wasn't wicked?"

"Of course not." The rain darkens his coppery hair and runs in rivulets down his glasses, but he doesn't raise his hood.

"I'll take care of her now," Maura says. "She should get inside, where it's warm."

Finn leans down and kisses me, right there on the street. I kiss him back. I am a wicked girl, after all.

If the Brothers knew what I'd done, they'd burn me at the stake.

They might be right to do it.

"Good night," I say to him.

"Good night," Finn whispers, tucking a strand of hair behind my ear. "I love you, Cate Cahill. You are beautiful and brave and *strong*. Whatever happens next, we'll deal with it together."

I nod. Brenna is dancing up the marble steps to the front door, and I'm following her when there's a sound—flesh smacking against wet pavement—and I turn. Finn's on his hands and knees; he's tripped over the curb. He picks himself up, pokes his glasses into place, and walks back toward his carriage, but his gait lacks its usual gangly grace. He pauses, examining the carriage, looking as though he's puzzled by it.

"Are you all right?" I call down.

He looks up at me, then ducks his head. His ears are red with embarrassment. "I'm sorry, miss—is this my carriage?"

His voice is awkward, formal. As though he's speaking to a stranger.

His words echo in my head: *I'm sorry, miss.*

I thought I was numb before. This is worse. I'm not shaking anymore, but now I cannot move. I can't go to him, can barely breathe. Only the fast, horrified drumbeat of my own heart proves that I am still alive.

I don't understand. I glance around the empty street. It's only Brenna and me and Maura here—

Maura.

My sister stands on the sidewalk, eyes narrowed at Finn. My Finn.

She wouldn't do this.

Not my own sister.

"Yes, Brother Belastra, that's yours," Maura says, her voice ringing out in the rain. "You were about to return to your lodging for the night."

"My lodging. Yes. Quite right." Finn puts a hand to his head. "Sorry, I'm feeling a bit muddled. I've got a splitting headache."

I stumble down the few steps. "Finn—"

Maura gives me a warning look, but Finn offers up a shy smile, rain dripping off his nose. "Oh. I know you, don't I?"

"Yes." My breath catches. He has to remember me. No matter what Maura's done, it can't have erased *me*.

"You come into the shop, sometimes. Get books for your father. Not much of a reader yourself." Finn snaps his fingers. "It's Miss Cahill, isn't it? Or—pardon, is it Sister Cate now?"

Sister Cate. My eyes fill with horrified tears.

"Yes, Sister Cate. And Sister Maura," my traitorous sister says sweetly. "You came to call on us, inquiring about news from home. I'm sorry you're not well. Why don't you get into the carriage, out of the rain? We'll fetch our coachman, and he can drive you."

"Well, I don't want to be any bother," Finn says, "but my head does ache something fierce. I can hardly see straight."

"No, it's no bother. Not at all. Robert can walk back; it's

only a few blocks. I'll send him right out." Maura ushers him into the carriage while I watch, stricken.

Our first kiss, feathers and the gentle touch of his hands on my back: gone.

Talking about pirates in my garden: gone.

Asking me to marry him, giving me his mother's ruby ring: gone.

Sneaking out to meet me at the convent gate: gone.

Showing me my very first library and the signed copy of *Arabella*: gone.

All of it has been erased. Everything that makes us Finn-and-Cate.

Maura clears her throat. "I'm sorry, Cate, but—he's a member of the Brotherhood. He's the enemy. He can't know our secrets; you heard how he reacted about the council. You never should have told him about your magic."

But that's everything. Our romance and my magic have been intertwined since the very beginning. If I weren't a witch, if I'd had no need to protect my sisters from the Brotherhood, I would never have sought out Finn or the banned books in his mother's bookshop.

If I weren't a witch, I wouldn't be the woman that he loves.

I understand that now.

I raise my head. Ice tumbles through my veins. "Do you hate me so much?"

"It isn't about you," Maura says, but her eyes fall to the rain-darkened sidewalk. "Inez asked me to do it. To prove I could put my feelings aside and do what needs to be done. And when my visions start . . ."

I look at Maura, her red hair the only color in the New London night, and I know that she is the child who used to run after Paul and me, begging to play with us; she's the girl who hid romance novels under her floorboards and dreamed of far-off adventures; she's the sister I would have done anything to protect.

Now I feel nothing for her but a weary contempt.

"They won't," I say. "You aren't the oracle. It's Tess. It's been Tess all along. I wanted to tell you, but she wasn't sure she could trust you. She was right, obviously; you cannot be trusted."

Maura staggers backward, as though I've slapped her. "No."

"Yes." I give her a glittering, serrated smile. It is not Cate's smile, but then I feel very little like Cate at the moment.

Finn looked at me as though I was a stranger. As though I'm not the girl he kissed and called beautiful five minutes ago. As though I'm not *his* Cate.

And I'm not. Not anymore. Countries are forged by war; perhaps girls are, too. New England and I will be reborn together in this war between the witches and the Brothers. Between Maura and me.

I am newly wrought—a girl of steel and snow and heart-rending good-byes.

My magic is renewed by my heartbreak. It spills out my fingertips, swirling around me. The wind picks up, bitter cold now. The rain turns abruptly to snow, haloing the gas streetlamps like iron angels. Enormous snowflakes begin to fall—fast, faster—obscuring my sister, hiding her and Brenna and the carriage and the gray stone building that has become my home.

I am all alone in a sea of whirling white.

It feels right that it should be so.

ACKNOWLEDGMENTS

BUILDING A BOOK AND SENDING IT OUT
into the world to meet its readers is such a complex process—more so than I ever dreamed before I was published. Thank you to everyone who's helped with the Cahill Witch Chronicles. Special thanks to:

Jim McCarthy, my agent, for answering all my newbie questions and paying me lovely compliments when I most needed to hear them.

Ari Lewin, brilliant editor extraordinaire, for pushing me to never settle for less than my absolute best. I worked harder on this book than I've ever worked on anything ever, and I'm so proud of what we've done. Paula Sadler, for your genius contributions and for sending me the best packages ever. Anna Jarzab and Dana Bergman, for your helpful notes. Ana Deboo, whose fabulous copyediting makes me realize my own writerly tics. Elizabeth

Wood, for my gorgeous covers. Eileen Kreit and Jennifer Bonnell and the rest of the paperback team, for putting together a truly lovely new look. Elyse Marshall, Jessica Shoffel, and the rest of the marketing and publicity teams for all your hard work connecting the Cahill sisters with readers.

Andrea Cremer, Marie Lu, and Beth Revis—for being such generous, funny, and talented ladies to tour with.

My early team of readers—Kathleen Foucart, Andrea Lynn Colt, Miranda Kenneally, Caroline Richmond, Tiffany Schmidt, and Robin Talley—for asking clever questions, being fabulous cheerleaders, and talking me down when I need it.

All my friends—but especially Jenn Reeder, Liz Auclair, Laura Sauter, and Jill Coste—for being supportive every step of the way and recommending my books far and wide.

My parents, Connie and Chris Moore and John Emanuel. My sisters, Amber Emanuel and Shannon Moore. And my grandparents—Helen and Jack Emanuel, Mary and Frank Scott, and Norma and Gene Moore—for helping instill in me a love of stories of all kinds.

This book is dedicated to my husband, Steve, because without him reading new pages and reassuring me that it was getting better, I would have given up in a fit of despair. Thank you for believing in me even when I don't.

To the wonderful booksellers, librarians, sales reps, and bloggers who've helped connect my books with readers. I may not know all of your names, but I am thankful for you every single day.

And to my readers, especially those who've taken the time to tweet, message, or e-mail me to tell me how much they love Cate and her sisters and Finn. I'm so privileged to write stories and share them with you. Thank you for choosing to spend your time with us.